As she walked to the window, she heard a loud report and a scream rose in her throat when she recognized it as a pistol shot. She peered through the study window but the curtains, partially drawn, obscured her vision. In terror, she hurried back to the ballroom where the orchestra was still playing loudly and couples were still dancing, oblivious to what was taking place in the room next door.

She was mindless of the stares of the dancers as she shoved roughly past them, breaking into a run when she reached the hallway, tearing toward the study. She threw open the door and gasped in disbelief.

LOVE'S PROUD MASQUERADE

Nomi Berger

LEISURE BOOKS ❧ NEW YORK CITY

A LEISURE BOOK

Published by

Nordon Publications, Inc.
Two Park Avenue
New York, N.Y. 10016

To my parents,
for believing

PART ONE

chapter 1

Thundering hoofbeats shattered the silence. To the bleating of the huntsman's horn, the riding party broke into the open. The horses' hooves tore up grassy clods of earth as they hammered up a gentle slope and streaked across the meadow toward a crumbling stone wall. Each rider eased his mount into a springing leap, clearing the wall, and plunging steadily on. The yelping of the lead dogs grew louder as they narrowed the distance between themselves and the red fox dashing for cover.

Melissa Howard, her auburn hair streaming in a copper cloud behind her as she rode, crouched lower over her horse's neck. Exhilaration flushed her golden skin and her topaz eyes glowed with excitement as she followed her father's lead. She scarcely felt the spray of icy water as they splashed through a shallow brook and climbed up the opposite bank where she overtook her father at last, riding neck and neck with him. At his sudden scowl, she smiled impishly, aware of the thoughts lurking behind the eyes so like her own. She blew him a kiss and watched his mouth twitch into a grudging smile. Then she edged her horse ahead of his, concentrating once more on the scrambling dogs and their helpless quarry.

Cornering their prey at last, the dogs set up a frenzied barking and the riders finally slowed their horses. Melissa reined in her chestnut mare and headed away from the group, content to know that the hunt was completed. She pitied the pathetic animal which had provided them with such a splendid chase. Dismounting, she tethered her sweating horse to a low-hanging branch of a giant oak tree, then leaned back against the trunk, waiting for her breathing to slow, her rapid pulse to ease.

"Ho, there! Melissa!" shouted an approaching rider. She scowled, recognizing Philip Wentworth trotting over to where she was standing. "Not staying for the kill, Melissa?" he asked, his blue eyes glittering expectantly.

"I fail to find it as satisfying as you do, Philip," she returned coldly, hating the eagerness she saw in his eyes.

"But it is all part of the sport, dear Melissa, is it not?" he persisted.

Instead of answering him, she turned her back to him, wishing he would leave her alone. She felt hot and sticky. Impatiently she tugged at the white scarf binding her throat and tossed it to the ground. Mindless of her white jodhpurs, she sank down onto the grass with a sigh of relief. Then she unbuttoned the scarlet jacket she was wearing and threw it down beside the scarf.

Philip's eyes followed her movements; the ripple of the shirt as it hugged her full breasts, her arching body as she stretched her cramped muscles before lying back in the sweet-smelling grass. Melissa glanced up at him, catching his bold scrutiny and she flinched beneath the intensity of his gaze. A slight smile was fixed on his thin mouth and his full blond moustache twitched imperceptibly. She shifted uncomfortably on the grass and his smile widened.

"Such a tempting wench, and so very modest, Melissa," he laughed. "But then, a man prefers the woman he intends to marry to show some modesty, especially when there are so many others close at hand."

She bit down on her lower lip to prevent herself from speaking out and telling him once again that she did not want to marry him. In spite of her father's insistence and his own persistent pursuit of her, she wanted no part of Philip Wentworth, his title, or his estate.

"Melissa! Philip!"

Her relief was audible as her father hailed them. She hastened to sit up before he chastised her for sprawling about. But she was too late.

"Good Lord, daughter!" roared Sir Edmund Howard, reining in his horse beside Philip's. "Are you hurt, Melissa, or merely attempting to drive poor Philip here mad?" Despite his blustering tone, there was a twinkle of amusement in his eyes and Melissa smiled guilelessly up at him.

"Neither, father." And with that, she gathered up her scattered clothes and mounted her horse again. She continued to ignore Philip's silent scrutiny and turned instead to her father. "I'll race you back to the house, Sir Edmund."

Without waiting for an answer, she spurred her mare to a gallop and headed for home. But her troubled thoughts kept pace with her horse's pounding hooves. She could not shake Philip from her mind. She had known Philip all her life. Their estates shared common boundaries. They had shared the same tutors, rivaled each other in sports, and executed their first awkward dance steps together. And so, it had been taken for granted that the sole surviving heir to the vast Wentworth fortune would one day marry the only child of the smaller, but no less respected house of Howard.

But Melissa had stubbornly refused to give in. She clung to the notion that she might still have the opportunity to marry a man for love, and not for prestige. A man she herself fancied, and not one chosen for her by another. Even though that very choice had been made by the father she adored, she did not love

11

Philip Wentworth. And the prospect of spending the rest of her life with him frightened and dismayed her. He was a man whose ruthlessness and greed were alien to her, for her own father had always been a gentle and giving man. Philip's possessiveness was like a blanket threatening to smother her, while he admitted readily to numerous flirtations of his own. She shuddered. And then she set her mouth in a determined line. No one would force her into a marriage she did not want. Not even her father.

She finally topped the rise which overlooked the clipped green lawns and formal gardens surrounding Howard House. How she loved this view. The magnificent gray stone mansion, its facade draped with twisting ivy, rose proudly before her. A semicircular drive swept past the front portico, its graceful columns reached upward to the second story. Mullioned window panes glinted in the fading spring twilight and Melissa noticed the tentative flicker of candlelight already shimmering within the house.

The sound of approaching hoofbeats sent her charging down the hill, determined to win the race with the man who was even now calling out to her. It was only when she neared the stables that she slackened her pace. Flinging herself from the saddle, she handed over the panting horse to one of the grooms who had hurried out to meet her.

"Good race, daughter," said Sir Edmund as he finally drew up alongside her. "Good race indeed. If I had placed a wager on every contest you have taken from me, I would be a far poorer man today."

"Does that mean that the pupil has finally managed to surpass the teacher?" she teased him, watching as he slowly dismounted.

"It simply means, young lady, that your father is getting old." He clapped an arm affectionately about her shoulder.

"Nonsense," she scoffed, nestling close to him.

"You, dear father, will never be old. You possess more energy than men half your age."

His laugh was soft, almost pained. She looked over at him sharply, seeing again the sadness in his eyes which had been there quite often of late. Her chest constricted with fear.

"Come, daughter, let this energetic old man walk with you back to the house."

His steps were slow, much slower than she remembered. But as they climbed the steps to the front porch, he bowed gallantly before her and pushed open the heavy oak door. Relieved, she swept him a low curtsy and entered the house ahead of him. He pecked her on the cheek and walked toward his study while she headed for the staircase. Suddenly the voice of their housekeeper, Letitia, rang out and Melissa froze.

"One moment, young miss." The plump woman waddled toward her, broad hips swaying beneath her crackling skirts. "Just where would you be going with them rumpled clothes in your hand?" She was critically eyeing the riding jacket and trailing scarf Melissa was holding. Then her nose wrinkled disdainfully. "And what about that horsey smell? Will you be wearing that to dinner with your lovely new gown then?"

"Oh hush, Lettie, how you do carry on." Melissa laughed and handed the woman the soiled garments. "Would you be a dear and have Rosemary draw me a bath and have the cook send up a plate of cold turkey? I am simply ravenous."

"And how will you be fitting into your gown after filling yourself so close to dinner?" the housekeeper persisted. But Melissa ignored the woman and bounded up the stairs, taking them two at a time. "A lady never runs up the stairs that way," Lettie bellowed in exasperation. But Melissa ran all the way to her room.

She unbuttoned her damp silk shirt, tugging it free of the clinging white breeches she was wearing. She smiled, recalling her father's fit of temper when she had appeared at a hunt three years earlier, immaculately attired in a man's tailored riding habit. She had adamantly refused to ride sidesaddle, hampered by the cumbersome black skirts worn by other women. Her father, admitting the futility of arguing with his daughter, had finally capitulated. He had even managed to bear, with considerable dignity and good humor, the cutting remarks of many of his friends. For he had long ago resigned himself to losing every dispute to his fiery-haired Melissa.

Poor father, she mused, as she tugged off her breeches and flung them onto the bed. How disappointed he must have been when she was born. For, after two stillborn sons his delicate wife had at last succeeded in producing a healthy child—albeit a girl. Melissa sighed deeply, for she scarcely remembered her mother. Her only recollections were of a musty bedroom with the window draperies tightly drawn, the pungent smell of medicines, and the ashen face wreathed in clouds of faded blonde hair lying still against the stark whiteness of the bed cushions.

Despite her frailty, Abigail Lathrop Howard had forced her stubborn body to provide her husband with the heir he so desperately wanted. But the two stillbirths had taken their toll, and after Melissa was born, she would try no more. She had turned away from her husband and her infant daughter, and sought her release in death.

She eventually refused all food and took to her bed. She lay there quietly, like a soiled and broken doll, her emaciated body buried beneath the stifling covers, as she passively waited for the end. One night, with a gentle whimper of relief, she died.

"Your bath is ready, Miss Melissa." Rosemary's soft voice shook Melissa from her thoughts. She hastily slipped out of her lacy underclothes and, taking up a fragrant bar of rosepetal soap, lowered herself into the steaming tub. She leaned back, her tousled ringlets

14

trailing in the water, her body gradually relaxing in the soothing warmth.

As the fatigue drained from her body, Melissa began to vigorously soap herself. Humming softly, she smiled in anticipation of wearing the first of the new gowns hanging in her wardrobe. The following day she would be celebrating her nineteenth birthday with a gala masquerade ball and this evening Sir Edmund had planned an intimate dinner with Philip Wentworth as the only guest. She shuddered apprehensively, realizing that Philip would use the evening to press her to accept his proposal of marriage. Her father, of course, would side with him again, and she would be hard put to make the evening a pleasant one.

Her bath water was cooling, so Melissa rinsed herself and reached for the fluffy towel Rosemary had left her. Stepping from the tub, she caught a glimpse of her long, tumbled hair reflected in the towering cheval glass across the room. A mischievous smile tipped the corners of her mouth as she decided to provoke her father by brushing her hair freely about her shoulders, instead of wearing it in an elaborate coiffure for the evening. Sir Edmund was continually admonishing her for her long, unbound hair, castigating her for her refusal to conform and behave more like a grown woman, as was fitting and proper.

But Melissa abhorred propriety and lived as she pleased. As a child growing up alone and privately tutored, she had balked at receiving only the traditional schooling of young ladies and had added riding and marksmanship to her education. She had long ago abandoned her childhood girl friends, preferring instead the companionship and the competition offered her only by the men she knew. Melissa knew that her father, despite his grumbling, secretly admired her unique high-spiritedness, and this knowledge bound them closer.

Iridescent water droplets spun into the air as she

dried herself. She dropped the towel to the floor and walked to her mirror, as the reflected image stared back at her. Although she had always considered herself unfashionably tall for a woman, she had been grateful for her height as her body had matured and ripened. Lustrous auburn hair, tinged with golden streaks, hung to her narrow waist. Her topaz eyes, tilted provocatively at the corners, were fringed with thick, dark lashes. Her nose was slim and straight, the nostrils flaring slightly, and her sensual mouth, with its full lower lip, was drawn back in a lazy, appreciative smile, revealing straight, white teeth.

She flushed as her eyes traveled lower. Never quite prepared for the fullness of her firm, high breasts, she was startled each time she gazed at herself. But the graceful neck and slender torso, softly rounded hips, and long tapering legs, taut from years of riding, provided her with an exquisitely proportioned young body.

A knock at the door sent her scurrying for the towel. She snatched it up, hastily covering herself. Rosemary walked in, a frown on her face as she glanced at the untouched turkey and her mistress's state of dishabille.

"Miss Melissa, if you be wanting me to fix your 'air, we'd best 'urry," she exclaimed.

"We have plenty of time," Melissa said, calming her maid. "There will be no fussing with my hair tonight. Just dry it, please, and brush it down." Her eyes sparkled as she watched the effects of her words on the girl.

"But your father," she said, "and it being your birthday and all. . . ."

Melissa's bubbling laugh cut her short, and she settled herself onto the chair in front of her vanity table, gaily waving her hairbrush.

"Brush away, dear Rosemary," she instructed, "we would not want to keep them waiting, now would we?" The girl reluctantly took the silver brush and obediently began to smooth the tangled mane of auburn hair.

When Melissa was satisfied with the effect, she stood patiently while her maid helped her slip into her filmy undergarments and the loathsome corset which would be laced to ensure that her small waist appeared even smaller than it was, and that her full bosom peeked enticingly over the top of her dress. She sighed luxuriously as she stepped into the coolness of her gown. Fashioned of amber silk to offset her honey tinted skin, the gown hugged the supple curves of her body. The sleeveless bodice dipped to a low vee, exposing her tempting cleavage. The skirt fell in gentle folds, skimming the amber satin shoes she wore. Full, draped panniers were gathered across her hips, sweeping into a flowing train at the back.

Rosemary wistfully fingered the clusters of amber silk roses which would have entwined Melissa's curls if only she had formally dressed her hair. Noticing her young maid's woebegone expression, Melissa snatched up one of the silken blooms and grinning devilishly, she tucked it into her hair over one delicate ear. Then, with a soft rustling, she swished from the room and made her way downstairs.

The sound of angry voices emanating from her father's study brought her to a halt outside the door. She could recognize Philip's precise, clipped tones as the quieter of the two, while Sir Edmund's voice was booming loudly. Curious as to the nature of their dispute, she knocked discreetly and immediately threw open the door, hoping to catch them off guard.

She was met by hostile silence as both of the men glared at her. Philip, immaculate in a dark evening suit, frowned at her intrusion and set his mouth in a grim, hard line. He seemed unaccountably nervous and his long, thin fingers tugged continually at his trim blond moustache.

She gazed questioningly at her father, who was sitting on the edge of his massive oak desk, absently

17

twirling a wineglass in his hand. He seemed to be more relaxed than Philip, but the rapid rise and fall of his broad chest belied his composure. He reached for a heavy crystal decanter and poured himself another full glass of wine.

Melissa rustled her skirts, inviting their attention, but she was rewarded by uncomfortable silence. "Does the birthday girl not merit a glass of wine, gentlemen?" she finally asked, her tone striving for lightness to mask her rising irritation.

"Of course, Melissa, I'm sorry," Sir Edmund apologized, his voice somewhat strained. He hastily filled another glass and handed it to his daughter. "I would like to propose a toast to the most beautiful daughter a father could hope for, on the eve of her birthday and her betrothal." He and Philip raised their glasses but Melissa stared from one to the other in disbelief.

"And to whom am I betrothed?" she demanded, her voice taking on a harsh and strident tone.

"Surely, Melissa, you must be jesting," Philip answered smoothly, his hand straying to his moustache once more. "You knew it was simply a matter of time before we made it official between us. And what better opportunity than tomorrow evening at the ball with all of our friends in attendance?"

"What better time indeed," Melissa snapped, turning to her father again. "You have never made my mind up for me in the past and I should think it a trifle late to begin now. How could you do this to me?" The last words were more of a wail as she fought back her tears.

"Now see here, Melissa," her father barked, his own temper flaring, "I have long berated myself for allowing you to twist me around your little finger, for giving in continually to your whims and capriciousness. But I warn you that I shall remain firm on this matter and win at least one battle from you." His naturally ruddy face was splotched with rage and he slammed his fist purposefully against the top of his desk.

"I can scarcely believe you would do this, father; forcing me into a marriage I have never sought."

"Believe it, child, for it is done!" he roared.

"And that is your final word?"

"It is." He filled his glass once more.

Melissa stood there, her mind reeling, her body cold. Without another word, she stumbled from the room, the untouched wine in her glass splashing onto the bodice of her gown. With a wrenching sob, she hurled the wineglass to the floor and ran up the stairs to her room, throwing herself across the bed. The sobs tore at her chest, plucked at her very core, and she cried out in rage and betrayal.

She heard the footsteps only when they neared her, and Sir Edmund sank down onto the bed beside her and pulled her into his arms. "There, there, Lissy," he crooned, "hush now. Forgive me for taking you so completely by surprise." He smoothed the tendrils of her hair back from her face. "But my mind is made up, child, and fight as you will, I doubt that you can change it."

Melissa tore from his grasp as the tears coursed steadily down her cheeks. "I despise Philip Wentworth," she hissed. "I find him thoroughly unscrupulous and grasping, and he stops at nothing to get what he wants. But even though he wants me, father, I vow he shall never have me, in spite of what you say."

"Philip has his shortcomings, like all of us," Sir Edmund reasoned, reaching for his daughter again. "But consider the advantages of being married to a man with his enormous wealth and position. Why, Wentworth Hall makes Howard House look like a caretaker's cottage by comparison."

But Melissa refused to be consoled. She squirmed from her father's embrace and walked unsteadily to the window, pulling aside the heavy satin draperies. Looking out onto the grounds below, the trees and flowers and rolling parkland silhouetted in the pale spring moonlight, she was enveloped by a frightening sense of loss. And the pain and outrage she felt because of her father's callous abandonment was more than she could bear. With a shuddering sigh, she turned to face him, and she employed her last and most potent weapon—his fear of losing her.

"Well, father," she began, forcing her voice not to quaver, "since you seem to have made up your mind, I suppose that, short of running away, I shall have to obey you. But mark me well. The day that I become Mrs. Philip Wentworth is the day I shall no longer have a father. You will not be a guest in my house, you will never hold your grandchildren, and I shall never speak to you again."

At her words, his face seemed to crumble, his handsome features suddenly creased with the intensity of his anguish. With a wrenching sob, he finally heaved himself from the bed and staggered from the room. She fought the urge to call him back, to retract her words, but she remained still, standing mutely as he closed the door. She had played her trump card and surely he would be forced to reconsider his decision.

Sagging into a chair, she rocked back and forth in an effort to comfort herself. The minutes passed with agonizing slowness as she waited for her father to return. The sound outside her door sent her racing to open it, but there in the doorway stood Rosemary, bearing a tray laden with silver serving dishes.

"Your father said you would most likely be missing dinner so the cook prepared a tray for you." As Melissa shook her head, the girl pleaded with her. "But it's your birthday supper, Miss Melissa, and the cook will be upset knowing you 'aven't tried any of it."

"Take everything back downstairs, Rosemary." She gestured wearily. "I have no appetite." With a shrug of resignation the girl backed away and Melissa shut the door.

She pulled off the stained and crumpled gown and left

it in a heap on the carpet. Adding her underclothing to the snarl of discarded finery, she stretched out across the bed again, the satin coverlet comfortingly cool against her burning skin. She lay there, limp and still, while scalding tears trickled silently down her cheeks and she stared blankly up at the satin canopy above her. Idly, she wound an auburn ringlet around her finger, starting as she touched the silk rose still fastened in her hair. She tugged the flower free, glumly regarded the delicate bloom. She watched in mute satisfaction as she pulled the rose apart, petal by silken petal.

She tossed and turned all through the long night, crying wretchedly into her pillow, pounding it ferociously with doubled fists. In her despair, she thought of the masquerade ball and her father's intention to announce her betrothal there. How she wished it were not too late to cancel it, but their guests would be arriving throughout the day from every part of Kent, and it would be impossible to get word to them in time. She railed bitterly against her father, weeping inconsolably until her temples throbbed and her throat was raw.

Exhausted, she finally fell asleep shortly before dawn.

chapter 2

When Melissa awoke, buttery sunlight was spilling in through the open window. She lay sprawled across the coverlet, her head pounding, her throat stinging each time she attempted to swallow. It was her birthday, she noted grimly, a cause for celebration, and she should have been happy. Yet all she felt was a gnawing ache inside of her and an overwhelming sense of desolation. She slid from the bed, and shrugging into a brocade dressing gown, rang for Rosemary.

When the girl knocked, Melissa flung open the door to confront not only her maid, but a scowling Lettie as well. Ignoring the housekeeper, Melissa started to ask Rosemary to bring her a pot of tea, but her words came out as hoarse croaks.

"Well, well, young lady," clucked the housekeeper, her disapproving frown taking in the disheveled girl and the cluttered room in a glance, "you certainly have done yourself proud. The guests will be arriving soon with no hostess to greet them. Only a red-eyed rasping toad."

"Lettie," Melissa whispered, tugging plaintively at the older woman's sleeve, "please have the cook prepare some hot tea laced with honey. Then bring me those lozenges Dr. Ashby left for father when he was sick last winter." Nodding curtly, the housekeeper restrained her waspish tongue and bustled off down the corridor.

22

"Quickly, Rosemary, lay out a nightgown and bed jacket for me," Melissa urged, swallowing several times in an effort to ease the pain in her throat. "And please tell father that I am indisposed."

"But, Miss Melissa," the girl began, only to be silenced by Melissa's warning frown as she turned and flounced back to bed.

Donning a filmy yellow nightgown and matching jacket, she settled back against the pillows. When Rosemary returned with the tea and lozenges, Melissa began gingerly sipping the scalding brew and sucking on the bitter tablets. Suddenly the bedroom door opened and her father strode into the room. His handsome face was drawn, his eyes bloodshot. Silently he pulled a dainty slipper chair to the bed and perched his large frame precariously on the seat. Raking his fingers through his hair, he gazed deeply into his daughter's troubled eyes.

"I am here to beg your forgiveness, Melissa," he said softly. Melissa was so astounded that she could only stare wordlessly back at him. "I was wrong to try and force you into accepting Philip's proposal, for I had no idea how loath you were to marry him. He and I spoke together long into the night and I finally convinced him of the senselessness of such a match. You see, my child—" and his eyes filled with tears— "I could never bear to lose you. But then," he concluded bitterly, "you knew that too."

Melissa, grappling with her own emotions, released a hoarse sob and joyfully threw her arms around her father's neck. He held her close to him, stroking her burnished hair, and Melissa felt as if her heart would burst with relief and gratitude. If she had seen the stricken look on her father's face, she would have held a tighter rein on her feelings, for his face was that of a defeated man.

"Now rest quietly, Lissy," he cautioned, pressing her gently back against the cushions, "and look like my

23

princess tonight. In the meantime, I shall make your excuses to our guests."

Nestled safely in bed, sipping the remainder of her tea, Melissa felt her sense of dread give way to a contented calm. She dozed on and off throughout the day, gulping hot tea when she awoke, and listening to the carriages drawing up to the house. The spare bedrooms of Howard House along with the estate's smaller guest house filled quickly with laughing, chattering men and women, who would rest awhile and then change their clothes in preparation for the evening's festivities.

Toward dusk, Rosemary arrived to assist Melissa. The young maid's expert hands artfully arranged the long, shining hair into elaborate curls and ringlets and Melissa smiled approvingly. As she stepped into her evening gown, she began to experience the first flutters of anticipation, for surely after the fiasco of the previous evening, her masquerade ball would more than compensate for it.

She fidgeted restlessly as Rosemary fastened the gown's tiny buttons until the girl stepped aside and Melissa viewed herself in the gold-framed mirror. Her gown of tissue-thin silver cloth was cut along simple Grecian lines, the gauzy fabric hanging in softly pleated folds from a neckline completely baring one shoulder. Clips of glittering brilliants adorned the silver slippers she wore, and after powdering Melissa's hair to disguise its copper glow, Rosemary worked similar sparkling clips through the cascading ringlets piled atop Melissa's head and winding across her bare shoulder. She tugged on a pair of elbow-length silver gloves and fastened a delicate diamond bracelet on each wrist. Both of the bracelets had belonged to her late mother, and were given to Melissa as her birthday present by Sir Edmund. The finishing touch to the ensemble was the spangled silver mask which Rosemary slipped carefully into place. A touch of lip pomade was the only cosmetic

Melissa required as her skin glowed golden against the shimmering silver enfolding her.

She stopped at the head of the winding staircase and gazed down at the sight unfolding before her. The floor of the hallway was obscured by dozens of brightly-costumed couples moving about. She marveled at how well Lettie and the household staff had managed without her assistance during the day, and she clapped her hands in delight at the garlands of flowers looped over the doorways and the giant bouquets flanking the front door.

Sir Edmund stood patiently at the foot of the stairs. Dressed simply in a black evening suit, he had decided against wearing a mask in order to welcome their guests and tend to their comfort more easily throughout the evening. He smiled up at his daughter and her heartbeat quickened as she slowly descended the steps, aware of several people turning to watch her. She gratefully accepted his proffered arm and he handed her a glass of champagne and walked with her through the crowded hall.

Strains of a waltz drifted from the ballroom and Sir Edmund claimed his daughter for the first dance. Entering the room, Melissa gasped, for the ballroom had been transformed into a lush, fragrant bower. White trellises covered with twining leaves and tiny pink roses had been placed at intervals along the walls, and garlands of white daisies spanned each high cur-tained window. Melissa and her father joined the couples already spinning around the floor, the glimmer of candleshine reflected in the whirling silks and satins and winking jewels.

"How very beautiful you are tonight, Melissa," Sir Edmund beamed appreciatively at her.

Against the music and the noisy chatter, she merely smiled her thanks, indicating her stubborn throat. Nodding sympathetically, he smiled back at her, but as he glanced over toward the doorway, his gaze suddenly clouded.

"There's Philip coming in now," he muttered. As if responding to her unasked question: "He told me what he intended to wear tonight."

Catching sight of them, Philip made his way across the room. Dressed as Horatio Nelson, resplendent in dark blue with gold epaulets and elaborate naval decorations, he doffed his hat and bowed low over Melissa's hand.

"Milady," he said mockingly, straightening smartly and settling the hat back on his head. "Need I say how exquisite you are despite your foul temper and astonishing display of bad manners last night?"

"Then, sir, if my manners so offended you, why did you bother to appear this evening?" Melissa returned hoarsely.

"Your daughter seems to have lost not only her temper but her voice as well, Sir Edmund," Philip remarked snidely, seeming to relish the older man's discomfort. As Melissa watched the two men, she was aware of the same undercurrent of tension she had sensed in the study the previous evening, and she frowned as her father tugged nervously at his tie.

"Father?" she whispered, placing a hand on his arm.

"I'm fine, my dear, although I think I might step outside for some air," he said. Despite her look of alarm, he headed toward the French doors leading onto the garden.

Philip calmly stroked his moustache, his eyes glinting maliciously behind his small blue mask. "It seems a pity you were so unreasonable, my dear Melissa. You are costing your father a pretty penny indeed."

"If you mean this party," she began, but something in Philip's gaze told her otherwise. She grabbed at his arm as he turned to leave.

"Philip, what has been going on between the two of you? What are you hiding from me?" she demanded, her voice breaking. "Philip," she pleaded. But with a

26

withering look, he plucked her hand from his sleeve and walked away.

Bewildered by his behavior, she found it difficult to force the incident from her thoughts and she wandered moodily among her guests. She grudgingly accepted a dance from a masked archer and in spite of her apprehensiveness, she found herself whirling about the ballroom floor, enjoying the music at last, and relaxing enough to finally drive Philip and her father from her mind. Swinging from one costumed partner to another, she eventually grew tired and bored, and her throat ached mercilessly from her vain attempts to be heard above the noise and the music.

She made her way into the dining room where two long tables had been set with an elaborate buffet. Large silver platters were filled with thin slices of smoked ham and turkey, green salads, shimmering aspics, rich puddings, and cream-centered pastries, and Melissa eagerly sampled the rich fare while idly glancing about the crowded room. Suddenly, she caught sight of a man who appeared out of place there. Although masked, he was not in costume and he was standing alone, leaning casually against the wall. His tall, muscular frame was accentuated by the clinging doeskin breeches and high boots he was wearing, and his white linen shirt was open at the throat, exposing the dark curling hair on his chest.

He seemed to sense her curious stare for he raised his glass to her in silent salute and smiled. She flushed and hastily lowered her gaze. A faint fluttering began somewhere deep inside her and her skin seemed to warm with a strange heat. She was certain that she could feel the intensity of his eyes on her even as she studiously concentrated on the hem of her gown.

"An exquisite goddess," commented the deep voice at her elbow, "and such a shy one at that." She felt herself stiffening at the slight mockery in his tone. With deliberate slowness, she turned to look up into his grinning, sun-bronzed face. Her breath caught in her throat. She found herself trapped by a pair of silver-gray eyes which glinted at her like twin slivers of ice. A shivering tremor took hold of her, shuddering through her entire body as she forced herself to look away again and break the compelling hold he had on her.

"Does the goddess have a voice?" Again he was mocking her.

"She does."

He threw back his head and laughed. A deep, rumbling sound which further unnerved her. "I think she's lost her voice."

She clenched her fists together, feeling her cheeks flame even as she found herself looking at his face again. It was a rugged face. And she followed his straight, strongly defined nose and finely chiseled lips down to the firm, square chin. Again she felt a quickening heartbeat and she silently cursed herself for such weakness.

"Are you memorizing my face for any particular reason?" he asked, swallowing the last of his champagne. Melissa squared her shoulders and faced him defiantly, ignoring his question.

"You are obviously not British," she whispered. "Just where are you from?" She was wondering how he came to be at her party.

"I'm from Maryland," he answered smoothly. Then he grinned maddeningly at her. "It's in America, you know."

"I am quite aware of the geography of our former colonies," she retaliated. The force of her reply made her cough and she felt mortified. He simply stood there and seemed to enjoy her discomfort. What a beast the man was! But she was curious about him all the same. "Are you holidaying in England?" she asked.

"Not this time." He was so curt, abrupt, and she was taken aback by his peculiar manner. His eyes narrowed then. "By the way, do you know which one of these men is Sir Edmund Howard?"

"Yes, of course." She hesitated momentarily, somehow wanting their little charade to continue without his knowing who she was. And so she simply pointed her father out to the stranger and said nothing. Did her father know this man? Did they have some business dealings together? Her suspicions aroused, she was about to question him when she felt a nudge at her side.

"I believe you owe me this dance, my pet," Philip said to her, attempting to draw her away from the table. The American seemed to sense Melissa's reluctance and immediately stepped over to them.

"I'm afraid the young lady promised this dance to me," he announced to an astonished Philip. And before Melissa could even protest, she found herself being propelled from the dining room. She stumbled on the hem of her gown and he steadied her, the brief contact with his body sending a spark of fire coursing through her. He led her into a waltz and as his arms encircled her, she allowed him to hold her close. Much closer than propriety permitted. And yet, she was helpless to do anything else.

He danced remarkably well, she thought, for an American. And since she had always imagined them to be a rather backward and clumsy lot, she was pleasantly surprised by his expertise. She moved smoothly with him, following him easily, as he guided her about the floor. She soon forgot her suspicions and thought only of the music and the way his body felt pressed up against hers. The vague tingling which had begun when he had first looked at her spread slowly throughout her entire body until she felt that if he released her, she would surely collapse.

But he did not let go of her through dance after dance. Although many masked and costumed men sought to claim her, they remained together. And Melissa, in the newness of these wonderful feelings, began to grow afraid. Unschooled by a mother's words, a mother's advice, she wondered if love began this way. And she shivered.

"Are you cold?" His voice was a whisper. She could feel his warm breath against her ear and she shivered again. Somehow she managed to shake her head. She heard him chuckle softly, his arms tightening about her again.

He must think me a silly fool, she chastised herself. He seemed so certain of himself. And of her. Suddenly, she felt that she could no longer bear his closeness. She tugged herself free of him, struggling to maintain some of her dignity as she tripped again on her gown in her haste. Her ears stung with the sound of his mocking laughter which trailed after her as she fought her way through the crowded room and out into the emptier hall.

"Whatever happened, my pet?" Philip called out as he hurried over to her. "Did that half-clad savage tread on your toes?" Melissa pushed past him and contented herself with a glass of cool champagne to soothe her dry throat and steady her trembling nerves. Her head was beginning to throb and she found herself confused and frightened again. She slammed the goblet down onto the table and made her way back through the ballroom once more. She desperately needed some fresh air. Approaching the double doors leading onto the terrace, she flung them open and stepped outside into the cool evening.

"A walk in the moonlight, madam?"

Melissa frowned and looked around her.

"Over here," instructed the voice. She followed the sound, but she could still not find him. And then she started in fright as the tall figure of the American appeared from the shadows behind one of the glass doors.

"Do you always throw open doors without looking to see who's being flattened behind them?" He was laughing at her again and anger flashed a warning in her topaz eyes.

"What right do you have to be skulking about out here?" she screamed at him. And then, to her chagrin, she began to cough again. He came over to her and unceremoniously began to pound her on the back with the flat of his hand. She shrugged herself free and walked away from him. But he followed closely behind her. She felt his arms on her shoulders and then he was turning her around to face him. She held her breath.

"I have just the cure for that cough of yours," he said. She looked up at him questioningly. And then he pulled her into his arms and pressed his lips against hers. She was so astounded that she simply stood there, staring up at him, her arms rigid at her sides. Then as his kiss deepened, she began to fight him. She pummeled him with clenched fists, straining to break his hold on her. And then she pushed at him with all of her might and watched as he staggered backward. She was free at last.

"How dare you?" she sputtered, rubbing her hand across her mouth. In her attempt to erase the telltale signs of the indiscretion, she succeeded only in smearing the remaining lip pomade over the back of her glove. This set her fuming again while he stood there, his arms folded across his chest, smiling at her. She forgot about the ruined glove and whirled to face him again. She raised her hand, aching to slap the smug grin from his face. But he caught hold of her wrist and drew her up against him once more.

"I don't take kindly to a woman lifting her hand to me," he growled. "But you're such a tempting little morsel that I might forgive you after another sample of your kisses."

"Let me go, you despicable animal," she spat as he sought to claim her lips once again. In a last vain effort, she turned her head from side to side to avoid his invading mouth. But his kisses then landed on her cheeks, her ears, and then her throat.

Suddenly his scalding touch aroused a returning

31

ardor within her and she felt her control slip completely away. When his mouth met hers again, she gave herself up to the desire flooding through her and kissed him back. Hungry, yearning, she clung to him, her arms slipping around his neck and holding him fast. Never had she known such a glorious feeling. She marveled at how the simple meeting of two mouths could create such wondrous sensations.

His lips, sensing her acquiescence, grew more tender, and his strong teeth nibbled at her lower lip, teasing her, playing with her. And then he covered her mouth again with his and probed her soft warmth with his tongue. Startled, she drew back, but he tugged her back again. She relented, shyly meeting the thrusts of his tongue with her own. And then, all too soon, he released her. She wavered slightly, her thoughts tumbling chaotically around her, her dazed eyes having difficulty focusing on his. Her wanton response to this stranger shocked her. But her young body, newly awakened, craved more of him.

To her dismay, he backed away from her, his voice once again light and bantering. She felt herself begin to shrink up and grow suddenly cold. "Well, my lovely lady, you may consider yourself properly kissed." His smile was brief, mocking, and then he was bowing with a great flourish before her. She stood there, horrified, as he turned and stepped back into the ballroom, leaving her alone and trembling.

She was stunned. Her head was reeling, as much from the effects of his kissing as from his abrupt dismissal of her. How could he have been so passionate one moment and then so coldly disinterested the next? She was humiliated and she cursed him for having used her so shamelessly. How dare he treat her as if she were no more than a common trollop! Whoever he was, she intended to speak to her father about him and have him ejected, by force if necessary, from their home.

With a determined toss of her head, Melissa gathered

her skirts and hurried back into the house. Then she stopped. She must look a sight. How was she to explain her disheveled appearance to her father without arousing his suspicions as to her own part in this misadventure? She would first have to freshen her face and change her gloves before she sought him out.

As she climbed the stairs to her room, the sounds of raised voices reached her. Turning, she was startled to see her father standing near the door of his study, locked in an obvious argument with Philip and the man she was seeking to evict. Philip's face was flushed with rage as he said something to Sir Edmond and stalked off. Then, to Melissa's dismay, her father opened the study door and ushered the stranger inside.

She was seized by a terrible foreboding as she entered her bedroom. What did that man want with her father? She shivered, suddenly cold, and stepped in front of her mirror. Tugging off her soiled gloves, she ran the tips of her fingers over her face, frightened by what she saw there. Her mouth was puffy, her eyes bright, and her skin was covered with a fine sheen of perspiration. Hastily dampening a linen handkerchief with perfume, she patted her arms and face, cooling her stinging flesh. She pinned up several of the offending ringlets which had come loose, added a touch of lip pomade to her tender mouth and located a fresh pair of gloves to wear. She powdered her arms and struggled into the clinging gloves, patiently smoothing them and refastening the diamond bracelets.

She studied herself in the mirror again, wondering if her face betrayed the conflict of emotions raging inside her. But her reflection revealed only a new glow to the golden warmth of her skin and a limpid quality to her eyes. She turned away from the glass. Fighting down the strangely disquieting feeling within her, she left the room, prepared to do battle with the objectionable American who somehow had her father's ear.

Pausing outside the study door, she listened for

sounds of activity within. But the music was too loud, the people too close, and she gave up, finally returning to the ballroom. There a group of young men impatiently waited to claim their dances with her. She was spun around the dance floor with a different partner for each set. Despite her attempts to lose herself in the music and the gaiety, she found it impossible, and her eyes darted restlessly about, seeking a tall masked figure clad in pale doeskin breeches.

Tiring at last, she excused herself and walked alone out into the garden. She followed one of the shrub-trimmed paths down to the small ornamental pond filled with tiny goldfish. The sounds of scuffling and muffled voices coming from the shadowed bushes made her feel especially lonely. She sighed and sat down on a wooden bench beside the pond, watching the moonlight dapple the gently rippling water and spark an occasional shimmer of gold as a small fish caught the light. A breeze cooled her and stirred the filmy layers of her gown, brushing them against her in a soft caress. Closing her eyes, she imagined herself back in his arms and, as he crushed her to him, he protected her from the loneliness enveloping her.

When the wind seemed stronger, Melissa realized that she had remained outside longer than she had intended. She rose stiffly from the bench and headed back toward the house. As she approached, she glanced over at the window of her father's study, startled to see light filtering through the curtains, for she had assumed that his talk with the American would have long been over.

As she walked to the window, she heard a loud report and a scream rose in her throat when she recognized it as a pistol shot. She peered through the study window but the curtains, partially drawn, obscured her vision. In terror, she hurried back to the ballroom where the orchestra was still playing loudly and couples were still dancing, oblivious to what was taking place in the room

34

next door.

She was mindless of the stares of the dancers as she shoved roughly past them, breaking into a run when she reached the hallway, tearing toward the study. She threw open the door and gasped in disbelief. Her father lay sprawled on the floor near his desk, a gun resting on the carpet beside him. Her hoarse screams brought people rushing into the room and, in horror, she watched as one of the men pressed a hand to Sir Edmund's neck, seeking a pulse there. Glancing up at Melissa, the man shook his head. With a cry of anguish, she knelt beside the still form of her father, tears streaming down her face as she ripped away her mask.

"Call Inspector Humphreys from the ballroom," she cried as she stooped to retrieve the gun. But a pair of arms restrained her. She turned to stare up into the shocked face of Philip Wentworth.

"Philip!" she gasped. "He's dead. My father is dead. Why would someone have wanted to kill him? Why?" Sobs wracked her body as she allowed Philip to draw her into his arms. Curious guests stood gaping in the doorway until a tall, heavyset man brushed them back and closed the door after them. Suddenly, Melissa tensed, straining in Philip's embrace. She looked wildly about the room, feeling his ominous presence everywhere, seeking the tall masked figure with the mocking gray eyes.

"What are you looking for, Melissa?" Philip demanded.

"The American. Did you see him leave? He and father were alone here . . . for so long . . . and then the shots . . ." her voice trailed off. And before Philip could form a reply, the door opened and the stocky, balding figure of Inspector Luther Humphreys stepped into the room.

"So you believe that some American fellow might have had reason to harm your father, Missy girl?" boomed out the dear, familiar voice. And she broke

35

away from Philip and flung herself into the arms of her father's oldest friend and her godfather.

"He killed my father, I know it, Luther. He killed my father." She wept as she forced herself to remember exactly what he looked like. She could feel him holding her and kissing her even as she spoke. She stumbled over her words and felt a swirling sickness take hold of her.

"Quickly, Philip," barked Humphreys, "get some men together out there and thoroughly search the house and the entire grounds."

Melissa heard the door slam and she shuddered, pressing herself up against Humphreys. "There, there, Missy child. I promise you that we will get to the bottom of this." Then he released her and stooped over the body of Sir Edmund Howard to examine the small, oozing wound at the side of the man's head. He picked up the pistol, sniffed at it, and then laid it down again. He stood slowly and returned to Melissa, taking hold of both her hands, feeling their clammy coldness in his.

"Melissa, I regret that at the moment it would be impossible to state positively that your father was the victim of foul play." He paused awkwardly. "We cannot overlook the possibility of suicide."

At his words, Melissa began to shake uncontrollably. She felt her knees give way beneath her and she slumped toward the floor. No, no, no, her numbed brain screamed. Her father would never have killed himself. He had loved her too much. He would never have purposely left her alone. Never. In spite of their disagreements, in spite of her refusal to marry Philip, he had loved her. And he would have never chosen to abandon her, not without saying goodbye. She could never believe that of him. Not ever.

"Is this his gun, Melissa?" she heard Humphreys asking her as he forced her back into a chair. All she could see was her beloved father lying there. So still. Gone from her forever. Snatched so cruelly away,

36

leaving neither of them the time for proper farewells. She began to cry again, certain that her heart was breaking, wishing that it would, so that she would not have to remain behind alone.

"Is this his gun?" The question clattered in her ears. She looked at the pistol and shook her head. He had had so many guns. It looked like one of his, but she could not be certain. And she told Humphreys that she was not certain. He grunted to himself and turned away from her.

Where was Philip? What was taking them so long, she wondered. Surely, they would have found the American by now. She closed her eyes against the pain, and felt herself drifting in his arms again; felt once more the beautiful tenderness of his mouth on hers. She cursed herself and him. Then she laughed out loud. Love. She had actually imagined herself to have been falling in love with him. All the time he had been wooing her, teasing her, had he also been plotting her father's death? Where was Philip? When he returned with the stranger, Inspector Humphreys would have his murderer and she would gladly watch him hanged.

She closed her eyes again and waited. It seemed that an eternity was passing before her and then she heard someone call her name. Father? She looked up hopefully. But the tired brown eyes and drooping moustache of Inspector Humphreys loomed in front of her. She swallowed hard and tried to concentrate on his blurring face. He was shaking his head.

"I'm sorry, Missy. There was no sign of the fellow anywhere about. Not in the house nor on the grounds. A complete search will be impossible now until daylight, for there are many acres of forest to cover. To begin now would only prove futile."

"Where is Philip?" she whispered.

"He returned to Wentworth Hall." The man looked puzzled. "He mumbled something about some papers and promised to come back here forthwith."

Melissa was finding it increasingly difficult to concentrate. Papers, he had said. How could Philip have been thinking about papers when her father was lying there dead? She looked down at the floor. He was gone. Only a deep red stain on the carpet was left to bear witness to what had just happened there. Then suddenly, Philip was there. She saw the papers in his hands; formal-looking documents, dripping with red seals and bits of ribbon. A cold fist of fear closed around her heart.

"Perhaps this is not the most appropriate moment, my dear Melissa," Philip began in a subdued voice, "but I fear no time would be suitable for what I have to tell you." He paused. "Howard House and all of its surrounding lands and dwellings now belong to me. These are the deeds and letters of intent, signed over to me by your father to prove it."

She felt as if she had been flung back into the chair and a searing pain knifed through her. Somewhere she heard someone screaming and when she felt Inspector Humphreys' slap across her cheeks she realized that the screams were hers. She watched in horror as Humphreys took hold of the papers and scanned them hastily. "Papers," she screamed again. Papers, when her father was dead and his murderer had eluded them?

"No!" she cried hoarsely. "I refuse to believe you, Philip. It is simply not possible. It cannot be possible."

"But it is possible, Melissa, and if you will have a look at these documents, you will see for yourself that what I have just told you is the truth." He held the thick sheaf of papers out for her but she swiped at them with her hand, scattering them across the floor. With a muttered curse, he bent down and began to pick them up again.

"How could you?" her pathetic voice rasped. "How could you confront me with this at such a time? My father is dead, Philip, dead. And you come to me now and tell me that this is no longer my home?" She felt herself begin to grow faint again but she fought it back, even though the pain was more than she could bear.

"I regret to inform you, dear Melissa—" Philip's voice was cutting, cold— "but your father was hopelessly indebted to the bank when he came to me for assistance. He had used up all of his capital and had drawn heavily from the bank, counting on the Howard name to secure great loans. And when even that failed, I paid off his debts." His eyes narrowed then. "Howard House was his collateral. You lived in grand style, Melissa, but your father was not a businessman. You lived in a pretty world bolstered mainly by Wentworth money."

"My God." She shook her head in disbelief. "Why did he not tell me? I had no idea . . . we were so close . . . how could he not have trusted me enough . . . Philip, why would he keep this from me? All these years?"

"I offered him a solution, Melissa, but you spoiled it for him. For all of us, I might add. I told him that I would affix our lands and that he could remain at Howard House for the rest of his life. On the condition that you marry me." Melissa gasped. "But you, my proud and stubborn beauty, defied him to the end. And now see what a sorry state you are in."

"But he would never have chosen to kill himself. We would have faced this together, he and I, just as we faced everything together in the past. He would never have left me alone. Never. He is dead and someone has killed him." The image of her father sprawled on the study floor danced crazily in front of her. And then she heard the stranger's deep voice in her ear, felt the heat of his breath on her skin. And she shuddered with sudden loathing. "The American. Find him and you shall find the reason for my father's death. You must find him for me, Luther," Melissa whispered fiercely. Her eyes, alight with her hatred, bored into Humphrey's. The man flinched.

She felt his arms around her as they danced, and the

hunger in his mouth as he claimed hers. She saw herself reflected in his silvery eyes as he laughed at her and courted her, then left her standing alone on the terrace. It was as if her very flesh were alive with her longing for him and her loathing of him.

"That man killed my father. You cannot convince me otherwise. Find him, Luther, or I will hunt him down on my own."

"You had better heed her words, inspector," Philip cut in, his mouth twisted in a sneer. "Our Melissa is willful enough to do exactly as she has threatened."

She stared up at Philip, uncertain as to whom she hated more, the American or him. They had both used her and then betrayed her. And the one man who should have been her comfort through it all, the guardian of her honor, was dead.

"All right, Melissa, I will see to it. I promise you." The man slowly nodded his head. "But right now, I will see you up to your room. You must get some rest."

He helped her up from the chair and she sagged weakly against him. As Philip offered her his own arm in an effort to support her, she slapped him away, recoiling from the very nearness of him. How she despised him and the glint of triumph glittering there in his steely blue eyes. With a shrug, he walked from the room and into the strangely quiet hall. All of the guests had left, fleeing the tragedy, seeking the safety and comfort of their own homes. Never before had Melissa felt more alone.

She lay sleepless on her bed, enveloped in her agony. Her father was dead. Murdered. Of that she was certain. Her home was gone. Philip had proven himself to be a greater adversary than she had ever imagined. And he had taken everything from her, leaving her nothing. Once more she felt the silvery eyes of the stranger holding hers. His body glided with hers across the dance floor. She rubbed her hands over her eyes, trying to blot out his haunting image.

She knew then that she would never be free of him. Not until she had avenged her father and her own honor. All that was left to her now was her pride. And so, with the memory of her father as her witness, she vowed to seek out the American and punish him for what he had done to them. Bolstered by the promise of revenge, Melissa felt an icy calm settle within her. Maryland was a part of another world, an ocean away from her. But she would find that mocking stranger again, and kill him.

chapter 3

The days passed in a wavering blur of pain and tears, of visitors received, condolences accepted. Inspector Humphreys returned to report their failure to locate the missing American even though men had been dispatched throughout the county in an effort to find him. Melissa greeted the news with cool detachment, guarding her feelings well, and carefully laying her own plans.

On the morning of the funeral, cloaked in black and shielded from prying eyes by a heavy veil, Melissa watched her father's casket lowered into the ground of the Howard family cemetery. Scattering a cluster of spring flowers onto the coffin, she turned away and stumbled back to the house, just as the first clods of earth rained into the grave.

It was that night, as she tossed fitfully in her sleep, that the dream began. Melissa found herself kneeling beside the goldfish pond in the garden, staring at her reflection as it bobbed about on the glinting surface. Suddenly, the water darkened and she could not see herself anymore. But as she scanned the inky depths, a man's face appeared, replacing hers. Terrified, she looked behind her but found no one, yet when she gazed back into the pool, his image still shimmered there.

She splashed frantically at the mocking face and

although it rippled and wavered, it refused to disappear. Then it began moving toward her like some disembodied ghost, growing larger as it drew closer, and she fought in vain to push it away. Then she saw his gray eyes and heard his taunting laughter and she awoke screaming, her thin nightgown plastered to her clammy body.

"What is it, child? Whatever is the matter?" Lettie called out as she stood in the doorway. Raising her lamp, she spotted Melissa sitting bolt upright in bed, tears streaming down her face, her eyes wide and staring. Rushing over to the distraught girl, she placed the lamp on the bedside table and drew Melissa into her arms.

"Oh Lettie," she sobbed, "it was awful. His face . . . it kept coming closer and closer until I thought I was going to suffocate."

"Whose face, Melissa child? Was it your father?" the housekeeper questioned.

"Not father," she moaned. "His face, the American."

"Hush now," the woman said, soothing her. "Lettie will see that no harm comes to you. Now lie back and let me sponge your face and bring you a fresh nightgown."

Melissa gratefully complied, and as Lettie hovered protectively over her, tending and soothing. Melissa's breathing relaxed, her fluttering heartbeats eased. With the housekeeper promising to stay with her, Melissa fell asleep again and slept undisturbed until morning.

Shortly before noon, Philip Wentworth arrived at the house and Lettie ushered him into the study where Melissa was looking through her father's vast collection of books. She glanced up as Philip strode purposefully into the room and something cold seemed to clutch at her insides.

"I must say, Melissa, that black is hardly your most flattering shade," he remarked as his eyes arrogantly swept her body. "And here I had always hoped you would one day wear white for me, my dear, it suits you much better."

"I resent your attempted humor as much as I dislike this intrusion, Philip," she returned bitterly. "So would you be so kind as to remove yourself from my house?"

"Your house, is it?" he sneered. "My, my, how quickly we do forget. Howard House is mine now, dear girl, and it is only because of my respect for your late father that you have remained here as long as you have."

"Respect," she scoffed, her mouth twisting contemptuously. "You besmirch the very word."

"Nonetheless, Melissa, the papers are in my hands as you saw the other night, and the house is indeed mine."

She drew herself up proudly and forced herself to answer him in a cold steady voice. "You have nothing to fear from me, Philip, for I shall take little of what is here. I was simply deciding on which of father's books I might keep. That is, if you have no objection."

"Take whatever books you want," he replied with a disdainful wave of his hand. "They hold not the slightest interest for me." Then his voice suddenly softened. "Ah, Melissa, if only you had been less stubborn. How different things would have been. If only you had loved me a little, we could have shared everything."

"What a liar you are, Philip," she hissed. "Even as a child you never knew what it meant to share. You have always wanted everything for yourself." She turned her back on him then, staring out the study window at the familiar view she would soon relinquish. Tears filled her eyes. Philip had wanted it all and now he had it. And yet she was grateful for one small thing. He did not have her. She would belong to no man. Ever.

Composed again, she turned to face him, studying him carefully as she asked, "What do you know about

44

the American, Philip?"

"What exactly do you mean?" He appeared startled by her question and began drumming his fingertips against her father's old desk.

"You and father were speaking to him outside the study that night," she continued. "You left them, looking extremely agitated. Why, Philip?"

"I suppose I was a bit peeved that they wanted to be alone together," he said shrugging. "Nothing more than that, dear girl."

"What had you three been talking about?"

"Nothing of consequence, merely polite chatter." He smiled slightly. "I haven't the foggiest recollection of what was said, so obviously it could not have been of any consequence."

"Then why were you so angry?" she persisted.

"Dammit, Melissa, I refuse to be interrogated like this," he shouted. "It is over and done with and whether it was a suicide or murder hardly matters now, does it? Nothing can change what has happened. Nothing."

"But it does matter, Philip. It matters to me. Perhaps the inspector is looking for the wrong man." Philip looked at her sharply. "Perhaps you killed my father, Philip, knowing it might be years before you could take possession of our lands. Perhaps you feared that I might marry someone else and save our estate. And then what would you have gained? Nothing. You would have lost me and the estate."

"What preposterous nonsense," he bellowed. "You insult me by the very insinuation. I am ambitious, yes. Clever, yes. Devious, perhaps. But a murderer, never. I was in no hurry for your lands, Melissa. They would have come to me in due course. And if not, there are other estates hereabouts."

She turned away from him, wondering if she should believe him. All the time, a pair of silver eyes looked into hers and cramped her belly with pain and yearning. Again she hardened her resolve, believing Philip, and knowing what she still had to do.

"Besides, Melissa, I was in the ballroom dancing at the time your father died. Inspector Humphreys has already questioned the young lady who was my partner at the time." She heard what he was saying and searched her memory for corroboration. She vaguely remembered the distinctive hat of Horatio Nelson somewhere in the crowded ballroom as she hurried through it on her way to the study. Her shoulders sagged.

"I must leave you now, Melissa." She looked at him again. A cruel half smile lit his face. "But one final thing. I want you gone from this house in two days' time." He turned on his heel and strode from the room. She stood there stunned.

Lettie hurried into the study as soon as Philip had left the house. "I heard what that no-account scoundrel said to you, child. Two days?" she groaned. "Where will you go, with no family left now that your dear papa is gone, God rest him. And what of us? Are we to be thrown out too?" she wailed, wringing her gnarled hands despairingly.

Melissa grimly studied the woman before she replied. "I spoke with father's solicitor, Mortimer Dowling, and he has assured me that Mr. Wentworth will employ anyone wishing to stay on. Anyone choosing to leave Howard House will receive adequate compensation and a letter of recommendation."

"And what of you, my poor Melissa?" the house-keeper whispered, tears welling up in her eyes.

After a moment's hesitation, Melissa said simply, "I have planned a sea voyage for myself, dear Lettie."

The elderly woman stared quizzically at her mistress, but Melissa refused to elaborate. Lettie's shoulders slumped and she shuffled slowly from the room.

Melissa crossed the study, her gaze trained on the large globe set in the heavy oak stand beside her father's desk. She idly twirled the painted orb, watching it turn, spinning it faster and faster until continents and oceans blended together in a patchwork swirl. Abruptly, she stopped the globe, her eager eyes at last locating the name she sought, nestled there on the east coast of America, and she pressed her finger on the spot. Slowly she traced her way back to England, across the vast expanse of turquoise ocean still separating them, and a smile ignited in her topaz eyes.

Melissa hastened upstairs to collect the few belongings she would take with her. She thought bitterly of how little had been left to her, and how only memories would have to suffice her for a lifetime. With an aching heart, she carefully wrapped the diamond bracelets, knowing that she had worn them for the first and last time. In London she would sell them, and with the money she received, she would book passage on a ship bound for America.

Once she arrived, she was certain she would find work as a governess for some wealthy family or as a riding instructor at a girls' academy. She silently thanked her beloved father for allowing her to learn more than the gentle arts of conversation and needlepoint, for she would require more practical skills in order to survive, until she accomplished what she was setting out to do.

She spun through the following two days, her grief-worn mind mercifully occupied with last-minute preparations. The morning of her planned departure dawned cool and cloudy and she walked alone through each room of the only home she had ever known. Then she made her way to the cemetery and, kneeling beside her father's grave, she placed a small bouquet of spring flowers on the freshly turned earth and tearfully whispered her farewell. She struggled to her feet and trudged wearily back to the house to collect her small valise.

Handing the portmanteau to Walters, the family

coachman who had insisted on driving her to London, she turned to face the household staff lined up solemnly in front of the steps. She hastily bid them all goodbye, fearful of a final encounter with Philip Wentworth should she tarry. When she approached Lettie, she clung to the weeping woman, her own tears beading on her thick lashes, her eyes dangerously bright.

"God bless you, child," the housekeeper whispered brokenly, tearing from Melissa's arms and hurrying back into the house.

Walters helped Melissa into the carriage and closed the door. She leaned back against the red plush-velvet seat and pressed a hand to her throbbing head. With a sudden lurch, the carriage jolted forward and Melissa turned to look back at her home. She watched as it slowly receded behind them, until it was dwarfed by the surrounding trees. When she could discern only a single tall chimney, she finally looked away, and the distance gradually increased between the gray stone house and the carriage speeding toward London.

chapter 4

It had been three years since Melissa's last visit to London. For her sixteenth birthday, Sir Edmund had surprised her with a week-long stay, booking rooms in one of the luxurious hotels overlooking the Thames. They had dined in the finest restaurants, enjoyed the best of London's superb theater, and shopped in the most exclusive establishments in the city. How different it all seemed to her as the carriage wound its way through the crowded streets of London's teeming waterfront. There would be no fine hotels, no extravagant dinners for Melissa this time. The meager amount of money she had tucked away would afford her only the most modest of quarters near the harbor. But as the carriage clattered over the cobblestones, Melissa began to question her decision, for the odors of fish and garbage hung heavily in the air, and she pressed a perfumed handkerchief to her nose, breathing in its welcome freshness.

It had already grown dark by the time they reached a freshly painted hotel which appeared more suitable than the rows of decaying inns they had been passing, and Melissa ordered Walters to stop. He handed her down and she climbed the sagging steps of the wooden building to confront the stooped man behind a small battered desk. Ignoring his leering appraisal of her appearance, she managed to reserve a room for herself and had Walters fetch her bag. He carried it up the creaking, uncarpeted stairway to a dingy room with one cracked window overlooking the harbor.

Melissa shuddered apprehensively as she studied the bed with its worn, lumpy mattress. She pulled back the thin spread and found that, despite its inferior quality, the bedding was clean. The room boasted a rickety chest of drawers, a roughly hewn oak night stand, and a faded screen behind which rested a chipped chamber pot.

"Begging your pardon, Miss Melissa," Walters said, clearing his throat uneasily, "but are you meaning to stay in a place like this by yourself?" His face reddened in embarrassment.

"I fear so," she sighed, "but I hope it is only for a day or two." He dared not ask her of her plans and she remained silent, so he merely nodded his head sadly and wished her well, leaving her alone and suddenly frightened in the dreary room.

In an effort to occupy herself, she immediately unpacked her valise, hanging her dresses and slipping her underclothes and toiletries into the chest's small drawers. Wearily she tossed her hat onto the bed and unpinned her hair, running her fingers through the tangled mass of auburn curls. She looked around the room, grimacing at the peeling gray paint and the patched curtain fluttering in the slight breeze through the broken window.

Her growling stomach reminded her of the late hour. Slipping into her long, jersey cape and clutching her precious reticule, she left the hotel in search of a respectable place to dine. The crude sidewalks were pitted and broken and she stumbled as she walked, catching her heel in the wide cracks of the pavement. The stench of fish assailed her nostrils as the dockside smells were borne aloft by the wind. The vast expanse of the wooden wharves was crowded with boxes and crates of varying sizes, many covered with crumbling fish

50

nets, and kegs and barrels lined the fronts of weather-beaten sheds and sloping warehouses. Filthy water sloshed against the barnacle-encrusted pilings, sending foul-smelling spray into the air.

Melissa was jostled by a drunken man who slammed up against her, his mouth hanging open in a lopsided toothless grin. He belched loudly and staggered past her, weaving his way down the street. She drew her cape more tightly around her, uncomfortably aware of her incongruous appearance, and hurried on. Several women gaped at her as they passed, their crudely painted faces and garish clothes marking their profession. Melissa stared back at them. One of the women smiled craftily, exposing a dark gap between her front teeth and moved menacingly toward Melissa. She quickened her pace, mindful of the woman's raucous laughter following after her.

"Them girls laughin' at ya', dearie?" cackled a voice near her. Melissa started and looked down into the grotesque face of a man with jagged scars seaming his puckered skin. He was balanced precariously on a barrel and when he grinned, his mouth revealed small rotted stumps of teeth. "Ol' Jack wouldn't laugh none if ya' came 'ome wid 'im." She stared at him in horrified fascination and then broke into a run.

In her panic, she was prepared to abandon her search for a place to have a meal and return to the hotel to wait for daylight. But she fought down her fears and forced herself toward the welcoming glare of a taproom's lighted window. Clutching her small purse to her chest, she tripped up the steps and pushed open the heavy door. A chorus of loud catcalls greeted her entrance, but she straightened up haughtily and, with studied dignity, made her way to an empty table.

"Tired 'a walkin' them streets, girly?"

She glanced over at the table near hers and the sailor who had spoken gave her a broad wink. She turned away quickly and looked down at her hands, clasping and unclasping them in an attempt to calm herself.

"Whatsa' matter, ducks, we ain't good enough fer yer ladyship?" he demanded, his voice rising unpleasantly. She smarted beneath the curious stares of some of the men as they turned in her direction. She began to shake, her hands growing clammy as she battled the rising urge to scream. As other voices joined in to taunt her, she finally pushed herself away from the table and ran outside, covering her ears to blot out the sounds of the whistles and jeers at her hasty departure.

Through a veil of tears, she looked desperately around her and then she started to run, her head bowed against the lashing wind that whipped her cloak uncomfortably about her ankles. Rounding a corner, she charged headlong into a large, beefy man, who stumbled back slightly, pulling her against him.

"'ey, mate," he called out to his companion, "look what we 'ave 'ere. A bloomin' princess." He held her in a pair of muscled arms covered with tattoos and as she protested, squirming away from him, his grip tightened.

"Let me go," she cried, "let me go, I beg you."

"'ear that, mate?" the man bellowed, his whiskey-laden breath hot against Melissa's face, "'er ladyship be beggin' us to let 'er go. What think ya', me boy?" He shoved her towards the smaller man who caught her and pawed viciously at her, his filthy hands grappling with her cumbersome cloak. She gasped, outraged by his audacity, and struck him in the face.

Startled by her action, he loosened his hold enough for her to break free. Running along the street, she frantically sought a place to hide as she heard the men clambering after her. She upset a metal trash bin, sending it crashing to the ground, papers and rotted vegetables spilling across the pavement. Her heel snagged suddenly in a crack and her ankle twisted, sending her sprawling to the sidewalk. Picking herself up again, she began limping towards a cluttered alley when she felt herself grabbed roughly from behind.

Straining and clawing futilely at the air, she opened her mouth to scream, but her body was propelled brutally forward. Her head connected loudly with the side of a heavy crate and her world spun into blackness.

chapter 5

Melissa was caught in a swirling mass of inky fluid, swimming feverishly against the current holding her down. She heard voices and tried moving toward them, battling her way to the surface and burst of light which struck her full in the face. Opening her eyes, she blinked against the sudden glare.

"She's awake, Meg," a man whispered. Then the blurred face of a woman was peering down at her and Melissa squinted in an effort to clear her sight. She wet her lips with a thick and furry tongue and the woman called out for some water.

"There you are, child, just little sips now," the voice soothed, holding a cup to Melissa's parched lips. She tried to raise her head, but a blinding stab of pain sent her reeling back.

"What is wrong with me?" she moaned. "Where am I?"

"You 'ad a nasty 'it on the 'ead, child," the woman explained, "we found you lyin' on the walk just outside 'ere."

Melissa groaned and gingerly pressed her fingers to her head, wincing as she felt the large bump there. She managed to drink some of the water the woman offered, and she curiously studied the homely face bending over her. Although the woman's leathery skin seemed old and worn, her snapping cornflower-blue eyes were bright and lively. Gray-brown hair frizzed in casual disorder about her head and the tip of her broad nose was red and slightly bulbous from years of drinking.

"Studied me enough then?" the woman chuckled. Melissa flushed, lowering her gaze. "Never you mind, girl, we've 'ad ourselves a time of it examinin' you, to be sure." Throwing back her head she laughed until she broke into a hacking cough and the man behind her pounded her roughly on the back. "Stop it, Joe," she finally gasped, "you'll be beatin' the life outa' me one day, you will."

The man called Joe was short and squat with the mangled face of a one-time pugilist. An eye was partially closed, his nose was broken and one of his front teeth was missing. A scar ran down one cheek, lining the swarthy skin and lending a ferocity to his overall appearance. Melissa looked away from his battered face and turned her attention to the sparse room in which she found herself. Following her gaze, the woman explained, "You're in a bedroom top a' the little tavern we own—The Three Kegs we calls it—Joe 'ere tends the bar an' me, I keep the customers 'appy. You know, a little song 'ere an' there, a lively spin around with one a' the fellows," and she added proudly, "I also do some pretty fair cookin' fer them that wants to eat while they's drinkin'."

Melissa nodded, trying to absorb what she was being told, but the pain in her head was worsening and she was growing faint. When the woman suddenly asked why she had been wandering about the docks, Melissa tried to answer her, but she was unable to concentrate. Her head began spinning violently and she felt herself slipping backward. She threw out her arms in an effort to save herself, but she fell back with a splash into a cold, swirling pool.

But this time she was not alone. Beside her, reflected in the waves was a masked face, his silvery eyes piercing her with their icy glare. Then the face moved toward her, growing larger until her entire world seemed bounded by a pair of flashing gray eyes. She clawed at the face and began to scream, struggling against the weight pinning her down.

Joe was leaning over her, his forehead beaded with perspiration as he held her down against the covers.

"No!" Melissa cried out, "no, don't kill me! I promise not to scream again, but please don't kill me too!"

"Easy there, missy," he cautioned her, gripping her flailing arms, "ain't nobody tryin' to kill you. You 'ad a bad dream, that's all. Quiet now an' ol' Joe will see to it that no one 'urts you." He gradually relaxed his hold on her as Melissa's rigid body slackened and she lay limply back against the cushions.

"Should we send 'round fer ol' Doc Timmens?" Meg asked, wringing her hands. "The girl mighta' scrambled 'er brains real bad in that fall."

"Nah, Meg," Joe answered, rising from the bed where Melissa lay subdued and breathing more calmly, "I seen worse an' all they were needin' was sleep."

The woman shrugged and sighed. "I 'ope so, Joe. She's too pretty to be locked up in one a' them crazy 'ouses."

"You stay 'ere, Meg, I gotta' be gettin' back to me bar 'afore them louts take to drinkin' me ale fer free."

Melissa slept as if she had been heavily drugged and when she finally awoke, Meg brought her a bowl of clear broth and a thick slice of black bread smothered with rich butter. Plumping up the pillows, Meg stepped back to watch Melissa eat. When she had cleared away the empty dishes, she saw the questioning glance in the large topaz eyes regarding her closely.

"Is it morning or afternoon now?" Melissa asked, straining to raise her head.

"It's just past noon, child. You been sleepin' off an' on fer two days now," Meg answered softly.

"Two days?" Melissa echoed incredulously. As she fought to recall what had happened to her, her mind remained unbearably blank, barren of thoughts, with only a persistent dull throb to remind her of her injury.

56

Her gaze raked the room, searching for something, and she began to get up from the bed. She then realized that she was naked and, flushing with embarrassment, she tugged the blanket around her again.

"Don't you fret none," Meg laughed, "I undressed you meself an' 'ung away yer dress. "Melissa smiled wanly, but she was still confused. Something was still missing.

"Are you lookin' fer this?" Meg asked, returning to the bed, the small purse in her hand.

"Yes, yes." Melissa sighed with relief and clutched the soiled pouch to her chest. Hastily opening the little bag, she gasped in dismay. It was empty.

"What's 'appened then?" Meg demanded.

"Everything has been taken," Melissa whispered.

"It was lyin' near to where you was found that night. I never looked inside it an' neither did my Joe. That be the God's truth, I swear it."

Melissa flung herself down onto the bed, her body shaking with the force of her sobs. She had now lost everything which connected her to a past she could not remember. It was as if some vague shadow were hovering over her, setting her adrift in an alien world, with little hope of return. And then, in the shimmering darkness of her mind, she saw a face. Masked, his silvery eyes sought hers and his mouth moved as if in slow motion, repeating to her a single word, urging her to comprehend and follow. Maryland . . . Maryland . . . Maryland. . . .

It spun around her, repeated itself inside her brain like a tantalizing litany. Maryland . . . Maryland . . . and she found herself repeating the word, whispering it aloud, hoping to awaken that sleeping part of her. But the name seemed to hold no meaning for her. She opened her eyes and the dizziness abated. Once more she said the name and wished she understood.

"What are you sayin', child?" Meg's voice distracted her.

"Maryland," Melissa mumbled and her voice grew

louder as she said the name over and over again, until something whirred and clicked inside her tortured mind and she began to remember. "Maryland," she cried, color flooding her waxen cheeks. "I was on my way to Maryland. I must have been boarding a ship when I fell that night."

Meg watched the transformation in the girl and felt the sting of tears in her own eyes. But her relief was short-lived as she stared at the empty purse Melissa held.

"Did you 'ave yer ticket in there then?"

"Ticket?" Melissa repeated, frowning in concentration. "No, I . . . I had no ticket. I was going to purchase one with the money." She paused again, trying to recall. "The bracelets, I was supposed to sell the diamond bracelets my father had given me for my birthday." It was as if those last words had finally managed to thaw her frozen mind, and although her head pounded angrily, she forced herself to repeat what she had said, and suddenly the pain and the anguish of her recent tragedy flooded back into her consciousness.

Bit by bit, the pieces of the splintered puzzle tumbled into place and Melissa fell back weakly against the cushions, her eyes closing once more. Meg tiptoed from the bedroom, leaving Melissa alone with her memories. She trembled, recalling her father lying dead at her feet, and she searched the room with anxious eyes for someone who should have been there. But he had gone. A stab of pain pierced her and her mind seemed suddenly to rebel again. A man's masked face flickered tauntingly before her, but as she reached out to him, he eluded her, slipping safely behind the door which slammed shut again within her head.

He was lost to her now, lost behind that closing door which would separate them until the time when she would choose once again to remember. Torn by her love for her father, her refusal to believe him dead by his own hand, and drawn to a stranger to whom she had so recklessly given her heart, Melissa's troubled mind sought refuge in forgetting. Desolation swept over her. She could recall none of the events marking her father's death. The man whose face she had glimpsed was now a mystery to her. But as the pain in her head worsened, the name Maryland whirled around her, beckoning her, driving her.

She knew only that she had to reach Maryland, although the reasons now lay hidden within the spiraling vortex within her memory. Further thought was denied her, as a whirling darkness engulfed her, and she gave herself up to its soothing tide.

The following morning, Melissa forced herself out of bed and, as her legs began to quake, she clutched the bedpost for support. She wrapped the thin blanket around her just as Meg strode into the room, carrying a basin of steaming water.

"I thought you'd be wantin' to wash," the kindly woman said, hoisting the basin onto the table. "I'll be back with some buckets 'a water an' you can 'ave yerself a proper bath."

Melissa moved unsteadily over to the window and leaned out into the warm spring air. Breathing deeply of the fish-tainted air, she looked out over the waterfront with its large wooden docks alive with people and produce. Ships with tall masts and lashed sails bobbed up and down on the gentle river and sooty smoke rose from the stacks of a steamship making its way across the water. The cries of birds mingled with those of the fish vendors and vegetable hawkers, and everywhere she gazed, there was bustling activity.

For the first time since her father's death, she felt her heart lighten, as the pulsating life around her stimulated a revival of her own high spirits. She turned from the window as Meg returned with a young boy in tow, each of them clenching a handle on a giant cauldron of hot water. They poured the steamy water into a shallow tub in the corner of the room and Meg handed Melissa a bar of harshly scented soap.

"It prob'ly ain't what you been used to," she apologized, "but I'll wager it does as good a job."

When they had gone, Melissa threw aside the ragged cover, testing the water with one foot before she lowered herself into the tub. With a sigh, she leaned back and closed her eyes, stretching her body to ease her tensed muscles. She began washing her hair, wincing as the soap rubbed against the bump on her head. Proceeding more cautiously, she worked up a rich lather and then rinsed it away with the water in the basin.

Picking up the bar again, she gently soaped her body, slowly following the curve of her throat and shoulders, the rising peaks of her breasts, down to her tiny waist. Soaping the golden patch between her legs, she closed her eyes once more as a warm tingling seeped upward through her body. She moaned as the feeling grew, but suddenly she envisaged a pair of gray eyes looking into hers and her head began to throb. She shivered in spite of the heat of the bath.

Hastily stepping from the tub, patches of soap still clinging to her skin, she fought to rid herself of the image troubling her. She dried herself with a large rough towel. Finding a brush, she sought to unsnarl her long, thick hair. Then she stepped to the small clothes cupboard and took out her gown and hurriedly dressed. She was surprised by its freshly pressed appearance and she silently thanked Meg for the obvious pains she had taken to clean and iron it.

She was about to set out in search of the woman when there was a rap on the door and Meg walked in, smiling approvingly at the girl before her.

"You surely are a beauty," she said, beaming, but the smile faded as she asked, "And what will you be doin' now, child?"

Melissa frowned, remembering her ransacked purse. "I have no idea," she murmured, "I have no money now and I dare not return to the hotel without the money to pay for my room." She thought of the dingy little room and wondered what would happen to all of her belongings. The man at the desk had probably already sold them, she thought bitterly, when she had failed to return.

"I 'ave an idea," Meg broke in, " 'ow's about workin' 'ere with Joe an' me? Our last girl up an' run away with a sailor off one a' them clipper ships. She might be in China now fer all we know. Cleaned out the till, she did, before she left, the bloody tart. Well, what do you think then?" She squinted at the astonished girl. "We'll pay you proper an' you can 'ave this room, it was 'ers before. She even left 'er workin' dress behind, an' with a little takin' in an' lettin' out 'ere an' there, it should fit you fine."

A thousand disparate thoughts whirled through Melissa's mind as she pondered her reply. A bar maid, she grimaced, and then she laughed aloud. If Philip Wentworth could have seen her there, would he still be as eager to marry her? A bar maid in a public house. She cringed at the very idea, but without any money or clothing, she knew that her choices were few. She accepted the only offer standing between her and starvation.

Melissa and Meg spent the remainder of the afternoon altering the skirt and ruffled blouse left behind by the former bar maid. Meg had carefully washed and pressed the garments before she had stored them so that once the repairs were completed, Melissa stepped immediately into her borrowed clothing. The white blouse, with its full, puffed sleeves, was cut so daringly low that Melissa feared her breasts would tumble out when she leaned over.

"I think we made a mistake with the blouse," she said, eyeing her exposed cleavage.

Meg laughed at her discomfort, assuring her that the men would heartily approve of the display and show their appreciation by leaving her larger tips. Melissa grimaced, realizing that it was too late to alter the blouse again. She tugged at it in a futile attempt to raise the plunging neckline. The black skirt provided her with further misgivings when she noted its length—it fell in folds to well above her borrowed black shoes, exposing her shapely ankles.

"Them blokes love to see good legs," Meg insisted as she caught Melissa's look of consternation. Meanwhile Melissa busied herself by tying a starched, white apron about her narrow waist. At Meg's insistence, she left her hair trailing down her back.

"Makes you look less the lady, if you know what I mean," she explained, and Melissa nodded mutely.

With a few final instructions from the woman, Melissa was ready. She took a deep breath to steady herself and obediently followed Meg's swaying form down the dimly lit stairs to the noisy taproom. A blast of hot smoke-filled air greeted them as they entered the crowded room. From behind a bar, Joe was hurriedly filling tall mugs with foaming ale and passing them around to the men facing him. Most of them appeared to be sailors and dock workers, and were either slouching forward from their narrow stools or leaning heavily against the bar with their dark, muscular bodies.

Melissa studied the dingy place, lit by swinging oil lamps which cast flickering shadows on the cracked plaster walls. Small, crudely made tables and chairs were scattered about, all of them taken by grumbling, belching, noisy groups of men. As she gazed uneasily about her, she became increasingly aware of the curious glances of some of the men, and she forced herself to finally walk over to the bar.

Joe winked encouragingly at her as she picked up a small, round tray. She smiled weakly back at him despite the pang of uncertainty she experienced as she watched Meg disappear into the tiny, cramped kitchen, leaving Melissa completely on her own. A loud burst of applause, accompanied by appreciative whistles, followed her as she strode over to a group of sailors and took their orders.

Dipping and swaying among the tables, she felt more at ease as the evening wore on, and as she relaxed, she managed a faint smile for the men she served. Balancing her tray gracefully, she placed glasses of the frothy ale before the thirsty men and quickly cleared away the empty mugs, moving swiftly and efficiently. As she slipped comfortably into the routine, she began to concentrate more on dodging the large rough hands reaching out to pinch and grab her as she passed.

She was managing to evade the greedy clenches, smiling impishly and scurrying out of reach, when she was suddenly caught unawares and spun roughly onto a sailor's lap. Her tray clattered to the floor, the shattering of the glasses echoing loudly.

"'ow's about a kiss, luv?" the drunken voice roared, drawing a crow of laughter from his drinking companions. Melissa's captor was a stocky man, wearing a striped jersey and scratchy wool trousers, which burned through the thin material of her skirt as she attempted to free herself. She writhed impotently against him.

"'ey, mates, this beauty's a fighter, ain't she? What say you to ol' Rob givin' 'er a good kissin'?" As he planted a wet, foul-breathed kiss on her neck, Melissa tugged at his greasy brown hair in an effort to force back his offending mouth. But he grabbed her hands, pinning them behind her back. He leaned forward trying to capture her lips, when a voice close to Melissa's ear spoke up calmly.

"I wouldn't do that if I were you."

The drunken man glanced up in surprise and Melissa found herself instantly released with a shove which almost sent her sprawling onto the floor. Regaining her balance and some of her dignity, she looked for her rescuer.

"Down here, miss," came the deep, accented voice again, and as she looked down, she gasped in disbelief at the tiny man staring up at her, a mischievous smile lighting his swarthy face. Despite the smile, displaying dazzling white teeth in a generous mouth set below a thin black moustache, the large, glinting knife he held forced her to take an involuntary step backward. The knife swiftly disappeared inside his jacket.

"My name is Marco," the little man said, sweeping her a low bow.

Before Melissa could recover from her shock, Meg appeared at her side. She braced herself for a tongue lashing as she thought of the broken glasses, but Meg ignored them.

"Are you all right, child?" she asked, a worried frown on her face. "I shoulda' warned you about some a' them lugs before this 'appened. But Marco 'ere will make sure it don't 'appen again." And without further explanation, she swished away, her long skirts crackling as she walked briskly back toward the kitchen.

Melissa felt a tug at her arm and she followed Marco over to a quiet corner of the room. He gazed up at her earnestly. "I work here for Joe to make certain things are peaceful," he explained. "When someone causes trouble, I always manage to convince him to leave. You see, in spite of my size, I am most accomplished with a knife, having spent many years using the knife in my profession." He laughed at her startled expression. "I was part of a traveling show in my native Italy. We were touring London when I took a walk one night and saw a man being beaten by two sailors in a nearby alley. My knife and I came to the man's defense and, in gratitude, he offered me this job. By then I had grown tired of the show and I readily accepted his offer. That was ten years ago." He swept her another bow and turned to walk away.

Melissa finally found her voice and called after him. He flashed his wide smile at her and she smiled her thanks in return. She watched his tiny black-suited figure, perched on high, black boots, disappear into the crowd.

The rest of the night passed without further incident. When Melissa finally staggered up the stairs to the small bedroom, her feet ached, her back was stiff and her eyes stung from the heavy smoke. She rubbed the back of her hand across her throbbing forehead, closing her eyes against the return of the steady drumming in her head. Her weary body cried out for a hot bath, but she lacked the energy to carry up a pot of water and it had grown too late to disturb Meg and ask for assistance. So she stripped off her clothes, splashed her face with the tepid water in the porcelain pitcher atop the wash stand and flopped onto the bed. She was immediately asleep.

The days began to take on a routine. She slept late each morning then bathed and ate a light meal. If Marco were available, the two of them would stroll along the waterfront together. Joe had forbidden her going out alone, not wanting to risk a repetition of the incident which had brought her to their doorstep. Melissa grudgingly agreed, disliking the curtailment of her freedom, but she owed them her life. She would obey them, if only for the time being.

And so the tall, auburn-haired beauty and the black-clad dwarf became something of a curiosity along the docks. Sailors and dock hands took to nodding as they walked by and the fish vendors and vegetable peddlers smiled their gap-toothed grins at the unlikely twosome. Melissa found herself smiling back, warming to the astonishing display of affection she and Marco received.

She grew accustomed to the medley of sounds and smells permeating the circumscribed world in which she lived. She and Marco explored the crooked little alleys curving between the ramshackle wooden houses which leaned precariously against one another as if hovering together for support. They walked the cobbled streets among the decaying snarl of buildings, guessing at the contents of the massive red-brick warehouses and peering in through dusty broken windows.

Many of the buildings they passed housed families on the upper floors and either dance halls or public houses on the ground floors. Children with sunken eyes and hollow cheeks, dressed in filthy rags, begged on street corners, and as carefully as Melissa was hoarding her money, she could seldom resist the tear-streaked faces looking up at her so plaintively.

Sometimes she and Marco would simply sit on a bench in front of one of the taverns and look out at the busy harbor. Bare-chested men heaved kegs and barrels from the wharves and placed them in the holds of the seafaring ships, while other men emptied the holds and stacked their wares in huge piles on the pier. Sailors, with their peculiar rolling gait, ambled by, their arms thrown about one another, singing sea shanties. Prostitutes sauntered along, ogling the brawny men, luring them back to their squalid rooms nearby.

And each night, Melissa would dress and serve the men and smile at their lewd remarks and expertly withdraw too friendly hands from around her waist. She had grown increasingly adept at avoiding affectionate pats and attempted kisses. Despite her aloofness, the men liked her, roaring their approval when she stepped into the room each evening and tipping her generously. At the end of each gruelling night's work, she forced her bone-weary body up the long flight of stairs and, before undressing, she added the evening's coins to the growing pile hidden in the little purse, tucked beneath her mattress.

chapter 6

It was early May and down to the already crowded dockfront came the flower vendors, dotting the dismal wharves with bright splotches of color, adding sweet fragrances to the pungent odors of decay. Melissa delighted in purchasing bunches of the delicate blooms to enliven her drab little room, filling the air with their gentle perfume. During the lengthening days, dappled with warming sunshine, she began to feel the first stirrings of restlessness within her.

One evening before she was to begin her duties, she slipped secretly out of the tavern, making her way down the cobbled steps to the river where the waves lapped softly against the embankment. Under the glow of a gas lamp, she crouched, looking out at the water, its surface covered with the dark silhouettes of masts and riggings, funnels and limply fluttering flags. Absently she picked up a handful of loose pebbles and began tossing them, one by one, into the river, watching the spreading circular pools radiating from them as they sank to the muddy bottom. Wearily closing her eyes, she allowed her thoughts to drift back in time, and then, unbidden, a pair of silvery eyes appeared, bobbing silently on the currents within her mind.

Her eyes flew open in panic and she blinked to dispel the image still haunting her. She gazed down again into the dark waters, feeling herself inexplicably drawn forward, lured by a will not her own. Under the wavering flicker of the lamp, she watched as her own image, hazy and undulating, rose up and fell back with the gentle current.

There was a loud shout and then a pair of arms were forcing her back, hauling her away from the bank. She half fell into Joe's powerful grasp as he began to curse her stupidity, pulling her against him.

"What the 'ell are you doin' out 'ere alone?" he thundered, "you tryin' to drown yerself, you crazy wench? Why'd you come 'ere when I told you never to be goin' no place without ol' Marco?"

She flinched under his scathing attack, her eyes downcast, her teeth gnawing nervously at her lower lip. She admitted to herself that he was right, but she had grown tired of being his prisoner, tired of being guarded like a piece of priceless porcelain. Aching for release from her unwilling bondage, she raised her eyes to meet his and an amber flame danced brightly in her gaze as her temper flared to the surface and exploded.

"I am growing tired of being locked away!" she shouted, her hands clenched tightly at her sides. "I am a free woman and I refuse to be trifled with and ordered about like a servant. Do you understand me, Joe?" she demanded.

He merely looked back at her, a smile curling about the edges of his mouth. "That's just what you be, ain't it, missy? A servant."

And Melissa's retort died on her lips. Burning with humiliation, she turned and ran back to the tavern, almost tripping over the prostrate body of a drunk who was lying at the bottom of the steps. And she silently cursed the man and all the others like him who nightly littered the stairs and the alleys like so many discarded human dolls.

As she stormed into the taproom, Meg bustled over to her, glowering, wiping her hands on her tattered apron. "Where were you, child? Marco says 'e turns 'is back an' the next thing 'e knows you've disappeared on 'im. Joe went lookin' fer you, madder than a fightin' cock."

"I apologize for worrying you, Meg," Melissa replied crisply, "but I felt the need for some air." She flounced off, with her head held high.

During the long evening hours, she noticed Joe carefully watching her and, under his scrutiny, she grew irritable and rebellious. Deciding to spite him, she began affecting outrageous, wanton gestures as she moved among the tables. Weaving her way around the playful pinches and outstretched arms, she began to exaggerate her movements. To the surprised delight of the men, she leaned across the tables, displaying more of her voluptuous curves than ever before. As her hips swiveled, sending her skirts swishing from side to side, her face glowed and her huge topaz eyes sparkled teasingly.

She ignored Meg's troubled stare and its silent warning, but as she was filling an order at the bar, Joe suddenly leaned forward, grasping her wrist and squeezing it. Melissa winced and glared at him but he held her fast.

"You better watch who you be teasin', missy," he snarled, abruptly releasing her, as his eyes wandered to her rounded breasts heaving below the plunging neckline of her scanty blouse.

She drew back from him, revolted and frightened by his actions. She hurriedly placed the mugs of ale on her tray and continued to serve the men, but something had died again in her eyes and her flirting airs of a few moments before quickly vanished.

That night, Melissa tossed and turned on her lumpy bed. She finally got up and walked to the open window. She leaned against the sill, and stared into the moonlit night. Her body ached with loneliness as she thought of her home, yearning for the life she had known. Bitter tears welled up in her eyes and spilled onto her cheeks, tracing burning paths to her quivering chin as she gazed out at the sleeping harbor below.

The skeletal masts of the ships riding at anchor were outlined against the high, yellow moon. The wharves, laden with their cargo, cut jagged shapes in the star-spattered sky. She watched the occasional drunk lurch and stumble across the cobblestones. The yowling of a cat echoed eerily and the faint sounds of laughter drifted upward from an all-night gambling parlor.

Watching the ships, Melissa longed to board one that night, but her pile of coins, although mounting, was still not enough to secure her passage. From listening to the sailors in the tavern, she had yet to hear them mention the destination she sought. She sighed despondently; she would have to continue to be patient a while longer.

She stumbled listlessly about in her room all morning and then she located Marco and convinced him to walk with her along the waterfront. The little man, his dark eyes sparkling, happily consented and they began making their way through the familiar streets, crowded with the usual vendors and their wares. Melissa hummed softly as they walked along and she stopped to purchase a large bouquet of flowers, gladly parting with one of her precious coins.

Breathing deeply of their delicious fragrances, she buried her face in their perfumed brightness. Marco laughed in delight as he watched her and Melissa plucked a bright red flower from the bunch and struggled to slip it through a button hole in his shirt. His chest puffed out with pride at her gesture, his swarthy face beaming with happiness as he gazed adoringly up at her.

Engrossed, laughing together, they failed to notice the open carriage rapidly bearing down on them. Only the angry shout of the driver alerted them at the last moment. Marco instantly pushed Melissa to the side of the road where they both fell heavily together in a tangle of skirts and twisted flowers.

"Are you hurt, miss?" a concerned voice inquired as Melissa endeavored to disengage herself from Marco. She accepted the hand offered her and, as she was pulled to her feet, she found herself staring into a pair of sapphire-blue eyes. She blushed at the open admiration in those eyes and selfconsciously began adjusting her dress. He repeated his question and Melissa hastily recovered her speech.

"I am quite all right now, thank you," she murmured, venturing a closer look at the man. He was not much taller than she was, with thick, curly, blond hair and elegantly carved features, and as he smiled at her, a dimple creased his right cheek.

"Melissa, I've saved all of the flowers," came the soft, almost plaintive voice behind her. Melissa whirled to face the little man, chastising herself for having forgotten him. She bent down, accepting the somewhat rumpled blossoms, and planted a tender kiss on his dark, perspiring brow.

"Jeremy," a woman's sharp voice rang out. Melissa glanced toward the carriage to see the young woman there impatiently signaling to the man. "We shall be terribly late, dear, so do hurry." Her beautiful face was marred by the sullen pout of her full, red lips as she glared at the unlikely trio. She angrily opened and closed her flower-sprigged parasol with small, white-gloved hands and, as Melissa watched the exquisitely gowned woman, she felt a pang of jealousy, realizing what a pitiful sight she herself must be in her only dress covered with dust and dirt.

The young man bowed slightly to Melissa, a smile still playing about his lips, and returned to the carriage. As it started forward, he leaned out and waved back at her and Melissa returned the wave. She watched as the coach continued down the street and she wondered what had brought the couple down to the harbor. Perhaps they were leaving on a cruise, she thought enviously, as she and Marco walked silently back to

The Three Kegs, the afternoon somehow spoiled for her.

That night the tavern seemed especially crowded, filled with many faces Melissa did not recognize. When she asked Meg, the woman shrugged, suggesting that there might be a new ship in port. Melissa's heart fluttered expectantly and as she walked among the tables, she listened carefully to the talk of the men.

Setting down drinks before each unfamiliar face, she lingered longer than usual, smiling and flirting, hoping to catch bits of their conversation. Her patience was finally rewarded as she caught the name she had long been seeking. She sidled over to the sailor who was amusing his companions with stories of his latest voyage aboard an American clipper named *The Sea Belle*.

"An' would ya' believe it, boys," the blustery, bewhiskered man was saying, "but two days outa' London, the captain gets hisself a case o' what we all thought was poisonin' from cook's food. Turns out it's 'is appendix an' it bursts on 'im before we get in to port. All the days we been 'ere, an' 'e's still laid up, an' we gets us a new captain just outa' knee pants." He bellowed with laughter, the men around the table joining in.

"And when will you be sailing again, might I ask?" Melissa spoke up boldly, swaying her hips and saucily eyeing the sailor.

"Ya might indeed ask, me pretty," he laughed, wiping ale from his stubbled chin with a rough, calloused hand. "Three days hence we be leavin' fer Baltimore." He gave Melissa a sound whack on the buttocks and sent her off for more ale. With a pounding heart, Melissa watched as Joe filled the mugs, hoping he could not read her eyes. He seemed oblivious to her excitement as he was greedily staring at her firm high cleavage, his lips moist, his eyes glittering.

Melissa's thoughts sped far ahead of her as she served

her final customers and hurried upstairs to her room. Emptying the contents of her purse onto the bed and adding the evening's tips, she hastily counted the coins she had saved. She wondered if she had collected enough for her precious ticket as she happily whispered the name of the *The Sea Belle*, delighting in its melodious sound. Scooping up the coins, she stuffed them back into her purse and tucked it under the mattress again. She joyfully hugged herself at the thought of her long-awaited freedom.

She slept fitfully, her mind filled with images of ships tossing about on the ocean and of the handsome young man named Jeremy and the way he had smiled at her. In the morning, she found it difficult to force herself out of bed and as she lackadaisically brushed her long hair in front of the small mirror, she noticed the faint violet smudges of fatigue below her eyes. She wound a green ribbon around her hair, pulling it back from her face, for the weather was growing warmer and the thick auburn mane lay heavily on her slender neck.

After lunch, Marco accompanied her along the docks. This time, however, Melissa carefully scanned the names of each ship they passed, searching for *The Sea Belle*. When she had despaired of ever locating it, and Marco had begun to complain of the distance they had covered, her heart leaped excitedly as she finally read the name on the hull of a sleek, newly painted clipper.

"Why are we stopping here, Melissa?" asked the little man as he mopped at his forehead with a large purple handkerchief.

"I have never seen a clipper like this one." She chose her words carefully as she spoke. "Last night the sailors were boasting of her speed. Imagine, Marco, some clippers have been known to cross the ocean to America in less than five weeks."

The little man grunted, impatient to begin the long walk back to the tavern, but Melissa could not be hurried. She had to speak to the captain.

"Marco," she said sweetly, "if someone is about, perhaps they could take me on a tour of the ship. In the meantime, you could have a cool drink at the taproom across the street." Marco's eyes brightened as he thought of shade and a refreshing ale. To her relief, he readily agreed. With a jaunty salute, he sauntered away and Melissa made her way up the gangplank.

Just as she stepped onto the deck, she was halted by a loud shout and a sailor came lumbering toward her.

"'ey there, miss, where d'ya think yer goin'?" The lanky sailor, his red hair closely cropped, loped to her side.

"I would like to speak with the captain," Melissa answered, attempting to keep her voice steady. She resented his studied scrutiny of her and she flushed uncomfortably at his rudeness. "Is the captain aboard?" she repeated, her irritation getting the better of her.

The sailor's gaze finally rested on her upturned face. "Nah, the captain's ashore with mosta' the men, gettin' food an' the like afore we set sail. What would ya be wantin' with the captain anyways?" His eyes narrowed suspiciously as he stared at her.

"I would like to book passage aboard this ship," she replied matter of factly, unprepared for the sailor's reaction. He threw back his head and roared with laughter. "Just what do you find so amusing?" she demanded, bridling. "Stop it!" She lashed out at him and was pleased at the immediate effect of her anger on the startled man.

"We ain't takin' no passengers this trip, miss," he barked, "not unless ya wants to be kept company in the 'old by a lotta tea an' such."

"But you must take me with you," Melissa insisted. "I have money to pay for my passage and I must leave on this ship."

His eyes were suddenly suspicious again. "Now why would ya be needin' a ship in such a bleedin' 'urry?

The police lookin' fer ya?"

"No, of course not," she snapped. "The matter is personal and can only be discussed with the captain. Now if you would tell me when I might be able to speak to him . . ."

"Speakin' to 'im ain't gonna make no diff'rence," he interrupted. "There ain't no passengers an' that's that. 'e's new to this 'ere ship an' ya can be sure 'e'll be goin' by the rules this trip. So off with ya now, girly, I got me work to do." He turned and stalked off.

Melissa was close to tears. She stood there helplessly watching the sailor walk away, and then she noticed Marco coming toward the ship. As she joined him, she forced herself to appear calm. She explained that since the captain was away from the ship, she was to return the following day for a tour. Marco groaned but he promised Melissa that he would accompany her back to the boat again. As he chattered gaily, Melissa's thoughts were elsewhere, desperately devising some plan to get her on board the clipper.

As they reached The Three Kegs, Marco began to mutter under his breath and Melissa followed his frowning gaze. A drunken sailor lay snoring against one of the large garbage bins outside the tavern. His mouth hung open, his dirty wool cap half covered his face, and one grimy hand loosely clung to an empty bottle. Melissa looked away in disgust, but as she entered the taproom, the seed of an idea took root in her mind.

The following day she and Marco returned to *The Sea Belle*. Unlike the previous day, she found the decks alive with men as the sailors hauled supplies on board and stored them away in the huge, darkened hold. Melissa peered about for the red-headed sailor but he was nowhere to be found, so she approached another man and inquired as to the whereabouts of the captain. The answer was the same. He was ashore for the day and there were to be no passengers that trip.

Fighting down her panic, Melissa walked back to the tavern where Marco was contentedly sipping his ale. She waited impatiently for him to finish his drink and as they strolled back to The Three Kegs, she told him of her tour and how truly impressive the ship had been.

That night, as she changed into her working clothes, she neatly folded her few possessions, tying them together with a worn shawl Meg had given her. She buried her purse, bulging with its hoarded coins, deep inside the bundle. She had only one chance to board *The Sea Belle* and she was counting on Marco's affection for her to help her plan succeed.

The hours seemed to crawl by. Melissa's hands were trembling so badly that several times she spilled the drinks as she placed them on the tables and once she dropped a tray of empty glasses. She cringed as Joe reprimanded her, cursing her clumsiness, threatening to deduct the cost of the glasses from her wages. But she paid scant attention to his words, knowing that if all went according to plan, she would have nothing to fear from him again.

When she had thankfully served her final drink of the evening, she signaled Marco to join her. Together they walked outside and Melissa hastily pulled him toward the alley running alongside The Three Kegs. There she could speak freely, without fear of being overheard.

"Marco, there is something I must tell you," she began uncertainly. "I hope to leave here tonight. With luck I can board the ship I visited today." She stopped, expecting an outburst, but the little man stood quietly, his arms folded across his chest, gazing up at her. "You must have known I would leave one day. Now the time has finally come. But, Marco, I need your help." She waited, scarcely daring to breathe until he slowly nodded his head.

"I'll help you, Melissa," he murmured, "but it

breaks my heart to do so." She released her breath in a loud sigh and hugged the small figure to her breast. Her plan was a simple one and, as she outlined it for him, he nodded and smiled, his eyes twinkling in anticipation of adventure.

He walked briskly away, disappearing into the shadows, and Melissa returned to her room. Pacing the floor in her bare feet, she counted the number of steps from the door to the window and back again, over and over. Then she sat on the bed, springing up again at every sound coming from the street below, scampering to the window and scanning the night for some sign of Marco. What if he failed, she worried, what if he lay hurt in some alley. Guilt nibbled at her as she waited and she feared that, unless he returned shortly, she would go mad.

There was a soft rapping at the door and she flew to open it. Marco slipped into the room and she closed the door behind him.

"It went even better than planned," he whispered. "I found a sailor. Just the right height, too. He was snoring away in one of the alleys not far from here. He'll be a little cold when he finally wakes up, but I left him a few shillings for the use of his clothes, so he shouldn't raise too much of a fuss."

The little man laughed softly as he handed Melissa the worn garments and then he turned his back while she undressed. She tore a broad strip from her petticoat and bound her breasts to hide their fullness. Then she slipped on the scratchy wool trousers, the striped jersey and the battered black shoes. Hastily braiding her hair into a long pigtail, she wound it around her head, pinning it securely, and then pulled on the dark woolen cap.

"Marco," she whispered, stifling a laugh as she scratched at the wool trousers, "how do I look?"

She watched the expression on his face as he studied her transformation from a voluptuous young woman into a lanky, seedy-looking sailor. "Remarkable," he murmured, shaking his head, "simply remarkable. But I think you need some dirt to smudge onto your face. You look too clean, as if you've never shaved." He winked at her.

"All right," she concurred, "we can do that on the way to the ship." Then she burrowed into her small clothing bundle and extracted the purse. She gave several coins to Marco and, as he balked, she pressed them into his hand and closed his fingers over them. "You must accept them," she insisted, "after all, you left money for the sailor. This is simply to pay you back."

"But it's much more . . ." he protested.

"Hush now, no arguments." Shrugging, he pocketed the money. "And this is for Meg and Joe, to make up for my not saying goodbye properly, and to pay for the glasses I broke tonight." She gave him several more coins and returned the purse, considerably lighter than before, to its place in the clothes bundle. Marco blew out the single candle and the two of them crept stealthily down the stairs and out into the cool night air.

They walked quickly, keeping to the shadows and avoiding the groups of late-night drinking sailors drifting past them. Melissa stopped once, scooping up some earth and smearing it onto their cheeks and chin. When they reached *The Sea Belle* at last, the ship was dark and seemingly deserted as she had hoped. All that remained for her to do was to board the ship and hide below in the hold.

"So this is goodbye then, Melissa," Marco said softly, seizing her hand and pressing it to his lips.

"Yes, dear friend, it is," she answered, her voice catching as she felt his kiss on her hand. She bent forward and kissed him tenderly on both cheeks and when he looked up at her, his large dark eyes were awash with tears. His smile trembled on his lips and, before she could say anything more, he quickly turned and walked away.

She whispered her thanks to the little man as the darkness enveloped him and, with a tremulous sigh, she stole noiselessly up the gangplank and boarded the sleeping ship.

chapter 7

Nestled on the floor between towering stacks of crates, Melissa managed to steal several hours of sleep. But due to the darkness of the ship's hold, she had no idea of the time. Her stomach growled hungrily and as she stretched her cramped body, she heard the muffled sounds of sailors' voices as they prepared to weigh anchor and set sail. She got to her feet and lurched against a crate as she felt the ship begin to move. Her heart began pounding with fear and excitement and she fought the impulse to sneak up on deck to watch the ship sail up the majestic Thames on its way to the sea.

Her stomach grumbled again and she wished she had thought of packing some bread and cheese in her little clothing bundle. But she had dared not alert Meg or Joe to her plans and had contented herself with an especially large dinner instead. As the ship's movements settled down to a rhythmic rocking, Melissa groped her way along the floor in an attempt to reach the door of the hold. Suddenly the heavy door was flung open, letting in a shaft of light, which caused her to blink against its glare as she darted behind a stack of wooden boxes.

"Put 'em in 'ere, mate," instructed a growling voice, "ol' cook's crowded enough as it is now."

There was a grunting noise as someone put down a heavy burden, then the sound of barrels being pushed into place. Footsteps receded and returned several times before the door was finally slammed shut. Melissa waited a few minutes more before peering out from her hiding place. The room was back in total darkness which, because of the bright stab of light a few moments earlier, seemed even darker than ever, and Melissa felt the first stirrings of panic inside her.

Beads of perspiration stood out on her forehead and she became increasingly aware of the scratchy wool cap and trousers she was wearing. Suddenly her whole body seemed to itch and as she tore frantically at the offending clothes. She battled against losing complete control of herself. Only her desperate determination to undertake the voyage kept her from scrambling to the door and bursting onto the deck and its precious daylight.

She crouched on the floor, taking deep breaths to calm herself. When she had regained some of her composure, she felt her way along the crates until she found the new stack of barrels the men had just stowed away. She ran her fingers over them in an effort to determine their contents. To her delight, one of the barrels was open and her searching fingers found tightly-packed oranges inside. After working feverishly, she managed to pry loose the top of another container and discovered piles of hard, dry biscuits.

Taking several of the oranges and stuffing a generous supply of biscuits into her pockets, she replaced the tops of the wooden boxes and crept back to her hiding place. There she sat down, her back propped up against one of the larger crates, and devoured her meal. When she had eaten her fill, she lay down on the floor, her clothes bundle as her pillow, and, growing drowsy again, she drifted off to sleep.

When she awoke, her body ached, her muscles cramped and stiff. She groaned with each movement she forced from her reluctant joints and vigorously massaged her arms and legs to restore the circulation in them. Then, climbing to her feet, she straightened slowly, rubbing the small of her back and stretching her body until she eventually felt some relief.

Wondering if it was nighttime, she pondered the idea of slipping onto the deck for air. Her quarters were becoming increasingly stuffy and she felt the rising prickles of panic on the back of her neck. To remain below, hidden in the clammy darkness, was something she dared not consider, especially if she were to survive the entire crossing. She craved air, and throwing caution aside, desperate to escape the smothering feeling threatening her again, she made her way to the door and opened it slightly.

To her relief, it was indeed night. Her straining eyes glimpsed the far-off constellations. She opened the door wide and tiptoed up the stairs onto the rolling deck. Clutching the railing, she gazed up at the luminous stars winking above her and she took in deep, grateful breaths of the damp night air. Closing her eyes, she leaned against the rail, feeling her body sway with the soothing rhythm of the ship.

The sound of distant footsteps sent her scurrying back down the steps and into the imprisoning hold, where she leaned back against the door, her heart hammering in her chest, fearful of imminent discovery. But as the minutes passed, she gradually relaxed, realizing that she was safe. She found her hiding place again and, untying her clothing bundle, she bunched up the dress and the shawl, fashioning a thin cushion for herself, affording her some modest protection from the hard and bruising floor. With her body pressed onto the skimpy pallet, she allowed the gentle sway of the ship to lull her to sleep.

Melissa's days and nights soon blended into an endless stretch of twilights. She nibbled on oranges and biscuits, slept fitfully, awakening with her body stiff and aching. She was grateful that, as time passed, no one returned to the hold for the supply of food there. At night, she would walk the deck, breathing life back into her sluggish body, gulping deeply of the freshness before being plunged back into her solitary darkness once again.

But as the days passed, she grew conscious of the rank odors filling the hold, odors comprised of orange peels, the cargo, and her own unwashed body. Scratching at her dirty clothes, she found herself growing increasingly uncomfortable, longing for a bath and clean clothing and a brush for her hair still bound in its filthy pigtail.

One night she sat bolt upright, tossed from a deep sleep to sudden awareness. She had slithered from her usual position due to the awkward pitching of the ship and, as she tried to get up, the boat tipped to one side and she barely stifled a scream as a crate near her crashed to the floor. The ship righted itself, shuddered convulsively, and rolled to the opposite side, sending another crate plummeting to the ground.

Shaking, Melissa finally struggled to her feet only to lose her footing as the ship lurched again. She was thrown heavily, scraping her side against a stack of boxes as she fell. Lying amid the splintered wood, whimpering in pain and fear, she wondered if the ship were about to sink; if, after all of her clever scheming, she had climbed aboard *The Sea Belle* to die. Sobbing, she sprawled helplessly in the dark, her body flung about by the capricious tossings of the ship.

And then the first wave of nausea struck. She gagged and moved herself into an upright position, hoping the feeling would pass. But as the clipper arced wildly, Melissa's aching stomach began to heave and, as spasm after spasm ripped through her body, she was sick. Crying and retching, she found herself wishing death would indeed release her. But then, in her pain, she thought of Lettie, feeling again her comforting arms, hearing once more her soothing voice, and her terror

83

lessened.

When the spasms finally ceased, she lay exhausted and panting in a crumpled heap. Then with a great effort, she dragged herself as far as she could to the other side of the hold until her strength deserted her and she collapsed weakly. As she huddled there, she felt the ship slowly ease its fevered pitching and resume a gentler rhythm. Worn out, Melissa slept.

She smiled as she was rocked to sleep, not by the rolling ship, but by her beloved Lettie. At last she would be safe. Then looking up from Lettie's lap, she noticed someone staring down at her, his eyes holding hers, their silvery depths glinting as she felt herself drawn toward him. He bent closer as if to meet her and she grew frightened and reached up to claw his smiling face, screaming for Lettie to protect her.

She fought to wake herself and found that she could not move. Opening her eyes, she gazed in terror into the faces of a group of bearded, leering men. Her arms were pinned at her sides by brawny arms and a lantern's merciless glare sent stabbing pains rocketing through her head.

"By God, it's a woman."

"'ow'd she get in 'ere?"

"Musta 'idden away afore we left port."

"Whew, there's a mighty stench down 'ere, ain't there?"

Stunned, Melissa cowered under their scrutiny and then she began grappling with the man holding her arms. She was hauled to her feet and, as she lashed out fiercely, she was seized and lifted up into another pair of arms.

"Better take this 'ere baggage to the captain, mates," ordered one of the sailors, and Melissa was borne away from her hiding place to face the wrath of the captain she had twice attempted to see. Fearing the worst, shaking with fear and trepidation, she sagged against the powerful chest of the sailor carrying her until she was dumped unceremoniously onto the carpet in a paneled cabin.

"We brung you a stow'way, cap'n," bellowed the man, prodding Melissa with the toe of his shoe, "an' believe it or not, under them rags is a woman."

"That will be all, Jenkins," the captain said crisply. Melissa lay in a pathetic heap at the man's feet, still not daring to face him. "Can you stand, ah, miss?" he asked, but she hung her head and refused to move.

"Are you injured?" he asked when she failed to respond. "Well then, what the devil is the matter?" His voice cracked at her like a whip.

Reluctantly, Melissa raised her head, her eyes widening as she gasped in disbelief. Standing over her, sapphire-blue eyes flashing, was the man named Jeremy.

chapter 8

Melissa's startled exclamation caused him to raise an eyebrow questioningly. "There is something wrong then," he commented wryly. "Is it me? Am I that fearsome as to warrant that expression on your face—what I can see of it, that is." He stood with his arms folded across his chest, his legs planted wide apart, an infuriating smile on his mouth as he considered her.

She yearned to scratch the grin from his face, but she was acutely aware of her frightful appearance, the filth and grime of her body and clothes, and it was little wonder that he failed to recognize her. Limp and worn from her bout of seasickness, still reeling from the shock of being discovered, she hunched dejectedly before him.

He finally pulled her to her feet and she swayed weakly against him. "I'm thirsty," she rasped hoarsely, averting her face, ashamed of her stench.

"So she speaks after all," he exclaimed, leading her toward a low leather chair. He filled a glass of water from a pewter jug and handed it to her.

"Sip it slowly," he cautioned as she gulped the water down. Her stomach protested immediately and a spasm of nausea coursed through her once more. She covered her mouth with her hand, her face burning in humiliation, and looked around her. He sprang to fetch a basin and as she retched violently, he muttered, "Stubborn little wench, aren't you?"

Then he gently lifted her from the chair and carried her across the cabin to his bunk. She felt herself sink into the softness of the mattress, freed at last from the brutal hardness of the hold's rough planking.

"I'll have a tub filled for you," she heard him say as she succumbed to the drowsiness enveloping her. "You may bathe first and then we can talk." She heard nothing more.

She slept until she was roughly prodded into waking. The sailor gestured to the tub of steaming water which had been placed in a corner of the cabin. She nodded sleepily and when the man had closed the door behind him, she gratefully peeled off the reeking clothes and dropped them onto the carpet. Walking to the tub, she caught sight of her reflection in the wood-framed mirror above the wash stand. She gaped at the sight of the ugly bruises mottling her delicate flesh. Dark smudges ringed her eyes and her face was pale and gaunt.

Sinking into the water, she worked to unravel the matted pigtail hanging heavily down her back. She soaped herself thoroughly and lathered her hair until it framed her face in a foamy white cloud. Luxuriating in the heat of the water and the sweet-smelling suds frothing around her, Melissa felt like a child as she gathered handfuls of the iridescent bubbles and blew them into the air, watching them pop and vanish. Then she lay back, rinsing the soap from her body and hair, submerging her entire length in the tub's blissful warmth.

When the water began to cool, she toweled herself dry and wrapped a second towel, turban fashion, around her wet hair. Naked, she padded about the cabin in search of a brush and, finding a pair of matched silver brushes on the wash stand, she brushed the snarls from her hair until it lay like a molten cape, encircling her.

"Botticelli himself could scarcely have improved on

such perfection," drawled the voice from the doorway.

With a start, Melissa dropped the brush and whirled to face the captain's appraising stare. Then, as if suddenly aware of her nakedness, she lunged for the discarded bath towel. But he was swifter and snatched it away before she reached it. Fuming, she raced over to the bed and pulled the covers up to her neck.

"How dare you intrude upon my privacy, sir!" she screamed. "How long were you standing there without having the decency to make your presence known?"

"Which question would you prefer I answer first?" he asked. At her hostile silence, he shrugged. "Very well then, as to the first question, you are a stowaway and scarcely merit any privacy. In answer to the second, I was standing here long enough to appreciate some, and I emphasize some, of your obvious charms."

She sat there, sputtering with rage and indignation, when she heard a loud rapping on the cabin door. The captain opened it and returned with Melissa's rumpled clothing. He tossed it disdainfully onto the bed beside her.

"I'm afraid we lack adequate laundering facilities, my dear, so you will just have to make do."

She untangled the shawl and the badly creased gown, wondering how she could wear them again. Aware of how little choice there was, she spread them out on the bed and attempted to smooth the wrinkles with her hands. As she moved, the blanket fell away from her, revealing the rounded fullness of her pink-tipped breasts. The sharp intake of breath from the captain drew her attention first to him and then back to herself. Hastily she drew up the covers again.

"Have you always lacked good manners?" she shouted at him then.

"Have you always screamed like a damned fishwife?" he countered and stormed from the cabin.

Grateful for her reprieve, Melissa wriggled into her dress and then settled despondently back on the bunk, worrying about what would become of her. She gazed out of the porthole at the pulsating ocean, its torquoise-blue waters stretching to meet the haze of the distant horizon. The motion of the ship was steady, the sea calm, and she hoped that her seasickness would not occur again.

She was jolted from her thoughts by the sound of the door opening again. A young cabin boy appeared, bearing a tray laden with fresh fruit, cheese, and cold meat. With a cry of delight, she accepted the food and the light wine accompanying it. Amazed by her ravenous appetite, she made short work of the meal and was contentedly sipping the last of the wine when the captain appeared again.

"I see that you managed to eat something," he remarked sarcastically. Melissa chose to ignore his comment, scarcely aware of his presence, her head spinning from the wine. As she attempted to stifle a yawn, he spoke again. "Before you fall asleep, my dear, I think it time we had our little chat." He settled himself beside her on the bed.

She felt unaccountably warm and she feared that it was not due solely to the effects of the wine. She sniffed at the faint scent of his cologne and her eyes boldly scanned his trim body, clad simply in dark blue trousers and an open-neck white shirt.

"Have you quite finished your appraisal?" he demanded harshly, and she hastily dropped her gaze. "I demand to know who you are and why you were hiding aboard my ship." His voice was rising menacingly, but Melissa remained passive until in frustration, he gripped her arm and wrenched it behind her. "Will you answer me or do I turn you over to someone better schooled in handling uncooperative prisoners?"

"Am I your prisoner then, captain?" she inquired, straining to break his hold on her arm.

"You will be if you fail to provide me with some answers," he threatened, twisting her arm more tightly.

"If you would unhand me, sir, I would endeavor to explain," she said sweetly. With a grunt, he released her and she slowly massaged her arm, deliberately provoking him with her continuing silence.

"Madam, I warn you . . ." he said.

"Enough, sir, you win," she smiled, staying his mounting impatience with a slight wave of her hand. "But before I divulge anything, might I at least know the name of my captain?"

"Jeremy Ransome," he mumbled irritably.

"Well, Captain Ransome," she rolled his name softly off her tongue, "you insult me by not remembering me."

"Remember you?" he repeated, frowning at her. "If, madam, we had indeed met, do you think I could forget such beauty?" he recovered smoothly.

"How glib you are," she retorted, "for we have indeed met and you have indeed forgotten, sir. Your carriage nearly ran me down while I was walking with a friend near the harbor in London."

She watched him carefully as he puzzled over what she had said and then he astounded her by bursting into throaty laughter.

"Yes, of course," he snickered, regaining his composure, "the young lady and her dwarf."

At his mocking laugh, Melissa had felt a cold fist tighten inside of her, squeezing the breath from her lungs. As she glared at him, he began to remind her of Philip Wentworth, a comparison which boded ill for Jeremy Ransome.

"I fail to understand your humor, captain," she said coldly, "but it further proves what I had already assumed. You are certainly no gentleman."

"I'm sure that my wife would hasten to agree with you, my dear," he chuckled, eyeing her cautiously. "But my patience is wearing thin and I suggest you now answer my questions."

Staring boldly into his deep blue eyes, she stated,

"My explanation will be brief, Captain Ransome. Until recently I was employed as a bar maid at a taproom along the waterfront. I managed to save enough money to book passage on a ship bound for America, and that ship chanced to be *The Sea Belle*. When I learned there were to be no passengers on this voyage, I grew desperate and hid aboard the boat before you sailed."

"Your name, please," he demanded.

"Melissa," she answered.

"I regret to say, Melissa, if indeed that is your name, that your story sadly lacks detail. Are you running from the authorities?"

"No," she replied honestly.

"Why did you choose *The Sea Belle?*" he persisted.

"Your ship is bound for Maryland and so am I," she admitted. He ran his fingers agitatedly through his thick, blond hair, grumbling to himself, and Melissa regarded him thoughtfully, wondering at his distress.

"Damn, why the hell did you have to choose my ship, especially on this crossing," he muttered, looking scathingly at her. "Damn you, woman, for your poor timing."

"I would be pleased to absent myself from this cabin, captain," she replied tartly, "for I seem to be causing you considerable discomfort. If money can buy me some privacy in some small corner of your ship, then I will gladly pay you for it."

"You may keep your money, madam, for you will find no privacy on board. This is scarcely a pleasure cruise, nor have my men been schooled in the fine art of chaperoning young women." His hands continued to rake angrily through his hair until he finally faced her again, with an air of cool detachment. "Well, my dear, I find that you leave me no alternative but to place you in protective custody, for your own safety of course." At her stricken look, he smiled slyly. "I myself will ensure that no harm befalls you, for I shudder to think of the consequences should my crew gain access to you. What

91

better protection could you find than being with the captain himself?"

"And where do you propose I sleep?" she demanded, indicating the narrow bunk and the smallness of the cabin.

"I would have thought you were more imaginative than that, my dear," Ransome returned, his eyes wandering casually over her body.

"I think, captain, that I prefer to take my chances with the crew than subject myself to your private form of captivity." With that, she leaped from the bunk and strode haughtily toward the cabin door. Ransome was upon her before she could turn the knob.

"Don't be such a stubborn little fool," he said. "You wouldn't survive a night after they finished with you. Shall I enumerate the various ways you might find yourself abused?" She covered her ears, refusing to listen to his scathing words, but he seized her arms. Resentfully, she looked up at him, her huge eyes glinting brightly through her tears, her lips vulnerable and quivering. Like an eagle swooping down on its prey, Ransome claimed her mouth with his in a long, hungry kiss.

She stiffened, attempting to fend him off, but the ship suddenly pitched, slamming Melissa up against him. His arms tightened relentlessly around her and, as his kiss deepened, his tongue teasingly probed her yielding mouth. Her arms hung limply at her sides, her clenched fists relaxing, her heart pounding faster as she felt a tremulous fluttering within her. Her lips seemed to possess a will of their own and they followed where his led.

Their gazes locked and she closed her eyes against the desire she saw in his. His wandering mouth grazed her ears, his gentle breathing echoing through her and, as he burrowed in the hollow of her throat, she thought of another's lips kissing her the same way. Her mind reeled, aching to remember, and lighted for her the image of a shadowed face whose silvery eyes held hers. With a wrenching cry, Melissa pushed Ransome away from her and flung herself sobbing across the bunk, ashamed of her response to the man, haunted still by the memory of some stranger she could neither remember nor forget.

"What the devil is the matter?" he demanded, crouching beside her shaking form, stroking the wild tangle of her coppery hair. "Are my kisses so unusual that they warrant such a violent reaction?"

Infuriated by his insolence, she flew at him, straining to rake her nails across his face. But he caught her flailing wrists and held her fast until she ceased her futile struggle. She glared at him with undisguised loathing.

"You are quite the fighter, my dear," he chuckled, the dimple in his cheek deepening as he grinned at her. "But sheathe your claws for now, my little wildcat, for although duty calls me elsewhere, I shall return. Our private battle has just begun." And he planted a light kiss on the tip of her nose and left her, seething with fury, on the bunk. She ran to the door shouting after him, and cried out in frustration as she fought the stubborn knob, for the door had been locked from the outside.

Ransome returned early in the evening. Spying her sulking on the bed, gazing out of the porthole, he attempted to soothe her ruffled feelings. He stooped to kiss her but she whirled around to face him, almost knocking him off balance.

"How dare you keep me locked up in here," she cried, "I am not your prisoner and I shall go mad for want of some fresh air." Watching as his eyes hardened spitefully, she lowered her voice. "I promise to make myself as inconspicuous as possible if you would only allow me to walk about on deck."

"Shall we negotiate the terms of an arrangement then?" His eyes flashed triumphantly and Melissa realized that she had trapped herself. "What is it now?" he questioned, sensing her withdrawal. "Surely you're not giving up before the negotiations have even begun."

"What is it you want, captain?" she said dully, growing weary of the battle.

"The pleasure of your company when I dine and the warmth of your lovely body in my bed," he answered easily.

"You said we could negotiate, did you not?" she responded. "Well then, I am prepared to dine with you but, as for sharing your bed, I find the floor more to my liking."

"Suit yourself, my dear," he shrugged, "but the hard floor will drive you to fulfill the second part of our bargain more swiftly than you imagine." He then rose from the bunk and led her into the small dining room where two places had already been set at the round mahogany table.

Suspicious of his abrupt capitulation, Melissa attempted to be an entertaining dinner companion, regaling him with stories of her life at The Three Kegs, while cautiously avoiding any references to her past. As Ransome downed glass after glass of wine, his own tongue loosened and she found that, in spite of her reservations, she was quite charmed by the young sea captain.

"Consider yourself most fortunate, my dear, to have found me rather than Trevor Talbott in command here," Ransome was saying. "That old sea dog would have fed you to the fish by now, after first sampling you himself, of course." He hiccuped and drained the wine from his glass. His face was flushed, his eyes bloodshot, and his speech was becoming slurred.

"Uncle Bryan, my father's younger brother, owns this beauty of a ship," he continued as he poured himself another glass of wine. "He left England twenty-five years ago and set out to build himself the largest clipper fleet on the east coast of America. Needless to say, he succeeded. Brilliant chap, Uncle Bryan." He raised his glass in a drunken salute. "But he never forgot his family and, thanks to him, I spent many summers in Maryland, learning everything he could teach me about sailing. He's promised me that after this run—" and he leaned toward Melissa, whispering conspiratorially— "I'll be off to China my next time out." He swallowed the last of his wine and reached for the near empty decanter.

"You've had quite enough wine, captain," she commented, more sharply than she had intended.

"Spare me your concern, dear Melissa," he slurred as he filled his glass. "You're beginning to remind me of dear, sweet Arabella."

"Arabella?" she echoed.

"Yes. Arabella Elizabeth Susan Whitley Ransome, my lovely and very rich wife," he informed her. "She's expecting our first child and is tucked safely away at home." He failed to notice the shocked expression on Melissa's face as she heard the name of his wife. Arabella Whitley, youngest daughter of Lord Stephen Whitley, was Philip Wentworth's second cousin, and at one time had been considered a suitable bride for him. But the headstrong Arabella had reportedly run off with a young sea captain, and Melissa smiled bitterly at the cruel coincidence which placed her across the table from that very man. She knew she would have to guard her tongue carefully and keep her own identity hidden from the inquisitive Jeremy.

A cabin boy finally removed the remains of their dinner and Ransome jerked unsteadily to his feet.

"I must make an appearance on deck," he muttered, "and if you promise to be a good girl, I'll take you up there with me." She happily followed his lurching form, grateful for the opportunity to at last walk freely about, to breathe the freshness of the air again.

Outside on deck, shivering in the chill night air, she

stared wonderingly up at the ship's towering spars with their giant masts framed against the pale moonlight. The vast spread of white sail reminded Melissa of a huge white bird, dipping and soaring above the sea. The billowing canvases crackled in the wind, snapping tautly as the ship cut powerfully through the inky water. Melissa leaned against the wooden railing, searching the star encrusted skies for familiar constellations, drawing deeply of the salt-spray air.

Ransome finally returned to escort her back to the cabin and she reluctantly loosened her grip on the rail and followed him silently to the small room once more. He seemed to have sobered somewhat and as he began to tug off his clothes, Melissa stared at him, horrified by his nonchalance. She cleared her throat in a bid to gain his attention and he turned to face her.

"I expected you to be eager to retire, my dear," he said, "and yet, there you stand still fully clothed. Do you require my assistance or are you modest and prefer if I extinguish the lamp?"

"I thought I had made myself understood before, Captain Ransome," she stated calmly. "I have no desire whatsoever to undress in front of you either with or without the light. Now if you would kindly give me a blanket, I could make up a bed for myself."

"We have an agreement, Melissa, and I intend to see that you honor it," he stubbornly insisted.

"On the contrary, captain," she retorted angrily, "I consented only to dine with you and you seemed content with that arrangement before we sat down to dinner."

"I was merely attempting to avoid unnecessary arguments before dinner. I detest eating after a row, it plays havoc with one's digestion," he said haughtily, but his voice hardened again. "If it's a fight you want now, my dear Melissa, I promise you that it will be shortlived. As captain of this vessel, I am privy to greater means of persuasion than you are."

"You swine!" Melissa said, "I'll see you dead before you touch me again." She looked wildly about for some weapon, determined that he would not have his way with her. Aware of her intentions, he sprang at her, wrestling her to the floor, where he pressed his full weight upon her squirming body.

"I warned you, little Melissa, that our fight had but begun, and fight you I shall. And I will win."

She forced her body to relax then, collapsing limply beneath him. Taken aback, Ransome raised himself cautiously on one elbow and gazed down at her face, her tender mouth gone suddenly slack. Wondering if it was a ruse, he studied her closely, but as she continued to lie there, he worried that she had indeed fainted. He pulled himself slowly from her still form and then bent over to take her up in his arms. The full force of Melissa's doubled fist caught him in the face and he fell backward, clapping a hand to his bleeding nose.

She was instantly on her feet, lunging for the pistol she had previously sighted on his mahogany desk. Cocking the gun, she aimed it at the dazed man who, thunderstruck by her action, glared hatefully at her and hurried to find a towel.

"I warn you, captain, that I am an expert shot," she said coldly, her hands steady, "and I would not hesitate to kill you if you dare try to touch me again."

Pressing a dampened cloth to his swelling nose, Ransome turned his back on the woman before him and stretched out on his bunk. "You bitch," he cursed her through clenched teeth, "it's far from over between us." And he lay back, dabbing at his sweating, aching face, groaning as he touched his nose, praying that it was not broken.

Melissa lowered the gun, slipping it into the pocket of her gown. Then she set about finding a linen chest. In a narrow cupboard, she finally found extra bedding, and hauling out a blanket and a pillow, she prepared a makeshift bed for herself in the large leather chair behind the captain's brass-bound desk. Settling the blanket on top of her, she nestled down in the chair, placing the gun in her lap.

From the opposite end of the cabin, Ransome watched her, hatred and lust mingling in his pain-filled eyes. He eased himself from the bed and splashed some cool water on his face, studying himself in the mirror, wondering how to explain his appearance to the crew. Moving carefully about the cabin, he blew out the lamps, and with a final belligerent glance at Melissa, he crawled back onto his bunk.

An uneasy calm settled between them as the ship plowed on through the peaceful, starry night.

chapter 9

Melissa and Ransome shared the same cabin and the same table for meals while observing a guarded silence in the days that followed, each carefully avoiding a confrontation with the other. Melissa carried the loaded pistol with her at all times and maintained a discreet distance from the rest of the crew as well. Ransome had explained away his bruised face by saying that he had been drunk and had fallen against the side of his desk. The men nodded their heads sympathetically while exchanging knowing winks the moment his back was turned.

Snuggling beneath a wool blanket, Melissa spent her days observing the sailors at their work and admiring the sleek, graceful vessel they so capably manned. The clipper, streamlined as she was for speed, stripped of any excess weight which might otherwise slow her down, cut through the water under full sail at all times. As a result, she could log more nautical miles per day then any other ship afloat. Due to the enormous expanse of her sails, the clipper's crews were also larger, and the men, clad in their woolen jerseys and dark bell-bottomed trousers, scrambled deftly about, checking the sails and the three sets of main masts, climbing aloft and keeping *The Sea Belle* rigidly on course.

Melissa often walked the deck alone, clinging to the guard rail, her flowing hair lashing her face, her skirts whipping about her legs. The ship excited her, stimulated her, the way only riding had been able to do, and she felt intoxicated by its rushing freedom. Sometimes she would wander into the ship's saloon, where the massive chart table stood covered with maps, the detailed parchments held open by strategically placed paperweights, while others lay curled inside long board cylinders. She pored over the maps, trying to comprehend their intricate markings. She idly toyed with the sextant and chronometer while Ransome wrote in his heavy logbook, ignoring her presence and her insatiable curiosity.

A week out of Baltimore, the Atlantic suddenly turned an uglier face, transforming herself into a seething, bubbling cauldron. Struck by an early summer storm, the ocean raged and fumed like a woman possessed. Gale winds tore at the sails, lightning forked through darkened skies and walls of indigo water crashed onto the clipper's open decks. Because of her delicate construction, *The Sea Belle* was no match for the warring forces surrounding her and she pitched and tossed frantically, fighting for her life against the sea which threatened to envelop her.

Ransome performed brilliantly, supporting and encouraging his men, working alongside them. Men scurried aloft to the yards, lowering sails and lashing them to the masts before they could be ripped apart by the howling winds. If a man was unfortunate enough to be washed overboard, he knew there was no chance of being recovered. Each sailor moved skillfully and cautiously, aware that a careless step could be his last.

Rigid with terror, clutching the sides of the bunk, Melissa lay alone in Ransome's cabin. Lamps had been forbidden for fear of starting fires and Melissa flailed helplessly about in the darkness. She had just thrown up her supper and she lay doubled up in pain, fighting the cramps in her empty belly and the fear screaming through her.

Suddenly the door of the cabin was flung open and, through a gust of wind and rain, Ransome stumbled into the dark clammy room.

"Melissa," he called into the darkness.

"I'm on the bed," came the weak reply. He fumbled about in the blackness until a flash of lightning revealed the bunk and the terrified girl huddled there. He made his way over to her, sinking down onto the covers, his clothes wringing wet, water pouring from his hat as he tore it off and ran his fingers through his wet blond hair. A bolt of lightning illuminated him momentarily and Melissa saw the fatigue and worry etched in his face. His nose had healed completely and their battles seemed forgotten as he attempted a weak smile.

"We'll make it, Melissa. I promise you that." His tired voice was almost tender as he tried to console her. "I've been through worse storms around the Horn. *The Sea Belle* is a good ship and the men are seasoned sailors, and together we'll beat this storm."

Melissa looked up into the face she could only dimly make out and she wished that she could believe him. But she could find little comfort in his valiant words, and so she lay back again, alone in her fear, as Ransome got to his feet and made his way across the cabin. He cursed loudly as his head struck one of the overhead lamps, but he finally reached the door, tugged it open and disappeared into a curtain of rain.

Melissa dozed off only to awaken with a start, her heart pounding in her chest. Claps of thunder rocketed overhead and the lightning flashed continually and with greater intensity, lighting the cabin in eerie false daylight. She glanced toward the door as it opened and Ransome hurled himself into the room again.

Oblivious to her, he stripped off his clothes and reached for the blanket tossed onto the floor from Melissa's sleeping chair. Transfixed, Melissa stared at his naked form as he dried himself. In flash after flash of

101

lightning, he glowed golden, the fine blond hair on his chest flickering with a bronze fire, the muscles in his body rippling as he worked the cumbersome blanket back and forth.

He grew aware of her then and sapphire eyes burned into topaz eyes, and he dropped the blanket to the floor. Melissa watched him moving toward her, his eyes holding hers, pinning them beneath his own unwavering gaze. As the ship pitched, he lurched against the bed and Melissa drew back and away from his nearness. She smelled the sea as he reached for her and she pressed back against the wall, trapped there. A loud clap of thunder muffled her scream as he touched her and then the ship spun into the air and, with a terrible shudder, crashed down heavily into a frenzied trough between the swells. Melissa knew then that they were going to die and, as Ransome's lips closed over hers, she ceased her struggling.

She waited for the cold arms of the sea to engulf her. But until then there was Jeremy, and Jeremy's arms were warm and pulsating with life. And she clung to him and the promise of life he held out to her, and he stripped away her rumpled gown and pulled her against the hard lean length of him. His hands smoothed back the clinging tendrils of auburn hair and he kissed her face, her throat, her shoulders, teasing a whimper from somewhere deep within her.

His tongue scorched her with its touch and blazed a fiery trail to her quivering breasts. He captured them in his hungry mouth, sucking the pink-hued tips until they rose hard and tingling to meet his lapping tongue. Melissa's arms tightened around him, feeling the smoothness of his back as their bodies clung together in tender desperation. He freed a hand and sent it wandering over her silken skin, and she tensed as he caressed her gently-swelling hips and her firm, taut thighs. She stiffened as his fingers grazed the moist, warm patch no man had ever touched before, but his lips swiftly returned to hers, his tongue fondling hers and she relaxed again beneath his expert touch.

As she lay back in tentative acquiescence, his fingers pushed beyond the red-blonde fur and probed the tender bud buried there. She arched against him as a wave of delicious feeling rippled through her and she tore her mouth from his, gasping as the feeling grew and threatened to explode inside her. She moaned at the unexpected delight born of his intrusion, giving herself up to the building agony he was creating within her. She perched on the threshold, drew back, aching to crest, and moved feverishly against the fingers humming inside of her.

And then he was on top of her, parting her thighs, his stiffness begging entry. And Melissa cried out, watching as a different pair of eyes bore deeply into hers. His face was hidden by a mask but he was laughing, laughing as he rode her. Melissa screamed and tried to tear away the mask, but he held her down, thinking that her cries were those of her release and he pounded at her glorious welcoming, drenching himself in her body's flowing tide until his cries joined hers. He burst amid a scattering of love petals and lay still above her.

Melissa stirred uncomfortably beneath him. Reluctantly he moved away from her and, nestling down beside her, he promptly fell asleep. She backed as far from him as the narrow bunk allowed. Her body felt numb. Remorse gnawed at her as she tasted the salty bitterness of tears on her flushed cheeks. She stared into the darkness, watching the lightning flash and vanish like some celestial beacon, and she wondered at the changes within her. Her first taste of loving had left her with a stinging soreness between her legs and the telltale stickiness from the loss of her maidenhead. But it had also left her disappointed, her body throbbing with frustration, feeling incomplete. Lonely and abandoned in the aftermath of such passion, she sobbed wretchedly until, exhausted, she fell asleep, the tears slowly drying on her upturned face.

When Melissa awoke, it was morning and she was alone in the cabin once again. She immediately sensed a difference in the ship as, to her relief, it was no longer tossing about. Crouching on the bunk, she peered out of the porthole at the sun shining in a cloudless sky and reflecting upon the calmer waters of the sea.

She looked down at the tumbled bed, her eyes widening as she noticed the stained sheets. Tearing them from the mattress, she rolled them into a ball and carried the bundle to the cupboard. Stuffing the linens into the back of the closet, she then found fresh sheets and hurriedly remade the bed, casually throwing the blankets across it.

A knock at the door sent her diving back under the covers as the cabin boy staggered into the room, carrying a large pot of water. After several trips, he bowed shyly to her and left. Melissa hastened to the welcoming bath and, twisting her hair into a loose knot atop her head, she settled into the tub.

She scrubbed at her skin until she had washed away all traces of the previous night. Remembering sent the blood rushing to her cheeks and she wondered how she would face Jeremy after her shameless abandon in his arms. Would he expect a repetition of their lovemaking or would he be satisfied enough with having won the fight as he had sworn he would?

She rose from the soapy water just as the cabin door opened, and she grabbed up a towel and wrapped it around her. Jeremy stalked into the room and when he noticed her, knee deep in the cloudy water, the towel scarcely covering her glistening skin, his scowl relaxed into a grin.

"Come, come, Melissa," he teased, "surely it must seem a trifle late for modesty now. After last night, I would have thought you cured of such prudishness." He laughed as the color deepened in her cheeks. "Shall

I help to dry you off before you catch a chill?" he inquired with mock solicitousness, beginning to edge toward her.

"Stay where you are, Jeremy. Please," her last word was more of a plea than a command and he stopped abruptly, considering her obvious distress.

"Ah, Jeremy at last is it?" he noted smugly. "That in itself shows some progress, dear Melissa."

She eyed him warily as he crossed the cabin and seated himself on the bunk. "What a bloody shame you are still so shy about that magnificent body of yours," he muttered, his eyes caressing her as she stood shivering in the cooling bath water. He leaned back on the bed. "I would, however, suggest that you leave your precious tub before you turn the color of the sea out there."

She tossed her head defiantly, spinning rainbow drops of moisture from the coppery curls at the nape of her neck, and stepped from the tub. Tauntingly, she lowered the towel and under the steady scrutiny of Jeremy's blue eyes, she teased him with the body he seemed to crave. She moved slowly, each gesture seductive as she arched her body, stretching gracefully as she drew the towel across her wet skin.

Each full breast was carefully patted dry and as the towel slid lower across her abdomen towards the auburn triangle between her legs, she heard Jeremy's strangled gasp. She smiled lazily, the grin of a sleek tawny cat, and bent forward to dry her legs, her breasts bobbing invitingly in front of his tortured gaze, as she worked her way up from her slim ankles to her thighs.

"Enough, Melissa," he groaned, rising from the bed, "enough. Your teasing is driving me mad." And before she could escape him, he had pulled her into the circle of his arms. The wool of his jersey tickled her breasts as he crushed her to him and she could feel the effects of her performance in the hardness pressing against her legs. He kissed her savagely, all tenderness gone, so great was his need. And Melissa, ashamed of what she had done, regretting that it had gone too far, struggled in vain to ward him off.

"Oh no, my beautiful temptress," he growled, straining to hold her still, "you'll not escape so easily." And he bit one of her delicate earlobes, his teeth digging viciously into its soft fleshiness until she cried out in pain. He wrenched the towel from her body and swept her up into his arms, carrying her across the room and tossing her onto his bunk. He pinned her down there while he fumbled with his trousers and she bucked and thrashed beneath his weight.

"No, Jeremy, not again," she panted, pleading with him. "I was merely provoking you, I meant no harm, please. Please stop this madness." Her breath was coming in short gasps as she fought him, but he remained deaf to her pleas.

He held her arms above her head, pinning them there with one brawny hand as he roughly spread her tensing thighs with the other.

"If you continue this way, Melissa," he rasped huskily, "you'll provide me with quite a ride indeed." He plunged inside of her, forcing himself deeper and deeper into the warmth and sweetness of her.

Melissa cried out at his first thrust, but her body treacherously spread itself open before his assault and bathed him as he probed her. She flinched at his brutal invasion, but as he drove inside of her, she was captured by the steady rhythm of his movements and she bent toward him, matching him stroke for stroke. Her eyes tightly closed against her body's sweet betrayal, she rode upward on a mounting wave and scaled the summit bordering ecstasy. Her body soared and dipped as Jeremy plundered her and, as she rose to cap that final wave, he shuddered and spilled himself inside her. And she slowly slipped back from the peak, bathed by the pool of his creation and not her own.

"Cap'n, you're wanted up top," shouted a voice from the doorway. Jeremy, instantly alert, tore himself from

106

Melissa's limp form. Straightening his clothes and without another glance at the bed, he rushed from the cabin, leaving Melissa alone and unfulfilled once more.

She pushed the damp hair back from her face and sat up. Feeling battered and abused, she limped toward the tub of filmy water and, mindless of its cold sting, she lowered herself into it and vigorously scrubbed at the flesh which had again betrayed her.

Melissa coldly faced Jeremy across the table at dinner that night, engaged in polite conversation and nibbled lightly at the heavy fare of meat and boiled potatoes. She allowed him to steer her about the deck for a brief stroll and, as they returned to the cabin, she slipped inside ahead of him, slamming the door and locking it. She laughed harshly as he hammered on the door, cursing and shouting at her until he eventually gave up and stormed away. Melissa slept alone in the bed that night while Jeremy bunked down with the crew.

The following night a pistol shot rang out and Jeremy marched triumphantly into his cabin, after having shot the lock from the door. Melissa sat calmly in the chair behind his desk, curled contentedly in a blanket, an enigmatic smile on her face.

"I thought you might find a way back in here, Jeremy," she murmured, the cold smile on her lips never reaching her eyes, "and as you can see, I prepared myself for that eventuality." He snickered contemptuously at her obvious reference to her makeshift bed, but his smile vanished when he noticed the gun lying once more across her lap. "Pleasant dreams, Captain Ransome," she whispered.

"So we come around full circle, Melissa," he remarked caustically as he turned away from her and set about extinguishing the lamps. The cabin was plunged into darkness, separating them, adversaries once again.

* * *

The remaining days of the sea voyage were spent with few words passing between them. Melissa was scarcely aware of the change in the rhythm of *The Sea Belle* as she left the open ocean and sailed up the protected waters of Chesapeake Bay, making for the bustling inland port of Baltimore. She spent the final day on board determinedly plotting a future for herself and hoping that in time the missing fragment of her memory, coupled with the reason for her voyage, would be restored to her as well.

When *The Sea Belle* docked in Baltimore's large harbor, Melissa changed back into the sailor's garb she had worn when boarding the vessel in London. As she gathered up her clothing, she felt a sudden stab of fear mingle with her feeling of anticipation and she took a deep, steadying breath before walking onto the deck for the last time to wait there with the rest of the crew.

"Have you a plan for yourself, Melissa?"

She froze as Jeremy neared her and she felt a sudden painful constriction in her chest.

"I believe so, captain," she answered curtly, avoiding his eyes.

"I wish you good luck then, my dear," he said formally, reaching for her hand. She backed away before he could touch her and he shrugged and lowered his hand to his side. As she moved toward the gangplank, he called after her. "Perhaps our paths will cross again someday."

She gave no indication of having heard his parting words and, as she walked from the ship to step onto the soil of America, Melissa refused to look back again.

PART TWO

Maryland 1885—1886

chapter 10

Melissa settled the green linen hat at a jaunty angle atop her shining auburn curls and carefully arranged the white silk flowers adorning the hat's narrow brim. Smoothing the coiled ringlets at the nape of her neck, she smiled at her likeness in the mirror. Awed by the large selection of ready-to-wear apparel in the dress shop near her hotel, Melissa had found it difficult to reach a decision, but as she studied her reflection, she happily approved her final choice.

The emerald-green muslin gown sported a high, closed collar and three-quarter sleeves edged in white lace. A froth of the lace spilled down the front of the fitted bodice and gathered in a graceful swirl encircling her hips. A large swath of lace bordered the hem of the gown, below which peeked a pair of green kid slippers.

Melissa pinched her cheeks to heighten their color and applied a hint of lip pomade to her mouth. Then, gathering up her white gloves and the small green purse which held her few remaining coins, she left the hotel room.

As she swung easily down the street fronting the noisy harbor, she eagerly anticipated her confrontation with the unsuspecting Bryan Halloway Ransome. Having decided to capitalize on her relationship with Jeremy Ransome, she had set out to locate his uncle, finding his offices in a large, red-brick building on the waterfront. Thus assured of the man's actual existence, Melissa had grudgingly parted with some of her precious savings to purchase an outfit to suitably impress the elder Ransome.

Reaching the building, its huge painted sign designating it as Ransome Enterprises, she began to feel apprehensive and paused in front of the door, suddenly unsure. After a moment's hesitation, she pushed open the heavy door and climbed the flight of stairs to the office she sought. Making her way through the spacious waiting room, she boldly informed the startled clerk that she had an appointment with Bryan Ransome. The bespectacled young man, swallowing nervously as he scrutinized her, finally managed to recover his composure.

"May I have your name please, miss," he muttered, having difficulty deciding which he would rather study, her face or her body, outlined as it was by the clinging gown.

With an imperious wave of her gloved hand, Melissa replied haughtily, "My name would scarcely mean a thing to him. Simply tell him that a friend of his nephew Jeremy wishes to speak with him." And she bestowed her most dazzling smile upon the perspiring young man, who promptly disappeared into a nearby office, leaving Melissa standing there, her mouth suddenly dry and her heart thumping loudly.

The door soon opened and a tall, powerfully built man strode forward to meet her. At fifty, Bryan Ransome was six feet tall with thick blond hair lightly sprinkled with gray. In a deeply tanned face, beneath brushy blond eyebrows, blazed a pair of blue eyes, much like Jeremy's. An aquiline nose leant a harshness to his face which was somewhat softened by the full sensual mouth above his firm square chin.

Melissa's proud resolve faltered but as Ransome smiled and reached for her hand, she brightened and flashed him a smile in return.

"Well, my dear," he said as he pressed her fingers lightly, "so you say you're a friend of Jeremy's. Why don't you join me in my office for a cup of tea, the one British custom I still maintain." He chatted easily as he guided her into his spacious wood-paneled office, which commanded a spectacular view of the harbor.

Over tea and small cakes, Melissa relaxed and finally explained the purpose of her visit. "You see, Mr. Ransome, Jeremy told me a great deal about you when he and I spent some time together aboard ship." She smiled tentatively at Ransome's arched eyebrow and hastily continued. "He greatly admires you, you know, and . . ." her words were cut off by a loud exclamation from the man facing her.

"Admires me, my foot!" he bellowed, his dark face growing darker. "That young pup would just as soon see me at the bottom of the sea as behind my desk here." His voice softened as he noticed her shocked expression. "You see, my dear, I have no sons of my own, and young Jeremy was always damned determined to make up for it, expecting me to treat him like my son instead of my brother's son. He's a fine sea captain, I'll grant him that, but knowing he's out sailing somewhere and not here trying to ingratiate himself with me, is when I feel most charitable toward Jeremy Ransome."

Melissa's voice was cold as she replied to the glowering man. "I know nothing of your hostile feelings toward each other, Mr. Ransome, or of your family fights. I am here at Jeremy's suggestion, hoping that you might have a position for me within your company or at your estate." She drew a deep breath and hurried on. "I was raised on an estate known for its fine breeding stock and I am an accomplished horsewoman and an excellent shot."

He seemed to be studying her closely as he sat silently across from her, calmly sipping at his tea. Melissa burned under his scrutiny and lowered her eyes, fumbling with her teacup as it rattled noisily against the

113

thin porcelain saucer.

"Don't allow my temper to frighten you off," he said, his blue eyes dancing as she confronted him again. "I'll wager that under that little hat of yours is a red-headed temper to match my own."

Her bubbling laughter eased the tension within her as she found herself liking this large gruff man, and she waited impatiently for him to make up his mind. Finally he broke the silence.

"I think it only fitting to know the name of a prospective employee before I hire her, don't you agree?" he asked, his eyes still twinkling. Melissa's heart surged with joy at his words but, as she was about to blurt out her name, she hesitated before replying.

"My name is Melissa. Melissa Howell," she uttered softly, feeling a twinge of guilt at the slight alteration of her name.

"Well, Melissa Howell, how patient a teacher are you?" he inquired. At her puzzled look, he continued, "I asked you that question because I have a daughter just about your age, who goes through riding instructors, grooms, and personal maids the way one tears through a meal. Not much left at the end but a pile of picked over bones. She's headstrong and willful with a temper to equal mine. But, if my instincts are correct, and they usually are, my Kathleen will have met her match in you." He chuckled as he watched Melissa's face for her reaction. To his delight, her small chin came up, her eyes glowed with determination and she nodded her head in acceptance of his challenge.

"Then, Miss Howell, consider yourself part of the Ransome household," he announced. "While we maintain a house in town, my wife and daughter spend most of their time at Laurel Hill, our country estate. During the fall social season, they join me here and spend several months in the city." His eyes narrowed as he carefully chose his next words. "I'm hoping that you and my daughter will get along, Miss Howell, for she

114

has few women friends. She has had more than her share of eager young suitors, but she's difficult to please and bends them all to her will like so many matchsticks." He set aside his teacup and rose to his feet. "Enough of this chatter, we'll have plenty of time for it all soon enough." Melissa stood quickly and waited uncertainly.

"I intend to return to Laurel Hill tomorrow, Miss Howell. Can you be ready to leave on such short notice?" She hastily nodded and gave him the name of her hotel. "Shall we say nine o'clock tomorrow morning then? It's a day's ride and I prefer to reach home before dinner."

"Nine o'clock will be fine," she agreed and turned to leave.

"Melissa." His voice halted her. "May I call you Melissa?" he asked and she nodded imperceptibly. "I'll undoubtedly be speaking with Jeremy before he sails again. Should I mention our meeting to him?" At her stormy look, he laughed understandingly, "I didn't think so. Until tomorrow then, my dear." His discreet wave was a polite dismissal and Melissa hurried out of his office and bounded back to her small room.

Joyfully she flung her hat onto the bed and whirled around the room, laughing and hugging herself, elated that her plan had worked so well. Her mind was flooded with images of life on a grand Maryland estate, where she would be free to ride again, to feel the rush of freedom tingling in her veins and soothe the lingering pain within her. She thought then of her father and her newfound joy was quickly tempered by a returning sadness.

That night she thrashed restlessly about in bed, her body taut with excitement, anticipating the trip to Laurel Hill. As she stared into the shadowy darkness, the room seemed filled with the presence of Jeremy Ransome, and she lived again their moments of loving,

115

locked in naked combat upon his narrow bunk aboard the sea-tossed clipper.

She closed her eyes, casting about for a comforting memory to soothe her, and as she drifted in the netherworld between waking and sleeping, she freed Jeremy from her mind and summoned forth another face. His features were obscured by a mask, but his silvery eyes glowed fiercely, bathing her in their icy glow and she shivered and sat upright in her bed.

She pulled the covers more tightly around her chilled body as a painful drumming began inside her head. Haunted once more by the glimmering specter, she tried again to prod his identity from her stubborn memory, to find the missing piece of the puzzle of her life which had shattered that night in a London alley. Try as she might, she was still no closer to the truth. With a deep sigh, she lay back again, and as the pain slowly eased, she allowed herself to sleep at last.

chapter 11

The morning dawned with sultry brightness and Melissa rose sleepily and splashed the tepid water from the china washbasin over her warm flesh. Then she powdered her body lightly and slipped into the green muslin gown, hoping it would withstand the day's journey through the countryside, for she had no other presentable dress. She brushed her curls up into a topknot and then, with a long hatpin, firmly anchored the small green hat to her thick hair. Packing her few possessions in the small portmanteau she had purchased, she walked downstairs to the lobby to wait.

She had barely seated herself in a comfortable chair when the front door swung open and an elegantly clad coachman approached her and took up her valise. He led her out to the waiting carriage and handed her up, where she sank into the thick plush seat across from a smiling Bryan Ransome.

"Good morning, my dear," he greeted her, politely tipping his derby, "I trust we haven't hurried you too much."

"Oh no, I was ready with time to spare," she reassured him. She settled back comfortably against the cushions just as the coach started off, the horses clopping noisily over the cobblestones.

Ransome seemed to forget about Melissa because he soon dozed off, his head nodding against his broad chest, his large hands relaxing in his lap. Content to observe the city as the carriage jounced along, Melissa stared out at the houses they were passing. Red bricked and strung together in long rows, they were reminiscent of many of London's townhouses. Most of the homes boasted high stone stoops and despite the early hour of the morning, many women were busily washing them down, splashing water over the porches and scrubbing them with large, bristly brushes.

It was not long before the carriage reached the outskirts of Baltimore and the scenery changed into the tranquil rolling countryside which Jeremy had once described to her. Spreading before her were lush, gently sloping hills, undulating like a vast green sea with herds of horses and cattle grazing on the fertile pastureland. They swept on, past fragrant meadows, startling the occasional animal which looked up at the intrusion, while continuing to munch contentedly on the sweet grasses and honeyed clover.

The way grew steeper as they headed toward the state's western shore that sprawled upland from the glistening waters of Chesapeake Bay. It was there that the hills provided the blue-green pasturelands which nurtured Maryland's vast horse-breeding operations. As they rode, Melissa stared wide-eyed at the huge estates with their adjoining breeding farms and stables and the magnificent horses she saw corralled there.

"Quite a sight, isn't it?" Ransome's voice startled her.

"It reminds me very much of my own home," she admitted wistfully.

Ransome stretched his long frame and tossed his hat onto the seat. Following her fascinated gaze, he explained, "Most of the land we're passing through is privately owned. That includes the cleared land as well as the forests. You'll come to appreciate our woods, Melissa, if you're as good a shot as you claim to be. We've got plenty of fox and deer around as well as

118

smaller game such as rabbit, raccoon, and 'possum.''

They rode in silence until Melissa found herself growing restless. She sought to pry some further information from her reticent companion.

"Tell me why you chose to call your estate Laurel Hill," she asked him.

"After the mountain laurel growing wild on our lands," he replied, squinting at her against the glare of the noon sun. "Most of the higher hills are covered with laurel, as you'll eventually see for yourself." He pulled out a handkerchief from his breast pocket and mopped at his forehead before continuing to point out some of the wildflowers they were passing. The fields and woods were speckled with the colors of wild geranium, phlox, and verbena, while the hills themselves abounded with wild columbine, witch hazel, and ground pinks.

As the sun climbed higher in the June sky, Melissa felt trickles of perspiration running down her back and she longed for some shade and a cool drink. Sensing her discomfort, Ransome suggested she remove her gloves and unfasten some of the tiny buttons fastening the high collar of her gown. She willingly complied and then stiffened apprehensively as he called up to the driver, who instantly halted the carriage.

"I took the liberty of having a small hamper of food prepared for us," he explained, unaware of her thoughts, and she immediately relaxed. "I also packed a bottle of wine in some ice, so let's hope it's remained cool enough to be of some use." The driver handed him a wicker hamper and then, to save time, Ransome suggested they eat while continuing on their way.

Settling the basket on the seat beside him, he filled a plate for Melissa, who gratefully accepted and began to sample the tasty chicken and vegetable salad. Ransome opened the bottle of wine and, filling a sturdy glass, handed it to her and then poured for himself. They ate in contented silence, as the carriage bounced its way over the rutted roads, and when they had completed their meal and finished the last of the wine, Melissa leaned back against the seat, drowsy and satisfied.

The steady clopping of the horses' hooves, the blazing sun, and the delicious wine all conspired to lull Melissa to sleep. Her head sagged forward, her hat tipped precariously, coppery curls springing free tumbling about her shoulders. Ransome chuckled as he watched her fighting to remain awake.

"Stop resisting, Melissa," he chided her gently. "Have a nap. We've still a long ride ahead of us." She unsuccessfully attempted to stifle a yawn and began to fumble with the hat pin in order to remove the troublesome little bonnet. Then, tucking her legs up under her skirts, she curled up on the seat, mindless of crushing the muslin gown. She soon fell asleep.

When Ransome nudged her awake, she sat up and stretched her cramped body and peered about her in the fading daylight. The carriage had drawn up before an imposing two story, red-brick mansion, its white, columned portico supporting a massive triangular pediment. Flowering shrubs were clustered beneath the first floor windows and twisting clematis was wound about the graceful pillars, carpeting them in purple velvet.

Melissa was handed down from the carriage and as she struggled to fully awaken herself, the heavy front door of the house opened. A tall, regal woman swept onto the veranda. Her lovely cameo face was framed by coal-black hair pulled back into a loose chignon. Her large, black eyes were filled with warmth as she hurried to meet the man climbing the steps to greet her.

"Bryan, what a surprise," she cried as he crushed her to him. "We weren't expecting you until tomorrow." He silenced her with a long, deep kiss, then set her from him as he turned to Melissa, beckoning her forward.

"Come here, my dear, and allow me to introduce you," he called to the sleepy and disheveled girl.

"Cornelia, my love, this is Melissa Howell, who has consented to take on the awesome task of schooling your niece in the art of horsemanship, among other things, we hope."

Melissa started, taken by surprise, for she had assumed that the woman he had so eagerly embraced was his wife.

"Melissa," he continued, unaware of her reaction, "this is Cornelia Simmonds, my sister-in-law." Melissa forced a smile to her frozen lips as she looked up at the woman who was eyeing her disdainfully. "I'm afraid my young traveling companion is still somewhat sleepy." He laughed, squeezing Melissa's hand encouragingly.

Before Melissa could respond, she was distracted by the sounds of shouting and whinnying horses coming from the back of the house. Ransome released her hand and hurried down the stairs, striding purposefully toward the commotion. Woodenly, Melissa followed after him, with Cornelia trailing behind her. Heading for the spread of whitewashed stables set back from the house, Melissa saw several figures engaged in a violent argument, while each one strained to hold onto the reins of a skittish horse.

"What in the name of thunder is going on here!" Ransome bellowed as he walked toward the knot of shouting people. Almost instantly, the bickering ceased, heads turning at the sound of his voice. Melissa watched dumbfounded as two of the figures released their horses, leaving two hapless grooms staring after them and then quickly scrambling to retrieve the fallen reins.

"Father!"

"Bryan!"

The voices called out together as the two black-suited forms approached, and Melissa stared incredulously at two handsome women, dressed in men's riding habits, descending upon the fuming Bryan Ransome. He

121

pulled himself free of their embrace and managed to knock the riding cap from one of the women's heads, sending a cascade of blue black hair streaming down her back.

"Whatever are you doing home? You weren't planning to be back until tomorrow," the woman exclaimed.

"So everyone keeps reminding me," he remarked scathingly. "What damned difference would it make. Today, tomorrow, you'd still be in one tangle or another. What is it this time?" he demanded and both women began shouting at once until he held up a hand for silence. "Enough, both of you. We'll try to straighten it out later. Now before you succeed in making complete fools of yourselves, there's someone I'd like you to meet. Melissa!" he barked, unaware that the astounded girl stood right behind him. She went to him and he thrust her forward to face the two women who were staring back at her.

"Melissa, may I present my wife, Amanda, and my daughter, Kathleen. This, ladies, if I dare call you that, is Melissa Howell who, my dear Kathleen, will help you with your riding and, if we are fortunate enough, teach you something about good manners."

Two pairs of eyes set in similar ivory-tinted faces studied Melissa. Amanda, whose black hair still lay tumbled down her back, was the mirror image of Cornelia, with the same large black eyes set below arching brows, the identical slender nose and finely chiseled lips. Kathleen's blue eyes, startling in their paleness, defiantly challenged Melissa, as the young woman scornfully assessed the rumpled interloper. Strands of silver-blonde hair escaped the confines of her riding cap and her pert nose flared haughtily above the full lips which pouted as she eyed Melissa.

Kathleen was the first to break the awkward silence and as she did, Melissa felt the sting of the girl's temper, as Bryan Ransome had warned she would.

"So, father dear, you feel your daughter lacks breeding," she commented, her icy eyes crackling. "Is that why you've decided to have one of your whores teach me better manners?"

Melissa paled and she watched Ransome's darkening face as he turned on his daughter. "It's exactly that type of remark which makes me see the wisdom of my decision, Kathleen," he snarled. "Perhaps it's not too late to silence your sharp tongue long enough to fool some poor devil into marrying you and relieve us of your continual unpleasantness."

He took advantage of his daughter's dumbfounded silence as he turned to his wife. "Amanda, I hope you'll see to it that Melissa is given a suitable room—in the family wing." Despite Kathleen's hostile grimace, he continued, "Melissa is to be considered part of the family for as long as she can bear us. I shall expect you all down for dinner in one hour." With a curt nod, he spun on his heel and tramped back toward the house, Cornelia hurrying to catch up with him.

"Come, Melissa," said Amanda in a surprisingly gentle voice, "I'm afraid we've given you a shocking impression of us." She moved to guide the girl back to the house. "We must have a talk, you and I, perhaps this evening after dinner." It seemed more of a statement than a question and Melissa mutely nodded her head.

She was dazed by the unpleasant episode she had just witnessed and she was still smarting from Kathleen's scathing remark. More puzzling was the off-hand manner Amanda affected concerning the blatant display of affection between her husband and her sister.

"Have your bags already been brought inside?" Amanda asked as she spotted the small valise still sitting on the veranda.

"I'm afraid this is all I have," Melissa admitted shamefacedly. "I left in rather a hurry," she finished lamely. With a wave of her slender hand, Amanda calmly dismissed the subject and hurried Melissa up the

123

steps and into the house.

The large front hall was dominated by a magnificent crystal chandelier suspended from the high ceiling. The walls were papered in pale-yellow silk, a warming note provided by the deep jewel tones of an oriental rug covering much of the dark-stained wooden floor. A graceful winding staircase curved upward to the second floor and tall pilastered doorways led into the rooms adjoining the hall. Tubs of flowering plants were placed about the room on small marquetry tables and Melissa's spirits lifted considerably when she saw them.

"You approve then, my dear?" inquired the cool voice of Cornelia Simmonds. "The cook wants you, Amanda," she said to her sister, "so I'll show Miss Howell to her room." As Amanda hastened toward the back of the house, Melissa found herself following the straight back of Cornelia up the stairs.

As she walked down the carpeted hallway, Melissa gazed inquisitively at the gold-framed oil paintings depicting race horses and pastoral scenes covering the walls. A pang of loneliness rippled through her as she was achingly reminded of her home. Tears welled up in her eyes. She collided with the woman ahead of her as she stopped abruptly and Melissa backed away in embarrassment, blinking back her tears. Cornelia's hard gaze softened and she gently guided Melissa into a large airy room.

"This will be your bedroom," the woman said matter-of-factly. "I think you'll find everything you need, although I'll have one of the maids bring you some fresh towels."

When Cornelia had gone, Melissa sagged onto the bed and gazed about the lovely room which was dappled in the fading colors of sunset. The wallpaper was printed with small nosegays of purple violets floating on a field of white. Fabric in the same pattern had been fashioned into long curtains to frame the tall windows and match the bed's scalloped tester and thick down coverlet. The furniture was painted white and a small vanity near one of the windows was bordered in layers of filmy white lace. Melissa felt as if she were adrift in a spring meadow as she marveled at the gay blossoms dancing all around her.

A knock at the door announced the arrival of the maid with an armful of fluffy towels, which Melissa gratefully accepted. The maid, her starched uniform crackling as she moved, nodded slightly in deference to the young woman whose position had somehow won her a bedroom close to the family members. Melissa shifted uncomfortably under the girl's studied appraisal of her and she was considerably relieved when the maid swept briskly out of the room.

She opened her small valise and hung away her old gown, watching it all but disappear inside the vast clothes closet. Placing her few undergarments in one of the bureau drawers, she then set about washing her hands and face in the flower-sprigged porcelain wash bowl. She sat down in front of the vanity's white-framed mirror and brushed out her hair until it fell in a burnished cascade to her waist. Smoothing the creases in her gown, plumping up the lace to free it from any remaining road dust, Melissa left her bedroom just as a tinkling bell sounded downstairs.

chapter 12

She stood uncertainly in the front hall when Bryan Ransome appeared, freshly attired in a velvet jacket and light trousers, and courteously took her arm to lead her into the dining room. The others were already seated as Ransome steered Melissa to her place beside Kathleen. The girl stared coldly at Melissa then turned away, showing her a disdainful snub-nosed profile.

Amanda smiled encouragingly from her place at the foot of the formally set mahogany table while Ransome settled himself at the opposite end. Cornelia appeared rather fragile and vulnerable seated alone across from Melissa and the woman seemed obviously distracted. As Melissa filled her plate with the mouth-watering food being passed by the serving maids, she could not help but compare the tense silence of the Ransome meal with the animated discussions which had always punctuated dinners at Howard House.

As the family continued to eat in stony silence, Melissa began shifting restlessly about in her chair, finally centering her concentration on the gracious room in which they sat. The dining room, like the front hall, boasted a spectacular crystal chandelier, its sparkling prisms reflecting in the ornate gold-framed mirror set above the long mahogany sideboard. The walls were painted a pale green and pale green brocade was swept into heavy swags to border the tall windows. White tapers flickered in silver candelabra set atop a Sheratonstyle buffet, and Melissa wondered at the cost of importing such exquisite furnishings from England.

"You seem to be rather curious," Kathleen remarked contemptuously, "does our home overwhelm you?"

Melissa, determined not to bow to the imperious young woman, replied in an equally contemptuous tone. "Quite the contrary, Kathleen, I'm rather pleased to find that you Americans have come to appreciate the beauty of our English design." She was granted the satisfaction of watching Kathleen's face redden.

"Bravo, Melissa!" came Bryan Ransome's approving shout from the head of the table. He merrily toasted her with his wine and Melissa, warmed by his support, raised her own glass in response.

"Father," Kathleen raged, "how dare you take the side of the hired help against your own daughter!"

"Stop this immediately!" Amanda's voice cut in sharply before Ransome could reply. "If this type of behavior continues, Melissa will no doubt be packing before the meal's over, and I must admit, I wouldn't blame her."

"What an idea, mother," Kathleen put in smoothly, looking tauntingly at Melissa. "I, for one, would even help her pack." She grinned slyly, blue sparks shooting through her light eyes.

Melissa sprang from her chair, unable to control the rage seething within her. Her face flushed, her eyes flashing, she faced them all. "What kind of people are you? Mr. Ransome hired me to assist his daughter with her riding and no sooner do I set foot on this place than I am accused of being a whore and then treated like some social pariah. I assure you that I am neither and I would prefer to seek employment elsewhere than to subject myself to further humiliation by such offensive people as you are." With that, she hurled her napkin onto the table and stormed out of the room. Ignoring the immediate surge of voices as she fled, she ran up the stairs and flung herself across the bed.

"Melissa?"

She raised her head and saw Amanda standing in the doorway, a sorrowful expression marking her lovely face.

"Melissa, dear, may I speak with you?" she asked, and without waiting for a reply, she seated herself on the bed.

"I don't know how to apologize for what happened, but the hostility here has very little to do with you. It's us, Melissa. It's something we've lived with for a very long time." At Melissa's quizzical look, Amanda continued, "As you might have guessed, Cornelia and I are twins, and as twins often do, we delighted in playing jokes on people, since few could tell us apart."

She sighed fretfully and clasped her hands tightly in her lap as Melissa regarded her thoughtfully. "Bryan was Cornelia's beau, a rather remarkable sea captain who was building an empire for himself, and although I was fond of him, I had beaus of my own to occupy my time. Then one night we were to attend a ball; Bryan was to be Cornelia's escort as usual. At the last moment, we decided to tease the men and we assumed each other's places. The evening passed pleasantly enough and no one was the wiser.

"Cornelia and I played this little game several times that summer until it finally went too far. I allowed Bryan to make love to me, and only when I discovered that I was pregnant did I confront Cornelia with the truth. She accused me of lying, of trying to steal Bryan away from her and, although nothing could have been further from the truth, my parents forced him to marry me." Her eyes filled with pain and her next words were whispered. "I miscarried two months after our wedding."

"But, Kathleen," Melissa murmured, staring at Amanda, stunned by the woman's revelation.

"Kathleen was born several years afterward, but by then Cornelia had married and moved out of the state. When her husband died several years ago, leaving her penniless, she moved in with us."

"But how can you tolerate having her here with you after what happened?" Melissa blurted out.

"It's easier when you have no feelings for your husband," she answered wistfully. "How they still feel toward one another has very little to do with me." Her eyes took on a strange glow as she smiled and her face was animated as she said, "My passion has been breeding and racing horses. We have some of the finest stock in Maryland and the walls of my tack room are covered with the ribbons our thoroughbreds have won at racetracks across the country."

"Does Kathleen know about . . . everything?" Melissa stammered.

"Yes, she does," Amanda admitted ruefully, the sparkle dying in her eyes, "and that's why I hope that you'll reconsider your decision to leave. Kathleen should have the chance to learn the gentler side of womanhood because what she has witnessed all these years has left her bitter and rather hardened. Although she's already twenty-one, she scorns one eligible suitor after another. I don't want her to be cheated the way her mother and her aunt were, Melissa, and I'm begging you to give us another chance before you decide."

Amanda rose from the bed and crossed the room, pausing expectantly with one hand on the door.

"I'll stay for now." Melissa's voice was barely audible. "If only because of you." She was rewarded with a dazzling smile which lit Amanda's face and brought a tiny spark back to her sad black eyes.

The following morning Melissa found herself alone at the giant table in the dining room. The others had risen early and were out examining the new horses Amanda had bought the day before. Wearing the same gown she had traveled in, Melissa fretted about finding suitable riding clothes, and she set off in search of the family, anxious to reach an understanding with her belligerent pupil and establish her position in the household.

Walking toward the stables, she encountered Bryan Ransome on his way back to the house. He hailed her with a wave and strode over to her.

"Good morning, Melissa, I trust you slept well."

"Very well indeed, thank you. My only problem now is finding myself a riding habit, since this dress is all I have." She paused, indicating her thin muslin gown.

"Of course, of course," he readily concurred, "Kathleen's about your size, except perhaps across the, ah, chest," he mumbled awkwardly as he scrutinized Melissa's full breasts straining against the bodice of her gown, "and I'm sure that, considering the size of my daughter's wardrobe, you're bound to find something suitable." He took her arm and steered her toward the house again.

One of the maids directed Melissa to Kathleen's bedroom but she stood indecisively outside the door. Reluctant to enter, she preferred speaking first with Kathleen in order to avoid any misunderstandings. As she was turning away from the door, she noticed Kathleen herself walking briskly down the corridor toward her.

"What are you doing lurking about there, Melissa?" she demanded, her eyes narrowing suspiciously.

"Your father suggested I borrow one of your riding habits," Melissa answered evenly, "but I decided against it and was just about to set off to find you."

"I see," came the guarded reply, "I appreciate your honesty," she admitted grudgingly, and then, as if weighing the importance of her decision, Kathleen said, "I have an outfit I intended to give away, but I think it might suit your purposes for now. Wait here." She brushed past Melissa and into her room, closing the door firmly in Melissa's astonished face.

When she reappeared, she was carrying a chocolate brown riding habit, consisting of a fitted jacket and jodhpurs with an ivory-silk blouse and a brown velvet helmet. Melissa was surprised at the apparent newness

130

of the ensemble and she could not understand why Kathleen was getting rid of it. She thanked the girl and hurried back to her own room to change.

Ransome had been correct in his assumption as Melissa could barely fasten the buttons of the blouse. But she tied the long ivory scarf around her neck and, by allowing the ends to trail down across the front of the shirt, she managed to mask the telltale snugness. The rest of the suit fit reasonably well and as Melissa pulled her hair into a tight knot and donned the stiff riding cap, she felt a surge of excitement in anticipation of riding once more.

At the stables she was greeted warmly by Amanda, who silently examined the girl dressed so becomingly in her own daughter's cast-offs.

"You look charming in brown, Melissa," she said approvingly. "It seems to set off those remarkable eyes of yours. But come," she said brusquely, taking Melissa's arm, "you must choose a horse for yourself."

Melissa followed the woman into one of the large horse barns, passing each stall and studying each horse, waiting for some spark to ignite between her and the one she would ultimately choose. As she approached one of the stalls, a golden palomino stretched a long graceful neck over the top of the slatted wooden gate and sniffed curiously at Melissa's face. She laughed as the sensitive nostrils quivered, tickling her, and she raised a hand to stroke the tawny silken mane.

"This is the one," she announced to Amanda.

"An excellent choice, my dear," she affirmed. "Her name is Honey and she was a foal of one of our thoroughbreds, Tiger Lily, who brought us a great deal of prize money in her time." She ordered one of the grooms to saddle the horse and left Melissa to wait while she supervised the saddling of her own animal. Melissa sauntered back outside where she met Kathleen.

"I hope you're almost ready," the girl pouted. "It promises to be another scorching day and I want to get in as much riding as possible before it gets too hot."

To Melissa's relief, the groom promptly appeared and led Honey over to the stepping block, preparing to offer Melissa a leg up. But she shunned his offer and expertly swung herself into the saddle, aware of Kathleen's observation of her movements. Kathleen mounted a handsome bay and kicking roughly at the horse's flank, started off, signaling Melissa to follow her. Melissa, accustoming herself to the feel of the saddle and the strange horse under her, was slow in starting after the other girl. Honey responded easily to Melissa's practiced touch and when she gave the horse its head, she caught up quickly with Kathleen.

The two girls cantered in silence across the rich green expanse of Laurel Hill, plunging through flowering fields of black-eyed Susans, daisies and buttercups and pounding through groves of red spruce and white pine. Melissa's heartbeat matched the thundering strides of her horse as she galloped ahead of Kathleen, taking the wind in her face, breathing deeply of its restorative freshness. Strands of auburn hair sprang free from her cap and licked at her face as she rode and she crouched over Honey's straining back, urging her faster.

They zigzagged through a meadow, its knee-high grasses slashing at the horse's sinewy legs. Following a dusty slash of road, they galloped toward a glinting stream. Melissa eased Honey into the air, clearing the rushing water in a giant leap. At the top of a hill, Melissa finally reined in her heaving mount and, awed by the panorama spreading before her, stared out across the distant plains towards the Blue Ridge Mountains, rising as a jagged purple haze.

At the sound of approaching hoofbeats, Melissa turned to see Kathleen, her face flushed and her ash-blonde hair streaming out behind her, spur her horse up the knoll and halt him beside Melissa. Panting, the girl glared at Melissa and groped about for her hat. Discovering it gone, she lashed out angrily.

"How dare you take off that way! You don't know your way around here and you could have gotten lost or hurt and then what would you have done!" the girl shouted, her face contorted with rage.

Melissa gazed in disbelief at the fuming girl and, unable to control herself, she burst out laughing. But her laughter was shortlived as Kathleen split the air inches from Melissa's face with a vicious swing of her riding crop.

"Don't you ever laugh at me, Melissa Howell. I'm warning you," she threatened, shaking with the force of her fury.

"I'm sorry, Kathleen." Melissa strained to keep a smile from her lips. "I'm afraid your reaction took me completely by surprise. I was scarcely prepared for such a childish outburst."

"I resent that remark," the girl snapped, raising her hand menacingly again. But this time Melissa was prepared and, as the crop came down, she grabbed it and tugged, wrenching the other girl from her saddle and sending her tumbling to the ground. Melissa dismounted immediately, the crop clenched in her own hand, warily eyeing the fallen girl who was struggling to her feet.

"Now I shall warn you, Kathleen," she said, her voice deadly calm, "never lift a hand to me again. And for your first lesson in horsemanship, so that I might be able to justify my wages, never let me see you use this crop on your horse. If you have the proper control of your animal, he will always respond, but beat him with this quirt or kick him with the heels of your boots as you do, and you will never be considered a good rider." With that she threw the crop to the ground, remounted her horse and leaving Kathleen standing there speechless, she headed back toward Laurel Hill.

Dinner that evening was as silent as the one the previous night. Kathleen refused to even acknowledge Melissa. Whatever brief attempts she made at conversation were greeted with cool disinterest. At the end of the meal, Melissa asked Ransome if she might borrow some books from his library and he happily consented. She spent several hours contentedly browsing through the vast collection, leafing through books on sailing, horse breeding and even poetry. The study, a masculine retreat from the light, feminine touches found throughout the rest of the house, smelled of pipe tobacco and leather and reminded her painfully of her father's library at Howard House.

She selected a number of books and was preparing to leave the room, when Ransome walked in.

"Well, I see you've found something to your liking," he observed, glancing at the titles she had chosen. "Oh, by the way, Melissa, I thought you might be interested in knowing that your friend Jeremy will soon be on his way to the Orient, skippering *The Highland*, the newest and fastest clipper in my fleet. A long trip like that should keep him out of mischief for a while, wouldn't you agree?" He winked broadly at Melissa, who simply shrugged her shoulders and hurried out of the study, ignoring the burst of laughter which followed her. As she walked back to her room, she fervently hoped that Ransome had kept his promise to her and not revealed her whereabouts to Jeremy.

The following days passed with a bland repetitiveness which irritated and worried Melissa. On occasion she managed to corner Kathleen for a riding lesson, advising the girl on her jumping techniques, but Kathleen remained unresponsive and hostile. Cornelia appeared only for meals and Amanda was involved with the intricate operation of her vast breeding farm. Melissa wondered how long she would be kept on at Laurel Hill since the women paid her little mind and Bryan Ransome seemed constantly preoccupied, busily dividing his time between the estate and the townhouse in Baltimore.

One particularly hot June afternoon, as she dressed for a ride alone, Melissa discarded the riding jacket and helmet and rolled up the sleeves of the silk shirt. Carelessly knotting the ivory scarf around her neck, she studied her face in the vanity mirror, scarcely believing the changes in herself since leaving *The Sea Belle*. Her pallor had been replaced by a golden tan, her face had filled out again, her topaz eyes gleamed with health and vitality, and her auburn hair was streaked with tawny glints from the summer sun.

Humming softly, she hurried to the stables, anticipating a long ride because Kathleen was away for the day with Amanda who was hoping to purchase another racehorse for the already overcrowded stables. Eagerly mounting her horse, she led Honey away from the estate, searching for new places to explore, and soon rider and horse blended easily together in a long-strided gallop, covering miles under the glare of the brilliant sun.

Melissa rode until her clothes clung to her and rivulets of perspiration bathed her heated body. Honey's coat was slick with sweat and she was panting from the unbroken pace of their ride. Spotting a tiny grove of birches, Melissa slowed her horse and headed toward the cooling shelter where a small brook was bubbling. Dismounting, she set Honey grazing beneath the trees while she tore off her scarf, unbuttoned her shirt, and knelt beside the sparkling water. Soaking the scarf, she mopped her face and let teasing droplets of water trickle down her neck and onto her warm breasts.

Then peeling off the clinging shirt, she spread it out on the grassy bank to dry, while she stretched herself out on her back, feeling the prickly warmth of the grass beneath her body. The breeze cooled her glowing skin, dried the moisture on her face and breasts, and rippled soothingly over her bare flesh. She drifted into easy slumber only to be awakened by a strange noise close to her ear. Opening her eyes, she saw a large black horse calmly grazing near her shoulder and with a cry of alarm, she sprang to her feet, searching frantically for her shirt.

"Looking for this?"

She whirled at the sound of a deep male voice and

hurriedly folded her arms across her chest. But his laugh set her trembling. "Too late, my beauty. I was lucky enough to observe you at my leisure while you were sleeping."

Seething with indignation, she watched as a tall figure moved out of the shadows and walked toward her, carrying her shirt as if it were a white flag of truce.

"How dare you sneak up on me that way," she cried, as he drew closer.

"I'd hardly call it sneaking considering the fact that you were sound asleep," he countered.

She ignored his remark and snatched savagely at her shirt, ripping the thin material as she tugged it from his hand. Turning her back to him, she fumbled with the torn blouse, hastily buttoning it and tucking it back into her breeches. Then she turned to face the intruder, only to find him standing beside his horse, preparing to mount.

"Were you about to thank me for finding your shirt?" he asked, casually toying with the reins.

"It was never lost," she retorted.

"How can you be sure when you were asleep?" His persistence coupled with his teasing grin only enraged her further.

"Do you make it a habit of always playing such childish games?" she shouted in frustration.

He dropped the reins and sauntered back to where she stood, hands on her hips, her chest heaving. He looked down at her with eyes filled with mischief. As she defiantly returned his stare, an uneasy shudder shook her. Despite the fact that he was a stranger to her, there was a disturbing familiarity about him.

The wind ruffled his thick black hair and under straight black brows glowed the opalescent grayness of his eyes. His nose was straight above a firm, strong mouth and the cleft in his chin deepened as he suddenly laughed, his teeth flashing white and even in his sun-darkened face. Melissa flushed, misinterpreting his laugh. He caught the flash of temper in her eyes and

136

attempted to ward it off.

"Whoa, lady, easy does it," he cautioned. "I was laughing at the absurdity of the situation, not at you."

"Indeed," she returned, her eyes drawn inexplicably back to his.

"Do I detect an accent in my lady's speech?" he teased, imitating her. "British?"

"Yes," she replied stiffly.

"And here I thought you people were known for your charm and hospitality."

"Some are, perhaps," she snipped waspishly, "when the occasion warrants it."

"I was just in England myself," he continued, despite her hostility, "and I found that most of the people there were exceptionally friendly." He lazily perused her body, his eyes resting on her straining breasts. "What part of England are you from?" he asked casually.

"I doubt that it is any of your concern," she charged. With a toss of her head, she turned and set out across the grass to retrieve her horse.

"Won't you at least tell me your name?" he called out after her. Receiving no reply, he shouted, "Perhaps I'll have the pleasure of meeting you again sometime."

"I sincerely hope not," she said over her shoulder as she swung easily onto Honey's back. With an impatient flick of the reins, she nudged her horse forward and galloped off with the stranger's mocking laughter ringing in her ears.

chapter 13

The following evening as Melissa was dressing for dinner, she heard hoofbeats pounding up the gravel drive toward the house. She reached the window in time to see a man disappearing up the front steps. Although she only glimpsed his hatted figure, there was something disturbingly familiar about him. Turning back to her mirror, she wondered about the identity of the rider as she continued to fuss with her hair.

She had pulled it into an elegant twist, freeing several long ringlets to nestle against her shoulders. Her gown, another in her growing collection of Kathleen's unworn and discarded finery, was of fine yellow muslin embroidered with white daisies. The sleeveless bodice was scooped enticingly low, displaying her tempting cleavage, before falling away into a full skirt. The muslin was gathered into graceful panniers about her hips, sweeping into a modified bustle. To offset the daring decolletage, Melissa tied a wide yellow satin ribbon about her slender neck and satisfied at last, she set out to join the others.

As she headed for the dining room, she was baffled by the sounds of boisterous laughter and animated chatter providing a startling departure from the usual tense calm pervading all Laurel Hill meals. At her entrance, the voices were abruptly stilled and Kathleen immediately relinquished the arm of the man with whom she had been urgently whispering.

"Melissa, my dear," Ransome roared, beckoning her to him, "we have a delightful surprise. An old friend of ours has just consented to stay for dinner."

For one sickening moment, Melissa feared she was about to confront Jeremy Ransome, but as she was ushered to their guest, he turned toward her and she raised her eyes to meet the gray-eyed gaze of the insolent stranger she had encountered the previous day.

"Melissa, this is our good friend and neighbor, Calvin Gabriel. Cal, this young beauty is Melissa Howell."

Melissa reluctantly allowed him to raise her hand to his lips, but his grazing touch further unsettled her and she hastily withdrew her hand, feeling somehow that she had been burned.

"Miss Howell." His voice was like a silken caress as he uttered her name. "I believe this belongs to you." From his coat pocket, he produced her ivory silk scarf.

"But how . . ." Her words disintegrated before his penetrating stare.

"How did I know where to find you?" he supplied, his grin widening. "It was easy. Honey's a fairly distinctive animal, considering that Tiger Lily was mated with one of my studs and Honey was the result of their pairing. As Bryan said, we're old friends."

"And I thought you stopped by on my account, Calvin," pouted Kathleen, placing a hand possessively on his arm. Melissa experienced a fleeting pang of jealousy as Calvin smiled down into Kathleen's up-turned face and stooped to kiss the hand resting along his arm.

"Come along, everyone," Amanda cut in, breaking the awkward silence which had descended upon the group. "Dinner is served."

Melissa moved mechanically to her place beside Kathleen and as Calvin first helped Kathleen into her seat and then turned to assist Melissa, she wrenched the chair from his grasp and seated herself, ignoring his snort of laughter. Kathleen snickered and Melissa threw her a withering look.

"Why didn't you tell me you'd already met Calvin?" Kathleen hissed in Melissa's ear.

"Because I didn't know his name nor did I care to under the circumstances," she muttered between clenched teeth.

"What circumstances?" Kathleen persisted, her eyes widening expectantly.

"Girls, stop that whispering," Cornelia reprimanded them, effectively silencing the inquisitive Kathleen, much to Melissa's relief.

Cornelia had been moved so that she faced Melissa while Kathleen was seated across from Calvin and although Melissa kept her gaze averted, concentrating on the food before her, she was acutely conscious of his occasional glances even as he spoke to Kathleen. She gratefully accepted a second glass of wine and, under Calvin's amused scrutiny, she downed most of the wine in a single gulp. A flush rose in her cheeks and she struggled to keep from coughing, refusing to further humiliate herself in front of the brash Calvin Gabriel.

"It's a privilege having you here for dinner," Amanda was saying as she focused her attention on their guest. "It seems so much like old times. Why did we ever stop those Sunday dinners? The only time we see people nowadays is at the races or at one of those stuffy dinner parties during the season in Baltimore."

"Children grow up, Amanda," Bryan interrupted somewhat pointedly, "and as adults, they usually prefer the company of others their own age." Amanda and Calvin exchanged puzzled glances before Amanda lowered her gaze. A strange light flickered within her deep eyes.

Cornelia sought to ease the mounting tension as she touched Calvin's arm. "Tell me about your father, Cal; has he recovered from his stroke?"

"Not completely, I'm afraid." He shook his head. "He's partially paralyzed on one side, but his speech has improved considerably."

"I'm sorry to hear that, son, I didn't realize how serious it had been," put in Bryan, as he poured himself another glass of wine and refilled Calvin's glass as well.

"Calvin," Kathleen murmured, her usually pale face flushed and glowing as she addressed him, "did father tell you of our plans to race Pebbles at Pimlico next season? He feels she should be ready by then and I get to choose the jockey. What do you think of Luis Alvarro?" She dimpled, leaning forward toward Calvin so that his eyes traced her movement to the frank display of her high small breasts, pressed together above her pale rose gown.

Melissa returned to contemplating the cold food on her plate, which she busily shifted about into small groupings with the aimless wanderings of her dinner fork. She was growing restless and not even Amanda's renewed attempts at conversation could draw her out of the dark mood descending upon her. She looked up to find Cornelia studying her closely, a half-smile curving her usually tight-set mouth. The older woman immediately shifted her gaze as Melissa challenged her, and they completed the meal in uncomfortable silence.

Ransome and Calvin retired to the study for after-dinner brandy and cigars, and Melissa excused herself and walked outside into the garden. She drifted leisurely down one of the paths to the small white gazebo, partially obscured by the rich tangle of wild rose bushes growing around it. Breathing deeply of their fragrance, she tenderly touched some of the plump, velvety flowers and then climbed the step of the gazebo, settling herself on the stone bench within the tiny structure. She trained her gaze on the stars, spattering the indigo sky with their winking brilliance, and she thought of Jeremy using those same stars to chart a course for himself as he crossed the ocean to China.

"First a wood sprite and now a moon goddess," teased a deep voice at her ear. "How many other disguises do you wear, Miss Howell?"

She whirled to glimpse the shadowed face of Calvin

141

Gabriel, his gray eyes flashing silver in the moonlight. She shivered as something flickered within her memory but, as she sought to capture it, it vanished, and before she could move from the bench, Calvin had seated himself beside her. He pressed an apricot-tinted rose into her hand, saying softly, "To match the glow of your skin."

She closed her fingers around the rose and threw it scornfully onto the floor. "Keep your flowers, Mr. Gabriel," she hissed, "I want none of your attention."

She rose to leave but he grabbed her wrist. "Let me go," she exclaimed. "You have succeeded once more in interrupting my privacy and I resent your intrusion. Now please let go of me."

"Not until I've exacted my price, Miss Howell," he laughed, squeezing her wrist more tightly.

"You have no price I care to pay," she spat angrily, slapping at him as he attempted to seize her other wrist.

"Why are you putting up such a fight?" he demanded, pinning both of her arms behind her back and drawing her up against him, her soft breasts flattening against his chest. "You know this is what you want, otherwise why would you have come out here alone?"

"I want nothing from you," she retaliated, "I consider you one of the most arrogant men I have ever met . . ." Her words were cut off as he crushed his lips to hers, bruising her with the intensity of his kiss. He forced her lips to part, lashing the tender inside of her mouth with his tongue. She strained against him and managed to bite his tongue with her teeth and he drew back with a cry but refused to relinquish his hold on her.

He forced her head back then, his fingers digging into her thick auburn curls, and he bent toward her, kissing her pulsing throat and the tops of her swelling breasts. Her body stiffened and then ignited with a burst of hungry fire and she moaned, trapped by her body's response, helpless to quell the awakening desire kindled within her. She sagged against him and from her weakening he drew his strength. He kissed the hollow of her throat again before caressing her yielding mouth, nibbling at her parted lips and coaxing her reluctant tongue gently with his own.

"Calvin! Are you out there?" Kathleen's voice shattered the spell, scattering the fragile web spinning around them and Melissa was abruptly released from the tempting prison of his arms.

"Damn," he cursed irritably, getting to his feet and straightening his clothes. He tossed Melissa a lopsided grin and shrugged. Then he stooped to kiss her hand. "A delightful interlude, Miss Howell," he murmured. "Until the next time then, my dear." He strode from the gazebo, calling out to Kathleen as he walked swiftly up the path toward the house.

Stunned by his hasty departure, Melissa sat there, trembling and confused. She ran a shaky hand across her lips and over her breasts, still feeling the sting of his passion on her tender flesh. Looking down, she noticed the rose she had thrown onto the floor and with a vengeful sob, she crushed it viciously with the heel of her shoe. Then she eased herself to her feet and made her way back to her room, scurrying up the stairs before meeting anyone who might question her rumpled appearance.

She undressed and slipped naked between the cooling sheets, welcoming their silky relief against her warm throbbing body. She tossed and turned, trying to relieve the burning deep inside her and, as she thrashed miserably about, she heard the sound of a horse clopping down the drive and away from the house. She thought resentfully of Calvin Gabriel and of his effect on her and she envisioned him with Kathleen, imagining them together and she ground her teeth in frustration, dispelling the disturbing image.

When she finally drifted into a troubled sleep, her dreams were filled with fearsome happenings, peopled with phantoms. She was enmeshed in an intricately woven web and the harder she fought to free herself, the more tightly bound she became. As she writhed and twisted, the gossamer tentacles wrapped themselves around her, threatening her with ultimate suffocation. Then as the breath was being squeezed from her, she felt someone ripping away the deadly threads to release her. She floated upward into the arms of a man whose face was burnished by brilliant sunlight. But as she shielded her sight from his blinding radiance, his eyes turned into twin pools of molten silver and she felt as if she were drowning in their depths. She screamed to waken herself.

Melissa lay tangled in the bedcovers, panting for breath as golden light streamed into the room. Her head was drumming painfully as she recalled her nightmare, but the ominous presence embracing her seemed to dissolve with daylight's soothing brightness. There was a knock at the door and Melissa hastened to straighten the sheets as Amanda peered into the bedroom.

"Is everything all right, dear?" she asked, her brow puckered with concern. "I heard you screaming."

"I was having a nightmare," she admitted, her voice tremulous as she plucked nervously at the lace edging of the sheet.

Amanda seated herself beside Melissa and smoothed back the girl's damp hair. "Do you think it might help if you shared your dream with someone?" she asked gently.

"Perhaps," Melissa admitted grudgingly, and in halting speech, she told Amanda of the event in London and how she had slipped in and out of consciousness before finally recovering most of her memory. "But there remains one part of my past I cannot seem to recall," she finished, heaving a plaintive sigh. "I only know that it involves the night of my father's death."

Amanda stroked the girl's hand comfortingly, saying nothing. Then watching the expression on Melissa's face, she asked casually, "What did you think of our Mr. Gabriel?"

Melissa's features tightened into a scowl and as her

eyes flashed belligerently, her words rushed out in a torrent. "I found your Mr. Gabriel to be one of the most arrogant and insolent popinjays I have ever had the misfortune to encounter."

"I'm surprised to hear you say that, Melissa," Amanda replied, masking a smile. "Every woman I know has set her cap for him at one time or another, including Kathleen now, I'm afraid."

"Why should that concern me?" Melissa retorted hotly.

"I suppose I'm simply trying to warn you of my daughter's interest," she sighed resignedly. "She grew up with a child's adulation of Calvin and even though she was twelve years younger than he, she spent a great deal of time with him, learning to ride and managing to fill many lonely moments with his help. Now I'm certain Calvin is the only man Kathleen will consider marrying."

"Then what is stopping her?" Melissa inquired bluntly, uncomfortably aware of the rapid beating of her heart.

"Calvin's disinterest in marriage," was the muted reply. "You see, Melissa, his father, Tyler, spent many hard years trying to make a success of his farm and I think his wife grew tired of hardship. When Calvin was eight and his brother, Edward, was five, their mother walked out on them and I suppose Calvin has never forgiven her.

"Nevertheless, Tyler gradually built up Stony Briar into one of the largest stud farms in the state. But in doing so, he had little time for two small boys. Edward, who is now a lawyer in New York, was practically raised by neighbors, while Calvin spent much of his time here at Laurel Hill after Bryan and I were married." Her voice trailed off and her eyes seemed to glaze over with unshed tears. Melissa shifted restlessly in the bed until Amanda seemed to visibly shake herself from her thoughts.

"I seem to burden you with our family problems,

don't I?'' she asked, smiling sheepishly, and without another word, she swept from the room.

As Melissa and Kathleen were mounting their horses later that morning, Melissa noticed a subtle change in the other girl. She was humming to herself, her face was suffused with color, and a faint smile tilted the corners of her mouth. Melissa felt an inexplicable loneliness as she regarded Kathleen's obvious happiness, and she unwittingly kicked Honey with her boot, startling the horse and causing her to rear, her forelegs pawing the air. Melissa sawed back on the reins, bringing the animal under control, and then she urged her forward to follow Kathleen's lead.

Calvin Gabriel became a frequent visitor at Laurel Hill in the weeks that followed. He still flashed Melissa his teasing grin and attempted to draw her into conversation, but he made no further moves to touch her. His attention, it seemed, was directed solely at Kathleen and the girl blossomed and preened coquettishly in his presence. She spent less time with Melissa as she spent more of it with Calvin and she soon began leaving the estate for extended shopping excursions into Baltimore. Melissa readily adapted to Kathleen's erratic schedule, cherishing her newfound freedom and filling her days with peaceful rides through the countryside. She still worried about her precarious position at Laurel Hill, but scant attention was paid to her lapsed duties. She found herself treated less like an employee and more like a member of the family. As a part of the family, she was expected to sit patiently in the parlor with the others while Kathleen spun past them in the ensembles created for her in the city. Melissa would force a smile to her lips and pretend to admire the magnificent array of finery, but beneath the frozen surface of her face brooded a distressing jealousy.

Bryan Ransome stormed about the house, raging at the extravagance of his daughter while Cornelia attempted to soothe and placate him. Kathleen argued that if he wanted to see her married and off his hands, her expenditures were temporary inconveniences he would have to put up with. Amanda seemed to be oblivious to the entire situation as she spent her days either attending horse shows upstate or supervising the hand breeding of her own thoroughbreds.

Kathleen was away on another shopping trip and Melissa was sitting alone after breakfast. The day was hot and humid with the promise of a thunderstorm in the air. She prowled about the house, picking up a book, leafing disinterestedly through it, putting it down and choosing another. Fighting off a headache aggravated by the oppressive heat, she grew more irritable and edgy as the day wore on. Hoping that a ride might ease the throbbing in her head and the restlessness within her, she changed into her shirt and riding breeches and headed out toward the stables.

"It looks like it's brewing up a storm, Miss Melissa," warned the groom as he reluctantly saddled Honey. "I wouldn't be riding too far if I was you."

"I appreciate the warning, Pete, but I've ridden in storms before," she assured him as she mounted and galloped off toward the darkening hills.

The stiffening breeze tossed her hair about her face as she plunged through a meadow strewn with clover and honeysuckle. She gulped the air which refreshed her, invigorated her, as she bucked against its rising force and felt the heaviness lifting from her aching head. At the first flash of lightning, Honey whinnied, breaking her stride, but Melissa soothed her in a crooning voice and urged her on. Raindrops began to fall, beating a gentle tattoo against horse and rider and Melissa threw back her head, allowing the droplets to pelt her face in a tender shower.

As thunder rumbled and the sky darkened further, Melissa turned and headed back toward Laurel Hill. The grass had become slick with the fast-falling rain and Honey skidded as she careened down a steep incline. Melissa struggled to keep her seat in the saddle and fought to control the horse as she slipped sideways down the hill. Honey regained her balance once she reached flat ground but, blinded by the rain, she floundered again, uncertain of her footing. Melissa felt a cold stab of panic as the horse set off again, streaking across an open field, and she tugged frantically on the reins. She screamed as a bolt of lightning struck close by and she headed Honey away from the blinding flashes.

Honey's frenzied hooves pounded heavily on the muddy ground as, lost, they thundered through a grove of trees and out into a clearing once more. Then, through the blurring rain, Melissa spotted a small wood cabin just ahead of them and she nudged Honey forward toward the welcoming shelter. In another flash of lightning, she noticed a horse hitched to a post in front of the cabin and she hoped that whoever lived there would forgive her intrusion.

Honey slithered to a halt and Melissa slid from the saddle, hastily tying the heaving animal to the post beside the large black stallion tethered there. Melissa hammered on the door with her fist and then, trying the latch and finding it unlocked, she hurled herself into the dimness of the cabin's interior. The figure crouched in front of a small stone fireplace straightened abruptly at the sound and turned around.

Melissa gasped as she stared into the startled face of Calvin Gabriel.

chapter 14

As his look of astonishment disappeared, a slow lazy smile spread across his handsome face.

"Well, well, a guest, and a very wet one at that," he drawled, moving toward her. He was shirtless and his muscled torso, with a brush of black hair matting his sun-darkened chest, gleamed in the firelight. His eyes, glowing silver as he watched her, lingered on the soaking shirt which hugged her breasts, the nipples protruding against its wetness.

She burned under his penetrating gaze and she backed up to the door, preferring the storm outside to the raging emotions gripping her. She railed silently against the fate which had brought her to the cabin. Calvin stopped her with the sharpness of his command.

"Stay right where you are, Melissa. You'd be a fool to try and find your way back in this storm." She stood uncertainly, her hand on the door latch, but as she began to shiver, he pulled her away from the door and steered her to the fireplace.

"Take off your clothes before you catch a chill. Now!" he barked as she stood there as if rooted to the spot. "All right, then, if you won't do it, I will." He began to unbutton her shirt until she found her strength and fought him off with fingers numb with cold.

"I can manage it," she rasped as her teeth started chattering. "Just turn your back, please."

He chuckled and turned away, stooping before the fire and adding another log to the blazing pile there. Melissa whimpered in frustration as she attempted to remove her riding boots and he glanced over at her.

"Let me help you," he offered. "Sit down on the floor and lean back against the wall." She did as he instructed, crossing her arms demurely over her chest as he tugged and pulled, finally managing to free her feet. He turned his back again as she wriggled out of her wet breeches and then she shyly handed him her dripping garments. He strode lithely across the room and spread her clothing out on the floor in front of the fire. Then he crossed the room to a small cot and grabbing up a blanket, he tossed it over to the cowering girl.

"Here, cover yourself up and then sit down in front of the fire," he ordered gruffly. She gratefully accepted the blanket and wrapping it around her, she timidly seated herself on the rough wooden floor beside him. She watched the leaping tongues of fire devour the crackling logs, sending showers of golden sparks raining above them.

"Whose cabin is this?" Melissa stuttered through her chattering teeth.

"Mine. It's on the boundary between Laurel Hill land and my property. I've intended for years to have it torn down, but today I'm pleased I never did." He scorched her with his gaze and she lowered her eyes, aware of her wet straggly hair plastered about her face and her state of deshabille. She shuddered convulsively then and her face seemed unbearably hot while her body remained icy cold. She shifted about beneath the prickly blanket, trying to ease her discomfort.

"What's wrong?" he asked her, as she squirmed about.

"I'm not certain," she replied, beginning to shake uncontrollably. "Why am I both hot and cold at the same time?"

"It's easy when you've caught a chill," he answered,

taking hold of her shoulders, "and I have just the cure for it." He drew her closer to him, but she pushed him back, the blanket falling from her as she moved. She struggled to retrieve it and he laughed aloud at her dilemma. "Which will it be, Melissa, keeping the blanket around you or fighting me off? You can't manage both, you know."

"Stay away from me," she hissed. "I prefer being cold than have you pawing at me like some demented beast."

"And here I thought I was providing you with some medical assistance," he teased. "How ungrateful you are, Miss Howell."

"Take your ministrations elsewhere, Mr. Gabriel, to someone who might appreciate them. Kathleen, for instance."

"Ah, yes, Kathleen," he repeated, frowning slightly. "You wouldn't be jealous of sweet little Kathleen, now would you?"

"Jealous!" she spat. "You flatter yourself. She is most welcome to you and your crude advances."

"Strange," he muttered, shaking his head, "I've never considered myself crude, but then, perhaps you're confusing me with someone else."

"And what do you mean by that?" she cried, outraged by his insinuation, and she sprang to her feet, clutching the blanket to her.

"Wouldn't you consider Jeremy Ransome to be crude?" he asked coldly as he got to his feet and faced her wrath.

"Jeremy! What has he to do with this?" she gasped, backing away from Calvin, stunned by the mention of Jeremy's name, and wondering why Calvin had said it. She was sickened by what he might know.

"Don't look so surprised," he taunted as he stalked her. "Bryan simply mentioned that it was through your friendship with Jeremy that you first came to Laurel Hill. And knowing Jeremy, it's not too difficult to

151

imagine just what kind of friendship it was."

Melissa cringed, feeling herself torn apart by the force of his words. She flung herself across the narrow cot, sobs wracking her body as she buried her head in the musty pillow. She cried in humiliation, cursing Bryan Ransome and his betrayal of her confidence, suffering once more the recurring terror of being trapped in a world so alien to her, living among people who knew only hatred.

"I'm sorry, Melissa." His voice was gentle as he sat down beside her, fumbling with her tangled mane of hair in an effort to placate her. "I should never have spoken to you like that, I'm truly sorry."

"Don't touch me," she sobbed. "Just leave me alone." She managed to avoid his fingers as she sat up then, her tear-streaked face flaming with the intensity of her anger as she lashed out at him. "What right do you have to speak to me as you do? You know nothing about me, nothing about my life at all, and yet you claim to know a great deal. You and the Ransomes deserve one another, you are all so filled with hate."

"I said I was sorry," he snarled back at her. "I need no lectures from a little snippet I could take across my knee and paddle."

"If you dare touch me again, I shall kill you," she warned, her voice tinged with deadly fury.

"Kill me with what?" he scoffed. "Your vicious little tongue? Or perhaps you've concealed a weapon somewhere on that luscious body of yours." With one brutal tug, he dragged the blanket from her and hurled it onto the floor.

His eyes flickered as he stared at the perfection before him. Tousled auburn hair, spangled with golden highlights, tumbled around her honey-skinned body, framing it in a rich copper glow. Her golden breasts, firm and round, were capped with rosy nipples, tipping saucily upward. He followed her taut belly to the auburn triangle between her thighs and scanned the

152

length of her slim, tapering legs.

"You're exquisite, Melissa," he said, one hand tentatively reaching out to stroke her, but she swerved away from his touch and bolted for the door. Throwing it open, she was greeted by a steamy gust of wind-driven rain. As she hesitated, Calvin hauled her away and slammed the door shut with his foot.

He carried her, clawing and kicking, to the bed and dropped her onto the worn mattress. Then he threw himself on top of her, momentarily knocking the wind from her, and as she lay panting for air, he fought to remove his trousers. Naked, he crushed her to him, her smooth firm body nestled against the scratchy hardness of his own. He gripped her head in his large hands and lowered his mouth to hers. She forced her lips together, denying him entry, but under his persistent probing, her twitching muscles weakened and his tongue plunged victoriously inside.

He kissed her until she lay inertly beneath him, attempting the same ruse she had successfully employed against Jeremy. But to her chagrin, Calvin continued to rain kiss after kiss upon her face and as he began caressing her throat, she tensed and again resisted his persuasive fondling. But she was suddenly seized by a spasm of desire and she found herself floundering helplessly in the throes of her awakening passion.

He teased tiny circles around one tender earlobe with his tongue and then he pressed its stinging tip into her sensitive ear. Blowing gently, he sent a whimpering shudder undulating through her and, as her mind floated upward on a cloud of delicious feeling, her body strained to meet it. Her arms slowly encircled Calvin's broad back. Her fingers, feather light, tripped up and down his muscled firmness as she held him.

She arched against him, beginning to move in a beckoning rhythm. He joined his body with hers and they rose and fell together, his hardness growing against the pouting softness which cushioned him. His lips sucked hungrily at hers and her tongue shyly answered the questing of his own. When he raised his lips, she felt abandoned but she gasped as he closed them around her breasts, playfully biting her nipples until they rose proudly before him.

As his hands moved across her stomach, she shivered in the trembling wake they left behind and she tugged his head back to hers, her lips begging for his. He chuckled softly at her reaction but lowered his head back to her belly once more, licking a fiery path down to the moistness glistening between her parting thighs. He caressed the silken fur protecting the lips he sought and as his tongue pressed inside her, she cried out, startled by what he was doing, ashamed of her own capitulation. He ignored her pleas and flicked his tongue in agonizing slowness across the tiny tensing bud, and Melissa quivered as he strummed inside of her. Throbbing heat radiated from her stinging core and spun upward until she thought she would burst from the glory of her feeling.

He raised his head at last and where his tongue had been, she felt his pulsing shaft explore before it plunged forward, capturing her and pinning her to him. He bathed in the moisture springing from her body's chasms and he plundered her yielding sweetness. Moaning softly against him, she matched his mounting stride, swinging upward and hurtling toward a blinding sun. She melted in the heat of her exquisite pain and as she reached the summit, he took her higher until they exploded together in a shower of cascading love drops and fell from dizzying heights to the placid calm awaiting them.

He rolled away from her and lay beside her, his breath coming in ragged gasps. Bathed in the afterglow of his loving, Melissa lay in tingling numbness, not daring to move and lose the glorious contentment she had never before thought existed. With shaking fingers, she touched his face, reassuring herself that he was there and that she had not been alone on her ecstatic journey. But even as she fondled him, she felt afraid, ashamed of what had happened between them and that he had participated in her wanton surrender.

Suddenly, he moved from the cot and slipped back into his trousers. He had not broken the silence between them and Melissa lay back, bewildered by his action and puzzled by his abruptness as he moved across the room toward the fire. He stared into its fiery heart before he turned to look back at her, and she flinched in sudden pain at his words.

"It was just as I thought," he said bitterly, "damaged goods."

Enraged, she drew a ragged breath and then she was on her feet, snarling like a wounded animal. "You loathsome creature," she screamed at him, "you dare to call me damaged when you are as deserving of the name 'stallion' as any of your own horses."

With an incensed cry, he unleashed his own fury and her head snapped back as he struck her, the flat of his hand connecting loudly with her cheek. She wheeled around to strike him back but he grabbed her wrists and held them.

"Don't try it, Melissa," he thundered and with a snort of disgust, he flung her from him. Gathering up the rest of his drying clothes, he stamped over to the cabin door and threw it open. The storm had eased considerably and without so much as a backward glance at Melissa, Calvin strode from the cabin, slamming the door behind him.

She stood in the middle of the room, tears winding a narrow path down her face. She rubbed the back of her hand across her smarting cheek and then began to dress herself in her damp clothing. Leaving the fire to burn itself out, she fled the cabin, mounted her shivering horse and began the long ride back to Laurel Hill.

The nightmare returned that night and reappeared with such frightening regularity that Melissa soon dreaded going to sleep. She tried to ease herself to sleep by reading late into the night by the light of a single oil lamp on her bedside table. When that failed to relax her, she would pace the floor, hoping to tire herself out enough to enable her to sleep without interruption. She grew irritable and lost much of her healthy appetite and as her time of the month came and went, she was sure she was pregnant.

Her nerves were stretched taut, almost to the breaking point, and at the slightest provocation she would burst into tears. When by herself she was unable to force Calvin Gabriel from her thoughts, and when in the company of others she remained taciturn and grim. Amanda attempted to learn what was troubling her, but Melissa dared not confide in the woman. Even Kathleen noticed the peculiar change in Melissa's behavior and used all of her wiles to extract the truth from her. Melissa remained silent.

One evening, after a particularly strenuous jumping session with Kathleen and a new horse she was training, Melissa returned to her room to change her clothes for dinner. As she shed her riding outfit, she began to weep with relief at the telltale staining in her undergarments. That night at the table, her appetite astounded everyone and a hint of color gradually crept back into her gaunt and haggard face. Part of the crisis had passed, but as she glanced across the table and caught Cornelia's hard-eyed stare, Melissa felt that somehow the older woman had guessed the truth.

As Melissa restlessly paced the floor that night, she heard a door closing and tiptoed over to her bedroom door and opened it. Hearing nothing, she moved stealthily down the corridor until she discerned that the light was still on in Bryan Ransome's room. Suddenly she was aware of voices arguing on the other side of the door.

"I'm warning you, Bryan," a female voice was saying, "there's something going on between Melissa and Calvin Gabriel."

"You're wrong, Cornelia," he replied. "That young scamp is panting all over Kathleen and I'll warrant my daughter is leading him a fine chase."

"You're a bigger fool than I thought," Cornelia commented harshly. "If you'd take the time to examine Melissa, you'd see something other than an interest in horses written all over that pretty little face of hers. I'd suggest you make your Kathleen an even riper plum for dear Calvin to pluck if you ever hope to get her off your hands."

Melissa could not hear his reply and she quickly stole back to her own room. With sinking heart, she pondered the conversation she had just overheard and she wondered why Cornelia considered her a threat to Kathleen and the girl's prior claim on Calvin Gabriel's affections. She doubted he dared treat Kathleen with the same contempt he had shown her, and with a resolute thump of her fist against her pillow, Melissa convinced herself that Kathleen was more than welcome to Calvin Gabriel.

But Cornelia's bitter words distressed her more than she dared to admit and that night Melissa could not sleep at all.

chapter 15

A week later, a breathless and flushed Kathleen accosted Melissa shortly after breakfast.

"I have the most exciting news," she bubbled. "Father has decided to launch the fall season here at Laurel Hill instead of waiting until we move into the city. In three weeks we'll be hosting a weekend of grouse hunting and riding competitions, with a huge ball on Saturday night." She clapped her hands excitedly, but her smile was quickly replaced by a scowl at Melissa's obvious lack of enthusiasm. "You must promise to work especially hard with me on my jumps, Melissa," she continued sternly, "because I want to be the best in the jumping competition."

Melissa nodded absently, wondering at her own disinterest, aware only of a continuing discontentment within her. Wearily, she pushed herself back from the table and followed Kathleen's swaying figure into the front hall. Kathleen halted abruptly and turned back to Melissa, attempting to mask the exasperation in her voice.

"You needn't look so glum. Father's generosity includes you as well. You and I are off to Baltimore now to keep an early appointment tomorrow morning with our dressmaker." With that, she swept grandly up the staircase, leaving Melissa standing dumbfounded in the hall below.

Despite her earlier reservations, she found herself gradually warming to the idea of a festive weekend, and her anticipation was further heightened by the prospect of selecting new clothes for herself. Buoyed by her newfound enthusiasm, she lifted her long skirts and skipped lightly up the stairs to pack a small valise for the overnight stay in the city.

But even as she readied herself, her bolstered spirits plummeted as she recalled Cornelia's advice to Bryan Ransome that night, and she wondered if the entire weekend was part of their plan to encourage the obvious courtship of Kathleen and Calvin Gabriel. She had little time to dwell further on the matter as Kathleen appeared at the bedroom door, a parasol in her gloved hands, gaily swinging a purse fashioned from the same material as her frothy white- and rose-flowered day dress.

"Come on, Melissa, do hurry," the girl prodded, "and don't forget to bring a parasol with you. Your skin is most unbecomingly dark." And with a toss of her shiny blonde curls, she pranced off down the corridor. Melissa snapped the bag shut. Leaving the dreaded parasol behind, she scuttled after Kathleen, catching up with her on the veranda just as the carriage drew up to the portico.

The long dusty ride into the city was taken up with Kathleen's incessant chatter. Melissa longed to cover her ears against the lengthy descriptions of the girl's outings with Calvin, the people they visited, the homes of his friends, and his own magnificent Stony Briar. Kathleen eventually sensed Melissa's growing indifference and lapsed into sulky silence, and the girls rode the remainder of the way exchanging only the smallest pleasantries.

It was nearly dusk when the carriage halted in front of the three-story brick house on Clarendon Street. As Melissa stepped from the coach and stretched her cramped limbs, she gazed up at the townhouse, one in a long row of similar structures, each one bordered by well-tended gardens and skillfully trimmed shrubbery. Following Kathleen inside, she was unprepared for the somber, somewhat stuffy atmosphere of the place, which presented such a remarkable contrast to the airy spaciousness of Laurel Hill.

Organized clutter seemed to characterize the large, high-ceilinged rooms as Kathleen steered Melissa through the house. On the second floor, Melissa scanned the bedrooms, each one dominated by a massive walnut bed with patterned head draperies matching both the quilted coverlet and the festooned window curtains. Several large upholstered chairs, a tall bureau, and a towering pier glass completed each room's decor. Kathleen laughed aloud at Melissa's exclamation of surprised delight when shown the separate bathroom, replete with a large zinc tub set in walnut and two marble sinks.

On the main floor were the parlor, library, and the dining room, while the vast kitchen occupied a wing to the rear of the house. The parlor was filled with easy chairs and sofas, upholstered in wine-colored velvet and heavily fringed. Small walnut tables scattered about the perimeter of the room, displayed hand-painted lamps and delicate china ornaments. The walls were papered in richly flocked rose silk and the heavy wine-colored velvet draperies were fringed and tasseled like the furniture.

As they peered into the library, Melissa wrinkled her nose at the lingering odor of stale tobacco which permeated the room. Barely discernible were the walls lined with ornately carved oak bookcases overflowing with leather-bound books. The royal blue velvet curtains were pulled tightly closed. In one corner of the darkened room stood a massive roll top desk, while in another corner two dark leather chairs faced each other across a small Persian rug, creating an intimate conversation area.

Melissa's brief glimpse of the dining room left her with the same oppressive feeling as the other rooms had. The long table and ten surrounding chairs were of carved oak, as were the great sideboard and twin china cabinets. The walls were papered in a deep green flock and rich green damask draperies hung beneath deep swags at the tall windows.

"Rather dismal, isn't it?" Kathleen remarked, as if reading Melissa's own thoughts, "but mother insisted on furnishing the house this way. She said it's very à la mode. I've come to learn, through visiting other homes in town, that they all seem to be furnished the same way." She shrugged delicately, led Melissa upstairs and waved her into one of the bedrooms. Melissa unpacked her valise and freshened herself in the wondrous bathroom before joining Kathleen again in the dining room.

She was surprised to discover the house fully staffed considering that Bryan Ransome resided alone there for much of the year. As she seated herself across from Kathleen, she smiled wryly to herself, thinking of the absurdity of only the two of them being seated at opposite ends of the vast table and being served by two kitchen maids. Her discomfort increased as the meal wore on because Kathleen remained silent and uncommunicative, and the girls slipped back into the accustomed constraint marking mealtimes at Laurel Hill.

Melissa was awakened early the following morning by Kathleen's impatient rapping on the bedroom door.

"Hurry up, Melissa," the girl instructed, as she poked her head into the room, "breakfast is already on the table and if we're late arriving at Madame Dufort's we'll probably spend the entire day there." She firmly closed the door and Melissa succeeded in dragging her sleep-numbed body from the bed.

She dressed in the lace-trimmed green muslin and,

piling her hair haphazardly on top of her head, she struggled with the green hat, finally managing to secure it with two large hat pins. She grabbed up her purse, into which she had determinedly tucked some of her earnings to offset Ransome's continuing generosity, and scurried down the stairs to the dining room. Kathleen was finishing the last of her coffee and Melissa quickly seated herself across from the unsmiling girl. She had scarcely begun to eat when Kathleen stood up and gestured for her to hurry. Resentfully, Melissa gulped down some scalding coffee and placated the other girl by munching on a hot biscuit on the way to the waiting carriage.

At Madame Dufort's small establishment, Kathleen was relieved to find that she and Melissa were the first customers of the day, and the petite russet-haired French woman and her two assistants immediately produced bolts of sumptuous fabrics, spreading them enticingly about on the carpeted floor. Fingering the exquisite materials, wading through yards of laces and ribbons, Melissa finally decided on a gown for the ball, a light day dress and an outfit for the day of the hunt. The dressmaker's mouth dropped open in astonishment as Melissa explicitly outlined the hunting costume. As Kathleen stared at her aghast and began criticizing her audacity, Melissa silenced her immediately.

"I refuse to creep about through the woods with long skirts trailing behind me, weighing me down," she forcefully explained, "and if you were wise, Kathleen, you would do well to follow my example."

"You don't mean to say that you're actually going to drag a shotgun about yourself?" she demanded, her eyes widening in mock horror. "Most of the women I know simply accompany their men and occasionally carry the ammunition to assist them. I, for one, will be perfectly content to let Calvin shoot those stupid little birds." She shuddered expressively." But then she narrowed her eyes and a malicious gleam flickered in their pale depths as she added, "I suppose it's different for you, Melissa, seeing as you have no man to hunt with. You'll have to attend to everything yourself, won't you?"

Melissa bristled at the cutting remarks and glared coldly back at the smirking girl. Then she hastily turned away as she felt a blush stealing into her cheeks at the sudden recollection of Calvin Gabriel and his passionate lovemaking, and she busied herself with selecting accessories to complement her new ensembles. But the disturbing warmth settled deep inside of her as an anguished pulsing between her legs. She squirmed uncomfortably, forcing her trembling hands through the tempting displays of shawls and fans and hair ornaments in a desperate attempt to deny the longing she had considered conquered.

After a hasty lunch, the girls returned to Laurel Hill. It was late in the evening when, dusty and exhausted, they climbed stiffly from the carriage. Melissa hurried up the steps ahead of the dawdling Kathleen, relieved to finally be freed of her company. As she passed Amanda's room, the found the door ajar and Amanda standing by the open window. Melissa called to her, watching the woman flinch slightly before turning around and acknowledging her. Amanda's face was flushed, her hair in tousled disarray, but it was the look in her luminous black eyes which drew Melissa's attention. Her eyes were limpid and gently misted, the eyes of a sated woman. As she returned Melissa's stare, she smiled faintly.

"Did you enjoy yourself in town, dear?" she asked, her voice muted and hushed. Melissa nodded curtly and acutely uncomfortable before the older woman, she edged away from the door.

"Mother," Kathleen's sharp voice echoed down the corridor as she hastened toward her mother's room. "Father just told me that Calvin stopped by. Why didn't you have him wait for me? You knew that I'd be

163

home this evening."

"He stayed for quite a while, Kathleen," her mother answered, one delicate hand gesturing vaguely in the air. "I showed him our newest thoroughbred and we spent some time at the stables. Since we didn't know exactly when you'd arrive home, he eventually left." She smiled distractedly at her perturbed daughter. "Now if you'll both excuse me, it's late and I'm very tired." She quietly but firmly closed the bedroom door.

Melissa glanced surreptitiously at Kathleen, wondering if she had taken note of her mother's unusual appearance, but the other girl seemed absorbed completely in her own thoughts. Without further hesitation, Melissa padded quietly down the corridor to the welcome privacy of her own room.

She lay awake in bed, agitatedly plucking at the bed sheets, unable to dispel the image of Amanda's face, bathed as it was in the obvious aftermath of loving. Most painful of all to accept was the realization that Calvin Gabriel was responsible for that glow.

chapter 16

The three weeks sped past in a flurry of activity as everything was readied for the Ransomes' weekend celebration. The house was cleaned from top to bottom, all of the brass and silver polished to gleaming perfection, the large oriental rugs aired and beaten, the draperies cleaned and rehung. The beautiful woodwork glowed beneath a fresh coat of wax and hundreds of white tapers were fitted into the crystal chandeliers and the silver candelabra in the ornate ballroom.

The floor of the immense room was waxed, the gilt-framed mirrors washed until they sparkled, and small white chairs were set up and fitted with pale green velvet cushions designed to match the draperies billowing at the tall, graceful windows. Marble stands, which would later bear vases of freshly cut flowers, were placed around the room and on either side of the two sets of glass doors leading out onto the landscaped terrace.

The dressmaker's assistants delivered Melissa and Kathleen their clothing and remained with the girls long enough to ensure that no further alterations were necessary. Melissa hastily hung away her new finery once she had grudgingly agreed to model her two gowns for the family. Amanda had attempted to persuade her to show them her hunting costume, but Melissa had been adamant in her refusal, throwing

Kathleen a warning scowl to remain silent. There would be time enough for their disapproval.

The morning of the planned grouse hunt dawned warm and sunny, but Melissa awoke feeling strangely subdued. Having lost herself in the whirl of hectic preparations, she suddenly was suffering misgivings about appearing at the hunt and the ball unescorted. She lay listlessly in bed even as she heard the first carriages arriving, the guests alighting and making their way into the house for the breakfast buffet.

She summoned one of the maids and ordered a bath drawn for her, and when she settled herself into the tub, she reveled in its protective confines. Her peace was short-lived as Amanda walked into the room, stunning in a dove-gray velvet redingote and steel-gray linen skirt. Her hair was twisted into a chignon and on her head perched a dove-gray velvet hat with a huge ostrich plume curling about the brim. She waved her gray gloves in annoyance as she approached Melissa, who lingered contentedly in the tub.

"You must be withering in there," Amanda rebuked her. "Everyone has finished their breakfast and are preparing to set out, and you're still whiling away the time up here."

"I'm sorry, Amanda," she replied, her voice taking on a harsh edge. "I know so few of the people invited and I feel too much like an outsider," she explained, thinking back to Kathleen's contemptuous remarks.

"That's nonsense," Amanda retorted, picking up a bath towel and handing it to Melissa. "You could have come downstairs to meet everyone instead of remaining up here all this time. But there's still plenty of time for introductions later, so be a good girl and get dressed." She swirled from the room as Melissa reluctantly climbed out of the tub.

She hurriedly dried herself and donned the hunting outfit, but as she surveyed herself in the mirror, she grimaced, questioning the wisdom of her choice. Her

166

auburn hair, pinned in a bun at the nape of her neck, was covered with a rust mesh snood. She wore a rust silk shirt, open at the neck. With no undergarments to conceal her breasts, their fullness was provocatively outlined. Tight ivory breeches clung to her long legs and soft doeskin boots completed the daring costume. She slung a large leather pouch across her shoulder and with a last wavering glance at the mirror, she left the room.

Edging soundlessly down the wide staircase, she hoped to be able to steal from the house unnoticed and join the others already collecting their shotguns and assembling the packs of hunting dogs. But as she reached the last step, a low whistle rang out. She froze, returning the penetrating stare of Calvin Gabriel, who leaned casually against the doorframe of the dining room.

"That's quite a remarkable outfit, Miss Howell." His smile flashed mischievously in his handsome face. Affecting indifference, she allowed her own gaze to roam over his body, his long muscled form garbed completely in caramel buckskin, from the open-necked shirt to the breeches tucked into boots so like her own.

"I see we have similar taste," he remarked off-handedly, aware of her traveling appraisal. "That's a definite point in your favor."

"I had no idea you were keeping score, Mr. Gabriel," she countered smoothly.

Before he could reply, Kathleen swept into the hallway. "Calvin darling, I've been looking everywhere for you," she exclaimed, rushing toward him. But as she spied Melissa standing there, her mouth dropped open in astonishment. "I didn't think you'd actually have the nerve to wear that outfit today. I can't understand why a woman would prefer to dress like a man, can you, Calvin?" she purred, linking an arm possessively through his. Calvin nodded imperceptibly at Melissa as he allowed Kathleen to lead him off.

Melissa hesitated momentarily. Then determined to make the most of the hunt, refusing to be intimidated by Kathleen and Calvin, she charged from the house, grabbing a shotgun and ammunition from one of the attending stable boys. She grew conscious of the startled looks of the guests as she marched haughtily past them, and she ignored the frenzied whispers of the women and the blatant ogling of the men. With a hasty glance around her, she was almost relieved to find that the Ransomes had gone ahead without her. She hurriedly mounted Honey, galloping out of the stable area and off toward the hunt.

As she rode, she spotted a group of riders just ahead of her and spurred Honey on, crossing the broad expanse of meadowland and finally reaching that part of the estate where the grass gradually gave way to more steeply inclined, boulder-studded terrain. Nimbly picking her way up the slope, Honey followed the lead of the horses in front of them, but as Melissa recognized the buckskin clad back of Calvin and the royal blue velvet of Kathleen's riding jacket, she slowed Honey's pace, widening the gap between her and the rest of the small hunting party.

Reaching a copse where the other riders had tethered their mounts, Melissa dismounted and tied Honey securely to a small sapling. She picked up her shotgun, slung the ammunition pouch over one shoulder and set off into the woods. The air was almost still, with only a gentle breeze to ruffle the leaves as she strode through the lush undergrowth carpeting the forest floor. Bushy-tailed gray squirrels scurried past, their mouths filled with nuts to be stored away against the encroaching threat of winter. Overhead, the warbled songs of bluejays accompanied Melissa's hurried steps as she hastened toward other crunching footsteps echoing through the forest calm.

As she caught up with a small group of guests, she was chagrined to find she had reached Calvin and Kath-

168

leen's party, and she hung back, keeping to herself. As they progressed through the woods, Melissa watched with smug satisfaction as Kathleen's long blue skirt kept catching in the underbrush. The girl continually slowed the pace of the group as she stopped every few yards to tug her gown free from clinging branches and snagging brambles. The swishing skirts of the two other women fared no better and Melissa soon found herself striding alongside the men as the women fell further and further behind.

As they walked, following the course of a winding stream, Melissa trained her gaze on the underbrush for signs of the ruffed grouse which the sniffing dogs might flush out. She carefully scrutinized the small clumps of bushes bordering the brook, knowing them to be favored nesting spots for the small game bird they sought. Suddenly one of the dogs paused near a thicket and the hunting party stopped immediately. All at once there was a loud clatter as several grouse swept into the air, their wings beating furiously as they sought the shelter of the overhead trees. Shotguns were aimed and shots blasted off, sending two of the birds plummeting to earth.

"Mine," called one of the men, bounding over to the fallen birds.

"Mine," shouted another as he followed after the first. Suddenly Calvin's deep voice rang out.

"This just won't work," he shouted and heads turned to look at him, questioning his outburst. "I told Bryan he was going about it the wrong way. We'll have to divide ourselves into couples, otherwise we'll be spending the entire day arguing over these damned birds."

"He's right, you know," agreed a small, balding man as he dropped one of the grouse into his leather pouch. Then, amid much grumbling and muttering, they finally managed to break up into pairs.

"Well, that leaves the three of us," Calvin announced, indicating Kathleen and acknowledging Melissa for the first time. "We really don't need the dogs, so let the others have them." And he waved Melissa forward to join them but Kathleen's menacing glower again caused her to hang back.

As the hours passed, Kathleen began to complain about the heat and the tedious pace of the hunt. She continued to stop, jerking her skirt free of thorny bushes. She plodded on, perspiring and growing more irritable as the afternoon wore on. Melissa clamped her teeth tightly together in an effort to restrain her growing impatience with the irksome girl, but she found it increasingly difficult and her controlled temper soon threatened to explode. As Kathleen halted once more to untangle her gown, she collapsed onto a mossy tree stump and refused to budge.

"There must be another way to amuse ourselves," she whined. "I'm hot and tired and bored to tears. Just look at my gown, it's ruined." She glared accusingly at Melissa who stood watching Kathleen's discomfort with frosty, unsympathetic eyes. "How do you manage to tote that heavy gun around with you, Melissa, aren't you even tired?"

"Tired more of your complaining than anything else, I'll warrant," Calvin cut in sharply. "Look here, Kathleen, if this is all too much for you, I suggest you turn around and head back to the house."

"You'd like that, wouldn't you," she demanded, dabbing ineffectually at her face with a lacy handkerchief.

"If you two intend to continue bickering, you can do so without me," Melissa stated bluntly, and she stalked off.

It was not long before she became aware of the crackle of the dry fallen leaves behind her. Calvin came striding toward her while Kathleen limped behind him, gingerly holding up her trailing skirt. Melissa suddenly held up a hand for silence as she had spotted a slight movement just ahead of her. The others halted and a moment later, a grouse, with a noisy beating of wings, flew up into the air. Melissa traced its flight and expertly bagged the bird. She raced over to it, but hesitated slightly before bending over to retrieve the fallen prey.

"Good shot," praised Calvin, smiling warmly at her as he scooped up the grouse and deposited it in her hunting pouch. "I never realized how good you were." His mouth was twisted into a wry grin and Melissa backed stiffly away from him, as a slow warmth began to course through her limbs.

"Calvin," Kathleen called out, limping over to him, "you'll have to take me back now. I've blistered my foot and it's impossible for me to go any further."

"You'll just have to manage by yourself, Kathleen," he answered curtly. "There's still enough light left for some more good hunting and I won't stop now." He trained his gray eyes on Melissa. "Do you want to continue on with me?" he asked her.

"Calvin, you just can't walk away and leave me here alone," Kathleen shouted harshly.

"You won't be alone," he retorted. "You know these woods like the back of your hand, so stop acting like a spoiled child." Dismissing her with an impatient wave of his hand, he grabbed Melissa by the wrist and hauled her after him.

"Perhaps you should go back with her," she suggested half-heartedly, reading the fury in Kathleen's face.

"She's a grown woman and it's time she started behaving like one," he growled. Melissa glanced back in time to see Kathleen begin walking away, her even gait missing the telltale limp she had affected earlier. With a knowing grin, Melissa gazed covertly at the tall figure loping along beside her, but he seemed to have noticed nothing.

Calvin downed the next two birds and after several

poor shots, he finally ran out of ammunition. Melissa offered him some of hers, but he declined.

"I've gotten enough now, the next one is yours," he said.

"Such gallantry, Mr. Gabriel, it seems I underestimated you," Melissa teased, unprepared for the coldness in the gaze he turned on her.

"I'm sick and tired of your insinuating that I'm nothing more than a cloddish boor," he snapped.

"I meant you no harm by that remark," she countered. "What I seemed to have misjudged was your sense of humor." As his gray eyes clouded, their lightness turning darkly stormy, Melissa turned her back on him and stamped off through the woods alone.

She walked along for some time, her interest in the hunt strangely lessened by his absence, and she wished that she had not left so hastily. Finally deciding to double back and find him again, she retraced her steps and eventually came upon his buckskinned figure standing in a clearing, apparently examining a nearby cluster of rocks. Calling his name, she walked briskly toward him, but he shouted for her to stop.

"Don't come any closer. There's a timber rattler not one foot from me, and he's poised to strike."

She gasped in disbelief and immediately stood still, terror gripping her as she remembered that he was out of ammunition. Squinting, she could barely discern the shape of the deadly snake, and with her eyes riveted upon the rattler, she inched silently forward. Each cautious step moved her closer for a clearer shot—a shot which would have to be true if she were to save the man who stood, frozen like a statue, helpless to save himself.

When she felt that her lungs would burst from the pressure of her strained breathing, Melissa raised the shotgun, praying that her hands would ease their shaking long enough for that one shot. With the rattler in her sights, she took a deep steadying breath and gently squeezed the trigger. The snake seemed to disintegrate before her eyes, shattering with the force of the blast, and Melissa sagged to the ground, the smoking shotgun falling from her hands.

She felt herself being drawn into his arms, his strength encompassing her trembling frame, and she gave herself up to the warmth radiating through her as his lips claimed hers. She closed her eyes and as she held him, she felt a contentment she had thought never to experience again. He pressed her back into the long, fragrant grass, its sweetness filling her nostrils as the fervor of Calvin's kiss filled her being.

His mouth traveled across her throat, then lower to her thrusting breasts. His fingers tore at the buttons of her shirt and as her breasts sprang free, he captured them, teasing them with his exploring tongue. But Melissa grew frightened and twisted away from him, weakly gathering her open shirt around her.

"What are you doing?" he groaned as she staggered to her feet and began to fasten the buttons again.

Her voice was scarcely audible as she forced the words from her lips. "I refuse to be treated like your whore, Calvin. Not now, not ever."

He was instantly at her side, his face darkening with anger. "Why do you always play the innocent virgin with me, Melissa, when we both know you're neither innocent nor a virgin."

"So you continually remind me."

"I'm sorry if you don't approve of the way I chose to thank you for just saving my life," he commented bitterly.

"Perhaps I should never have bothered," she snarled.

He lunged for her then, catching her off guard and spinning her into his arms. His savage kiss silenced her, tearing the breath from her, but she squirmed and pummeled him with her doubled fists in a vain attempt to free herself. For an instant, he released her lips, but only to warn her.

"I've just looked death in the face, Melissa, and it made me very hungry for life. I want you and I mean to have you." He kissed her again and ravaged her mouth with his tongue until her mind reeled in a confusing whirl of revulsion and growing desire.

He drew her down with him onto the grass once more and she felt herself being sucked into a spiraling vortex, propelling her into a universe all their own. She found herself helpless against the intensity of his passion and she gradually answered his hunger with a hunger she herself could no longer deny. He tugged at her shirt and then fumbled with his own until she added her hands to his and between them they tore away their clothes, their naked bodies straining together, already misted with the dew of awakened loving.

He explored her mouth with his tongue and she released hers to follow his lead. He sighed as she kissed his burning brow and skimmed butterfly kisses tenderly across his face until he seized her mouth again, bruising it with his own. Her hands danced tickling circles through the thick black hair of his chest, and he tensed as she continued down across his taut abdomen to tentatively explore the matted hair below. Covering her hand with his, he pressed her inquisitive fingers lower and held them there to feel the heat throbbing through him. He guided her and she gently stroked his quivering flesh until he brushed her hand away, afraid that he would spend himself too soon.

He trilled staccato rhythms with his tongue across her nipples which peaked at his touch, and his hands caressed her thighs until they parted, inviting his intrusion. And he bathed in her glorious love font and stroked her until she spun through eddies of feeling so exquisite that she cried out for him to release her.

But he caught her in his tantalizing web and bound her to him until she sobbed, begging for deliverance, and he thrust himself inside her. Down they pitched through darkening tunnels until, skidding madly, their momentum hurled them upward and they careened toward the shimmering surface. Bursting through its tender barricade, they soared on their mutual climb to an uncharted paradise and when they had tasted more than they could bear, he finally released her. They shattered there among the stars as, sprinkled with their cosmic dusting, they slipped slowly back to earth.

Calvin stirred and flung himself down beside her on the grass. Melissa gazed at him through the langorous haze enveloping her, studying his handsome face, flushed and calm then in repose. The fading sunlight threw a shaft of dimming light across his features, and as he turned his head to look at her, his eyes gleamed silver, and icy fear clutched at Melissa's heart. For Calvin's eyes had become the eyes of the man who haunted her sleep, and she shuddered in the sudden cold and turned away from the frightening specter. When she dared to look at him again, the light had shifted, and stormy gray eyes bored into hers.

"Is something wrong, Melissa?" He had propped himself up on his elbow and was watching her curiously. "Why are you staring at me like that?" He leaned forward, stretching out a hand to brush a twisting strand of auburn hair back from her face. But she flinched at his touch, drawing back as if he had burned her.

"There *is* something wrong," he accused, his voice hardening. "Were you disappointed in my performance just now? Have I failed to measure up to what you've been accustomed to?"

"How dare you speak to me that way?" she flared, her momentary fear replaced by her rising indignation. "Why must you always assume you are one of my many lovers? If that kind of woman suits your fancy, then I suggest you find yourself one and leave me alone."

"That suits me well indeed, madam," he answered, scrambling to his feet and beginning to throw on his clothes.

She hastily gathered up her own scattered clothing, despising him for the cavalier way he always treated her, hating herself for having given in to him again, for allowing him to arouse her so easily. Tears of mortification stung her eyes as she pulled on her boots and looked about for her shotgun. Snatching it up, she slung it roughly across her shoulder and without another word, she strode off through the woods and back to her horse.

chapter 17

Melissa bounded up the stairs and flung open her bedroom door, stripping off her clothes as she moved, eager to rid herself of the lingering scent of Calvin Gabriel and his ardent lovemaking. She almost collided with the maid who was busily setting out Melissa's evening clothes and mindless of the girl's presence, Melissa tore off the last of her clothing. Wrapping herself in a silk dressing gown, she threw herself onto her bed. Lying back, she loosed her thoughts, reliving the turmoil of the afternoon and the uncanny resemblance between Calvin's gray eyes and those of the shadow figure in her nightmare. Once more she forced her stubborn memory back in time, picturing her birthday masquerade and the whirl of people flashing by. But once again she lost her way in the murky haze still protectively shrouding that terrible night. Her head hammering painfully, she abandoned her fruitless quest and drawing herself back to the present, she slowly rose from the bed and began to dress.

She sat before the vanity while the maid arranged her gleaming auburn hair into a fantasy of curling tendrils, entwining clusters of gold satin rosebuds through the intricate coiffure. Melissa then stepped into her gown and stood patiently while it was fastened. The folds were adjusted until they hung perfectly. The gown of tissue-thin gold cloth was suspended from broad satin straps, the bodice falling into a deep vee. The underskirt was fashioned from gold lace, while the panniers across her hips and the gracefully draped bustle were of the same shimmering cloth as the bodice. Her gold satin pumps reflected in the lamplight as she swirled about in front of the long cheval glass, watching the gown ripple with her sensuous movements. In spite of herself, she was still bathed in the afterglow of Calvin's loving. The luminous sheen in her eyes and radiant face was unmistakable.

When she reached the downstairs hall, she heard the gentle strains of music drifting from the ballroom, and guests were already congregating in small groups near the long buffet set up in the dining room. Melissa felt a tightening in her chest as she thought back again to that ball so long ago. With a great effort she pushed the troublesome recollections aside and strode into the noisy dining room in search of a light dinner.

"Well, Melissa, you're bound to create quite a sensation in that gown," remarked Bryan Ransome as he joined her. He was painstakingly balancing a plate heaped with food in one hand and a slender goblet of champagne in the other. "Will you promise to reserve at least one dance for me during the evening?" he asked, his eyes twinkling as he studied her.

"I doubt that you will have any difficulty claiming me," she answered ruefully, her eyes anxiously scanning the room and the many older couples moving about. "Most of the people here seem rather securely attached."

"The evening's just begun, Melissa," he admonished. "Take heart, my dear." He moved off to greet some of his friends. Melissa wandered to one of the tables and began to fill a plate for herself.

"May I help you with that?" inquired a deep voice at her side. She whirled around to stare into a face so like Calvin Gabriel's that she gasped in astonishment, almost upsetting her plate.

178

"Careful with that," he cautioned, his gaze lowering to the decolletage. "It would be a shame to soil such a beautiful gown." Finally meeting her startled eyes, he said, "I'm Edward Gabriel, but judging from your reaction, I assume you've noticed the family resemblance."

"I am Melissa Howell," she replied, recovering her composure enough to steady her tilting plate. "And if you bear more than a facial resemblance to your brother, I would prefer to end this conversation right now." As she inched away from him, he reached out and took her arm.

"Is that any way to treat someone you've just met?" he chastised. Seeing the flashing warning in her eyes, he hastily added, "I promise to release you if you consent to dance with me."

"You *are* just like your brother," she exclaimed, "and I don't care to dance at the moment, thank you. Now please let go of my arm," she hissed from behind gritting teeth.

"You'd better do as she says, little brother," ordered that too familiar voice as Calvin made his way to them. "She's one lady you shouldn't tangle with." The two brothers, suddenly oblivious to everyone else, threw their arms about one another, and embraced warmly.

"When the hell did you decide to come?" Calvin demanded as he stepped back and examined his younger brother.

"My case wound up earlier than I'd expected yesterday," Edward explained, "so this morning I caught the train and here I am. I plan to impose on your hospitality for a few days, visit with Pa, and head back to New York at the end of the week."

Further conversation was cut short as Kathleen, radiant in a sumptuous gown of pale blue satin encrusted with silver beads, sauntered over to Edward and linked her arm through his.

"What a pleasant surprise," she breathed, coyly studying his face from beneath her sweeping lashes. "Father neglected to tell me that he'd invited you."

"We thought we'd surprise you, Kathy dear, since I was never certain I'd make it here at all." Edward's frank gaze swept her body and a slight flush stained her cheeks at his admiring scrutiny. "Perhaps you could use your influence to convince Melissa to dance with me," he suddenly interjected. An icy coldness crept into Kathleen's eyes.

She shifted her concentration to Calvin then, running her hand along his arm before she replied.

"Why don't you dance with Edward, Melissa," she said tonelessly. "After all, we wouldn't want you to spend the entire evening by yourself. Would we, Calvin, dear?" She regarded the scowling figure beside her.

"No, of course not," he muttered in concurrence, tearing his eyes from Melissa's face. "Enjoy yourselves, children, while I get myself a drink." He tugged free of Kathleen's grasp and walked away.

Under Kathleen's contemptuous gaze, Melissa slid her untouched plate back onto the table and silently followed Edward into the ballroom. As he swung her out onto the dance floor, she studiously avoided his eyes, directing her attention to the people dancing around them. The couples whirling past were all dressed in the current fashion, the women in sculpted gowns of brocades and satins, wearing fanciful headdresses of ribbons, feathers, and precious jewels, while the men were attired in straight, precisely creased trousers, worn over side-buttoned half boots of dark leather.

"You're doing your utmost to ignore me, Melissa," Edward remarked as she moved stiffly about, following his lead. "If you continue dancing that way, you'll have one hell of a sore neck tomorrow. Why don't you try and relax?" he cajoled, pressing her closer as they moved. She found her body responding to his gentle persuasion and she gave herself up to the music's sweet melody as she settled more comfortably in his arms.

"That's much better," he whispered, his lips brushing her ear, sending a tremulous quiver through her.

"May I interrupt, little brother," Calvin's voice suddenly cut in. "Melissa's beginning to look too relaxed." With that, she found herself in Calvin's encircling embrace.

As they moved to the slower rhythm of a waltz, her heart began to pound and a tingling weakness began to spread through her limbs. She was aware of the lingering scent of tobacco and leather, traces her own body still bore, and she allowed him to hug her more closely to him.

"I understand your brother is a lawyer," she blurted out suddenly, attempting to ease the tension building within her.

His gaze was guarded as he looked down at her. "Do I detect an interest in brother Edward?" he inquired coolly.

"Not interest, simply curiosity," she retorted. "No one, except for Amanda, has ever spoken to me about him."

"Edward's an independent character," Calvin said, "and we inhabit two different worlds. His dream was to practice law while mine was to manage Stony Briar and breed thoroughbreds. He works with a prestigious law firm in New York City, loves the theater and fine restaurants. He comes home from time to time, just to visit with our father." He fell silent and before she could respond, a tall sandy-haired man tapped Calvin on the shoulder and whisked her away.

Bryan Ransome finally claimed a dance with Melissa and then she persuaded him to accompany her to the dining room where she was finally able to sample some of the excellent food before being swept back to the ballroom again. As she twirled from partner to partner, she soon discovered that Kathleen danced exclusively with the two Gabriel brothers. When she spun by in Calvin's arms, Melissa burned with a jealousy which surprised and dismayed her.

Her wine glass was continually filled by her attentive partners and she whirled giddily through the evening so that by the time Edward drew her into his arms again, she was dangerously lightheaded. When he spoke to her, she seemed capable only of nodding her head. She began to giggle inappropriately during lulls in his very awkward attempts at conversation, her head growing too heavy for her slender neck to support.

"I think you need some fresh air, Melissa," he finally rasped in exasperation as she leaned against his chest. He led her, stumbling over the hem of her gown, past the other dancers and out through the glass doors onto the terrace. At the rush of cool night air, Melissa took in deep breaths of its scented freshness and followed Edward's tugging hand into the lush gardens.

As they meandered down the twisting pathways, Edward maintained a firm grip on the tottering Melissa who lurched and threatened to fall as they walked. Approaching the small white gazebo, she faltered slightly, but Edward clamped his arm about her waist and led her up the step and into the tiny moonlit structure, seating her beside him on the cold stone bench.

"You're so very beautiful, Melissa," he murmured, kissing her forehead and then tracing the outline of her delicate nose with his lips. As they tentatively brushed against her own mouth, Melissa swayed against him and he drew her closer. As his kiss deepened, his tongue gently begged access to her soft mouth and she yielded to his urging pressure, welcoming him. He moaned, deep in his throat, and ran his fingers across the tops of her breasts and, following the cleft between them, he sought to release them from their silken prison.

Slipping the straps of her gown from her shoulders,

he lowered her bodice, exposing the golden firmness of her bosom to his caressing fingers. Then he moved his lips to her throat, nuzzling the fluttering pulse there, until he dipped to nudge her straining nipples into his questing mouth. She shuddered and leaned back against the startling coldness of the bench, arching her back as she held him.

"Calvin," she whispered, pressing him against her warmth, running her fingers through his thick black hair. She gasped as his head jerked away and she stared up into a face contorted with hurt and rage.

"Calvin, always Calvin," he hissed, pushing her away from him. She looked dazed, not quite comprehending what he was saying to her.

"Don't pretend you're so drunk that you don't know what you just said." As she shook her head, he roared, "Calvin! You called me Calvin!" She shrank from the contempt she saw in his stormy eyes and her hands groped nervously for the fallen bodice of her gown.

"Well, Melissa dear, if it's his manner you prefer, I'm sure that I can accommodate you," he snarled then as he ripped her flimsy bodice with a jagged tearing sound and Melissa huddled before him, naked to the waist.

He seized her head, crushing the delicate curls of her hair with his angry hands, and brought his face down to hers. Her arms flailed helplessly as she fought him and wrenched her mouth free, twisting her head to one side as she gasped for breath. Before he could silence her, she threw back her head and screamed with as much force as she could manage. He clapped a hand across her mouth but as she struggled against its bruising pressure, she heard running footsteps echoing down the stone path toward them.

"What's going on out here?" shouted a deep voice. Melissa, still grappling with Edward, failed to recognize the voice until it was too late. She felt the weight of Edward's body being dragged from hers and she shivered as the breeze struck her nakedness.

"What the hell . . . Edward. Melissa?" His voice was filled with outrage and contempt. "I should have known it wouldn't take you too long, Melissa," he snarled in disdain.

"Well, brother of mine," Edward interposed, his voice as cold as Calvin's, "it seems you're just in time. She's been calling for you." He shrugged himself free of his brother's grip and stormed from the gazebo. Melissa lay back against the bench. Her head was spinning violently and her shaking fingers were failing in their attempt to hold her tattered gown together.

"One brother couldn't satisfy you," Calvin said as he loomed over her shrinking form. "You had to go after Edward as well? Melissa, my innocent virgin, you disgust me." He left her there, alone with her shame and the emptiness flooding through her.

As she fought to clear her numbed senses, she thought she heard the sound of Kathleen's rippling laughter ricocheting eerily in the darkness. She sat in the cover of night, tears coursing down her cheeks, until she found the strength to stand up again. Pulling the torn gown around her, she stumbled back toward the house, stealing noiselessly through the back entrance and up the back stairs to her room. She staggered to the washstand just as waves of nausea rose in her throat. As she reached the basin, she was sick.

Her forehead bathed in perspiration, her knees weak from her ordeal, she managed to drag herself across the room to her bed, where she collapsed with a loud groan. She lay sprawled there, drained of all feeling but the spreading paralysis of despair. How would she be able to face the Ransomes again when they learned of her behavior? Would they dismiss her immediately, she wondered. Tortured by doubt, her head relentlessly thudding, she shuddered as a convulsive spasm tore through her. Tugging weakly at the coverlet, she finally succeeded in drawing part of it over her and she rolled into a tight ball in an effort to warm her chilled and trembling body.

Daylight stabbed mercilessly at her and she opened her eyes slowly, mindful of the dull throbbing in her temples. She was still curled up with her knees tucked under her chin and her body stubbornly resisted her faint attempt to move from her cramped position. Every muscle ached as she slowly straightened herself, managing to stretch over onto her back where she lay staring vacantly at the violet-sprigged canopy above her head. Her tongue felt thick and furry and her mouth had a dry, metallic taste. She moaned as she shifted her weight and lay on her side, puzzling at the amount of champagne she had consumed which made her so ill. The painful recollection of her drunkenness brought the evening's events rushing back again and she closed her eyes against the sting of tears against her swollen lids.

Someone had begun knocking softly at the door, but to Melissa, it resembled the loud thumping of a hollow drum. How could she admit someone when she still wore her torn and crumpled gown, she panicked as she tried to sit up. But she fell back against the covers with a defeated sob as the door opened and Kathleen walked into the room.

"Well, you're certainly a sight this morning," she remarked disdainfully as she surveyed the rumpled figure on the bed. "But you'll be pleased to know that your performance last night was concealed from everyone by a stupidly gallant Calvin. I wanted to inform my parents but Calvin insisted I keep silent. Edward left in a huff and if neither of them comes by today I'll hold you responsible and have you dismissed before the day's out. Now I suggest you make an appearance downstairs before my parents become too suspicious." She cruelly slammed the door behind her as she left.

Every movement was a jarring strain as Melissa forced

herself from the bed, stripping off her ruined clothing and halfheartedly sponging herself with a cloth dipped in perfume. The refreshing scent revived her somewhat as she rubbed the perfume over her skin. She pulled the remaining pins from her hair and coaxed her brush through the snarls and tangles until her hair fell in an even burnished mass about her shoulders. Tugging on her new day gown of ruffled green and white muslin, she fastened the tiny buttons and slid into a pair of green shoes with large bows on the instep.

Tightly gripping the carved bannister for support, she gingerly descended the stairs, each step echoing loudly in her head. When she reached the dining room, she was relieved to find it empty and she gratefully accepted a cup of tea from one of the maids. She was seated at the table, drinking a second cup of the restorative brew and nibbling her way through a freshly baked scone, when Bryan Ransome strode over to her.

"Good morning, Melissa," he boomed and she winced at his loud cheerfulness. "Kathleen told me you left the party early last night due to a bad headache." He cupped her pale face in his large hand and frowned with concern as he regarded her. "You look rather drawn, my dear, perhaps I should send for Dr. Standish and have him examine you."

"Oh, no, that really isn't necessary," she hastily demurred. "I'm ashamed to admit that my malady stems from nothing more serious than having enjoyed too much champagne." She attempted a wan smile. "I think a walk in the fresh air is all the medicine I require."

"If you're sure that's all it is, I'll take your word for it," he concurred grudgingly, "but if you still feel poorly this evening, I'll insist on your seeing Standish." He leaned over and planted a fatherly kiss on her forehead. "In the meantime, why don't you wander over to the west riding field. We've set up the hurdles there and some of the guests are already involved in the jumping competition.''

She nodded in mute compliance and finished the remainder of her lukewarm tea. The pain in her head had abated enough to enable her to stroll outside into the autumn sunlight with little discomfort. She ambled to the riding field where she spotted a group of riders circling the ring in smooth succession and then effortessly clearing the sets of wooden barriers. As each rider completed a full turn around the course, he waited along the side until the others had finished, and the bars were then raised another notch and the entire procedure began again.

A familiar figure astride a giant black stallion trotted past the spot where Melissa stood watching the activities. Calvin Garbiel wore a dark blue redingote which strained across his broad back. His muscular thighs, encased in cream colored breeches, tensed and relaxed as he posted gracefully. If he had noticed her standing there, he gave no such indication, and he rode across the field, his tall figure proudly erect in the saddle, to take up his position.

At the given signal, his great stallion sprang forward and Melissa closely studied his movements. Approaching the first hurdle, Calvin leaned forward in the saddle, the reins relaxing in his hands, giving the horse his head. As he soared into the air, Calvin raised himself out of the saddle, his weight in his heels, his knees firmly braced against his horse's sides. The huge animal, sleek and elegant, stretched its forelegs ahead, and as its hind legs cleared the post, it landed evenly, hurtling toward the next wooden rail without breaking his stride.

Melissa watched as Calvin completed his run and cantered to where another rider awaited him. She realized that it was Kathleen and her heart fluttered in her chest as Calvin bent forward to speak to the girl. He looked after her as she rode off to take her own turn. Following the suggestions Melissa had made to her during their lengthy riding sessions together, Kathleen began executing her jumps exceedingly well. It was only as she approached the last and highest of the hurdles that she resorted to the cruelty Melissa had so often warned her against.

As her horse seemed to break stride and balk at the oncoming obstacle, Kathleen viciously kicked at the animal's flank and whipping her with a short quirt, she forced it onward. The horse pulled back at the last moment, digging in just in front of the hurdle. As Kathleen sawed on the reins, the horse reared and the girl fought to keep herself from being thrown, struggling desperately to bring her skittish mount back under control. With a final rough jerk of the reins, she swerved sharply away from the offending barricade and left the field.

As Kathleen trotted past her, Melissa spotted flecks of foam forming at the corners of the horse's sensitive mouth and a thin trickle of blood which was coursing down its heaving flank.

"Kathleen," she called out, her fury mounting as she strode rapidly to the girl, "I suggest you return Bluebell to the stables immediately. In case you neglected to notice, she's bleeding." Fists tightly clenched at her sides to prevent her from striking the sullen girl, Melissa spun angrily on her heel and headed back toward the house.

She spent the rest of the day closeted in the privacy of her bedroom, sprawled out on her chaise, reading a book from the library. When she heard the first of the guests departing, she sauntered to the window and propped up against the ledge. She watched as the Ransomes waved them off. When she had assumed that all of the guests had gone, Melissa rang for the maid and asked for a tray of dinner to be brought upstairs. For the first time in a very long while, she wanted to be left completely alone.

chapter 18

A cool truce existed between Melissa and Kathleen as the weeks passed and the leaves fell steadily to the hardening ground. But even as the autumn days grew brisk, with a definite promise of frost hanging in the air, the two girls still managed to ride for several hours each day. Kathleen treated her instructor with studied indifference and Melissa began gloomily contemplating a long winter of inactivity.

One particularly dreary day, dampened by a cold drizzle which had plastered the fallen leaves to the earth in treacherous, slippery patches, Amanda summoned the girls to her sitting room. A fire was crackling in the grate and the room, furnished in soft blue with vivid touches of warm apricot, was bathed in a cheering glow. Amanda beckoned the two silent girls to the sofa, where they settled themselves beside the taciturn Cornelia, who scarcely glanced up from the intricate needlepoint she was stitching.

"I've decided it's time we opened up the house in town for the season," she explained. "Cornelia has chosen to stay on here until shortly before Christmas, at which time she'll join us in Baltimore." She turned then to consider Melissa and her voice softened. "Melissa, dear, you seem so much a part of the family now, that I hope you'll come into the city as well. I'm aware of how awkward you might feel, since you and

Kathleen won't be riding for several months, but Bryan and I both insist you spend the winter with us in any case." She laughed gaily then, "Who knows? Perhaps you'll snare yourself a husband at one of the parties we'll all be attending."

Melissa returned the woman's smile, scarcely believing her good fortune, greatly relieved at being spared the prospect of seeking another position elsewhere. She happily nodded her assent, daring a sideways look at the pouting Kathleen who sat grimly staring at the hands she had clasped tightly in her lap. With a defiant toss of her blonde head, she challenged her mother.

"Why must we leave right away," she demanded "when in a week Calvin will be traveling out of the state and I won't see him for a while? Can't we postpone moving into town until after he's gone?"

"I'd prefer to leave right away, Kathleen," Amanda retorted sharply.

"I thought you and father were anxious to have Calvin propose," she insisted stubbornly. "Why are you in such a hurry to separate us now?"

"I don't care for your tone, Kathleen," her mother remarked, her own voice rising. "As for you and Calvin, you'll have plenty of opportunity to see one another during the season. I want to leave now because I find this weather oppressive. I could do with a bit of a change." As if declaring the subject closed, she turned back to her own needlepoint, effectively dismissing further debate. The two girls immediately rose and left the room.

As the door closed behind them, Cornelia set down her work. Turning to face her sister, her eyes were coldly accusing. "Are you being completely truthful with them, Amanda?" she asked.

"What exactly do you mean, sister dear?" Amanda answered tartly.

Cornelia's smile was thin and edged with malicious cruelty as she replied. "I think you know what I mean,

190

sister dear," she mimicked. "Did you actually believe your little charade could continue indefinitely without detection? And now that he's grown tired of you and has directed his attention elsewhere, you're determined that he won't have Kathleen either."

Amanda's eyes widened in fear and disbelief as she gaped at her smug, complacent sister. "You've known, Cornelia?" she whispered in a strangled voice.

"Who else, dear? You don't imagine Bryan was astute enough to realize what was going on all those years?" Her laugh was short, tinged with cruelty. "Poor Bryan, and he always thought he was the only unfaithful one."

"I was so lonely, Cornelia," Amanda whispered, her tone pleading as she gazed wretchedly at her twin.

"And what was I?" came the snapped retort.

"Just what is it you want now, Cornelia?" Amanda inquired, attempting to still her trembling hands.

"What I've always wanted and have had to share all these years. Bryan."

"But why should anything have to change now?" Amanda asked. "We're getting a little old to start over again."

"I'd hardly call being forty-one old," Cornelia retaliated fiercely, "and I'm growing tired of waiting. What if I were to tell Bryan what I know? What chance would Kathleen have of marrying Calvin then, dear Amanda?" she persisted tauntingly. "I promise to keep silent about your affair providing you do nothing to jeopardize Kathleen's chances of marriage—to whomever she chooses. Then, once she is settled, you, Bryan, and I might be able to reach some kind of understanding together. Divorce might not be out of the question, then. Bryan and I could marry and you could live with your precious horses and bed whomever you wish. No one would care in the least."

In the stunned silence that followed, Amanda slumped in her chair, her face creasing in anguish. "Do you still despise me that much, Cornelia?" Her voice was scarcely audible as her sister scornfully ignored her and turned back to her needlepoint.

Two days later, Amanda and the girls left for Baltimore, with Bryan Ransome promising to join them later in the week. The weather was cool and crisp, and the three women burrowed beneath the protective warmth of large fur rugs for the long, cold ride into the city. They traveled in a closed carriage and as they bumped along over the narrow, winding roads, Melissa contented herself with viewing the passing countryside. Gone was the pastel sea of blossoms and rich greenery of her first trip to Laurel Hill. The heavily wooded areas were almost bare of leaves, the naked limbs of the trees twisting upward to the autumn sky. Even the sun's yellow warmth had dulled, drenching the woodlands in a paling silver glow.

Most of the summer birds had begun their long flight southward, while only the hardier wood thrush, oriole, and woodpecker remained to brave the encroaching winter. Flame-hued leaves fluttered softly to the ground and were crunched noisily beneath the rolling carriage wheels as the coach passed oak and hemlock trees, red spruces, and skeletal white pines. As the carriage dipped into gentle valleys and strained to the tops of rising hills, the withering grasslands appeared barren and forlorn without their brilliant coverlet of flowers.

By the time the coach drew up in front of the large brick house on Clarendon Street, the women were weary and sore from their tedious, unbroken ride. Seeing their luggage safely inside, they separated, each seeking the privacy of her own bedroom. Dinner was served amid polite silence and Melissa was grateful when the strain of the meal ended. She hurriedly retreated to her room once more.

Despite her fatigue, she was unable to fall asleep,

unaccustomed as she was to the bed and the strange surroundings. In exasperation, she finally pulled on a dressing gown and taking up one of the oil lamps, she padded downstairs to the musty library. She ran her eyes appreciatively over the vast collection of books there, settling at last on a heavy volume of Shakespeare's plays. Tugging it from the bookcase, she was startled to see a small book flop forward from its hiding place behind the cumbersome Shakespeare. Curious, she lifted the tiny book and discovered it to be a book of poetry. Opening it, she drew her breath sharply when she read the inscription on the frontispiece: 'To Amanda—with these poems, find me near you. Your loving Calvin.'

Her hands began to tremble so violently that she almost dropped the book. Then her gaze fell on the date, May 23, 1870, and she quickly calculated that he could have been no more than eighteen years old at the time. Her heartbeat slowed as relief flooded her. Of course, she reasoned, a young man's infatuation with an older, very beautiful woman was understandable, since he had spent so much of his youth with the family at Laurel Hill. But her initial uneasiness refused to dissipate completely, and she tucked the book back into its hiding place, returning the Shakespeare as well. She blindly chose the nearest book and taking up the lamp again, she scurried from the room.

The following morning, she accompanied Amanda and Kathleen to Madame Dufort's shop where they spent most of the day selecting materials for gowns and cloaks. Melissa, growing increasingly uncomfortable at the extravagant generosity of the Ransomes, again insisted on paying for much of the clothing herself, thus diminishing her garnered savings considerably. She chose her new ensembles carefully, acknowledging that she would have to content herself with a smaller wardrobe than either Amanda or Kathleen were planning for themselves.

They stopped for afternoon tea in a cozy tea room, abounding with the delicious aromas of spicy herbs and freshly baked pastries. Afterward, Kathleen grew restless and returned to the house while Melissa and Amanda strolled through the streets, peering into shop windows, examining in awed fascination the vast array of exquisite merchandise so temptingly displayed. Baltimore had long been noted for its fashion-conscious citizenry and its women prided themselves on being among the trend setters in the east. People from all parts of the country flocked to the port city for their clothes. Originally chartered in 1729 as a tobacco port, Baltimore had grown in importance until its advantageous location made it the center of importation for silks and satins from the Orient as well as for millinery and dress designs from Europe.

As they walked, Melissa glanced toward the distant harbor where tall masts dotted the horizon beyond the peaked rooftops of the buildings lining the waterfront. She was suddenly reminded of Jeremy, and she wondered if his ship would soon be returning to Baltimore, laden with more precious finery from the mysterious, far-off East. With a start, she realized that Amanda was speaking to her and she listened vaguely to the description of the city's social season. Names such as the Supper Club and Cotillion reeled about in her head as Amanda talked on.

As the days passed, the inevitable invitations to the dinner parties and gala dress balls began to arrive, and whenever Melissa returned to the house on Clarendon Street from one of her excursions about the sprawling city, she found the hallway littered with boxes from Madame Dufort, Amanda and Kathleen wading excitedly through mountains of tissue paper. When Bryan Ransome finally put in an appearance at the townhouse, Melissa greeted him with unbridled enthusiasm, for she was growing tired of the companionship of the other women and becoming increasingly bored by their idle chatter and constant bickering.

One morning as Ransome was setting out for his office, Melissa cornered him at the front door and asked to accompany him for the drive. He readily consented and swept her down the steps and into the waiting carriage. Settling herself across from him, she adjusted her billowing skirts and straightened her jersey cloak more comfortably around her. She glanced at him and found him intently studying her. Aware of her quizzical look, he dropped his gaze, appearing somewhat flustered. Melissa's heartbeat quickened as she read the unabashed admiration in his eyes, and she cast her mind back to her first encounter with Kathleen at Laurel Hill, when the girl had accused her of being one of her father's whores. She idly wondered if Bryan Ransome had indeed taken many mistresses over the years, and when she caught him observing her again, she realized that she had been staring at him. She blushed in embarrassment.

"We seem to be playing games with each other, Melissa, my dear," he remarked, his mouth curving into an amused grin. To her surprise, he reached over and clasped her gloved hands in both of his and pressed a kiss into her upturned palms. "I assure you, child, that you're quite safe with me." His eyes twinkled as he released her. "A father could hardly treat you with more respect." Her eyes suddenly misted as she twisted her hands together in her lap and blinking back her tears, she looked away from him and stared out of the window, feeling somehow transported in time.

The carriage finally jerked to a stop in front of the familiar red-brick building and, after bestowing a brief parting kiss on Melissa's cheek, Ransome hastened up the steps to his office. She gazed after him somewhat wistfully and then set off to explore the rambling waterfront area.

She wandered leisurely up and down the narrow,

cobbled streets, reading the names on the signposts—
Thames, Fleet, Shakespeare—all painful reminders,
harkening back to her own past life. As she meandered
about, following curving alleyways, peeking into grimy
storefront windows, she became aware of interested
eyes tracing her movements. As a group of sailors
ambled by, ogling her, they gestured for her to join
them. A coarse-looking man, a leather apron tied about
his sagging middle, called out to her from a doorway.
Recalling the incident in the London alley, she quickly
turned back toward the open dock area, where crowds
of people were milling about, moving among the open
stalls of freshly caught fish and decaying vegetables. As
she rounded a corner in front of a cluster of small
dilapidated shops, she heard shouting and the clatter of
running footsteps.

"Stop thief! Stop her someone."

Melissa saw a young girl racing down the street
toward her, a uniformed policeman and several irate
men charging after her. As the girl approached her,
Melissa stepped hastily aside, stumbling awkwardly as
she caught the heel of her shoe in the cracked pavement. The girl collided with her and they both fell to
the sidewalk in a clumsy tangle. Before Melissa could
recover her senses, she felt something being thrust into
her lap as the girl picked herself up and scurried down
the street.

"You all right, miss?" puffed the policeman as he
helped Melissa up. She watched as the other men
scrambled past and nodded absently, but the policeman's eyes were suddenly riveted to the ground at
Melissa's feet.

"Well, what have we here?" he muttered, stooping
to pick up a small pouch. She watched as he opened the
sack and spilled several sparkling jeweled brooches into
his open palm. "It seems we've just found what we were
looking for," he grunted. "Now if you'll come along
with me, please," he informed the astounded girl, who

then found herself being propelled along the street by a strong, muscled arm.

"What are you doing?" she sputtered, hobbling alongside the policeman on her throbbing ankle. "Where are you taking me? I didn't do anything, it was that girl you were chasing, not me." She shook her arm in an effort to free herself but the surly man held tightly onto her.

"You shouldn't have been so sloppy about holding onto that bag, miss," he grumbled. "You might have gotten away with it."

"But I had nothing to do with any of this," Melissa protested indignantly, tugging on the man's arm as his pressure increased on hers.

"You'd better not make such a fuss and come quietly," the man cautioned. "Being an accomplice in a robbery is serious enough without adding resisting arrest to the charge."

"Accomplice? Resisting arrest?" she echoed, her incredulous voice sounding harsh and tinny to her ear. "But I never saw that girl before she ran into me, you must believe me."

"The station's just around this corner, miss. You can do all of your explaining in there." She was unceremoniously hauled up the sloping steps of a rundown, gray stone building with two oversized gas lamps perched atop the stone pillars in front of it. Released in a small, dimly lit room, Melissa collapsed into a hard-backed chair, barely catching her breath before a second policeman walked in, curtly dismissing the man still hovering over the distraught girl.

She gazed miserably up at the large, ruddy-faced man whose light brown eyes were openly studying her. The bristly red moustache under his bulbous nose twitched continually as he chewed thoughtfully on the end of a battered pen.

"You must understand that your man has made a dreadful mistake," she blurted out, unable to bear the man's silent scrutiny.

"Has he?" he finally answered in a gravel voice, his eyes never leaving Melissa's anxious face.

"Yes, he has," she insisted, nodding her head emphatically, "He thinks I was involved in some robbery, but I assure you that I was not an accomplice. I was simply a most unfortunate bystander," she added bitterly.

"I see," he said, leaning forward across the table separating them. "And what were you doing wandering about on the docks by yourself?"

"I was taking a walk," she retorted crisply, her voice rising in spite of her efforts to remain clam.

"Isn't the waterfront a strange place for a young woman of your obvious means to be taking a walk?"

"My employer has his office near the harbor and I rode with him to the building and then set out to explore the area."

"And what were you hoping to find on this little exploration of yours?" he persisted, his voice hardening with suspicion.

"Find?" she repeated, perplexed by his question. "Nothing. I was merely intrigued by the shops and the ships in port and," she spluttered, "that's simply all there is to tell."

"Any particular ship in port?" he fired at her.

"No," she replied angrily.

"Tell me about your accomplice in the robbery."

"I had no accomplice. I was not involved. Why won't anyone believe me? Do I look as though I have to steal to support myself?" she shouted hotly, her temper finally getting the better of her.

"What is your name, young lady?" the policeman demanded abruptly.

"Melissa H-Howell," she stammered.

"Where do you live, Miss Howell?"

"I'm employed by the Ransome family of Laurel Hill."

His eyes widened at the name and be began tapping agitatedly on the table top with his pen. "Ransome," he repeated, muttering to himself. Then staring sharply at her once more, he nibbled away again at the tip of the tooth-marked pen. Melissa shifted uneasily in the straight-backed chair, wondering at his peculiar behavior.

"Are you acquainted with one Jeremy Ransome?" The question caught her off-guard and she started at the mention of Jeremy's name, a flush springing to her cheeks as she struggled with her emotions. "I can see the name means something to you then," he commented wryly, tapping the table with the pen again. "Just how well do you know him, Miss Howell?"

"I met him in England," she replied, choosing her words cautiously, "and it was through him that I joined the Ransome household here in Maryland." She stopped, waiting for her heart to slow its frantic pounding, puzzled by the policeman's interest in Jeremy when he seemed convinced she herself was a criminal.

"When was the last time you saw Captain Ransome?"

"I thought I was being questioned about a theft," she retaliated. "Why am I now being asked about Jeremy Ransome?"

"Shall I repeat the question, Miss Howell, or can't you remember what I just asked you?" His tone was menacing, his face darkening with anger.

"Several months ago," she mumbled.

"I see. And were you aware of his planned port of call once he left Baltimore?"

"Yes. His uncle mentioned something about the Orient," she admitted grudgingly.

A look of smug satisfaction settled across his coarse features as he nodded at her reply. "And that's all you know about it?" he asked, his voice dropping considerably as he watched her.

"Yes," she murmured, her shoulders sagging, her hands relaxing in her lap.

"Now about this robbery, Miss Howell," the policeman began again and her frightened eyes fixed themselves to his. "Being an accessory to a crime is as damning as being the actual perpetrator of that crime. Are you aware of that?"

"How often must I repeat myself before you believe me," Melissa fumed. He cut her short.

"Until you convince me that you are equally innocent of complicity where Jeremy Ransome is concerned," he thundered. "Perhaps if I leave you by yourself for a while, your poor memory might be miraculously restored."

Melissa sprang to her feet, knocking over her chair, and raced around the table to him. Clutching his arm, she cried, "How can you leave me locked up in here? I am no criminal and if you would send for Bryan Ransome, he could straighten out this ridiculous misunderstanding."

He brushed her hand from his sleeve as if she were an annoying insect and walked briskly from the room. She flung herself at the door just as she heard it being bolted from the other side. In desperation, she looked over at the room's one small window, but it afforded her little comfort. It was barred.

Fighting down a rising wave of panic, she righted her fallen chair and sagged into it, burying her face in her hands. Tears welled up in her eyes and she angrily swiped at them as they coursed down her cheeks. Wearily, she leaned across the table, resting her head against its cool surface, trying to make some sense out of what was happening to her. What had Jeremy done to have brought him to the attention of the police? And what possible connection could there be between his suspected activities and her being accused of theft?

As the hours passed, her apprehensiveness increased. She paced the floor and stared hopefully out of the grimy window, watching the lengthening afternoon shadows. Then she returned to the door and rattled the knob; tentatively at first, but growing more insistent as her indignation mounted. Her head had begun to pound and she was feeling faint from her confinement in the airless little room. Finally when she could no longer tolerate the situation, she started hammering at the door with her fists, shouting in an effort to gain someone's attention. When she heard the bolt being thrown back and the door creak open, she stepped away just in time to avoid being knocked down by the same beefy policeman as he hurled himself into the room.

"Well, are you ready to cooperate now?" he bellowed, waving her back to her chair again.

"I can add nothing further to what you already know," she answered evenly. "Have you managed to locate Bryan Ransome?" she asked, but the man shook his head. "But why not?" she demanded as she faced him, her eyes narrowing contemptuously.

His mouth twisted into a sardonic grin as he watched her and his voice was surprisingly muted when he finally spoke again. "There won't be any need to summon Mr. Ransome now, Miss Howell. In fact, you'll be pleased to know that we've managed to snag the little girl who stole the jewelry. Lucky for you she denied having a partner and admitted tossing the pouch into your lap to avoid arrest." Melissa's sigh of relief burst from her lips as she slumped forward in her chair. "As for the matter concerning Jeremy Ransome—" he paused, eyeing her warily again— "let's just say I'd like to believe your story. But for my own peace of mind, I'm going to have you watched from time to time by some of my men."

"But why?" she exclaimed, instantly alert. "I have no idea what this is all about."

"Quite simply, Miss Howell, your friend Captain Ransome has gotten himself involved in a large smuggling operation. Our information tells us that on his trip to China, he'll have picked up a supply of opium to bring back to America." Ignoring Melissa's gasp of dismay, he continued. "Apparently this is his first such attempt so he should be quite easy to apprehend, provided that he's not warned beforehand."

"But I still don't understand what all of this has to do with me," Melissa asked in bewilderment.

"We know there's a woman involved in the operation, and when you said you were acquainted with the Ransomes and were found out along the docks, well," he said, "you can imagine what went through my mind. While you were in here, I had one of my men track down our informant and get a description of this woman. You don't quite match it." He laughed wryly, his arrogant gaze roaming her body until she squirmed in discomfort.

"When is Jeremy's ship due back?" She spoke up boldly, and he was forced to return her burning stare.

"Not for another few weeks," he replied. "And I'd appreciate it if you said nothing about this to the family. It might raise a general alarm and we can't afford to take any chances. I hope you understand."

With a slight inclination of her head, she nodded her assent. Then she slowly rose to her feet and walked shakily to the door he held open for her.

"Goodbye, Miss Howell, and I'm sorry if we were excessively harsh with you," he apologized as she eased past him. She smiled wanly and walked out of the musty police station into the fading afternoon light. She hailed a passing hansom cab and traveled back to Clarendon Street in a state of shocked disbelief.

chapter 19

When Melissa entered the house, Kathleen met her in the hallway. Formally gowned in a dress of lavender velvet, she clicked across the lacquered floor, calling out impatiently. "Where on earth have you been? Mother was growing frantic because we're expected at Montgomery house at seven o'clock and it's now almost six."

"I apologize, Kathleen," she murmured, edging toward the staircase, "but I simply lost all track of time. Perhaps you should go on without me this evening."

"That's out of the question," Kathleen snapped irritably. "These dinners are carefully planned and without you there would be an extra man at the table. I'd advise you to be ready on time."

With a defeated sigh, Melissa trudged up the stairs to her room and stood before the giant armoire, trying to decide on an appropriate gown, her hand trailing absently over each of the elegant new dresses hanging there. But her thoughts were elsewhere and she could not make up her mind. She turned finally to the maid hovering over her and instructed her to select a gown for her. As the girl hastened to comply, Melissa sat down in front of the vanity mirror and began listlessly brushing out her long hair.

When her toilette was completed, she stepped into her dinner gown. Accustomed to the light materials of her summer frocks, she was scarcely prepared for the sudden weight of the moss green velvet as it was fastened and draped about her slender frame. She fretted with the heavily beaded bodice, wishing she had chosen a simpler design, and tugged at the tight-fitting long sleeves in an effort to relieve their binding snugness. The maid assisted her with the long moss-green cloak and then fumbled awkwardly with the stiff braided frogs which closed it. By the time Melissa swept down the staircase, she was perspiring. Her hair clung to her face in dampening tendrils, and she was in a foul mood, threatening to explode at the slightest provocation.

"Enchanting as always, Melissa my dear," Bryan Ransome beamed as he handed her into the carriage. Kathleen grudgingly moved over on the plush seat to allow Melissa enough room to sit down, and then proceeded to stare sullenly out of the window during the entire ride.

"I hope you like the Montgomerys," Amanda whispered to the scowling Melissa as they alighted before an imposing three story, gray stone mansion. "They're old friends of Bryan's and their dinners are among the most popular in Baltimore."

Melissa remained intractably silent as she tripped on her cumbersome cloak going up the stairs, before finally entering the house. The hum of quiet conversation and the cheery fires blazing in the marble-topped fireplaces in the vast hallway and formal parlor created a welcoming aura and Melissa began to relax. But her moment of relief was short-lived as a petite woman, her pale, brown hair piled into a towering combination of curls and winking jewels, lunged forward and embraced Amanda.

"I'm Cara Montgomery," she said, pecking Amanda on the cheek but addressing herself to Melissa. "Bryan and Amanda, how simply wonderful to see you both again. And darling Kathleen, still unmarried but so beautiful. And this must be Melissa, what a lovely young thing." Melissa winced as the woman seized her face with her two plump, bejeweled hands and squeezed her cheeks before stepping back and smiling broadly at all of them.

"But do come in and meet everyone," she tinkled. Before Melissa could protest, she was tugged forward and propelled by the tiny woman into the midst of a chattering group of men and women.

"This is Melissa Howell," she announced in her chirping voice, the large diamonds at her ears bobbing as she spoke. "She's a recent arrival from England, and I want you all to make her feel welcome here." She disappeared, leaving Melissa staring at the unfamiliar faces staring back at her. One of the men hastily scooped up a glass of wine from a silver tray atop one of the small mahogany tables and handed it to Melissa.

"A toast to the beautiful newcomer mercilessly thrown among us," he offered. Everyone laughed and obligingly raised their glasses, the tense silence pleasantly broken.

At dinner, Melissa found herself seated across from a middle-aged widower, who spent the evening alternately staring at her bosom and pulling off his spectacles to wipe them with the edge of his linen napkin. She tried gamely to engage him in conversation, but she ultimately abandoned the effort when he insisted on speaking of his dear, departed wife and his three children who needed a mother. Melissa shifted about in her chair, stifling a yawn with the back of her hand and yearning to be free of the tedium of the evening.

Suddenly she felt a hand touch her leg and as the pressure increased, she turned angrily to the thin, moustached man on her right. He leaned over and whispered conspiratorially, "You looked as if you were about to fall asleep so I thought I'd help keep you awake."

"I'm perfectly capable of staying awake myself, thank you," she hissed through gritted teeth as she slapped away his offending hand. He hastily withdrew and ignored her for the remainder of the meal.

After dinner the men retired to the study for brandy and cigars and the women made their way to the overheated parlor. Melissa was wedged uncomfortably between two older women on a small settee and as she sank deeper into the thick, down-filled cushions, she looked about her in dismay and caught Kathleen's penetrating stare. Both girls eased themselves from their seats and walked into the cooler hallway, where they fanned themselves ineffectually with their hands and grimaced together.

"I detest some of these dinners," Kathleen muttered, beginning to pace the hallway carpet. "Everyone here is so old and deadly boring." Melissa nodded in mute consent, keeping step with Kathleen's restless pacing. "And all of the unattached men," Kathleen scoffed in disgust. "Most of them are older than my father."

Before Melissa could answer her, they looked up and found Amanda signaling to them from the doorway of the parlor.

"Girls, you're being terribly rude," she rasped in a forced whisper. "Get back in here and try to show some better manners." They glanced helplessly at one another and slunk back into the stuffy room, spending the rest of the evening yawning behind their discreetly raised hands and listening to the women's unending patter.

When Melissa finally tumbled into bed that night, she vowed that if any of the other parties proved to be as tiresome, she would find a way of remaining home and avoiding them altogether. But despite her fatigue, her disgruntlement soon changed to worry as she thought of Jeremy Ransome, sea captain turned opium smuggler. As she fell asleep, she imagined him with his handsome face contorted in anguished death as he swung from the end of a hangman's rope.

* * *

Over the following weeks and in spite of her resolution, Melissa suffered one dull dinner after another, matched continually with uninteresting men whom she hastily discouraged from ever calling on her. The only promise of change came in the form of an invitation to a costume ball to be held at the beginning of November. Even Kathleen put aside her perpetual gloom and sparkled with enthusiasm, animatedly discussing the various costume possibilities. But her excitement increased with the arrival of a letter from Calvin saying that both he and Edward would be attending the ball as well.

After considerable deliberation, Kathleen finally decided to dress as the biblical Salome. She spent endless hours with Madame Dufort choosing the gossamer materials which would be transformed into the billowing veils to be worn over a slender sheath of apricot silk. Amanda was aghast at the idea of such a blatant display of her daughter's body, but she was assured by the harassed dressmaker that the long tube of silk would render the costume completely respectable. Amanda relented and busied herself with the preparation of her own costume, having chosen to appear as Queen Elizabeth I.

"I'm beginning to wonder if this was a mistake," she complained, struggling to fit her luxuriant black hair under the cap of the curly red wig she would be wearing. "I'll have a headache all night long with this awful contraption on," she groaned as she pulled and tugged until the wig was finally settled upon her head.

Melissa stood watching the two women in bemused silence, unable to muster any enthusiasm for the upcoming ball. While they stood patiently for their lengthy fittings, she wandered about the shop, fingering different materials and listlessly flipping through the pages of the many catalogues which pictured the most recent in European fashion.

"Melissa, for goodness sake," cried Amanda in

exasperation, "you've already wasted several precious days by moping about with that woebegone expression on your face." She pivoted before one of the long mirrors critically appraising the burgeoning efforts of the seamstresses. "Are you ever going to decide on a costume?" she continued. "If you are, I advise you to make up your mind today, because Madame Dufort will soon have her hands full with the rest of her clients, you know." She spun before the mirror again, Melissa completely forgotten.

Melissa sighed and put down the catalogue she was reading. Just then Kathleen whirled into the room, her body curves outlined by the clinging silk sheath suspended from her shoulders by thin straps, barely skimming the tops of her dainty slippers. One of the assistants followed after her, her arms lost in the swirling clouds of filmy material she carried.

"Mother, this will be even more successful than I had imagined," Kathleen exclaimed, pirouetting in front of the startled woman. "But if Calvin doesn't propose after seeing me in this, I might have to resort to what Salome did." She laughed wickedly as she saw the expression on her mother's face.

"And just what did she do?" inquired Amanda coldly.

"Why, dance of course, mother," she replied with a studied look of innocence. And she swished past them into the adjoining fitting room. Melissa felt a stab of jealous resentment as she visualized Kathleen twirling about in her seductive costume, clasped in Calvin's appreciative embrace. With her eyes flashing, she announced defiantly to Amanda, "I have made my decision at last." She paused until she was assured of the woman's attention. "I'll go to the masquerade as Cleopatra." And she hurriedly began searching through the myriad bolts of fabric for the materials she would need for her costume. She selected a fine white chiffon and heavy gold cloth for trimming and then

208

cornered the dressmaker, giving the woman her instructions and feeling at last the first stirrings of anticipation.

The evening of the masked ball finally arrived, but Kathleen's enthusiasm was dampened by a message she had received from Calvin explaining that he would be delayed due to Edward's late arrival from New York.

"Now I'll have to look for him among all those people at the party," Kathleen fumed, crumpling the note and hurling it into the fireplace. "I don't understand Calvin at all. His townhouse is only three blocks from here. Surely Edward can arrive by himself and allow his brother to come along with us. That man is impossible," she spat, clenching her fists and pounding them against the mantel.

"Stop carrying on that way, Kathleen," her father roared, throwing her a menacing glare. "Don't you think it's time you ladies were upstairs preparing yourselves?" He cast a quick glance at Amanda who promptly rose and signaled Melissa with a curt nod to follow her, and the angry Kathleen had little choice but to leave as well.

Melissa hurried through her bath and then dusted her body with a translucent, shimmering powder on the advice of Madame Dufort. The French modiste had explained that it was a custom adhered to by all of the French women of fashion when they desired a sparkling glow to their decolletage. She then slipped into the specially designed chemise which was the only undergarment she would be wearing and slithered into the chiffon gown itself, a simple floor-length tunic suspended from two ornate gold clasps at the shoulders and falling into a softly gathered vee both in front and in back. The filmy gown was slit up the sides and edged in gold braiding, allowing her long tapering legs to flash seductively whenever she moved. She stooped to fasten the laces of her flat gold sandals, twining the leather thongs around her calves and tying them just below her knees.

She stood still while the maid adjusted the small gold facemask. Then she leaned forward, squinting into the vanity mirror as she painted her lips a vibrant scarlet. Around her upper arms she fastened two broad gold armlets studded with large colored stones and then she bound up her long curls, pinning them securely before lowering onto her head the heavy wig of thick, straight, black hair. The finishing touch was a gold serpentine tiara which the maid fitted carefully over the wig and across Melissa's forehead. After sliding into a gold, cashmere-lined cloak, she walked back and forth across the room until she had accustomed herself to the flat-heeled sandals and the awkward weight of the head-piece.

The glittering masquerade, held in the stately mansion of the Clifton family, was well underway by the time Melissa and the Ransomes arrived. The house was bathed in candlelight, music filtered down from the third floor ballroom and richly-costumed figures filled the vast entrance way. As Melissa gingerly slid from the protection of her long wrap, she was acutely aware of the stares of some of the people around her. A woman gasped and turned away, fanning at her plump face with a huge, plumed fan while her partner adjusted the monocle in his eye and stared boldly at the half-clad young woman.

At the shocked reaction of the Ransomes, Melissa smiled nonchalantly and returned their glances with cool indifference. Kathleen, her blue eyes narrowing, turned to her mother accusingly.

"It seems you neglected to lecture Melissa about propriety. You reserved it only for me, dear mother," she snarled, gazing hatefully at Melissa before she stalked off, the pastel veils floating gracefully about her slim form. Her head, with its plaited hair ablaze with jewels, was held high.

"I must admit, Melissa, that for once Kathleen is right," murmured Amanda. "Your gown is shocking." She followed after her daughter as Bryan Ransome, awkward in the padded garments of Henry VIII, tottered after them both, leaving Melissa by herself.

She gathered herself proudly and glided toward the carpeted staircase, winding upward to the splendid ballroom where she could lose herself among the glittering blend of fanciful characters she would never have to know. Her entrance did not pass unnoticed, for no sooner had she drifted into the room when she was immediately claimed for a dance by a tall, masked knight. A giant, golden lion was enblazened across his tunic, a heavy sword dangled at his side. They joined the spinning couples on the huge dance floor of the mirrored ballroom and she gradually lost herself in the music and the arms encircling her. She spun delightedly from partner to partner, enjoying their extravagant compliments, flirting outrageously and coyly guarding her identity.

An Indian brave brought her a glass of champagne, but even before she could finish it, she was swept up into the arms of a laughing clown. She was claimed by a helmeted crusader for a waltz and she sipped at another glass of champagne handed to her by a frowning harlequin. A cowboy whirled her off for several dances, refusing to relinquish her to the masked figures attempting to break his possessive hold on the sultry Cleopatra. She laughed gleefully when she was tugged from his arms by a determined brown-cloaked monk and she moved from his embrace into the grip of a musketeer. She had taken but one step with him when she was snatched away by a glowering pirate sporting a gleaming cutlass. A large gold hoop dangled from one ear.

She smiled into his masked face, waiting for the flirting banter to begin, but he remained silent, almost grim as he held her against him, leading her expertly around the floor. A strange tingling rippled through her as she moved against him, feeling the muscular firmness of his body bruising her. A cavalryman attempted to cut in, but her partner shrugged him off, steering her toward a quiet corner of the room and a refuge behind several large potted trees. Her heartbeat quickened as she molded her body to his and she knew even before he spoke who her pirate was.

"Well, my beautiful Cleopatra," he murmured, "as always you're the center of attention."

"Calvin," she breathed, trembling as she whispered his name.

"Madam," he mocked, "is my disguise so poor that you fail to recognize the notorious Jean Lafitte?" But she twisted in his arms, daring not to trust her voice again, aching to be free of him. "Where do you think you're going, my little Egyptian temptress?" he demanded, refusing to release her, "Weren't you made for loving?" He tightened his arms around her, his lips hungrily claiming hers. Through the gossamer thinness of her gown, she felt his hardness driving into her. Waves of desire washed over her as she fought against his power, determined not to weaken and give herself to him again. He drew back from her then, regarding her quizzically with troubled gray eyes streaked with silvery glints. She gasped as an icy stab of fear pierced her.

A dull throbbing began in her head and a curtain fluttered tentatively within her memory. As if peering down a darkened tunnel, she caught a glimpse of two figures, masked and dancing together, before the curtain closed once more. And although she strained to penetrate the stubborn haze still guarding that missing fragment of her past, she could see nothing further.

"What's the matter, Melissa?" he asked, the hard edge in his voice gentled by concern.

"I'm not quite certain," she whispered, allowing him

to draw her back into the circle of his arms. "I was remembering something which always gives me terrible headaches." She finished with a nervous laugh, aware again of the awakening pulse deep within her as he held her.

"Would you like to sit down?" he offered, and at her nod, he ushered her to a sofa. He was about to sit down beside her when a woman's voice called out to him.

"There you are, you rascal. I've been looking all over for you," gushed a voluptuous blonde woman, dressed as Helen of Troy, her transparent gown hugging her full breasts, the dark nipples revealed by the sheerness of the cloth. "How typical of you to find someone else the moment you're out of my sight." She pouted prettily as she took his arm. "You don't mind, do you?" She smiled at Melissa. "He never did bring me the glass of champagne he promised me." Melissa sat there wordlessly as Calvin walked away with the woman, his arm slowly encircling her waist as he steered her through the crush of people around them.

She swallowed hard against the rising ache inside of her. Blinking back tears of frustration, she gladly accepted a dance with the harlequin once more. As he guided her about the floor, she strained to locate Calvin. When she finally spotted him again, she noticed that he had abandoned his Helen and was dancing instead with a striking Marie Antoinette. She forced her gaze away from them as the couple spun past. They were soon lost in the crowd and Melissa found herself handed over to a portly Julius Caesar.

"You and I were fated to have at least one dance together, don't you agree, my dear?" he insinuated, laughing loudly and breathing heavily into Melissa's face. She attempted to break from his suffocating grasp, but he was surprisingly strong despite his girth. He grabbed her buttocks with his meaty hands and squeezed her painfully. Her temper flaring, she shoved him away from her as he attempted to execute an intricate dance step. Caught off balance, he tumbled to the floor. Ignoring the startled cries of surprise from the couples nearby, as several men rushed to assist the fallen man, Melissa pushed her way through the other dancers and headed for the doorway.

Just then Calvin danced past her, his arms wrapped around a laughing Salome. As Melissa watched in dread fascination, Kathleen drew Calvin's head to hers and kissed him full on the mouth. Melissa whirled around, her eyes brimming, and collided with Bryan Ransome.

"I'm afraid your poor Henry is too fat to dance with you, Melissa," he grumbled as she tugged insistently at his sleeve.

"Please, Henry, please dance with me," she implored, her voice quivering. At his reluctant nod, she lured him onto the dance floor and as the music slowed to a waltz, he took her in his arms, moving gracefully despite his bulk.

"Did our Salome find her pirate?" he asked softly. If he noticed Melissa falter slightly, he pretended otherwise. "My little daughter still has it in her stubborn head to marry the man, but I fear she'll never snare him." He sighed deeply. "I pity Edward though, he's been in love with Kathleen all his life."

"Edward in love with Kathleen?" Melissa echoed incredulously.

"Why do you think he came down from New York for her ball at Laurel Hill that weekend? Why he's here tonight? Waiting for the crumbs she tosses him whenever she's been frustrated by Calvin," he finished, his voice tinged with bitterness. Just then he was tapped on the shoulder by an imposing Indian chief, resplendent in a full-feathered headdress. "Talk of the devil," Ransome grunted as he released Melissa to Edward Gabriel.

"I thought it was time I took my turn with the exquisite Cleopatra," he laughed as he studied her masked face. "You're the most beautiful woman here, you know," he confided as he tightened his hold on her.

"Even more beautiful than Salome?" she asked, unable to resist the barb. She was rewarded by a scowl creasing his handsome face as he suddenly loosened his grip.

"So Bryan's finally told you, has he?" he demanded, and Melissa regretted her words, feeling an unwilling empathy for the man whose eyes had filled with pain. But then, to her dismay, he leaned forward and whispered hoarsely in her ear, "A sorry couple, aren't we, Melissa dear, I want Kathleen and you want Calvin."

"I want no such thing," she hissed, pulling back from him. "Your brother is a cad and a boor and I want no part of him."

"If you say so, Melissa," he said knowingly, his mouth twisting in a sardonic grin.

He gradually drew her to one side of the room and settled her on one of the low sofas along the wall. Picking up two glasses of champagne, he handed her one and then raised his glass in a silent toast. She smiled tremulously and returned his salute, drinking deeply of the golden liquid.

"Melissa," he began hesitantly, staring at the glass he held as he sat down beside her, "I want to apologize for my behavior that night in the garden at Laurel Hill. I had no right to take advantage of you, even though you were very drunk and very tempting. I'm truly sorry for what happened."

Her reaction was spontaneous as she reached over and placed a hand over his. "I'm sorry too, Edward, for I was as much to blame as you were." He raised her hand to his lips and gently kissed her upturned palm. "You know, dear Edward, you're not half as beastly as Calvin," she said softly. "Kathleen is rather fortunate, don't you think, to have both brothers in love with her?" And a sob caught in her throat and Edward snatched the wineglass from her trembling hand and set

215

it aside. Then he gathered her tenderly into his arms and cradled her there. As she clung to him in their silently shared pain, she finally admitted to herself the truth she had so long been able to deny. She had fallen hopelessly in love with Calvin Gabriel.

chapter 20

Edward returned to New York the day after the masquerade ball and Calvin, who had taken up temporary residence at his townhouse, began escorting Kathleen about. Bryan Ransome was left with the responsibility of accompanying both Amanda and Melissa to the numerous social gatherings, for Melissa still stubbornly rejected the attentions of all of the men she encountered. She studiously avoided Calvin and bore her hurt silently, masking her agony before Kathleen's probing eyes, watching as the girl basked in the affection of the man she herself desired.

One cold December night, Melissa announced that she would not be attending the dinner scheduled that evening at the Montgomerys again. She had been suffering one of her recurring headaches during the day and she was grateful for the excuse to avoid the boring experience of another Montgomery party. Kathleen was peeved because Calvin had returned to Stony Briar to look in on his father and she would have to suffer her own father as her temporary escort.

"Traitor," Kathleen hissed as she passed by Melissa's open door on her way downstairs. Melissa smiled smugly and waved her off, then settled back in her comfortable chaise, tucking a light coverlet around her and sipping a cup of hot lemon tea. She picked up a book and leafed through it, content in the knowledge that she would be blissfully alone for the entire evening.

As the hour grew late and her eyes grew heavy, she set aside her book. She closed the bedroom door, drew off her dressing gown and tossed it across the chaise. Padding about in her bare feet, she opened the window slightly and closed the draperies against the cold, gusting wind which immediately tossed them about. Extinguishing the bedside lamp, she crawled into bed, nestling under the down coverlet for warmth.

She lay there curled up on her side, enjoying the silence, staring at the thin strip of light defining the partially opened window. The curtains billowed suddenly as the door to her bedroom was opened and quietly shut and Melissa sat bolt upright in bed, pulling the covers around her.

"Who's there?" she called into the darkness. Receiving no answer she fumbled with the matches for the lamp only to have them snatched from her hand. Before she could scream, a hand was roughly clamped over her mouth and she was forced back against the bedcovers.

"If you promise not to make a sound, I'll take my hand away," a man's voice whispered harshly as Melissa gasped for breath. "Will you stay quiet?" demanded the rasping voice again and, as she nodded her head, he uncovered her mouth. "Who are you?" he demanded tersely. At her hesitation, he lunged forward and shook her threateningly.

"M-Melissa H-Howell," she stuttered, half-smothered by his weight as he pressed her deeper into the pillows. She was abruptly released as she heard his sharp intake of breath and then a match was struck and the face before her was illuminated.

"Jeremy," she croaked, her throat suddenly constricted as she forced his name from her frozen lips.

"My own eyes are not deceiving me then," he murmured. "It is my little wildcat." He threw back his head and laughed until the match burned down and scorched his fingers. He stopped laughing and dropped

218

the match onto the quilted coverlet. "Did I not say we would meet again, my beautiful Melissa?" he whispered, running a calloused finger through a curling auburn tendril of hair. She stared speechlessly into the darkness and when he struck another match, the blue eyes in his weathered and bearded face bored into hers.

"Could we have the lamp on?" she asked him when she had found her voice once more.

"Make certain that the window is closed and the curtains tightly drawn first," he ordered crisply. She stumbled from the bed and made her way to the window. As she closed it and tugged the draperies together, Jeremy lit one of the bedside lamps, and in its faint glow, her filmy nightgown became a transparent covering for her honeyed skin, her body daringly revealed by its gossamer sheerness. Jeremy's eyes caressed her near nakedness as she moved back to the bed and hurriedly settled the coverlet around her again. . "Ever the shy virgin, Melissa," he teased, reaching out and capturing her face with his rough hands. She flinched at his touch and he drew back, laughing bitterly. "I'm not exactly the gentleman I once was, am I?" he snorted, indicating his worn sweater and trousers and the woolen cap pulled over his head. His face and hands were streaked with dirt and he appeared for all the world to be simply a common seaman.

"What are you doing here, Jeremy?" she asked then, her face composed, betraying none of the conflicting emotions she felt as she studied him.

"I should be asking the same of you, dear Melissa," he countered. With halting speech she told him briefly of her meeting with Bryan Ransome and her subsequent life at Laurel Hill. His mocking laughter echoed eerily through the room. "Well done, Melissa girl. Well done indeed," he approved wryly. "I knew you were suited for more than a barmaid's life."

"And you, Jeremy?" she persisted, wondering if his laughter could be heard in the third floor servants' quarters, shuddering as she contemplated the consequences if he were discovered in her room.

"I, dear Melissa, am escaping from the police," he finally replied matter-of-factly. "A fine turn of events for someone with my possibilities, isn't it?" he mused, his voice edged with self-pity.

"What sort of trouble are you in?" she prodded, feigning innocence.

"Nothing that need concern you, my beauteous wench," he snarled, his tone suddenly nasty. He slid off the bed and walked stealthily to the window, parting the draperies just enough to afford him a view of the street below. When he returned to the bed, Melissa noticed for the first time the two pistols tucked into the broad leather belt he was wearing.

"The police were waiting for us when the ship docked this evening," he mumbled as he toyed nervously with one of his guns. "Someone must have turned informer on us." He scowled. "But my men put up a bloody good fight and I was lucky enough to get away. I hid for a while in an abandoned warehouse and then managed to make my way here on foot." His voice changed then, taking on a harsh and desperate note as he glared at Melissa. "You have to help me now, my girl," he stated bluntly.

"Why should I help you, Jeremy?" she demanded, watching his eyes grow cold. And in answer to her question, he raised his gun and pointed it directly at her heart.

"This is why," he snapped. "No one need ever know I was here at all if you cooperate. There is a ship, *The Emerald Rose*, bound for England tomorrow at noon and I must be on board when she sails. It will be my only chance, Melissa, and you will see to it that I have that chance, won't you?" His smile was cruel as he jabbed her with the barrel of the gun. She nodded her head, her heart beginning to thump wildly as she realized he had nothing left to lose and shooting her would make little difference.

"I knew I could count on you, my sweet," he sneered as he slipped the pistol back into his belt and walked over to the large armoire. "There is a false back to this cupboard. Dear cousin Kathleen showed it to me once when this was my bedroom during my visits with the family."

"How fortunate for you the armoire is still here," Melissa commented frostily. He ignored her remark and continued.

"I am certain that the police will be paying you a visit fairly soon, and will insist on searching the house. Naturally you will know nothing of me or my whereabouts and when all is clear, you will signal me. In the morning I shall leave the house and board that ship without anyone being the wiser." He grinned, pleased with himself and his devious scheme. The smile suddenly vanished as he read the contempt in her eyes and his tone became menacing. "One final word of caution, Melissa; if you should have a change of heart and divulge my little secret and expose me, I promise that before they take me I shall kill you. I plan to get away from here and if it means disposing of any members of my beloved family to do so, I shan't hesitate. So think twice before you decide to turn me in, dear girl." He flung open the massive wooden doors of the clothes cupboard, fumbled among her dresses for the hidden spring releasing the false back and quickly disappeared into the depths of the armoire.

Melissa climbed from the bed and hastily rearranged her clothing before closing the doors again. Then she put out the lamp and crept back into bed, settling back against the cushions to wait. It was not long before she heard a carriage pulling up to the house and she turned over onto her side, closing her eyes and feigning sleep, willing her heart to slow its frantic pace.

She could hear voices raised in heated debate as they came closer, as the Ransomes made their way down the

221

corridor toward her room. The voices were lowered to whispers as they stopped just outside her door. There was a soft knock and then a bolder one. When she did not respond, she heard the knob turn. She kept her eyes tightly closed against the invading shaft of light from the hallway.

"She's asleep," Amanda whispered.

"Then wake her up, dammit!" came Bryan Ransome's irritated rasp.

"Bryan, really, I see no sense in waking her now," the woman replied.

"Then stand aside, woman, and let me do it," he fumed, loping over to the bed and roughly shaking Melissa's exposed shoulder. She roused slowly and opened her eyes and seeing Ransome standing there, she blinked in surprise.

"What is it? Is something wrong?" she mumbled, forcing a wide yawn and blinking again.

"I think you'd better get up and get dressed," he ordered crisply.

"Why?" Melissa persisted.

"Dammit, girl, stop asking questions," he thundered. "Put something on and come downstairs to my study as soon as you're dressed." He stormed from the room, brushing past Kathleen who hurried in, her face flushed with excitement.

"Melissa, hurry up and light a lamp," she exclaimed, and Melissa quickly complied. In the light she could see Kathleen's face sparkling with animation, her pale eyes dancing. "You'll never guess what has happened," she cried, but she halted abruptly to admonish Melissa. "Hurry and get dressed while I speak to you, otherwise father will be furious if you take too long." Melissa sprang from the bed, all pretense forgotten. As she pulled open the doors of her clothes cupboard, she reached in blindly, extracting the first gown that came to hand, and began to change.

"We were sitting in the parlor after dinner," Kathleen began again as Melissa slid out of her nightgown, "when father rushed in with one of the clerks from his office. He then told us that my cousin Jeremy Ransome had attempted to smuggle opium from China into the country, but that the police raided the ship as soon as she docked and Jeremy managed to escape."

"My goodness," exclaimed Melissa at what she hoped was the appropriate interval.

"If you had ever met my handsome cousin Jeremy," Kathleen continued, Melissa hastily lowering her gaze, "you wouldn't be surprised by this at all. I've never known anyone so unscrupulous and greedy."

Melissa made a vague attempt to brush out her hair as Kathleen finally ceased her rambling, but the girl immediately grabbed away the hairbrush and hurried her out of the room. Downstairs in the study, Bryan Ransome was pacing the floor and gulping noisily from a large snifter filled with brandy while Amanda sat quietly in a chair, her hands folded in her lap, her brow puckered with worry.

"Damn that hot head," Ransome muttered, the brandy sloshing dangerously about in the delicate glass as he charged about. "I knew he'd do something stupid like this one day. He couldn't wait, the selfish bastard. If he dares show up here begging for my protection, I'll drag him off to the police myself."

"Bryan dear, please calm yourself," Amanda said, but he waved an agitated hand in her direction and continued his restless prowling.

"The next thing you know they'll implicate me in some way. They'll say that since Jeremy's ship was one of mine, that I'm ultimately responsible for the cargo she was carrying. That damned fool," he blustered, shaking a fist in the air. "If I get my hands on him, I'll kill him." He downed the brandy and poured himself more.

Melissa and Kathleen had seated themselves on the velvet settee in front of the window facing the street.

223

Kathleen kept turning around and parting the curtains to peer outside, anxious to catch the first glimpse of the police. Melissa fidgeted nervously, twining her hair absently around her fingers, biting at her lower lip as she pondered her predicament. Jeremy had promised to kill anyone standing between him and freedom, and she had no doubt but that he had meant it. She wondered if she dared chance telling the police, hoping that they could apprehend him before he was able to carry out his threat.

As she sat there, contemplating her choices, she cast her thoughts back in time, remembering when she had stowed away aboard *The Sea Belle* and he had kept her alive, kept her away from the crew and had not turned her over to the authorities once the clipper had landed in Maryland. Perhaps she owed him his chance to escape, she thought. She suddenly squirmed in her seat, recalling his lovemaking. A heat rose within her and her face flushed uncomfortably. She looked up at Bryan Ransome and kept her tortured silence.

"Kathleen, for the love of God," Ransome bellowed, interrupting her thoughts, "stop sticking your head out between those damned curtains. Sit still before I order you out of here!" Kathleen scowled as she straightened her skirts and stared defiantly back at her father until he turned away with a muttered oath.

The sound of a carriage drawing up to the house sent him hurrying into the front hall only to return momentarily with three men. As they walked into the room, Melissa stifled a gasp of dismay as she recognized the ruddy-faced man who had questioned her that day at the police station. He appeared not to know her as he bowed politely to Amanda and acknowledged Ransome's hasty introductions of both Melissa and Kathleen.

"I'm Sergeant Strothers and these two gentlemen are my assistants, officers Denworth and Findley," the red-moustached man announced. The two officers nodded slightly as they were introduced, then took up positions on either side of the study door. "We're here to search the premises, Mr. Ransome," the man said bluntly, "in case your nephew Jeremy has decided to hide out here— without your knowledge, I would hope." He directed his penetrating gaze at Bryan Ransome, inviting his response.

"Your assumption is correct, sergeant," Ransome answered crisply, taking another gulp of his brandy. "My family and I were attending a dinner party this evening. We were told of the incident by one of my clerks who was waiting for *The Highland* to dock with the shipment of silks we were expecting. Naturally, as soon as I learned what had happened, we returned home."

"Was everyone in this room at the dinner party this evening, sir?" Strothers asked, his eyes suddenly lighting on Melissa, with her tousled hair and casual day gown.

"No, as a matter of fact, Miss Howell hadn't been feeling well and chose to remain at home," Ransome answered and Melissa felt her stomach lurch peculiarly as she faced the inquiring eyes of the policeman again.

"Miss Howell," he began, walking to the sofa and gazing intently at the troubled girl, "did you see or hear anything unusual this evening?"

"No," she answered sharply, forcing her eyes not to waver.

"Where did you spend the evening, may I ask?"

"In my bedroom. Reading."

"And you heard nothing? No sounds of someone tryng to gain entry to the house?" he persisted.

"No, I had a terrible headache and put out the light early," she answered, her voice steady as she regarded the man towering over her. He nodded his head, apparently satisfied with her answers and signaled the two officers at the door to begin their search of the house. Urging Bryan Ransome to join him, Strothers followed after his men.

Melissa rose to her feet, swaying imperceptibly as she moved toward Amanda. "May I have a glass of brandy?" she inquired, her voice suddenly hoarse and strained.

"Of course, dear," Amanda replied, springing to her assistance and gripping her arm. "Are you all right, Melissa? You look very pale to me." But Melissa smiled weakly and filled a brimming snifter of brandy for herself and immediately took a large swallow of the amber liquid.

"I think I could do with a bracer as well," Amanda declared, reaching for another glass. "Will you join us, Kathleen?" she asked her daughter, who had begun edging toward the study door.

"Thank you, mother, but I think I'd prefer to tag along after the others. It would be a shame to miss the chance of seeing Jeremy humbled at last if he were to be captured here after all," she said, her lips tilting upward into a malicious grin as she swept from the room.

When Melissa finished the last of her brandy, she left Amanda still sipping hers. She reached the second-story landing just as the policemen were entering her room. Taking a deep breath, she trailed after them and watched as they searched the bedroom, wondering if Kathleen would remember about the false back to the armoire and alert the men. But the girl stood there as if transfixed, her pale blue eyes trained on the policemen, saying nothing as she stared at them. As they swung open the doors to the clothes closet, Melissa held her breath, observing them rifling through her gowns and finally closing the doors once more. Only when they had moved into the adjoining room did she let out her breath, sinking wearily onto her bed, and waiting for the trembling in her limbs to abate.

She heard the men finally descend the stairs and exchange a few more words with the Ransomes before the front door was slammed shut. Moments later, Bryan

Ransome appeared at her door, running an agitated hand through his thick hair, his face seemingly older and lined with fatigue and despair.

"Strothers is posting officers to guard the front and the back of the house," he explained. "He thinks Jeremy might be desperate enough to make his way here sooner or later, and if he does, they want to be ready for him. The damn fool," he growled, pounding the door frame with his fist. "Well, my dear, try to get some sleep now. I have a feeling this little drama is far from over." He closed the bedroom door.

She waited a few minutes, then stealthily tiptoed over and locked it. Then she opened the armoire and rapped lightly against one of the sides before returning to the safety of her bed. With a noisy rustling, Jeremy appeared, stepping out of the cupboard and into the room, a triumphant smile on his grimy face.

"Bravo, my faithful Melissa," he beamed, saluting her with one of his drawn pistols. "You have proven yourself most admirably." He tucked the gun back into his belt and drew a dirty hand across his brow. "God, but it was stifling in there. Lucky for me they left when they did. Otherwise I might have given myself away by hitting the floor in there in a dead faint." He continued wiping at his perspiring forehead with the sleeve of his ragged sweater until he noticed the porcelain washbasin and pitcher and, hastening over to the washstand, he vigorously scrubbed the dirt from his face and hands.

"What do you think of my beard, Melissa?" he asked, as he turned to her and dried off his hands with one of her towels. But she remained grimly silent, observing him warily as he walked toward her. Only the slight flickering in the depths of his sapphire eyes warned her of his intentions, and then suddenly it was too late for her to react. He was upon her with catlike speed, silencing her protesting outcry with his lips as he pressed them against hers. His beard scratched her delicate skin and as she brought her hands up to claw

227

at him, he caught her wrists and pinned her arms above her head. She heaved her body upward in an effort to throw him from her, but he was too heavy and his body forced hers deeper into the plush richness of the downy coverlet.

With one strong hand clasping her wrists together, he fumbled with her long skirt with his other hand, running his fingers along her bare legs and up toward her lacy undergarments. Impatiently he tore at the flimsy cloth and cupped the warm mound between her straining thighs. She moaned beneath the pressure of his bruising kiss and he raised his head, covering her mouth with his hand as he did. "Nothing has changed, has it, hellcat?" he panted. "You still prefer to put up a fight first. Well, so be it, for it only whets my appetite and makes its appeasing that much more rewarding." He drew his hand from her lips and held them captive once more with his own demanding mouth.

He massaged her silken thighs and, raising himself slightly, he managed to wedge a knee between her legs, forcing them to open. Then he hoisted her skirt up to her waist and lowered himself on top of her again, the coarse wool of his trousers chafing her as he rubbed up and down across her body. Under his scalding kiss, abused by his probing tongue, Melissa felt as if she were choking, and tears stung her eyes as she lay trapped beneath him, wincing and squirming as his finger pressed inside her.

Her reluctant warmth began to spill around him as he worked back and forth across her sensitive awakening bud, but she tensed, refusing to capitulate, refusing to give in to the delicious tingling which flamed through her legs and seeped upward into her belly. Jeremy fought with the buttons on his trousers and then she felt him, hard and throbbing, springing out against her. And as she thrashed about in a last desperate bid to escape him, he penetrated her softness and plunged inside her. Thrust after thrust met no resistance as she

228

forced herself to lie still beneath his assault, willing her treacherous body not to respond. She released her tormented mind, sensing it fleeing her degradation, so that there could be no witness to her shame.

With one final battering push, Jeremy released his stored up fury, spending his anger and his hunger in a splintering burst within her. Melissa, writhing in the anguish of her violation, gulped back the bitter tears coursing down her cheeks and sagged with relief when he hurled himself down beside her. Flinging an arm across her body, he was instantly asleep. She slid from the pressure of his arm and stumbled from the bed, her legs almost buckling under her as she crept to the washstand, and peeled her soiled gown away from her damp skin. Fighting back a wave of nausea, she bathed her face and body and without even drying herself, she splashed the entire contents of a bottle of perfume onto her burning skin, erasing the telltale scent of Jeremy's slaked lust.

Moving noiselessly to the window, she drew back the curtain and looked outside. She could see the lone policeman walking back and forth in front of the house and she wondered if she dared attempt to attract his attention. But just then Jeremy stirred on the bed and she hastily released the curtain, tiptoeing to her chaise and slipping into the dressing gown she had left there earlier in the evening.

"Melissa?" Jeremy's voice suddenly rasped. She heard the cocking of a pistol as he sat up and glared at her. "What the devil are you doing over there?" he demanded suspiciously as he motioned her toward him with a wave of his gun. As she walked back to the bed, staring into his scowling, bearded face, she was overwhelmed by guilt and she despised herself for having protected him, for having refused to inform on him when she had been given the chance. As she stood before him, her eyes narrowed to cruel, glimmering slits and her words were biting and scornful.

"You'll not escape now, my clever Jeremy," she spat. "The house is being guarded and any slight provocation will have the police rushing in here." Her laugh was cruel and taunting as his eyes widened in disbelief. With an angry curse, he leaped from the bed and strode to the window.

"You knew about this all along, didn't you, you deceiving bitch!" he railed, hurling himself across the room and seizing her by the shoulders. He shook her so violently that her head snapped back and forth, bright bursts of pain exploding before her eyes as he viciously rocked her. "I could kill you for this right now, but I think I shall save that pleasure for later," he snarled as he threw her back against the covers. "In the meantime, my treacherous Melissa, I will have to find some way out of here and you had better pray that I succeed."

chapter 21

Through the long hours of that night, Melissa lay cowering in a corner of her bed while Jeremy either paced the floor or sprawled out wordlessly beside her, one hand always clutching a pistol. He would rake his fingers through his tousled blond hair and tug at his bristly beard as he frowned in concentration. As the first pale rays of morning filtered into the room, he climbed from the bed, his eyes gleaming triumphantly.

"I have just devised a plan to get me out of this hornets' nest, my dear, and I am counting on your complete cooperation. You will cooperate, won't you, Melissa?" he smiled, tapping the tip of her nose with the cold barrel of the gun. She jerked her head back and whispered her compliance. He hauled her to her feet.

"Now get dressed," he ordered brusquely, and she stumbled forward on legs weak with tension and fatigue. "And get me a long cloak with a hood," he added. Her trembling fingers pulled out two long capes and a simple cashmere gown for herself and Jeremy snatched one of the cloaks from her hands and began to tug it on. She hastily donned her undergarments and slipped into the gown she had chosen before she gathered the bulky cape around her.

"Now pull up your hood," he commanded her, drawing his own hood down to shield his face. Being almost of the same height, Jeremy, in his flat-heeled shoes, was assured of his cloak brushing the floor and hiding his trousers and he studied himself in the mirror with a satisfied grin before ordering Melissa to the bedroom door. She opened it slowly and peeped out into the corridor, finding it empty and dark.

"There's no one about," she whispered and he waved her forward, following behind her with his gun drawn. They crept along the hallway and on his instructions, she tiptoed down the staircase, signaling to him when she was certain that they were still alone. They proceeded together to the front door. Following his orders again, she opened the door and he stepped quickly behind it. The policeman on the sidewalk below hastily drew his gun and hurried up the walk as Melissa appeared in the doorway.

"Officer," she whispered, beckoning him toward her. And as he climbed the steps, drawing nearer to her, Melissa frantically mouthed the words "Emerald Rose" in a last attempt to thwart Jeremy's carefully laid plans.

"What did you say, miss?" the man asked. Melissa cringed, silently cursing him as she moved her lips once more, willing him to comprehend. But Jeremy, sensing that something was amiss, threw back the door, shoved Melissa out of the way and slammed his pistol against the side of the policeman's head before the man could protect himself. He crumpled to the floor with a loud thud as Jeremy grabbed Melissa by the throat.

"You almost succeeded, you two-faced bitch!" and he struck her across the face with the back of his hand before pushing her ahead of him down the stairs and onto the sidewalk. "Now run, damn you, run," he shouted.

The two hooded figures ran through the deserted streets until Melissa finally limped to a halt.

"I can't run any farther, Jeremy, please let me stop," she gasped, her sides heaving, her hair falling into her eyes.

"Not yet," he barked. "Now move before I shoot you right here."

"And lose your hostage?" she demanded sarcastically, fighting for breath, her chest aching painfully from the long run.

Jeremy, meanwhile, was gazing off down the street to where a carriage had just pulled up in front of a large brick house. "Come on, hurry," he urged her, "just a little farther and we can get to the waterfront in grand style."

He dragged her after him as he headed down the street. They slowed to a sedate walk as they neared the elderly driver who had climbed down from his seat and was hobbling toward the house. At the sound of their approaching footsteps, he turned and doffed his hat to the two cloaked women and continued up the stone walk. As soon as he had entered the house, Jeremy pushed Melissa into the coach and vaulted up into the abandoned seat, grabbing up the reins and slapping the startled horse.

They lurched away from the curb and Jeremy slashed at the animal, forcing it faster and faster until the coach was hurtling over the cobblestones, clattering eerily through the silent streets. Melissa was bounced and tossed from side to side as the vehicle jolted its way toward the harbor, careening dangerously around corners, righting itself again for a moment and then leaning precariously to the other side as they rounded another bend. Only when they neared the waterfront did Jeremy slow the horse's pace to avoid arousing suspicion among the vendors setting up their carts or the sailors milling about on the dock. The carriage rumbled over the uneven pavement of the ancient streets and then ground to a halt, sending Melissa crashing to the floor with a bruising thud. Jeremy sprang down from his perch, threw open the door, and pulled Melissa out of the coach. He had already discarded his disguise and as he hurried her by the panting horse, she noticed her cloak lying in a crumpled heap on the floor of the driver's box.

He forced her along the street toward a crumbling wooden structure, its windows covered with jagged pieces of wood and metal, its battered door sagging on rusted hinges. As Jeremy opened the door, it gave easily with a piercing screech and Melissa found herself inside a clammy, abandoned warehouse, its musty interior still reeking of tobacco and fish.

"This served me well last night and it should do so again, Melissa dear," he smirked as he led her to a pile of damp, moldering straw hidden behind a stack of rotting crates. "Now this isn't too different from the hold aboard *The Sea Belle*, is it, Melissa? But if you are lucky, you might spend less time here than you did in that stinking hole." And he laughed, a cold, mirthless laugh, as he pushed her down into the straw.

"What are you planning to do with me, Jeremy?" she whispered, her voice failing her.

"Why nothing, my sweet, except assure myself of your silence until I am safely away from here. Now be still," he cautioned as she squirmed to avoid his touch. "You are no longer a threat to me and I see no sense in harming you, Melissa. Now take off your petticoat."

"No, please," she whimpered, grappling with him once more, but he again forced her back into the straw.

"Do as I say!" he thundered. With shaking hands, she forced the satin slip down her legs and allowed him to snatch it up, tearing it into broad strips. Then he rolled her onto her stomach, the sickly smell of the straw penetrating her nose and mouth and causing her to gag. He wrenched her arms behind her back and as he began binding her wrists tightly together, she tried to turn over and fight him off. But he pressed her face down into the hay and she gasped and gagged again, terrified that she would be sick. He bound her ankles together and then tied a wide strip of the material across her mouth, effectively silencing any attempts to scream.

He then stood up and surveyed the bound girl writhing at his feet, and he smiled ruefully down at her.

"Alas, Melissa girl, this is farewell once more. But this chance encounter with you was more than I had ever expected when we last parted company." He bent and kissed her forehead, straightening the soft hood which had fallen and twisted around her neck. "Wish me luck, little wildcat." He smiled and with a jaunty salute he turned and walked across the creaking floor, puffs of dust rising from the filthy wood as he moved. The door creaked open and then closed, and he was gone.

Sprawled uncomfortably in the hay, Melissa fought against the urge to retch, for with her mouth so tightly bound it would mean her death. But to breathe meant to inhale the putrid smells around her and so she arched her body and rocked from side to side in an effort to roll over onto her back. As she moved, she covered herself completely with the slimy straw so that the sickening stench seemed to envelop her, permeating her clothing and her skin. Beads of perspiration stood out on her forehead as she finally propelled herself onto her back, and she lay there in the hay, breathing heavily as she slowly surveyed her surroundings.

Daylight was filtering in through the cracks in the boarded windows and she could discern the bulky shapes of boxes silhouetted in the half-light in a corner of the warehouse. Most of the floor was littered with rotting boards and chipped bits of rock, all of which was covered in layers of fine dust. Ragged mounds of straw jutted up at intervals throughout the giant structure and planks of wood were stacked haphazardly nearby. Craning her neck, she strained to locate a sharp metal tool or panes of shattered glass, anything which might help sever her bonds and free her. But in the dimness she could see little hope for herself.

The muscles in her neck began to cramp and she finally lay back again and closed her smarting eyes. She

235

felt exhausted, drained of strength, still reeling from her harrowing experience with Jeremy, and trying to convince herself that it had actually occurred. Her limbs seemed to be growing numb, pinned as they were beneath her body, and the musty sweetness all around her made her feel dizzy and lightheaded. Her tingling body began to drift, spinning in whirling circles as she slipped into the twilight world of half-sleep and she battled against the swirling blackness welcoming her to its protective womb.

She floated aimlessly, buoyed by the gentle waters of a woodland stream, her upturned face warmed by a tender sun. Drifting past swaying clusters of marsh flowers, she watched them wave at her from their sinuous stalks on the grassy bank beside her. Suddenly, the current changed, growing stronger, shifting, until she was caught in the rhythmic circling of a whirlpool, lashing around and around, whirring out of control. She flailed about, clutching a clump of the marsh flowers, tugging on them in an effort to escape the imprisoning eddy. But as she pulled, their stems grew longer, stretching into heavy tentacles which wrapped themselves around her wrists and climbed insidiously up her arms toward her throat. Struggling only bound her tighter and as she began to choke, she screamed and woke herself, bathed in terror, her mouth bruised and bleeding from her chafing bonds, her arms and legs still held captive.

Whimpering against the cloth cutting into her mouth, Melissa swallowed hard, gagging on the blood, its metallic taste causing her to shudder and her stomach to heave. But she battled to regain her composure and as her ragged breathing gradually eased and the contractions in her throat subsided, she forced herself into a sitting position. Looking around her, she found the room much brighter than before, the stronger rays of the sun penetrating the rotting wood and illuminating areas she had failed to notice earlier.

As her gaze traveled about the floor and the walls, she discovered at last her means of escape—a rusty spade leaned up against a pile of crates some distance from her. Slowly she began edging toward it, mindless of the filth and the splinters of wood ripping into her clothing as she wriggled away from the protective nest of straw.

Carefully making her way across the grimy floor, arching and straining like a giant inch worm, she managed to reach the stack of crates. Breathing heavily, she rested momentarily before shifting about to position herself in front of the spade, wedging it between her body and the boxes behind it to hold it still. She turned slightly, angling her arms so that her bound wrists touched the side of the rusted tool, and began working her hands up and down against the blunted edge. She worked patiently until her arms started to ache and she was forced to stop and rest. Then she began again, sawing away at her bonds until they eventually seemed to loosen. Excited by the progress she was making, she increased her speed, her heart racing and her face bathed in perspiration, until, with a loud snap, the bonds were severed and her hands sprang free.

She rubbed her aching wrists, mindful of their redness and the deep indentations from the strips of cloth. Then she worked to free her mouth and she massaged her stinging lips and throbbing cheeks until the circulation was restored again. Her shaking fingers then set to work untying the knots in the material binding her ankles. After several vain attempts and a split and bleeding fingernail, she managed to undo one knot. The second came away more easily and finally her legs, too, were freed. Gingerly rising to her feet, she steadied herself against the crates, waiting for the rushing wave of dizziness to pass before she dared to move again.

Then she removed her foul-smelling cloak and beat as much of the clinging hay from her gown as she could. Releasing her hair and shaking out the bits of straw

237

imbedded there, she wound the tangled curls into a knot again and pinned it securely at the nape of her neck. Picking up the filthy cape, she walked slowly to the door of the warehouse and pulled it open. Flinching against the strong sunlight which stabbed at her, she squinted against its glare and hurried into its welcome brightness.

As she gazed around her, she realized that she was only a block from the wharves and she hobbled across the street, trying once more to get her bearings. Seeking some familiar site, she finally spotted a small white-washed building with a brilliant orange door which she recognized as being several blocks from Bryan Ransome's offices. Pulling the begrimed cloak snugly around her and bending into the cold wind which whipped up the murky waters of the harbor, she headed in the direction of the red brick warehouse.

Shivering in spite of the warm cape, shaking from hunger and fatigue, she edged more closely to the dockside buildings to gain some protection from the bone chilling breeze. A sailor passed her, giving her a knowing wink as she tottered by, reeling as if she were drunk. Her eyes narrowed against the stinging gusts and the bits of paper and loose garbage being tossed about through the air. She finally glimpsed the building she was seeking and hurried her steps. Reaching the familiar red brick structure at last, she dragged her reluctant body up the long flight of stairs to Bryan Ransome's office.

As she stumbled sobbing into the main reception room, Sergeant Strothers immediately sprang to his feet, shouting for Ransome to join him. The office door was flung open and Bryan Ransome rushed into the room. On seeing Melissa wavering there, he dashed over to her.

"Well, she's back," grunted the policeman. "Now maybe she can answer some questions for us."

"Later, Strothers," Ransome snapped, brushing the

man aside and drawing Melissa into his arms. "My dear child, you gave us all quite a scare," he crooned, stroking her snarled hair. "It was Jeremy, wasn't it?" She miserably nodded her head, and sagged weakly against his chest. He gently nudged her toward a chair and brought her a cup of steaming tea. As she thirstily gulped it down, Strothers's bulky frame loomed over her and his husky voice interrupted her momentary peace.

"I understand you whispered something to our man," he stated crisply and she nodded. "Well, when he finally regained consciousness, he kept babbling something about emeralds."

"Emerald Rose," Melissa broke in then. "That was the name of the ship Jeremy hoped to board for England."

"We figured it might have been something like that after we'd questioned Mrs. Ransome and her daughter about the possibility of there having been a jewel theft at their home," Strothers said. "But we were out of luck, beause by the time I'd dispatched some men to check the harbor, it was too late. She'd already sailed. If our man hadn't been out for so long we might have nabbed the scoundrel," he declared vehemently, chomping viciously on the end of his pen as his penetrating gaze bored accusingly into Melissa's.

She cringed inwardly and looked away, leaning wearily back in the chair. Her body was aching, it reeked of the vile odors of the filthy warehouse, and she longed desperately for a bath and a change of clothing. But Strothers had not quite finished with her and his rasping voice again intruded into her thoughts.

"Miss Howell, I'd like to know exactly what happened last night with Jeremy Ransome," the man stated, settling himself into a chair across from her. Recalling his brutal examination of her at the police station, Melissa doubted he would ever believe what she was about to reveal, but she began, in halting words,

to reconstruct her horrible experience. She omitted
nothing save the fact that Jeremy had raped her. When
she had completed her account, she looked beseechingly into Strothers's unreadable eyes and waited for
him to attack her story. But to her surprise, he remained
still, his teeth firmly clamped around his familiar
battered pen. And then with a slight grunt, he shook his
head and rose to his feet, offering to take her back to the
house on Clarendon Street. But Bryan Ransome interceded, insisting on escorting her there himself, and
both men assisted Melissa from the chair and down the
stairs to Ransome's carriage.

When they reached the townhouse, Melissa descended awkwardly from the coach and passed two
silent policemen flanking the large front door as she
made her way up the steps and into the welcome
warmth of the house. Amanda and Kathleen met her in
the hall, questions spilling anxiously from their lips, but
Ransome waved them off and led Melissa to her room.

"A bath," she murmured as she staggered into her
bedroom, "I must have a bath." And Ransome immediately rang for the maid and then left Melissa alone.

As she was luxuriating in a deliciously fragrant tub,
Amanda entered the room carrying a large silver tray.
She smiled and set down the tray on the bureau and then
quickly walked out again and closed the door. She and
Kathleen had been warned by Ransome to allow
Melissa some time to herself before beseiging her with
their questions and forcing her to relive her nightmare
all over again. After she had bathed and slipped into a
fresh nightgown, Melissa wolfed down the tempting
meal Amanda had left her and crawled contentedly into
her warm, clean bed. She slid beneath the covers,
reveling in their silken smoothness. She was soon
asleep.

She slept soundly until well past noon the following
day. When she awoke it was to a cold, bleak day with
clouds scudding across a gray, forbidding sky. Wrap-

ping herself in a wool dressing gown, she seated herself at her vanity table and began brushing out her hair. She stared at her pale face reflected in the mirror, noting the faint smudges of fatigue under her eyes and the tiny cuts at the corners of her mouth. Sighing deeply, she put down the hairbrush and ran her hands gently over the curves of her body, somewhat startled by its familiar sameness, for she had almost expected to find it changed, matching the battered lifelessness she felt inside. Her traveling fingers prodded awake the memory of Calvin Gabriel and as she whispered his name, her body responded, throbbing in defiance to her troubled thoughts, yearning for the exquisite release which only he could give her.

She padded quietly to the bedroom door, opened it, and, finding no one about, hurried down the hallway. She was hungry and hoped she might be able to steal into the kitchen, convince the cook to prepare her a light lunch, and then slip back unnoticed into her room again. As she passed the closed door of the parlor, she could hear Kathleen deep in conversation with someone. Calvin. Melissa's heart began thudding wildly. She glanced down at her dressing gown and spun quickly toward the staircase, scampering back to her bedroom and flinging open her armoire to choose a more suitable gown.

As she was trying to decide between two day dresses, there was a knock at the door and her breath caught in her throat. She hastily splashed perfume onto her wrists and at her throat, pinched her cheeks to force some color into them, and ran a brush hastily through her tousled mane of hair. Then, moistening her lips with the tip of her tongue, she drew a shaky breath, formed a smile with her quivering mouth, and opened the door. Her smile wobbled and faded as she looked up at Edward Gabriel, his handsome face examining hers with concern.

"Edward," she managed, as she attempted to mask

her obvious disappointment, "what a surprise."

"Only because you were hoping for someone else," he laughed, his gray eyes dancing. "Alas, fair Melissa, 'tis only I." And he clasped both hands over his heart and dropped to one knee, staring balefully up at her. She snorted with laughter and tugged him to his feet, throwing her arms about his neck and hugging him close to her.

"Thank you, sweet Edward, for making me laugh," she whispered as she nestled against him. "But what brings you to town?" she asked, slipping finally from the warmth of his embrace.

"Business," he replied, "but I thought I'd stop by and see Kathleen before heading back. She told me what had happened with Jeremy." His eyes clouded and he grasped both of her hands with his. "It must have been terrible for you," he murmured. "But it's over now and in time you'll forget all about it." He squeezed her hands reassuringly and then released them. His tone was light again as he said, "Just think, you'll probably become the talk of the city once word of this gets around." He grinned at her look of consternation. "Sure, you'll be something of a celebrity, flooded with invitations to parties just to tell everyone about your one night spent in the evil clutches of a mad opium smuggler."

She grimaced, shuddering at his imaginative ravings, and unwittingly drew her dressing gown more tightly around her body. Sensing her growing agitation, Edward immediately ceased his bantering and sobered once more.

"Well, Melissa dear, having assured myself that you're fine now, I guess I'll be on my way." He tenderly brushed her lips with his and hurried back down the corridor.

True to Edward's teasing prediction, the number of dinner invitations multiplied once Jeremy's adventures became common knowledge. But Melissa declined each request, refusing to attend any of the parties and be the object of speculation and idle gossip. Resentful, she brooded about spending more time alone and watched, with bitter longing, as Kathleen dressed for her evenings with Calvin, evenings which became routine again on his arrival in the city from Stony Briar. To Melissa's chagrin, he studiously ignored her on his first visit to the house on Clarendon Street. Smarting from his hurtful snub, she took to her room each night thereafter to avoid him.

Preparations, meanwhile, had gotten underway for the upcoming Christmas festivities. The Ransomes were planning to host their annual open house on Christmas Day, and the lengthy process of cleaning and polishing the large home began in earnest. A week before Christmas, Cornelia arrived from Laurel Hill and was installed in a bedroom across the hall from Melissa's. The older woman acknowledged her with a slight smile and a curt nod as she moved into her room. Melissa returned her frosty greeting and then took great pains to keep out of the woman's way.

It was just before Christmas that the shocking news reached Baltimore of the sinking of *The Emerald Rose*. The ship had reportedly broken up in high seas in the midst of a raging winter storm and every man had been lost. Bryan Ransome reacted to the news of his nephew's fate with stunned disbelief, railing angrily at the senseless loss of the man who should have lived to inherit his fortune. Melissa was stung by the news, but despite a fleeting pang of genuine regret, she could not help but feel that somehow she had been avenged.

chapter 22

Christmas arrived amid snowflakes and a flutter of last-minute gift purchasing. A giant spruce tree was installed in the Ransomes' parlor and the family spent most of Christmas Eve elaborately trimming the tree with garlands of painted pine cones, clusters of red velvet bows, and large, glittering silver balls. Then everyone tripped busily up and down the staircase, heaping their gaily wrapped presents beneath the spruce's spreading branches and chattering excitedly. After that was done, they set to work decorating the mantelpieces throughout the house with boughs of fragrant pine and bright red candles. Warmth and cheer radiated everywhere. But for Melissa, spending Christmas among virtual strangers, the house remained bleak and cold.

Early on Christmas morning, while the servants were busily preparing all of the food and readying the house for the guests stopping by through the day, the family began to open their presents. Tissue paper, boxes, and satin ribbons and bows soon littered the large carpet in the parlor as the women unwrapped their gifts of fruits, perfumes, scarves, gloves, bolts of exquisite cloth, and jewelry. Bryan Ransome contentedly eyed his mounting collection of cigars, gloves, cravats, pipes, and leather-bound books. The traditional Christmas breakfast astounded Melissa. Spread before her was a mouth-watering display of fruit, oatmeal, waffles, hot rolls, spicy Sally Lunn cake, and coffee. She left the table feeling slightly sickened by the extravagant fare, all of which she had hungrily sampled.

The maids scurried about the parlor, picking up all of the debris from the gift opening and Melissa piled her assortment of presents together and tottered upstairs to her room. Depositing her gifts on the bed, she laid out her emerald-green velvet gown with its matching slippers and then, stripping to her undergarments, she sat down at the vanity to brush her hair. Fumbling with the long curls, she was despairing of ever managing them, when there was a knock at the door and one of the maids slipped into the room.

"I've just finished helping the cook," the girl explained, "and I thought I might slip away and help you dress."

With a sigh of relief, Melissa handed her the brush and watched in fascination as the girl's hands fairly flew through her hair, expertly gathering up the lustrous auburn strands and pinning them into cascading ringlets.

"I envy you such skill," Melissa murmured as the girl worked, finally anchoring a last heavy curl with a tiny hairpin. As the maid turned to leave, Melissa sprang from her chair and hurried over to her bureau, withdrawing a small beribboned box and handing it to the astonished girl. "Merry Christmas, Marie," she smiled warmly, "and many thanks for your help." The young maid's eyes filled with sudden tears as she hesitantly accepted the gift. Bobbing a shaky curtsy, she hurried from the room. Melissa sighed, turning back to her toilette, and then slipped into her gown.

She worked patiently at the small covered buttons fastening the long, close-fitting sleeves and then concentrated on the buttons running down the front of the gown's low pointed bodice. Draped panniers were gathered across her hips, falling into a simple train and she carefully adjusted the rich folds of the heavy velvet. The underskirt of white satin was embroidered with green leaves and tiny red berries and she tucked similar sprigs of satin leaves and berries into her elaborate coiffure. Her spirits lifted as she surveyed herself in the mirror and she silently approved of the gown which heightened the honey glow of her clear skin and showed the tops of her swelling breasts to such advantage.

She roamed restlessly about the dining room, awaiting the arrival of the family, eyeing the sumptuous display of pastries and fruit cakes, plum puddings and mince pies, assorted jellies and nuts set in silver platters on the dining room table. Red candles glowed atop the bough-strewn mantel and a blazing fire snapped and sizzled in the massive fireplace, warming the room with its golden light. The scent of the candles mingled with the pine boughs and Melissa was swept up by an overwhelming surge of homesickness as she breathed the rich fragrances enveloping her. She wiped at the tears gathering in the corners of her eyes.

"Are you all right, Melissa?" Kathleen, breathtaking in a gown of deep purple velvet, amethysts glinting at her ears and throat, called softly from the doorway.

"A little nostalgic, I think," Melissa admitted, suddenly feeling ill at ease with the other girl.

"Then let's have a cup of eggnog before everyone else comes downstairs," she suggested amiably, bustling over to one of the laden sideboards and pouring some of the rich, creamy brew into glass cups. "This is father's own recipe, you know," she confided, handing Melissa a brimming glass. "He prepares it himself in the kitchen and refuses to share his secret with anyone."

They sipped at their drinks until they heard the door chimes announcing the arrival of the first guests. As they entered the house, they were swiftly followed by other guests. Before long, people were crowding about in the hall and making their way into the dining room for Bryan Ransome's legendary concoction. Melissa floated through the day in a gentle haze created for her by the delicious eggnog. As she was returning to one of the punch bowls she started at the sight of Calvin Gabriel filling a cup for himself. He turned as Melissa warily approached and he shot her a lazy, appreciative grin.

"Melissa, my sweet, you're lovelier each time I see you." He raised his glass to her in salute and drained most of the rich eggnog in a long gulp.

"You're drunk," she scoffed, moving quickly to another bowl.

"Only slightly, my dear." His words slurred together as he spoke. "This is the third home I've visited today and wherever I've been, the hospitality has been most generous."

She turned her back to him, willing her heart to slow its rapid pulsing, and shakily poured some eggnog into her cup, spilling it down the side of the glass and onto her hand. Calvin was instantly at her side, brandishing a linen handkerchief, which he dabbed against her skin before brushing the moist patch with his lips. She closed her eyes at his touch, feeling as if she were toppling backward, the warm tingle of his mouth on her hand spreading like a fire through her entire body.

"Calvin darling, here you are." Kathleen's voice broke the closeness of the moment and Melissa's eyes flew open as Calvin hastily released her. "Oh, did Melissa hurt her hand?" she inquired sweetly, suspiciously regarding the girl who was clutching Calvin's handkerchief.

"No, Kathleen," Melissa reassured her in a hushed voice, "I spilled some eggnog and Calvin came to my aid."

"Is that all?" she breathed, slipping her arm through his. "Come, darling, there's someone here you should meet. He came with the Harringtons. His name is

Enton Perry. He's just bought the old Waterston farm and plans to begin breeding his own thoroughbreds. What better person to speak to than you?" As the couple moved off, Melissa lost interest in her drink and wandered into the parlor.

There she found Amanda and half-heartedly attempted to draw her into conversation, but the woman seemed agitated, constantly scanning the room as she spoke as if looking for someone. Her behavior began to unnerve Melissa and she finally asked Amanda if there was something wrong.

"No, nothing, dear," she said, her reply somewhat distracted. "I'm just trying to see to it that everyone is mingling and that their glasses are being kept filled," she murmured, her eyes still searching about. When her wandering gaze suddenly halted, Melissa turned in time to see Kathleen and Calvin entering the parlor, and she realized with a sinking feeling that it was Calvin the woman had been seeking. She hastily excused herself and walked away, passing the front door just as it opened. Edward hurried in, brushing a light dusting of snow from his thick black hair, then handing his overcoat to one of the maids. Although slightly shorter than Calvin, Edward's build was no less muscular and lean, his well-tailored dark gray suit hugging the contours of his body and deepening the gray of his eyes. He caught Melissa's appraising stare and walked over to her, kissing her cheek and squeezing her tiny waist with his hands.

"As beautiful as ever, Melissa," he said, allowing her to steer him toward the dining room, where he poured himself some eggnog.

"Your compliment pales, sir, in light of your brother's extravagant claim," she teased, smiling impishly. "He said I grow *more* beautiful each time he sees me." Aware of the coldness seeping into Edward's eyes, she hastily sought to soothe his ruffled feelings. "But he was drunk when he said it, so I prefer your compliment instead." And she gazed coyly at him through her lashes, aware of the danger of such a flirtation but reluctant to stop.

"I think you're a little drunk yourself," he replied, looking somewhat uncomfortable as she edged closer to him. He tensed and backed away and she stopped in her attempt, suddenly embarrassed. "Please, Melissa," he said softly, "I don't want a repetition of that night in the garden. You're too beautiful and too damned tempting." He gulped down his drink and hastily poured himself another cupful.

"Of course, Edward, forgive me," she replied stiffly, stung by his rebuff. Humiliated, she turned away, colliding with Calvin, the eggnog in her glass sloshing onto the front of his jacket and shirt and dribbling onto his trousers.

"I'm sorry, how clumsy of me," she blurted out, her face reddening with shame.

"That's all right, Melissa love," he mumbled, weaving unsteadily as he faced her. "If you'll just give me back my handkerchief I'll repair the damage." It was then that she realized that she had kept it and, mortified, she tugged it from her sleeve and handed it back to him. One of the maids appeared with a dampened towel for Calvin's suit but the thick cream had ruined his cravat and soaked through his clothing.

"It seems to be worse that I thought," he muttered, wiping ineffectually at the sticky staining on his clothes. "I guess I'll go home and change. Ladies." He executed a wobbly bow first to Melissa and then to a furious Kathleen and, lurching slightly, he ambled from the room.

"Stop pouting, Kathleen, it was an accident," chided Edward as the girl glared at Melissa who had grown alarmingly pale.

Her head was spinning and her body had begun to shake as she wavered uncertainly on her feet. Ignoring the look of concern on Edward's face, Melissa pushed

249

past him, staggering from the dining room in search of a cool and more quiet place to sit down and escape the noisy crowd all around her. She stumbled down the corridor leading toward the rear of the house where the kitchen and the spacious cloak room were located. She sagged gratefully onto a chair which had been placed just outside the entrance to the cloak room and closed her eyes, waiting for the sickening dizziness to pass.

"What an enchanting sight."

She opened her eyes to find Calvin, his overcoat thrown casually over one shoulder, looking down at her.

"I thought you had gone home," she said crossly, aware of the acceleration of her pulse once again.

"I certainly intended to go home," he growled, "but I made the stupid mistake of trying to find my own coat instead of allowing one of the maids to do it." He shrugged. "And now that I've managed to locate it, I'm on my way."

But something in her eyes held him back and he gazed down at her questioningly. She blushed and averted her gaze, her heart hammering so loudly that she was certain he could hear it too.

"Melissa?" he whispered, and the eyes she raised to his were filled with tears and the ache inside of her intensified, threatening to overwhelm her. Then he was drawing her to her feet and wrapping her in the protection of his embrace, holding her against him. As his lips touched hers, she clung to him, and in her desperate longing, she murmured his name and hungrily returned his kiss, knowing that she was lost.

"Come home with me," he urged, burying his face in the curve of her shoulder.

"Impossible." She shook her head.

"Please, love," he insisted, searching her eyes, and her defenses dissolved before the yearning in his gaze. "Go upstairs and find a cloak. I'll wait for you here."

"No, Calvin," she gulped, "it would be wrong.

250

Please. Please understand," she pleaded with him, wanting him.

"Why start worrying about that now?" he snarled, shoving her away from him. "It's a little late for such pangs of remorse, isn't it?"

It was as if he had thrown cold, sobering water into her face. Stunned by his cruelty, she fled, hurtling down the corridor and away from his taunting laughter. She stood alone on the fringes of the large group still massing in the parlor until she noticed a man openly studying her. He reminded her of a fox, with his light, bushy eyebrows slanting upward over hazel eyes, a narrow nose and pencil-thin lips set above a pointed chin. She shifted uncomfortably under his brash scrutiny, fearing the malevolence she read in his glinting eyes. But before she could move away, he began walking toward her and she glanced indifferently at the wiry framed man. His casual brown suit seemed so out of keeping with the formal attire of all of the other men there.

"I haven't had the pleasure," he insinuated smoothly, his thin lips drawing back to reveal small, pointy teeth. "But your beauty hasn't gone unnoticed." His gaze dropped to her breasts cresting above her low-cut gown. Revulsion swept through her and she took a step backward. But he reached out and caught her wrist, holding her fast.

"I'm Enton Perry," said the small man. He cocked an eyebrow, waiting for her own introduction, which she grudgingly mumbled. "Oh yes, Miss Howell." His grin widened. "I understand you and I are about to become neighbors."

"You recently purchased the Waterston property," she murmured, recalling Kathleen's words and hoping that if she were civil to the man, he would let her go and avoid creating an unpleasant scene.

"How quickly news travels, Miss Howell," he replied, showing no signs of relinquishing his hold on her. "I just met another neighbor of mine, Calvin Gabriel, and since he's one of the best authorities on horse breeding around here, I intend to take full advantage of his experience," he stated bluntly. "I'll probably be calling on you folks at Laurel Hill once I get settled. Just to be neighborly, you know." Again his gaze lingered on her decolletage. Unable to bear him any longer, Melissa wrenched free of his grasp and hurried away.

She found Amanda standing alone in front of the fireplace in the parlor and rushed over to her.

"I just had the dubious pleasure of meeting our new neighbor." Melissa grimaced as Amanda glanced at her.

"You mean Enton Perry?" the woman asked, rolling her eyes upward. "Charming fellow, isn't he?"

"You find him charming?" Melissa squeaked incredulously.

"I meant quite the opposite, I assure you," Amanda laughed. "That man gives me goose bumps just looking at him with his shifty little eyes always darting about the place."

"He reminds me of a fox," Melissa confided, "and I would dread having someone like him for an enemy." The other woman nodded in agreement and then glanced past Melissa toward the doorway where Edward stood talking with Kathleen.

Her expression softened as she gazed at her daughter. A careless smile flitted about the corners of her mouth. Melissa stood there silently, again confounded by Amanda's peculiar behavior, and quickly decided that she needed another cup of eggnog. Returning to the dining room, she filled her glass with the foamy liquid and watched it bubble precariously over the rim. Gulping several mouthfuls as it spilled, she then sauntered toward the kitchen, wondering about Calvin, momentarily regretting her refusal to accompany him home.

She blinked in amazement as she saw a figure rushing into the cloak room, and she held her breath as he reappeared, running a hand through his snow tipped hair. Catching sight of her standing there, Calvin grinned broadly.

"Changed your mind, Melissa?" he laughed, his white teeth flashing in his dark face, deepening the dimple in his chin. She stared open-mouthed at him. "Speechless at the mere sight of me?" he teased, pulling her toward him and kissing her lightly on the forehead. His breath fanned her glowing skin, his nearness sent tremors rippling down her spine and the cup of eggnog tipped dangerously as he hastily set her from him.

"We wouldn't want another accident, would we?" He frowned as she wobbled uncertainly. "I'll soon run short of clothes if you keep this up, Melissa, love."

"Your impudent behavior demands just such a penalty, Mr. Gabriel," she taunted, a sly smile on her lips, as she raised her glass menacingly.

But he seemed to find little humor in her jesting and he glowered at her. "That's what I find so appealing about you, Melissa, your fine manners and ladylike demeanor."

She was taken aback by his abrupt change in mood, resenting once more his offhand treatment of her. Anger guided the hand which coldly emptied the contents of the glass onto his freshly changed clothes. Momentarily stunned, he stood rooted to the spot, and then he lunged at her, forcing her back against the wall and knocking the glass from her hand.

"All right, Melissa, love, you and I will both make the trip back to my house this time," he seethed. "I should have you launder my clothes for me as well, but I think I shall exact my price some other way." He pushed her into the cloak room, blocking her path of escape as he threw on his overcoat. Then he randomly chose a woman's long fur-trimmed cape and tossed it to her. "Put it on," he snarled. But she just stood there, watching as the cloak slid to the floor. As he bent to retrieve it, she ducked past him, but his foot rested on the train of her gown and she was jerked to an immediate halt. With the cloak in his arms, he drew Melissa against him and draped it over her even as she grappled with him. Then he picked her up and carried her through the kitchen, the servants staring blankly as he strode past them.

When the first snowflakes pelted her upturned face, Melissa began to kick her legs and beat at his chest with her fists. "Put me down, you heathen," she cried. "Calvin, put me down or I shall throttle you until you do," and she aimed a blow at his unprotected face.

As she swung her fist, he dropped her to her feet on the wet sidewalk. "My shoes," she squealed as he grabbed her wrist and hauled her after him. Her long skirts trailed behind her through the slush and he watched indifferently as she stepped off the curb into a deep, icy cold puddle.

"I am now soaking wet," she moaned as he dragged her mercilessly on.

"Now you know how I've felt twice today, thanks to you," he retorted as he led her up a path toward a house very similar to the Ransomes' townhouse, and one hand clasped her wrist while with the other he fumbled to fit his key in the lock of the front door. Then he shoved her ahead of him into the darkened hallway, pulling off her cloak and tossing it onto a chair as he drew her into the study. His house was a replica of the house on Clarendon Street and as he noticed her wandering gaze, he said curtly, "Amanda helped me furnish this place. I never had the time." She felt as if the breath had been knocked from her and she thought back to the slender volume of poetry in the Ransomes' library. She suddenly felt sick to her stomach. Fighting down the nausea, terrified of humiliating herself in front of him, she turned away as he crouched before the fireplace, touching a match to the kindling there and watching the first tongues of flame leap upward.

She began to shiver, wondering if she dare bolt for the door and run out of there, but he seemed to sense her intentions and straightened up quickly and caught her to him. His lips claimed hers, gently at first and then more determinedly as he drove his fingers into her tumbling hair and pressed her head to his, deepening their kiss, binding her to him. Then just as abruptly, he released her. He stepped to a crystal decanter and filled a glass with brandy.

"Here, drink some of this," he offered, his voice subdued, all harshness gone. She sipped obediently and he then swallowed a large mouthful before allowing her another sip. He drank from the side her lips had touched, his gray eyes never leaving hers as he passed the glass back to her. They shared the brandy until the glass was empty and then he cupped her face between his large hands and lowered his mouth to hers. He parted her lips with his tongue, tasting of brandy, as he probed the tender insides of her mouth. The tiny flame already ignited by the scalding brandy leaped higher, stretching from the pit of her stomach outward through her limbs and she encircled his back with her yearning arms.

He released her mouth and looked into her smoldering topaz eyes, whispering, "We're alone, love." He kissed her tenderly once more.

But she began to panic, worrying that her absence had been noticed by the Ransomes. "This is madness," she gasped, frantically trying to quiet her growing desire before it was too late. "Calvin, please take me back," she whimpered. But he ignored her, silencing her pleas with his hungry lips until she arched against him and drew his head down to her breasts. He nuzzled her, burying his face in their sweet fullness.

"Let me undress you, Melissa," he pleaded, his voice hoarse, "we're both soaked through," and he nipped at her flesh with tiny biting kisses, teasing her, arousing her. "Undress me, love," he urged, and her fingers reached out tentatively toward him. She slipped the jacket from his shoulders and he shrugged out of it, letting it slide onto the carpet. As she worked at the buttons on his shirt and untied his cravat, she felt the bodice of her gown being lowered to her waist. She allowed him to free her arms from the long, tight sleeves constraining her. She removed his shirt and explored the smoothness of his skin and the black hair curling across his broad, dark chest. As he released the last of her buttons, her gown swirled to the floor at her feet and she stepped gracefully from the glimmering velvet pool and stood before him, clad only in her gossamer chemise. His fingers guided hers as she fought with the fastening on his trousers and they too joined the growing tangle of clothing on the Persian rug.

She dared not look at him as he slid the chemise from her shoulders. Her own fingers refused to move further, and with a soft laugh, he stripped the last of his clothes away and folded his arms about her once more. She moaned as his hands traveled up and down her back until they clasped her round bottom, kneading the soft flesh there, as he pressed her against his bulging stiffness. She grasped his neck with her slender hands and held his face to hers, their lips parting, their tongues hungrily probing, uniting.

Then he lowered her onto the thick warm carpet, and as he lay down next to her, one leg positioned between both of hers, his face and body glowed golden in the dancing flames and she could see the fire reflected in his silvery eyes. He began to kiss her again, slowly, tantalizingly, his exploring tongue sending ripples of heat through her body as he touched every part of her with his mouth and caressing tongue. She trailed her fingers up and down across his back and her own lips burrowed in the curve of his strong neck before lowering to nip playfully at his chest and continuing down across his tightening belly. As she hesitated, he gently drew her back to meet his lips.

He fondled her quivering breasts, rubbing the tender nipples until they stiffened, stretching upward. Melissa strained to press herself more completely against him as her legs parted, silently begging him to enter her. He sensed her urgency, but murmured huskily, "Not yet, my impatient one, not yet." As she groaned, his hand massaged her opening thighs and teased her until she reached for his hand and placed it where she wanted it to be.

He stroked back and forth inside the furry warmth of her, his fingers wading in the bath prepared for him, slipping over the rigid bud and sending flashes of tingling heat bursting through her. When she felt as if she could bear no more, he gathered her to him and guided himself inside her, sliding easily into the furnace of her being. She rose to meet him, pulling him deeper until she had taken all of him, and still she yearned for more. They rocked together and instinctively she wrapped her legs around his back and he drove harder and faster inside of her.

Melissa's mind seemed to float free from her writhing body, drifting in some timeless corridor in a whirling universe. As she soared toward completion, she felt her body lifted up to join her spinning mind. She tensed, every muscle straining taut, and with a whimpering cry, she crested in a stinging burst of ecstasy. A tingling pool spread out in widening circles from her throbbing core, washing her entire body in its trembling wake. Her muscles slowly relaxed as, drained and limp, oozing in their melting state, mind and body were reunited in shimmering tranquility.

Melissa lay there, wrapped in a blissful contentment she had never know before, so satiated that she could not move. Gone were all thoughts of Amanda and Kathleen and Calvin's place in their lives. Gone, too, were the shameful memories of her moments with Jeremy, as she clung to the only man who could ever share her passion and her love.

Calvin raised his head and looked into her limpid eyes. Then he tenderly kissed her parted lips and untangled himself from her arms, dropping down beside her on the carpet. He lazily traced the curves of her body with his hand. She arched expectantly and reached out for him again.

"So eager, Melissa love," he breathed, caressing her rounded breasts. "God, but you're beautiful." He pulled her up against him, kissing her hungrily, crushing her to him with a sudden desperation as if knowing that he would soon have to let her go. She felt a sob tear at her throat as she sensed his need, and she hugged him close and whispered his name, running her fingers through his hair, desperately staying the inevitable.

"I think I'd better take you back now," he finally said, but she refused to unwrap her arms from about his neck. Laughing, he pried himself loose and tugged her to her feet, lightly spanking her on her firm buttocks. "No more, love," he commanded sternly. "Now get dressed and be quick about it." He began to sort out his clothing from the snarled finery heaped on the carpet. "Damn," he muttered irritably, "I have to find myself another shirt." And he hurried from the study as Melissa reluctantly dressed and tried to put some order to her hair.

When Calvin returned to the room, buttoning a fresh shirt, he seemed distracted. Watching him shrug into his jacket, Melissa felt as if he had already forgotten she was there. Pain twisting her heart, she agitatedly nibbled at her lower lip, aware of the ache beginning to gnaw away inside her belly. Wordlessly, he escorted her back to the Ransome house where they entered again through the kitchen. It was deserted and Calvin hastily removed her cloak, saying brusquely, "I'll put the cape back while you run upstairs and fix yourself up a bit." He planted a kiss on her yearning lips and turned and strode from the room.

Gathering up her damp and spattered skirt, she raced up the back staircase to her bedroom and quietly closed the door behind her.

She unpinned her straggling curls and brushed out her hair until it fell smoothly about her shoulders. Then she patted on fresh lip pomade to disguise the telltale puffiness of her mouth, kicked off her soiled pumps, slipped her feet into a clean pair, and returned to the party downstairs. No sooner had she entered the parlor than Kathleen sailed over to her, her pale blue eyes narrowing resentfully.

"Where have you been all this time?" she demanded, studying Melissa's loose hair and suspiciously scrutinizing her glowing features. "And whatever did you do to your hair?"

"I had one of my terrible headaches and I needed some air," she replied easily. "I walked about outside and the snow all but ruined my hair, so I simply brushed it out." She smiled innocently at Kathleen and walked away.

"Melissa, my dear." Bryan Ransome hurried over to her. "Our new neighbor, Mr. Perry, was quite taken with you it seems, and before he left he asked me if he could call on you and I agreed." Seeing the look of horror spring into her face as she recoiled at his words, he quickly asked, "Have I done something wrong, my dear?"

"Wrong?" she moaned. "That man sickens me, and if he ever dares to call on me I will leave word that I am indisposed and cannot possibly see him. Ever," she added vehemently and she flounced off, clenching and unclenching her fists in impotent rage.

She eagerly scanned the room for some sign of Calvin, missing him, still fretting over his brusqueness and their hasty parting, her body still warm from his loving. When she finally located him, he was deep in conversation with Amanda. The woman was speaking rapidly, her hand touching his arm and Calvin was looking around him, shifting uncomfortably from one foot to the other as he listened to her. He suddenly shook his head and Melissa cringed at the anger she could see contorting his face. He brushed Amanda's arm away and left her standing there, gazing after him with eyes brimming with tears.

Melissa started toward him but stopped abruptly, for Kathleen had found him again and he slid his arm about her waist. Melissa's stomach flip-flopped inside her as she watched them together. Swallowing her despair she marched determinedly to one of the punch bowls and filled a fresh cup of eggnog for herself.

chapter 23

During the months that followed, through a dreary, snow-spattered winter, Melissa was seldom afforded the opportunity of seeing Calvin alone again. He had escorted Kathleen to several grand balls during the Christmas festivities, but shortly after the start of the New Year, he returned once more to Stony Briar. Kathleen grew irritable and implacable in his absence, her vitality and enthusiasm being temporarily restored only by Edward Gabriel on brief visits from New York City. To Melissa's chagrin, Enton Perry came by to formally call on her on a number of occasions, but each time was given the excuse that Melissa was either out or indisposed. He eventually stopped his pursuit of her, heading back to the country to supervise the renovation of the Waterston farm which he had grandly renamed Twin Oaks.

At the end of March, the family returned to Laurel Hill, where to Melissa's continuing dismay, Perry again attempted to court her, but she always managed to elude him. Meanwhile, Amanda slipped back into the demanding routine of the horse farm and Kathleen renewed her interest in preparing her horse, Pebbles, to run in the Preakness Stakes at Pimlico, Maryland in May. She spent hours each day with the horse's trainer, watching Pebbles's workouts and conferring with the jockey she had chosen to ride her prized three year old. Luis Alvarro was a tiny man with swarthy skin and a shock of blue-black hair. Agile and lithe, he deftly schooled Pebbles until they were performing together as a smoothly coordinated team.

Melissa, free to ride alone, took full advantage of her time, covering endless miles each day and returning exhilarated, a fresh bloom high in her cheeks, her sense of well-being restored. The intense longing she had once felt whenever she thought of Calvin Gabriel had dissipated as the months had passed, and the abandon with which she rode each day all but banished him from her thoughts completely.

One day, as spring was painting the trees with greening buds and the hills with the pastel hue of early wildflowers, Melissa rode Honey into a valley unfamiliar to her. As they cantered steadily through the newly sprouting grasses, their progress was abruptly halted by a high fence, its wooden posts and intricate wire bars stretching out in front of her. Curiosity nibbling at her, she decided to follow alongside it. Large "No Trespassing" signs were posted every one hundred feet and just as Melissa rounded a corner of the giant fence, still tracing its perimeter, a shot rang out. She pulled up her horse sharply and looked off in the direction of the shot.

Galloping toward her was a man clutching a smoking shotgun. As he neared her, Melissa recognized Enton Perry, his wiry body clothed in leather breeches, a flannel shirt, and a plaid jacket. A red bandana was knotted around his neck. He reined in a large pinto and called out to the startled girl.

"Aren't you a ways from home, Miss Howell?" His eyes flickered menacingly as they roved over her tight-fitting redingote. "As you can see from the signs, trespassers aren't welcome here."

"I assure you, Mr. Perry, I was hardly trespassing," she countered, her temper flaring. "This was the first time I had ever been over this way and I was staying quite clear of your gruesome fence."

He seemed to relax, lowering his gun and resting it across the saddle in front of him. "It's a pity you never saw fit to accept any of my invitations, Miss Howell. You might have had the opportunity of viewing my property from inside this gruesome fence, as you call it." he continued to leer at her until she could bear him no longer and she wheeled her horse about and headed off in the opposite direction with his raucous laughter following the pounding of Honey's hooves.

With the peace of her ride shattered, she galloped directly back to Laurel Hill and handed Honey over to Pete. She spent the remainder of the afternoon moping about, following after Amanda and some of the hands while they exercised the horses. Then she witnessed for the first time the delicate hand breeding of a stallion to a mare in heat. On the initial try, the mare refused the stallion, but Amanda and the men patiently tried again until, amid a mighty thrashing of hooves and high-pitched whinnies from both horses, the stallion was finally guided up onto the mare's twitching hindquarters. His slender forelegs were locked around her back while his massive organ was slipped slowly and gently inside of the accepting female at last.

As Melissa turned away from the sight, she began to feel a familiar throbbing within her own body, an ache which she knew only one man could assuage. And despairingly, she realized that her need for him had not diminished at all and that her longing was as intense as ever.

That night, as she tossed and turned in bed, she could find no surcease for her yearning body and its burning hunger. She strained to recall each exquisite moment of their stolen time together at Christmas and she conjured up the feel of his flesh against hers, the touch of his hands as they caressed her body. And as she squirmed against the bedcovers, her nipples stiffened, her belly flamed with a building heat, and she felt herself dissolving. She hung suspended between full awareness and sleep, slipping into a netherworld between the two, and she saw his face before her, his gray eyes imprisoning her with their strange power, enslaving her, trapping her. She welcomed him, spreading open before him, and he massaged the tender core within her. She awoke, climaxing in her waking, her body brought to fulfillment by the phantom strokings in her dream.

The following morning she cornered Bryan Ransome as he was about to return to Baltimore for a week of business. He was just tugging on his gloves and heading for the front door when Melissa stopped him.

"Before you leave, I want to ask you about Enton Perry," she explained. "What exactly do you know about him?"

"Not very much," Ransome admitted, "except that he's from out west and obviously has a great deal of money which he seems to be spending rather freely. He's been enlarging the Waterston spread, rebuilding the house, fencing in some of the open land, and buying up some fine thoroughbred stock. Why the sudden interest in the man, my dear?" he inquired, his eyes twinkling as he noted the irate expression settling across her face.

"It has nothing whatsoever to do with interest," she retorted in a voice quivering with contempt. "I was out riding yesterday and happened quite innocently onto his property. Mr. Perry greeted me with a shotgun blast aimed above my head. There was a high fence around his land and 'No Trespassing' signs posted everywhere." Her eyes narrowed contemplatively and a deep frown puckered her brow. "I have a feeling that dear Mr. Perry is not the gentleman farmer he pretends to be. I think he is dangerous and the prospect of having such a neighbor frightens me."

Ransome pondered what she had just revealed to him, rubbing a hand thoughtfully over his chin, but he finally shook his head in bewilderment. "I wish I had some answers for you, Melissa, but I don't. My only advice is to stay away from his land." Planting a hasty peck on her cheek, he left the house.

In the days that followed, Melissa cautiously avoided riding near Twin Oaks terrain and there were no further incidents. It was already mid-April and spring was alive in the blossoming trees and the exuberant tangle of wild flowers springing up everywhere to carpet the valleys and rolling hills. Melissa had silently observed her twentieth birthday, keeping the occasion hidden from the Ransomes, the recollections of the year before still too painful, too fresh.

Riding back across the fields toward Laurel Hill one sunny afternoon, she spotted another rider some distance away, heading directly toward her. Fearing it was the despicable Enton Perry, she prodded Honey into a gallop and raced blindly across the open meadow back to the protection of the estate. As she rode, she heard the approaching rider shouting at her and gradually gaining on her. Frantically urging Honey faster, she careened recklessly toward the stables, bringing her panting animal to a grinding halt and instantly dismounting.

Glancing over her shoulder, she noticed the horseman reining in his heaving mount and again calling out to her. Calvin Gabriel swung down from the saddle and sauntered to where she stood, breathing heavily from her fright and reddening in mortification as she observed the mocking laughter in his eyes.

"Why the hell did you tear off like that?" he demanded. "You'd have thought the devil himself was after you, Melissa."

"It seems that he was," she returned, bridling at his insolence. She stalked away. She almost collided with Kathleen who was running toward the stables in great excitement and shouting to Calvin as she ran.

"Thank heavens you're here today," she cried.

"Luis is taking Pebbles out for some trial runs against the clock, and you must come and watch with me." Melissa hurried back to the house and stomped into the hallway, tugging off her jacket and flinging it across her shoulder.

"What's all the commotion about outside?" called Amanda from the dining room where she was busily arranging freshly cut flowers in a crystal bowl.

"Kathleen is about to impress Calvin with Pebbles's ability," Melissa replied caustically, leaning against the door frame and gazing at Amanda who hastily dropped the flower she was holding.

"Calvin's here?" she asked, her eyes lighting expectantly. "Good. There are a few things I meant to discuss with him before he leaves for New York."

"New York?" Melissa echoed bleakly, her heart sinking.

"Yes, he plans to run several of his horses there during the season. First at Belmont Park in June and then at Saratoga in August. He wanted to set up close to the tracks and work out the horses there."

Melissa felt her stomach begin to churn at the thought of not seeing him for the entire summer, and she watched as Amanda hastily wiped off her hands, ran them through her tumbling black hair, and strode briskly out of the house and toward the stables. She herself was curious about Pebbles, but she could not bear to watch as Calvin was smothered by the attentions of both Ransome women, and so she wandered dejectedly about the library in search of some book to amuse her.

It was late in the afternoon when she happened to glance out of the study window to see Kathleen heading toward the house. Since there was no sign of either Calvin or Amanda, Melissa hurriedly set aside her book and went to meet Kathleen in the hall.

"You could have shown some interest, you know,"

the girl blurted out accusingly before Melissa could even speak. "Pebbles performed superbly and you really should have been there." At Melissa's silence, which Kathleen mistook for disdainful indifference, she suddenly bristled and spat out angrily, "You certainly are high-handed for someone who's no more than a glorified servant." With that she stamped up the stairs, leaving Melissa dumbfounded at her outburst. With a shrug, she turned back to the library and picked up her book again, finding it somewhat difficult to concentrate, still smarting from Kathleen's attack.

Several minutes later, Kathleen clattered back down the stairs and announced from the hall in a loud voice, "I'm going riding if you'd care to join me, Melissa." As she sat there in stupefied silence, Kathleen appeared at the door. "I'm sorry about what I said to you before," she murmured contritely. "I suppose I was hurt because you didn't seem to care about what was happening." She turned to leave as Melissa bolted from her chair.

"Please wait for me," she called out, throwing her book down and picking up her riding jacket again. The two girls left the house together and walked back to the stables. Calvin's black stallion was still tethered to a post outside one of the barns, but there was no one in sight.

"I suppose they're all out exercising the horses," Kathleen sighed. "Come on, I guess we'll have to saddle up by ourselves."

Entering the dim interior of the stable, they halted, allowing their eyes to adjust to the sudden light change. Then they heard scuffling sounds coming from one of the empty stalls. Kathleen put a finger to her lips, cautioning Melissa, and they crept stealthily toward the suspicious noises. To her horror, Melissa heard a woman's cry and a man's low-voiced curse followed by sounds of sobbing. Kathleen seemed to have frozen in the spot where she stood and as Melissa drew alongside her, the low gate of the stall swung open and a bare

chested Calvin Gabriel stumbled out, clutching his
shirt and clapping a hand to the side of his face where
blood was oozing from a long scratch. At Kathleen's
sharp intake of breath, he glanced up and saw the two
girls standing there and a bitter grimace of pain twisted
across his face. As he moved toward them, he revealed
behind him the naked figure of Amanda crumpled on
the straw-covered floor, crying brokenly.

"No!" Kathleen screamed, her face white with
shock. "No, it can't be. Not you!" she cried, tears
filling her eyes as she faced her mother. Amanda
cringed, fumbling about for clothes to shield her body.
Kathleen began to scream, high pitched wails of agony
and betrayal, her beautiful face contorted into a mask of
intolerable suffering. Melissa felt as if her own legs
were buckling beneath her and her own cry of outrage
mingled with Kathleen's sobbing despair. Then the girl
began running out of the stables. Melissa forced her
rebellious legs to move and she staggered after her.

"Kathleen," she cried, "Kathleen, please wait." She
burst into the sunlight in time to see the fleeing girl
spring onto the back of Calvin's horse and viciously dig
her heels into his flank.

"No, Kathleen," Melissa screamed, "come back,
you'll never ride him." But her warning was lost to the
girl who rode off, crying and kicking savagely at the
frightened animal. Enraged, the stallion pounded
across the open fields with Kathleen's body being flung
about in the saddle as she gripped the reins. Melissa, in
her fear, began to run, running until she felt her lungs
would burst as she watched Kathleen clinging to the
frenzied horse. The animal swerved suddenly, heading
back toward the barn, but then he veered sharply again
and streaked off toward the wooden fence ringing one
of the paddocks. As Melissa ran, she saw the mighty
animal prepare himself to leap but Kathleen had lost all
control of the horse and as he soared, he faltered,
crashing heavily downward, breaking his body on the

splintering fence, sending Kathleen hurtling through the air, thudding to the ground.

Melissa reached her first. Kathleen lay limp and still, blood trickling from a gash on her forehead, her breathing rasping and labored. Her eyes flickered open and seeing Melissa's tear-streaked face gazing into hers, she mouthed the words, "My legs, I can't feel my legs." Her eyes closed again as she lapsed into unconsciousness and Melissa stumbled back to the house, shouting for help, not daring to look at Calvin's ashen face as she ran past him.

Kathleen was carried into the house, lain carefully across her bed and covered with blankets. Her head was bathed to cleanse the wound and when the doctor finally arrived, he brushed everyone from the room in order to examine the unconscious girl. When he emerged at last, his report was grim.

"She's regained consciousness now and I've bandaged the head wound, but I'm afraid we have more to worry about than that cut on her forehead. Kathleen is complaining of experiencing no sensation whatever in her legs, and from my preliminary examination, I'd have to conclude that she's paralyzed from the waist down." Amanda gasped and broke into tears. She ran back to her own room while Cornelia, her face an inscrutable mask, followed after her.

The doctor gazed thoughtfully at Melissa. "Has someone sent for Bryan?" he asked.

Melissa nodded. "One of the grooms has ridden into the city to fetch him."

"I want no attempts made to move Kathleen just yet," the doctor warned in a solemn voice, "but I would advise Bryan to get hold of Dr. Roland Mapes, one of the best doctors I know in Baltimore, as soon as possible. In the meantime, I have left something for the pain in her head and some tablets to help her sleep." He ambled slowly down the hallway, stopping outside Amanda's door, knocking softly, and letting himself in.

Melissa trudged wearily back to her own room and sank down onto the bed, her head in her hands. She had been so concerned about Kathleen that she had managed to temporarily erase the memory of Calvin and Amanda together, the brutal fact finally confirming her longstanding fear. Calvin had not even returned to the house when Kathleen had been borne inside. Instead he had stood near the paddock, dismally viewing his mortally injured horse. Then he had walked purposefully over to the straining beast and with a single bullet, ended its tortured suffering. Melissa winced in recollection as if the pain had been hers and she began to weep again, not only for herself but for all of them.

Bryan Ransome returned the following night and bellowed like a great wounded bull as he left his daughter's room, dazed by her adamant refusal to reveal the circumstances surrounding her accident.

"She won't say anything other than she was riding Calvin's horse and was thrown," he thundered, bringing his fist down with a powerful crash on the top of his desk. He glowered at the three silent women seated across from him in his study. "Will someone, for the love of heaven, tell me what Kathleen was doing trying to ride Calvin's horse? How, when she's a good jumper, did she manage to fall off?" Again his words met obstinate silence. "What are you all covering up here?" he demanded, his florid face reddening further as he raged on.

Melissa stared down at her hands, Cornelia gazed pleadingly at the furious man as she silently urged him to calm himself and Amanda stared vacantly ahead of her, her cameo face pasty white, her eyes bleak, all of the vibrant life squeezed from her.

"Melissa," he suddenly barked, "can you tell me what happened here?" But she shook her head, whispering, "It was an accident. She tried to ride Calvin's horse, but the animal got frightened and threw her."

"I already know that much," he countered sharply. Then with a defeated sigh, he lowered his head to his chest and began mumbling incoherently to himself. When neither Amanda nor Cornelia volunteered anything further, he straightened his shoulders and strode briskly from the room.

Amanda turned her waxen face to Melissa, a ghost of a smile lighting her mouth. "Thank you, my dear, for not betraying me," she murmured.

Melissa faced the other woman defiantly, barely managing to conceal the contempt in her voice as she replied, "I lied to protect *him*, Amanda, not you. He deserves to be spared any further hurt right now." She bounded from the room, unable to bear the presence of the two sisters any longer.

She sat with Kathleen awhile, watching over the girl as she slipped in and out of sleep, sometimes moaning and crying out, at other times lying so still that Melissa would lean forward to ensure that she was still breathing. Once her eyelids fluttered open, her eyes locking with Melissa's in unspoken understanding, and then she closed her eyes once more while tears trickled slowly down her pallid cheeks.

Several nights later, Amanda entered Melissa's bedroom, catching the girl unaware as she let herself in, and quickly closed the door.

"Melissa, I must talk to you," the woman pleaded, her beauty strangely faded, her young face lined with fatigue, suddenly old. "Kathleen refuses to speak to me or even allow me into her room and I'll go mad if I can't explain this to someone. Please, please listen to me." Her black eyes implored the topaz eyes glaring back at her in icy containment.

"Not this time, Amanda," she said springing from her chaise, her hands balling in controlled rage at her sides. "You see, I now know what I had always suspected." She spoke softly despite her raging turmoil

271

inside. "I discovered a certain book of poetry in the study in Baltimore." Amanda's shoulders slumped and she nodded imperceptibly as Melissa continued. "The night Kathleen and I returned from our first trip to the city last summer and he had been here. . . ." Her voice trailed off as Amanda raised her tortured gaze.

"That was the first time we had been together in two years," she whispered brokenly, "and the last. We had once needed each other very much, Melissa, don't you understand?" she entreated the girl. "But in the end, it was my need which was the greater and he refused me," she finished bitterly.

Melissa's heart wrenched with grudging compassion for the woman who stood sobbing quietly before her, and her arms slowly encircled Amanda's quivering shoulders, drawing her up against her. She gently patted the lustrous black hair until the sobs gradually subsided. Amands turned her tear-streaked face up to the younger woman's and her eyes transmitted her gratitude.

"You realize that it will be impossible for me to stay on here, now," Melissa murmured as Amanda finally tugged free of her comforting embrace.

"Where will you go?" she asked as she dabbed at her streaming eyes with a delicate handkerchief and daintily blew her nose.

"I need just a little more time to think about it," Melissa answered, walking over to the window and gazing out at the familiar grounds below. Her eyes filled with tears as she looked into the moonlit night. When she turned back to Amanda, she discovered that the woman had gone.

Melissa was sitting with Kathleen when Dr. Mapes arrived from Baltimore to examine the injured girl. Kathleen's terrified eyes held Melissa's as she rose to leave the room and she reassuringly squeezed the pale hands she held, watching as they dropped limply back onto the coverlet. She waited with the family in the study and watched as Ransome paced nervously back and forth across the floor, his hands clasped tightly behind his back.

"What the hell kind of life is she going to lead if she's paralyzed?" he blazed. "Of all the damned fool things to do. She had Calvin in the palm of her hand and she goes and destroys herself." Amanda and Melissa exchanged covert glances as he blustered on. "A healthy buck like him won't tie himself down to a cripple for the rest of his life, no matter how guilty he might feel. Damn that girl and her stubbornness," he ranted on, "if she'd married any one of the men chasing after her and this kind of thing happened, at least she'd have a husband to look after her properly."

"It seems to me, Bryan dear, what concerns you is not that Kathleen may be crippled for the rest of her life, but that you might have to be responsible for her care," Amanda charged, her voice shaking with ill-disguised venom. "You're blaming her for managing to inconvenience your life right now." Her accusing stare shifted to include Cornelia too.

"That's a damned lie, Amanda," Ransome thundered, glaring at his wife.

"Is it, Bryan?" she returned, her black eyes relentlessly piercing his until he looked away and resumed his restless pacing.

Melissa squirmed uncomfortably in her chair, loath to witness their confrontation. She was convinced that Ransome was still unaware of the true cause of his daughter's accident and Calvin had conspicuously stayed away from Laurel Hill since it had happened. But it was Cornelia's behavior which truly astonished her, for the woman had seemed to have undergone a curious transformation on that fateful day, exhibiting a gentle tenderness toward Kathleen which she had never shown before. The woman began to spend long hours each day with her ailing niece, bringing her

273

meals up to her and coaxing her to eat. She read to her each night until she was able to fall asleep. It was as if the roles of mother and aunt had been reversed with Amanda becoming the unwelcome stranger, supplanted by her sister in Kathleen's wavering affections.

The doctor appeared at the study door and signaled to Ransome. Several minutes later, he returned to the room, his face ashen, his body stooped, and Melissa sprang to her feet and hurried to him.

"What did he say?" she demanded, clutching his hand as he leaned heavily against her.

"It's just as we'd feared," he moaned, his tears flowing unchecked between the newly carved ridges in his handsome face. "Kathleen will never walk again."

Melissa remained long enough for him to steady himself and then she headed for the door. Bolting upstairs and running down the corridor, she burst into Kathleen's room glimpsing the pale face which seemed to have grown smaller, its last hope of life gone, seeming to collapse her inward toward a grieving soul and leaving behind only a thin and brittle shell.

"I suppose you've heard," came the muted voice from the living specter in the bed. "Well, I guess I won't be needing a riding instructor anymore, will I, Melissa?" A sob caught in her throat and her lower lip quavered as she tried to halt her tears. "Oh God, why couldn't I have died? How can I spend the rest of my life as a cripple, an invalid, someone that nobody will ever want?" As she cried, she began to beat her useless legs with her fists, hammering at them until Melissa ran over to the bed and grabbed Kathleen's wrists. She held her hands against her own chest, waiting for the girl's choking sobs to subside.

"Kathleen," she whispered, her own voice catching, "I am so sorry, so very sorry." She kissed the twisting hands of the writhing girl and gently placed them back against the coverlet. "Kathleen, I know it must all seem so hopeless to you now, but you can learn to begin again and fill your life with new meaning. You may never be able to ride again but you can still train and breed your own horses, and watch them wear your colors at the races. Oh Kathleen, there are still so many things you can do."

"But what man will want me now?" she wailed. "Calvin hasn't dared show his face around here since it all happened." Her thin body shuddered convulsively. "But you know, Melissa, I'm glad he hasn't come around because I don't think I could bear to look at him again. What a fool I've been," she whispered as her body was wracked with sobs once more and she looked plaintively up at Melissa through her glimmering tears. "Who will ever want me now?"

"Someone who loves you, Kathleen, I promise," Melissa answered, hoping in her heart that it was true, thinking then of Edward Gabriel and wondering if his love was strong enough to still want Kathleen Ransome. She eased herself from the bed and wearily sought the privacy of her own room, knowing that the time had come at last to plan her own course of action.

As she stared moodily out the window at the manicured lawns and the rolling hills, she thought wistfully of how she had come to regard Laurel Hill as home. But because of the cruel blow dealt Kathleen, her own peace had shattered. She would have to leave her second home just as she had been forced to leave her first. Then she thought of Calvin Gabriel, smiling, swaggering, loving her in brief interludes stolen from the turbulent world around them. Her body ached with the familiar sense of longing that the mere thought of him awakened in her. She knew that with the passage of time, his affair with Amanda would cease to hold any meaning for her, for she had come to understand the loneliness which must have driven them together so long ago. Sighing, she turned away from the window, startled to find her cheeks wet with tears, their salty taste bitter on her tongue.

chapter 24

Two nights later, Melissa was surprised by the sound of hoofbeats pounding to a halt before the front portico. By the time she reached the window, whoever it was had already dismounted, and in the dim light thrown by the porch lamps, she did not recognize the horse. She wondered who could possibly be calling at such a late hour—a visitor from the city, somebody from one of the neighboring estates, or perhaps it was Calvin at last. She waited until she could no longer contain her curiosity, then she stole along the corridor and crept silently down the staircase. Pausing at the bottom, she realized that the voices were coming from the study. She tiptoed to within earshot of the room in time to catch part of Bryan Ransome's words.

"It's very gallant of you to declare yourself this way, but I wonder if you appreciate the full extent of Kathleen's injuries."

"I do," came the deep male voice, slightly muffled.

"Marrying her would be committing yourself to a life far different from one with a normal woman."

"I'm aware of that," the man answered, stronger this time. Melissa gasped as she recognized him. It was Calvin.

"I hope you are, my boy, because my daughter's been badly hurt in many ways and it will take a great deal of time and patience to convince her that she can still lead a worthwhile life." Ransome paused for a moment before continuing. "I'd be a selfish fool if I didn't try to dissuade you, you know, but you seem to know what you want and I won't argue with the nobility of your intentions."

"Nobility has nothing to do with it. I want the chance to make up to Kathleen what she's lost."

"It's going to take a lot of loving on your part to make her feel you're not marrying her out of just pity. But you can rest assured that you'll have my full support behind you in this." A slight chuckle followed. "If it weren't so late I'd let you speak with Kathleen now, but she has so much trouble getting to sleep that tomorrow. . . ." His voice droned on, but Melissa was no longer listening. With her heart pounding in her chest, she stumbled back to her room. So Calvin was planning to marry Kathleen, to make it up to her, he had said. Melissa's stomach heaved, rebelling against the truth which ripped at her insides. She sagged against the washbasin, retching violently. Spasm after spasm tore at her until she was gasping from the effort of it. Tears slid down her cheeks and into her mouth and she gagged again. As she collapsed weakly onto the floor, the sound of hoofbeats echoed back down the drive, and all she could hear was the thudding of her heart.

She washed her face and rinsed out her mouth, then moved to her bureau, hastily pulling out the small, worn reticule into which she still placed her earnings. Counting out the money she realized that she had collected a goodly sum, enough to provide for herself until she found a position somewhere. Choosing a few simple gowns, a shawl and a pair of shoes, she folded them into a neat pile and wrapped them inside one of her capes. Then she blew out the lamps and sat down on her bed to wait until she was certain everyone was asleep before she dared leave the house.

The prospect of Calvin returning the following day to propose to Kathleen sent a fresh spear of pain knifing

277

through her and she knew that she had to place as much distance as possible between herself and the man she still loved before he married another. And so she sat, waiting in the blackness of her room until she finally opened the door and found the corridor dark, the house asleep at last. Picking up the bulky cape, she moved noiselessly down the stairs and toward the kitchen, where she carefully lifted the latch on the back door and let herself out into the starry night.

She pulled up her long skirts and ran in the direction of the stables. She would take Honey with her and when she reached her destination, wherever that might be, she would wire the Ransomes and tell them where they could find the horse. Making her way toward Honey's stall, she whispered the animal's name and then reached up to stroke her comfortingly so that she would recognize her and follow her quietly. The horse whinnied softly, nuzzling Melissa's outstretched hand, and then allowed herself to be drawn from the protective warmth of the stable. Once they were a safe distance from the house, Melissa swung up onto the horse's silken back, tucking her skirts around her waist and gripping Honey's flank with her bare thighs. Bareback, she rode off into the night, uncertain of her ultimate destination, but relieved to at least be on her way.

Moonlight filtered through the budding branches of the trees, sculpting shadows into writhing phantoms. Honey snickered uneasily as she picked her way cautiously over the rocks and stones, their shapes so familiar by day, but sinister and menacing at night. Melissa soothed the skittish horse with gentling whispers, stroking her neck reassuringly as she urged her forward. A night owl hooted from the depths of a giant oak and as the horse moved on, Melissa could hear the muted scampering of little feet as the tiny night creatures of the forest left the protection of their homes to hunt for food.

Melissa could not guess at the miles they had covered, but her legs had begun to ache from the effort of hugging Honey's sides and her arms were growing stiff and weary from gripping the reins. She blinked her weary eyes and they smarted from the strain of peering into the flickering darkness. Finally in the distance, she spotted a large structure and headed toward it, assuming it to be a barn on one of the estates bordering Laurel Hill's extensive property. As she approached it, the building appeared to be just one in a group of similar structures set far to the rear of a massive stone house. The house was dark and except for the occasional muffled neighing of a horse from within the stables, all was peaceful and still.

She slid from Honey's back and leading the horse gently by the bridle, she walked her to the first of the barns. Opening the door, she tugged Honey inside after her and closed the door again. As the moon slipped out from behind an obscuring cloud, the interior of the structure was lit sufficiently for Melissa to discern the stalls, each one already housing a resting horse. She coaxed Honey down to the far end of the building and tethered her to a wooden post before scooping up some hay and depositing it in front of the weary animal. Then she gathered several armfuls of the clean straw and heaped it together in the corner and untying the cape from her small bundle, she spread it over the prickly mound. Curling herself up on her improvised pallet, Melissa drew the edges of the cloak around her and was instantly asleep.

The echo of footsteps jarred her from her sleep and in the faint glow of a covered oil lamp, Melissa's incredulous stare focused on a gangling man roughly attempting to haul one of the horses from its stall. Burrowing further beneath the covering of her dark cloak, she prayed that the man would be too engrossed in what he was doing to take any notice of her. But she cringed as he suddenly called out to someone apparently positioned outside of the stable.

"Hey Luke, did he say to take the chestnut too?" His twanging drawl sliced the silence.

"Keep yer damn voice down, will ya, before we both get caught and hung," rasped an angry voice from outside. "Yeah, take the chestnut too. He's in the last stall there, Now git a move on."

Melissa crouched beneath her cape as she watched the man sauntering toward her. At first he seemed unaware of her presence, but as he battled with the horse who had reared up on his hind legs in an attempt to ward off the intruder, the man backed off and tripped over Melissa's huddled form. She immediately scrambled out from under the cloak and started for the door but her legs were pulled out from under her and she was sent sprawling to the floor.

"Well, well, lookie here," chortled the man, his grip tightening like a vise.

"Let me go," Melissa snarled, scratching at the man's filthy hands in an attempt to break his ironlike hold on her. She bucked and kicked but he held her fast as he shifted his position slightly, throwing his full weight on top of her and knocking the wind from her body.

"Wanna play, do ya?" he puffed, straining to pin her arms down. "Ain't ya the nasty little fighter though."

"What the hell's goin' on in here," came an exasperated cry as another man raced toward the two forms grappling in the straw. "What ya got there, Silas?" And the flickering lamp was held up to Melissa's face.

"Looks like we found ourselves a little filly, huh, Luke?" the man called Silas snickered. As he clambered off Melissa he tugged her to her feet beside him. She fought unsuccessfully with him again until he finally managed to capture her arms, yanking them behind her back and holding them there.

"Fights like a reg'lar tiger, don't she, Silas?" the other man chuckled as he stuck a long piece of straw into his mouth and began chewing pensively on it as he studied Melissa's tumbled beauty.

"What should we do with her, Luke?" he asked, wrenching Melissa's arms as she tried once more to wriggle free.

"We got no choice but to finish her off here," he grunted, still chewing on the straw, "or take her with us."

"Please just leave me here," Melissa panted as she squirmed in Silas's arms, "I know no one around here so how can I possibly be a threat to you?"

"She's got a point there, Luke, that there horse must be hers and there's a bundle of clothes tied up near them stacks."

"Nope, too risky." Luke shook his head and spat out of the side of his mouth. "What's a lady doin' runnin' around in the middle of the night fer anyways?" he demanded. "I say we bring her along and let the boss decide, that way he can't be blamin' us fer nothin'."

"Guess yer right," Silas conceded. "We better tie her up good and blindfold her. Can't have her knowin' too much, now can we?"

But Melissa viciously kicked out at him and his grasp loosened as he doubled over in pain. She threw her weight against the second man, catching him off guard, and sprinted for the door. But Luke recovered his balance and lunged for her, sending them both toppling to the straw-covered floor.

"Git a rope and be quick about it," he barked at Silas, "and let's git the hell outa here before we wake up the place."

They bound her hands behind her back and tied her ankles together with thick rope before stuffing a dirty handkerchief into her mouth. Then they wrapped a scarf around her head, covering her eyes. They carried her outside where she was flung sideways across the back of a horse. The horses sprang forward and she began to jounce painfully up and down as they moved,

281

her body lurching about precariously.

After what seemed to be hours of traveling and many miles spent being bumped and tossed about, the horses were slowed to a walk. One of the men called out to the other and the horse beneath Melissa's sagging body halted as a gate was unlatched and the animal started forward again, its feet scuffing against wooden boards, angling upward into what she presumed was another stable. As the horse stopped once more, Melissa was dragged from its back and her legs untied, the blindfold removed. Dazedly she looked around, squinting in the light of the oil lamps, viewing a newly constructed stable, watching helplessly as the stolen horses were led into the empty stalls.

"Git a move on there, girly," came the harsh snarl of Luke who prodded her in the back and pushed her out of the stable and into the faint pink light of dawn. Before she could study her surroundings, she was forced toward a large brick house which looked vaguely familiar to her.

As she was shoved rudely through the back door and into the kitchen, hurrying footsteps echoed across the bare wooden floor and a voice called out, "Everything go as we planned, Luke?"

"Yeah, boss, except we brung ya a little surprise," the surly man replied. "We caught us a mean little filly campin' out in the stable when me and Silas went to fetch them horses."

"What the hell. . . ." The exclamation died on the man's lips as Melissa looked into the ferretlike face of Enton Perry. The little man threw back his head and squealed with laughter. "Well, if it isn't Miss Melissa come a-calling." As he laughed, Melissa choked on the anger seething within her and she struggled against the bonds holding her, yearning to strike the hateful man leering at her, enjoying her humiliation.

"Hold her tight there, Luke, we wouldn't want our first houseguest to leave before we've shown her how hospitable we can be." He signaled the man to remove the gag from her mouth and bring her into another room. Prodded forward into a half-furnished study, Melissa angrily faced the smirking Mr. Perry.

"I demand to be released immediately," she blurted out as soon as the rag had been pulled from her mouth. In answer to her outcry, Perry thrust her roughly into a chair and eyed her craftily.

"I don't think you're in any position to demand anything, my dear Miss Howell," he remarked, his arms folded across his narrow chest as he leaned back against a large mahogany desk. "Luke," he snapped to the man still standing there, "how did you come upon the lady here?" he asked, and when Luke had hastily related what had taken place in the stable, Perry bellowed angrily, "You blundering idiot, you left her horse and clothing behind?" His lean face was contorted with rage and his hazel eyes glittered menacingly. "What do you have for brains, you imbecile."

"I'm sorry, boss." The man's head was bowed in contrition, "I guess me and Silas was so worried about her makin' a fuss that we jes' wanted to git them two horses outa there before she woke up the whole place."

"Well, it's too late to do anything about it now," Perry fumed, "but you'd better hope that nobody there recognizes her horse and starts snooping around asking a lot of questions." He shook his head in bewilderment. "The first job like this we try and there's already been a foul up. All right, Luke, get out of here." Perry turned his attention to Melissa who, during the entire altercation, had been listening attentively, attempting to make some sense of it all.

"Well, young lady, it looks like you and me are finally going to have that chance to get acquainted after all." He grinned at her. "But it was too bad I had to wait so long." He leaned forward, arrogantly studying her, before he ran the tip of his forefinger across one of her breasts, sending a shiver of revulsion through her. "I

283

guess I'll just have to be a bit patient with you until you get used to me," he smirked, and she squirmed as far back as she could in the chair. But he reached out and tugged a handful of her tousled curls, pulling her face close to his.

"As I said before, young lady, you're in no position to act so high and mighty with me anymore. I'm the one in control of things here." Before she could turn her head, he kissed her harshly, his breath reeking of stale tobacco, his tongue stabbing at her clenched teeth, forcing them open under its pressure until she thought she would be sick. When he drew back his head, his eyes smoldering as they raked her body, she worked a globule of saliva together and spat it full into his startled face. He swiped angrily at his wet cheek and then he slapped her viciously with his open palm, the force of which snapped her head painfully to the side, a red splotch instantly staining her tender skin.

"That's the last time I warn you about your manners, bitch. The next time you try something like that, I might not be such a gentleman."

"A gentleman?" she raged, blazing with indignation. "You are nothing but a sniveling coward, striking a woman, especially one whose hands are tied behind her back." He seemed about to slap her again, but he stayed the blow, and Melissa wondered if the evil little man had something more lethal in mind.

"We'll call it a draw for now, but your battle with me is far from over," he declared, taking the soiled handkerchief and stuffing it back into her mouth despite her strangled protests. "We'll just silence you until you get a more civil tongue in that pretty head of yours. Garth!" he roared then, walking over to the study door as a large, powerfully built man lumbered in. "Show our guest to a bedroom upstairs, the one next to mine to be precise, and lock her in." And he left the room as Melissa cowered in the chair, regarding the approaching giant who picked her up in his massive arms as if she were a doll.

Opening the door to a small, freshly-painted bedroom, he threw her down on the bed and withdrew, locking the door from the outside as Perry had instructed. Melissa tried to loosen the ropes cutting into her wrists, but they refused to give. Tears of frustration stung her eyes as she struggled with the stubborn bonds and soon she gave up, concentrating instead on the unfurnished room with its bare white walls and uncovered windows. The only piece of furniture was the bed; the only other objects filling the starkness were a porcelain chamber pot and a porcelain pitcher and basin, all set down on the freshly waxed and polished floor. Obviously Perry had only begun to furnish the house, preferring instead to concentrate first on the stables and the stealing of other people's horses. In despair Melissa wondered whose stables the men had plundered and who would claim the money and the clothing and the beloved horse she had been forced to leave behind there.

The sound of the lock turning interrupted Melissa's musings, and Perry sauntered into the room. A cold shiver tingled down her spine as he approached her, but she forced herself to appear calm, biding her time until she could either cajole her way out of his clutches or plot some means of escape for herself when he least expected it.

"I thought I'd check to see how our guest is enjoying her accommodations here." He smiled thinly, perusing her huddled form. The skirt of her gown rode high on her shapely legs, her breasts thrust against the tight bodice, their fullness accentuated by her arms pinned behind her back. "I apologize for the lack of suitable furnishings, but we weren't expecting houseguests quite this soon."

He sat down on the bed beside her, his rough-skinned hand running up her calf and along her thigh causing her to flinch. But again she forced herself to lie still.

285

"Such a beautiful woman," he muttered, his voice thickening as he continued his exploration. Then he stopped, resting his open palm on one of her firm buttocks. "Such a change from the spitting cat downstairs, Melissa. Is this some sort of trick or can you really be trusted to remain quiet? I wonder," he mumbled to himself, his hand gradually increasing its pressure until he had succeeded in pinching her flesh so cruelly that her body arched in pain. He chuckled deep in his throat and removed his hand.

"I'm glad to see that you haven't lost all of your marvelous spirit, because nothing bores me more than a compliant woman." He eased himself from the bed and bent over her. "If you think you can behave yourself now, I'll untie those ropes and get rid of that gag." She quickly nodded her head and he smiled his evil grin of smug satisfaction. Then he released her.

She sat up on the bed and straightened her skirt before massaging her aching wrists and tender, abused mouth. She was grimly reminded of Jeremy Ransome and just as he had ultimately been punished, Perry too would pay for his brutal treatment of her. The thought of the little man swinging at the end of a rope for kidnapping and horse stealing brought her a small measure of satisfaction and a tremulous smile warmed her lips. She was suddenly aware of his puzzled scrutiny and her smile vanished. Her eyes became veiled and guarded as she returned his stare.

"How long do you intend to keep me here, Mr. Perry?" she asked him then. He shrugged, looking down at his small hands as the ends of his fingers beat against one another in a steady tapping rhythm.

"That's a bit difficult to answer, I'm afraid," he replied. "You see, my dear Melissa, your stumbling into the midst of our delicate operation has been most unfortunate, for all of us. If we turn you loose now, you'll run straight to the authorities, and we can't afford to let that happen. So, for the moment, there seem to be only two alternatives; either you learn to enjoy our hospitality or—" he shot her a warning glance, his tapping fingers suddenly stilled— "we'll be forced to silence you permanently." His light, speckled eyes flickered briefly and Melissa gulped, her hands unwittingly clutching her throat.

"I see the second alternative doesn't appeal to you," he grunted. "Then I suggest you content yourself as quickly as possible with the first." He headed for the door, pausing as he opened it. "By the way, if you change your mind and decide to leave us, my men have orders to shoot you." With that he closed the door, locking it once more.

Melissa pushed herself from the bed and walked to the window. She opened it and leaned out, searching for some means of escape, either the bough of a tree or an abutment which might provide her with a foothold. But there were no trees near the window and the brick house dropped two stories to the ground without any obvious protrusions to aid her. She chewed at her lower lip in frustration and gazed off into the distance, her eyes skimming the leafing trees on Perry's property and the purplish range of mountain peaks on the horizon. From her vantage point, she could see a portion of the stables where several magnificent horses were being exercised in the paddock alongside the buildings, but nowhere was there anything which might help her.

As the day progressed, Melissa grew increasingly hungry. She tried knocking on the door several times in the hopes of attracting someone's attention, but to no avail. As the sky began to darken, she started banging her fists furiously against the door. She was finally rewarded by footsteps stamping up the stairs and along the corridor toward her room. Backing away from the door, she stood near the bed as the giant bulk of Garth stormed into the room and scowled down at her.

"It must be dinner time." Melissa spoke up haughtily before the man could open his mouth. "I hope Mr. Perry plans to feed me."

"The boss didn't say nothin' to me about your eatin'," he grumbled, his voice like a roll of thunder in his massive chest. "Jes' a minute." He closed and locked the door again and she heard his heavy tread rattling back down the hallway.

She was staring out of the window when he returned, motioning for her to follow him. Keeping at a safe distance from the man as they descended the stairs, she trailed after him into a large dining room. Perry immediately rose and assisted Melissa into a chair at one end of a long mahogany table and she shuddered as his hands lingered on her shoulders. Astounded by the formal place settings of fine china and silver, Melissa gazed wonderingly about the room. It was completely furnished, and with its original oil paintings, gold framed mirror, and large, sparkling chandelier, it appeared to be an exact duplicate of the dining room at Laurel Hill. Noting her amazement with gloating satisfaction, Perry's chest seemed to swell with pride.

"Do you think I've done a fair job of reproducing your former residence?" he inquired.

"You must have taken extensive notes on your visits there," she remarked cuttingly.

"Mrs. Ransome was a most obliging hostess and she seemed especially eager to make up for your own lack of manners," he returned sarcastically. "I'm working on completing the parlor now, and when that's done, I'll open my house to the families around here for some of the fanciest shindigs this county has ever seen."

"I doubt that your clever imitations will ever bring you the acceptance you crave, Mr. Perry," she stated frostily. "Breeding is something you can never buy."

His face livid, Perry slammed his wineglass down, shattering its delicate stem and showering the table and the pale green carpet with red wine.

"Do you see what I mean?" she remarked, her voice

icy with loathing.

A young girl, dressed in the starched uniform of a serving maid, scampered into the dining room as Perry bellowed for assistance. As she stooped to clean the spreading stain on the thick plush carpet, Perry pushed back his chair and strode to where Melissa sat watching him with cold amusement. Clasping her slender neck between his two bony hands, he tightened his grip until she gasped for air.

"Don't let me catch you laughing at me again," he threatened, "I could snap your neck in two right now if I had a mind to. But I promise you this, you'll pay for your little joke." He flung her back against the chair and ambled back to the head of the table.

Melissa rubbed her throbbing throat, swallowing with difficulty as she kept her eyes averted. She dared not look at the repulsive man opposite her who gulped contentedly at his thin, tasteless soup. Melissa touched a spoon to her lips and sipped at the soup, hastily returning the spoon to the bowl and staring dejectedly into the cloudy mixture. She fared no better with the rest of the meal, stabbing helplessly at the overcooked beef and managing only a forkful of the waterlogged carrots. As Perry cleaned his plate and finished two bottles of wine by himself, he belched loudly and wiped at the grease mottling his face with a white linen napkin. Melissa winced at his deplorable manners and as he pushed himself back from the table, he absently dabbed at the food stains on his shirtfront. Seeing her chance, Melissa hastily rose from her chair and headed for the doorway.

"Just where do you think you're going?" he demanded, tottering slightly on his short legs.

"Back to my room," she answered crisply. He muttered something under his breath as she raced for the stairs, running up them with skirts held high and tearing down the uncarpeted hallway to her bedroom. Pulling the key from the lock, she slammed the door and locked it from the inside. It was not long before Perry was at the door, angrily twisting the knob. As he cursed and shouted, she covered her ears with her hands, blocking out his foul obscenities, praying that he would not attempt to break down the door and punish her for defying him. When she finally uncovered her ears, it was quiet, but the peace was short-lived as Perry's roaring voice began to shout at her once more.

"You won't keep me out forever, Melissa," he cried. "But you're damned lucky that I just finished paying good money to have those doors built right, otherwise I'd kick the hell out of yours and break it down."

When it was still once more, she undressed in the dark and stretched out across the hard bed. Despite the stiffness of the new sheets, they were clean and fresh and she wriggled about in an effort to find a more comfortable position for her bone-weary body. Gradually accustoming herself to the strangeness of her new surroundings, she closed her eyes against the moonlight streaming in through the uncurtained window and allowed her thoughts to drift. Floating toward the peace of welcoming slumber, she felt herself being gathered into Calvin's embrace, and with him holding her, she fell asleep.

chapter 25

Melissa awoke with a start, uncertain of where she was until the bareness of the room reminded her. She quickly dressed and unlocked the bedroom door. Slipping the key into the pocket of her gown, she hastened down the stairs. Finding Garth eating in the large, bright kitchen, she immediately asked him for a lamp and a bar of soap and some towels. The large man merely grimaced at her and continued eating his enormous breakfast of eggs, cured ham and hot scones, while Melissa stood there gazing angrily at him, her hands on her hips, and her eyes flashing. With a snort of disgust, she spun on her heel and stormed about the house until she located the young maid busily dusting the furniture in the dining room. Approaching the girl with the same request, she was met with a blank look as the freckle-faced youngster shifted uneasily from one foot to the other.

"You'll have to ask Mr. Perry, miss, he says that nobody's to do nothing without first asking him," she mumbled, staring down at her red, work-worn hands.

"Then could you please tell me where I might find Mr. Perry?" Melissa asked, her patience wearing thin.

"He's out in one of the paddocks with the horses, miss," she replied in a faint voice, turning away and continuing her chores. Exasperated, Melissa swept from the room and headed for the kitchen again, ignoring Garth who was still consuming his meal, and flung open the back door to step out onto the newly landscaped terrace. She had just begun to make her way across the grass when she heard a rifle being cocked behind her. Whirling about, she turned to face the lanky figure of Silas who was lounging casually against the brick wall of the house, his gun pointed directly at her.

"Put that thing down," she ordered, "I was just on my way to find Mr. Perry."

"I'll take ya to him then," he answered, spitting out of the side of his mouth and bending over to pluck a long stem of grass which he then proceeded to chew on. She turned away in revulsion as he sauntered over to her. "Jes' follow me," he said, and he swaggered off ahead of her.

They walked toward the paddock Melissa had viewed from the bedroom window and as she neared it, she could see Perry and several hands busily leading a stud to a mare most obviously in heat. She recognized the stallion as the large chestnut stolen from the stable the previous morning, and an image of Perry's operations began to take shape in her mind. Reaching the wooden railing, she called out to him but he impatiently waved her away, returning his attention to the task at hand. But she refused to be intimidated and shouted out her requests, pleased to have him snarl back, "Silas, get her the hell out of here and give her whatever she wants."

"Sure thing, Mr. Perry," the man called back, chewing steadily on the length of grass and motioning Melissa back in the direction of the house again.

When she reluctantly descended for dinner that night, she nervously patted the key hidden in her pocket, wondering if she would again be able to evade Perry's forced attentions. Her hair was washed and sweet smelling, her body warmly tingling from the luxury of a long bath and a vigorous toweling. She was relaxed and refreshed, but she was nonetheless wary of the man already seated at the dining room table. This time he did not rise as she entered, seeming quite oblivious to her presence, a fact which both pleased and worried her, for she feared that this apparent disinterest was merely a clever ploy to catch her off guard.

As she stared glumly at the stringy chicken and the lumpy mashed potatoes floating about in a heavy gravy on her dinner plate, she smiled wryly. If Enton Perry expected to entertain his wealthy neighbors and impress them with his worldliness, he would do well to hire himself a proper cook.

"The food not to your liking?" he remarked snidely from the opposite end of the table as he watched her toying with the hapless chicken.

"To be perfectly frank, no," she replied, staring boldly at him, seeing him flinch under her honest criticism. He looked up as Silas came striding into the room and bent down to whisper into his ear. A red flush of anger spread across Perry's features and he pounded the table with his fist. The wineglass tottered dangerously but it did not tip as his hand shot out and righted it. He waved Silas off with a muttered oath and began to mumble under his breath, his fingers agitatedly tapping against the top of the table.

"Of all the damned stupid things to go and happen now," he grumbled. "One of my mares is sick and it's me that'll have to tend her."

"Why not send for a horse doctor?" Melissa suggested, reaching for her glass of wine.

"And take the chance of having someone nosing around with those other horses stabled here? Not on your life, lady," he barked. "But then you'd like that, wouldn't you? Maybe you'd think up some way of getting out of here."

"Just why did you steal those horses, Mr. Perry?" she asked then, anxious to diffuse his rising temper.

"Because they're two of the best studs around and I

293

wanted them. Damn, but I wanted them," he growled, his brows knitting together in a sullen frown, "but at the auction, every time I bid, the bastard raised me, as if he had to prove to everyone that he was better than me, and that an outsider had no right to the best horseflesh around like they did." Then his narrow lips drew back in a malicious grin, his small teeth bared like the fangs of a deadly predator, "But I'll show him, I'll show all of them. Twin Oaks will be the stable to beat, the one all those high and mighty folks will have to pay their respects to."

"But there are other studs," Melissa interrupted, puzzled by the man's outraged determination.

"Not like those two," he retorted, his eyes gleaming, "and I'm in a hurry, Miss Howell, a damned big hurry to get the best as fast as I can."

"Stealing horses is a rather serious offense, Mr. Perry, or had you overlooked that fact?" she goaded him.

"I don't consider what we've done to be horse stealing, my dear," he answered coolly. "I've merely borrowed their services for awhile, and once they've served their purpose, I'll simply return them. I have several magnificent thoroughbreds being groomed right now for the stakes in New York, so that with my winnings, I'll be able to match any man's price next year." His eyes hardened craftily then as he continued. "I had some mares crazy in heat and the studs I wanted for them belonged to someone else, so you can appreciate how badly I needed them, can't you?" He glared at her as if awaiting affirmation for his actions, but she refused to dignify him with a response.

His mouth settled into a grim line as he rose from the table. "You may breathe easier, my dear Melissa, for you've won yourself a reprieve tonight. You can sleep undisturbed while I content myself with a pile of straw and a sick horse for company."

Melissa snickered at his remark and followed him

into the hallway. "Out of curiosity, Mr. Perry, whose horses have you borrowed for your mares?" she emphasized the word borrowed and watched his expression harden again. "Do I know the stable?" she persisted, wondering at his sudden reticence.

"You should," came the grudging reply. "Young Gabriel is a neighbor of yours, too. At least he was until you decided to run away." He finished with a peal of raucous laughter as he spun on his heel and headed for the stables.

Melissa stood there stunned, the room suddenly spinning before her eyes. She reached blindly for the doorframe and sagged against it. Calvin. She had been on Calvin's land that night, sleeping in one of his stables, and had never known it. With a bitter cry, she stumbled upstairs to her room, fumbling awkwardly with the lock because of the tears blurring her sight.

As she came downstairs for breakfast the following morning, she heard Perry and one of the other men locked in a vicious argument in the front hall. Unaware of her presence, they continued their heated words.

"And you was so sure he'd already left Stony Briar," the man, whom she realized was Silas, was shouting.

"How the hell was I to know his father would have another one of his damned seizures!" yelled Perry, his face purple with rage. "He'd told me himself he was leaving with his horses for New York."

"Well, his stayin' ain't none of my doin'," retorted Silas.

"And I suppose leaving her damned horse and all her clothes behind there wasn't any of your doing either, you fool!" Perry thundered, raising a fist and swinging at the other man. Silas blocked the weak punch in midair and grabbed hold of Perry's arm.

"I ain't no fool," he snarled, "and don't ya' go raisin' yer hand to me agin unless ya want it broke fer ya." He shoved Perry aside and thudded past him. It was then that Perry noticed Melissa, standing silently on the bottom step.

"What the hell are you gawking at?" he shouted. At her hesitation, he bellowed, "I asked you a question!"

"I was simply curious about what was going on," she answered tartly.

"Well, you heard what happened. Gabriel never left for New York like he said he was," he complained, nervously tugging at his gun belt. "Here I am, up half the night with that blasted horse and now I'm greeted with this piece of news. I'd figured that with him out of the way, if anybody came poking around here, I could handle them easily enough. But with him still at home, I might be in for some real trouble. Damn!" he muttered, raking his fingers through his light brown hair. "And the worst of it is, he's offering a thousand dollar reward for information leading to the return of the horses. The whole blasted county will be in on it now." Cursing his luck, he stormed off.

Melissa spent the day wandering around the property with either Luke or Silas constantly in attendance. She felt like a caged animal, prowling restlessly about, stalked by a man with a deadly rifle slung across his shoulder, waiting for her to break away and attempt to escape. But she stilled her mounting anxiety, biding her time, knowing that her chance would eventually come.

Toward evening, as Melissa fidgeted about in her room, she again overheard Perry and Silas shouting vehemently at one another. As the back door slammed, she scampered to the window in time to see Silas striding toward the stables. Dismissing the incident from her thoughts, she left her room only to stop outside the door with a startled exclamation of dismay. A burly man, a thin cheroot dangling from his lips, sat tipped back in a chair against the wall, a rifle resting carelessly across his lap. He threw her a long, appraising look as she gathered her skirts about her and sailed haughtily down the corridor, anxious to confront her host.

"I could hear you and Silas arguing again," she remarked casually to Perry as she settled herself at the table. He scowled at her, soup trickling onto his chin as he lifted his head.

"That idiot; if I weren't worried about him talking, I'd send him packing tonight."

"Why is there a man guarding my room?" she asked then, affecting indifference as she dug her hand into her pocket and tightly clutched the key to her bedroom door.

"I've decided not to take any chances, that's why," he snapped and continued slurping his soup with loud, smacking noises. Melissa grimaced and idly pushed her spoon back and forth in the brimming bowl, loathe to attempt even a mouthful of the lukewarm liquid.

Perry finally broke the silence. "I told Luke and Silas and I might as well tell you now," he began. "We're taking the horses back tonight. I can't be certain my mares have been bred but with Gabriel still around I can't take the chance and keep them here as long as I'd originally intended." He paused and poured himself a glass of wine, downing it thirstily. "And for added insurance, dear Melissa, you'll be coming along with us."

"But why?" she gasped incredulously.

"As I said, if things get a little rough, you'll come in handy."

"I refuse to be any part of this," she cried, rising from her chair, sending it crashing to the floor. But Perry was instantly on his feet, a small revolver appearing in his hand.

"Put the bedroom key on the table, please," he ordered, his voice icily controlled as he began walking toward her. "We wouldn't want you to try locking yourself in again. Not tonight anyways. Now put it on the table." Reluctantly she withdrew the key and sent it clattering onto the table top. But he kept walking toward her. She backed away from him until she felt the wall at her back and she stiffened, watching his glittering eyes as he pressed the barrel of the gun against her chest.

"You're far too beautiful to die, my dear, so I caution you to do exactly as I say. Go upstairs, leave your door open, and wait until I send for you." He refused to back away and allow her to pass, so that as she fled the room, she was forced against his wiry body, its insistent pressure sending a shudder of repugnance coursing through her.

She paced the room for hours. The guard had shifted his chair so that he sat directly in the open doorway, calmly puffing on his cigar, disdainfully flicking the ashes onto the floor, and watching her, his eyes never leaving her. Desperately devising one escape plan after another and promptly discarding them all, she seethed with frustration and anger as the night wore on. Flinging herself across the bed, she lay there until the guard thumped into the room and prodded her with the long barrel of the rifle he was carrying.

"Here, put them clothes on and be quick about it," he ordered gruffly, tossing a bundle onto the bed beside her.

"Must you stare at me all the time?" Melissa snapped irritably as the man lingered beside the bed. "I would appreciate some privacy, so either close the door behind you or be so kind as to turn your back."

The man grinned insolently at her and shuffled back to his post at the door. Settling himself once more in his chair, he pulled out a fresh cheroot, bit off the end and held a lighted match to the tip, puffing slowly and deliberately as his eyes caressed Melissa's rigid form. In exasperation, she snatched up the clothes, blew out the oil lamp and retreated into the darkest corner of the room to change.

Hastily shedding her gown and slippers, she pulled on a pair of black trousers and tucked them into a pair of large midcalf boots. Then she shrugged on a man's wool shirt and piling her long hair on top of her head, she managed to force it all underneath a battered stetson hat and tighten the cord under her chin. She was painfully reminded of a similar masquerade which had seen her clothed as a rangy seaman. She shivered apprehensively as Enton Perry called out to her.

"Are you ready yet?" he shouted from the doorway into the dark bedroom. "Get out here now, Melissa," he barked when she failed to respond immediately. She stepped from the shadowed corner and walked over to him. He caught her arm and forced her ahead of him as they moved along the corridor, down the stairs, and out through the kitchen into the summer night.

Outside the stables, Perry ordered her to mount up. As she did, she noticed that burlap sacks had been tied around the hooves of the horses to muffle their hoof-beats as they rode. Luke and Silas each gripped the lead of one of the stolen animals while Perry laid a heavy shotgun across the pommel of his saddle and trained it directly on Melissa.

"Everyone will have been asleep for hours by the time we reach Stony Briar, but if there's the slightest sign of trouble afoot, leave the horses and hightail it out of there," he instructed his men, then stared hard at Melissa. "I'll be keeping an eye on you, missy, and if you give us any problems at all, I'll make good on my promise to quiet you once and for all." His mouth twisted into a taunting smile. "But if it all goes the way it should, you and I are going to catch up on the nights we've missed out on." With a sharp burst of derisive laughter, he nudged his horse forward, signaling the small party to follow him.

They rode in tense silence through the dark night. The gibbous moon peeked out occasionally from behind its cover of clouds, and Melissa stiffened at the slightest sound, at every moving shadow which caught her eye. She could taste fear in the dryness of her throat and feel it in the painful thumping of her heart. Trickles of perspiration coursed down her skin and her arms began to tremble from her taut grip on the reins. Checking her horse's movements, keeping in cautious step with the others near her, she made her way toward Stony Briar in the early hours of the morning.

No one dared speak and the enforced stillness hung heavily among them, transmitting itself to the sensitive mounts they rode. Branches snapped underfoot, low-hanging foliage scraped past them, brushing spindly tips against their bodies. They splashed through a narrow stream and Melissa caught her breath as her horse slipped on a moss-covered rock and faltered momentarily. She urged him on and sighed with relief as he regained his footing and picked his way slowly up the opposite bank. A tentative beam of moonlight illuminated the path ahead of them and then a cloud swallowed up the silver rays, blotting out its feeble glow and plunging the woodland into inky blackness.

They rode into a vast clearing and Perry motioned for them to stop. He pointed straight ahead of him and in another faint glimmer of moonlight, Melissa could discern the outlines of several similar buildings. The stables, she reasoned, and her pulse quickened, knowing that Calvin Gabriel lay sleeping not far from her and that he would never know how close she had been to him. They nudged their animals forward again, making their way toward the stables. Melissa glanced over at Silas as he seemed to fall back, allowing Perry and Luke to assume the lead together.

She had only an instant to question his move for as they reached the stables, the doors were flung open, the glare of a dozen torches split the night and men on foot and on horseback seemed to appear from everywhere. Horses shied and whinnied, a shot rang out and Melissa crouched low in the saddle as Perry emitted a blood curdling scream and spurred his horse forward, his shotgun blazing. Luke dropped the reins of the stolen horse and reached for his rifle but he was cut down in a hail of bullets before he could fire a shot. Silas seemed to have vanished and in the glowing light and the careening figures all around her, Melissa kicked at her horse, tugging frantically at the reins and heading him toward the large stone house.

"One of them's getting away," a man shouted.

"I'll get him," yelled another and Melissa could hear the pounding of hooves close behind her. Terror urged her on, fueled by the fear that at any moment she too would be shot. She galloped furiously onward in a last desperate bid to reach the house and throw herself on Calvin's mercy. Tears blinded her as she rode and as she neared the house and slowed her pace, she glanced back over her shoulder just as the figure on the horse behind her sprang from the saddle and tackled her in a flying embrace. They thudded heavily to the ground, Melissa's body cushioned in its fall by the man beneath her.

Her hat flew and her hair streamed about her shoulders as she grappled with the man struggling to pin her down.

"My God," the man gasped, "a woman."

But Melissa scarcely heard him as she fought for air. Her breath was coming in painful spurts and the scene before her was growing indistinct, its edges blurring as she strained to retain consciousness. She forced her mouth open in an attempt to speak, but she could not breathe and the man holding her began shouting.

"Calvin, get over here quick. Hurry man, you won't believe your eyes."

The sound of a horse panting to a halt tore Melissa's dimming gaze from the man still clutching her shirt. And the icy stare of Calvin Gabriel was the last thing she saw before she fainted.

Melissa's eyelids fluttered open and her world tipped crazily. Blinking to clear her wavering vision, at last she met his silent, brooding scrutiny and the gray eyes holding hers bored deep into her very soul.

"Well, Melissa, it seems you've gotten yourself into

trouble again," he said as he settled himself into a chair across from the couch on which she was lying. "I'm waiting for some explanation, my dear." His voice was testy and she resented his officious manner.

"I have nothing to say which could possibly interest you," she retaliated.

"On the contrary, Melissa, I'm most curious to find out what turned you from a riding instructor into a horse thief. It couldn't have been the charms of the late Mr. Perry, could it?"

"Perry is dead?" she murmured, her eyes widening.

"You seem distressed, Melissa dear," he sneered. "Could I have misjudged the man's attractiveness then?"

"Don't be absurd," she snapped. "I despised the man. He was really quite mad and would have murdered me without a moment's hesitation."

"And yet you were a part of his operation," Calvin persisted.

"I was not!" she cried, "Perry's men forced me to go with them. But surely you found Honey and all of my clothes in your stable," she babbled, running her hands agitatedly through her hair as she struggled to regain her composure.

"You're right about that part of it anyway," he conceded, his expression still hard.

"How did you learn about his plan to return the horses this morning?" she demanded, and his eyes twinkled as a smile curved his lips.

"Money, my dear, has the power to erase most loyalties," he replied easily, "I simply offered a reward and your friend Silas decided he preferred a quick thousand dollars to the promises of Enton Perry. He rode over here last evening and spilled his guts. And that, my beautiful Melissa, was that."

Stunned by his words, she lay still, her eyes closed, her body suddenly drained, void of all sensation. But her momentary peace was shattered as Calvin nudged her roughly, forcing her back to him, insisting she explain away her participation in Enton Perry's mad scheme. She told him of her three days at Twin Oaks. He listened quietly, without interrupting her once, and when she had completed her tale he sat back in his chair and solemnly nodded his head.

"One more thing," he said, fixing her with his steely gaze. "Why did you run away from Laurel Hill?"

She was ill-prepared for his question and she turned her head away, staring bleakly at the wall. She refused to meet his challenging stare, hugging the truth to herself.

"Melissa," he murmured, his voice hushed. Its gentleness forced her to look at him again. "I couldn't go back there after what happened to Kathleen." She winced at the pain she read in his eyes. "I couldn't face Bryan and have him guess the truth. You understand that, don't you?" She nodded mutely. "You knew, didn't you, Melissa love?" he whispered hoarsely and again she nodded. "But what you didn't know was that Edward asked Kathleen to marry him and she accepted. They were married last night."

Melissa heard nothing more except the furious hammering in her head and the choking sobs she could no longer contain. Edward and Kathleen. Married. Not Calvin and Kathleen. It had been Edward's voice, not Calvin's. Edward all the time. Through her tears she knew that she was smiling and then she was laughing. The laughter echoed harshly in her ears and Calvin watched her cry and laugh until she had no strength left for either. He cradled her in his arms and helped her dry her eyes.

When she was finally calm once more, she pulled free of his embrace and rose shakily from the couch. She lifted her head proudly, raising carefully guarded eyes to his and said, "I would like my clothing back and the use of Honey until I reach some place and find work again." She managed to keep her voice even and gentle as she spoke. "And I would appreciate your keeping this incident from the Ransomes. Please." She turned to leave him.

"I'm afraid it's not quite that simple, Melissa," he replied, blocking her path. "I'm sure that the authorities will want to question you about Perry and I'd hate to be accused of harboring a criminal."

She stared at him dumbfounded. "But I explained what happened," she cried, panic seizing her again. "I am not a criminal and you know that. Why are you trying to frighten me like this?" Her voice was distraught, her attempts at control slowly crumbling.

"You're hardly in a position to argue, Melissa, considering that you stole a horse from the Ransome stables, conspired with Enton Perry to return two animals stolen from my property, and God only knows what else." She was thunderstruck by the change in his tone, the sudden harshness, the cold gruffness as he challenged her. He moved then toward the door and she bolted after him.

"Where are you going?" she whimpered, grabbing hold of his arm.

"I believe the local sheriff is still outside, sorting things out. No doubt he'll want to speak to you now."

"Calvin, please wait," she begged him, clinging to his arm and tugging him toward her.

"How can I prove my innocence?" she whispered, her eyes wide and pleading.

"If what you told me was the truth, you've got nothing to worry about," he replied easily. "But then, considering your part in the Jeremy Ransome business, I don't know how believable you'll be."

"Just what are you trying to tell me?" she demanded, her voice hardening as she dropped her arm from his sleeve. "Are you now insinuating that I helped Jeremy escape, that I willingly acted as his accomplice too?" Her eyes showered him with cutting, golden sparks as, hands on her hips, nostrils flaring, she prepared to fight him.

"Who really knows what happened between you and Jeremy that night?" He shrugged. "Again it's your word against a dead man's. But I have an alternative for you, Melissa. My father is resting comfortably now, and there's a nurse with him all the time, so I'm setting out for New York State tomorrow. Why don't you come with me?" At her disbelieving stare, he chuckled and continued, "I can keep an eye on you then, as a kind of guardian, just to make sure that you stay out of trouble for a while." He returned her smoldering gaze. "Who knows, you might even snare yourself a permanent guardian from among the swarms of eager young men you'll undoubtedly attract up there."

"I think I would prefer to speak to the sheriff, thank you," she returned frostily and started for the door.

"Don't be a fool, Melissa. Do you want to go to prison?" he barked.

"I doubt I shall go to prison," she spat, "I think you have been twisting everything around to suit your own ends as usual. Why are you suddenly so concerned with my welfare when you showed not the slightest interest in it before? Is it because Edward married Kathleen, or is it because you grew tired of Amanda and are casting about for some replacement?" Her voice was rising steadily, growing high-pitched and shrill as she taunted him.

"What is it you want then," he shouted, "wedding bells and vows and love till death us do part? Kathleen always knew Edward wanted to marry her but she decided to amuse herself with me when she knew damned well I'd never have her."

"Then go back to Amanda," she cried. "Let her be your whore again, for that is one role I shall never play for you." He slapped her then, catching her by surprise, knocking the breath from her as she stumbled backward, losing her balance. Regaining her footing, she came at him, aiming a blow for his head. He deflected

305

her arm, but with her other hand she clawed at his face, her nails drawing blood as they raked across his cheek. Seizing her arms, he pinned them behind her and smothering her body with the force of his, he hauled her up against him and crushed his lips to hers. She bit his lower lip and he drew back sharply. She tossed her head from side to side, refusing his mouth access to hers again. Tiny drops of blood trickled down his chin and onto her cheeks as he battled her.

He sought the vulnerability of her throat, his lips searing her with their heat, sending shivers spinning through her unwilling body. Then he captured her open mouth with his, pressing his tongue against hers, teasing and tickling, probing and withdrawing. Releasing her wrists to encircle her back with his arms, he thrust himself against her, his hardness bruising her yielding warmth. Melissa, weak with desire, melting beneath the determination of his assault, ached to hold him to her and return his kisses with equal ardor, but something held her passion in check. The unbidden image of Calvin and Amanda together floated before her closed eyes. As a wave of revulsion swept through her, she shoved at him with all of her strength and freed herself from his strangling closeness.

Staggering back, breathing heavily, she pushed a fallen strand of coppery hair from her eyes. "I want you to stay away from me, Calvin, and never touch me again," she panted, her voice quivering as he dabbed gingerly at his scratched face with a handkerchief. A lopsided grin was aimed indifferently at her.

"You never objected as strenuously before," he mused, his tone mocking. "But then perhaps someone else has helped you forget our times together." Furious with his insolence, she raised her hand to strike the smirk from his lips, but he easily stayed her blow. "That's quite enough, my little hellcat. As it is I'll bear your scars for some time to come."

"I should do more than scratch you, Calvin Gabriel,"

she seethed, wrenching her arm from his grasp.

"I pity the man who marries you, Melissa love," he scoffed, "for your tongue and claws will keep him constantly on his guard and leave little time for anything else." She turned her back to him and flounced back to the couch again, where she sat down with a dispirited sigh.

"Your time is running out, Melissa," his voice suddenly crackled, causing her to start. "Either you decide to come with me or I turn you over to the sheriff right now. I've no time left for games." He began walking toward her, his steps slow and deliberate as he paced them with his words. "Consider this before you make your decision, Melissa dear. Silas has disappeared with his reward money and both Perry and Luke are dead, so there's no one left to corroborate your story. As the mistress of a thieving opium smuggler, what are your chances of being believed?"

His words lashed at her cruelly, weighted as they were with scorn and contempt. She buried her face in her hands, humiliated by his accusations, terrified that he might indeed be correct and that she would never be able to exonerate herself. She finally turned a stricken, tear-stained face up to her tormentor and admitted her defeat.

"I will come with you," she whispered, lowering her head again before he could see the hatred written on her face.

"A wise choice, love, a very wise choice indeed," he answered as he stood over her huddled form. "Now don't you think we should seal our little agreement?" And he lowered himself onto the couch next to her and pressed her back against the cold leather. She lay limply beneath him as he tore at his clothes and ripped away the trousers she still wore. He took her coldly and dispassionately, oblivious to her pain and the tears which coursed unchecked down her cheeks.

PART THREE

New York 1886—1887

chapter 26

Melissa and Calvin were comfortably settled in a small hotel on Long Island near the Belmont Park racetrack. Calvin's four thoroughbreds were stabled on the premises and he daily supervised their rigorous training, clocking their running times, enforcing a strict regimen for their feeding and currying, and generally keeping a watchful eye on their handling. The four jockeys, carefully chosen for their ability, deftly schooled their high-spirited mounts, patiently working alongside the trainers to mold the horses and themselves into smoothly coordinated teams.

Calvin had made no further attempts to touch Melissa or even spend much time with her since their arrival at the hotel two weeks earlier. They had registered under separate names and maintained seperate bedrooms. Although Calvin was polite and courteous when they were together, he remained aloof and somewhat withdrawn. Several other horse owners were staying at the hotel, but they kept to themselves, their wives maintaining a discreet distance from the fiery-haired young woman and her brooding companion whose relationship was so blatantly questionable. Melissa lived in enforced isolation, wandering bleakly about the hotel grounds and idly watching the training of Calvin's horses.

One night over dinner, Melissa turned to Calvin in

exasperation. "I shall go mad if I continue to do nothing more than stare at your blasted animals each day and endure the snubs of every woman here." Calvin calmly set his fork down and studied her as she raved on. She caught the glint of temper in his gray eyes but chose to ignore its warning. "You pay no attention to me whatsoever and I find your manners deplorable."

"Why, is there something wrong with the way I eat, Melissa?" he teased, the flash of anger replaced by a spark of humor in his gaze.

"You know perfectly well what I mean," she fumed. "You treat me as if I were nothing but an inconvenience. Need I remind you that it was your idea to bring me here with you?"

"But I never promised you constant amusement, dear Melissa," he countered. "I simply thought that if I kept you out of mischief long enough, you'd lure some eligible fish into your net and release me from my duties. But so far, you've disappointed me completely." His brows knitted together in a frown. "You seem totally oblivious to everyone around you, and that worries me a bit because I had no intention of playing guardian to you forever."

"I never wanted you for a guardian, Calvin Gabriel," she snapped, flinging her own fork down in disgust.

"What role would you have me play then, since you've already told me that I fail even as a lover?"

A slow flush stained her honeyed skin and she shifted uncomfortably in her chair. He leaned back in his seat, seeming to enjoy her embarrassment, and lighted up a long cheroot, exhaling the acrid smoke slowly as he observed her. He continued to puff contentedly on the cigar as Melisa fidgeted about, trying to ignore him.

When he turned his head to look at a couple entering the dining room, she glanced up at him, feeling her throat tighten as she studied his profile; the thick black hair curling about the base of his neck, the straight nose and finely chiseled mouth, the proud bearing of his body and its muscled strength straining in the light-gray suit as he swiveled in his chair. Melissa idly followed his gaze and noted the beautiful woman being seated at the next table. She seemed suddenly aware of Calvin's interest, for she looked over and her full, red lips parted in a seductive half-smile.

Melissa toyed angrily with the napkin in her lap, a pang of jealousy stabbing relentlessly at her until Calvin straightened in his chair again, his face an inscrutable mask.

"Since we seem to have exhausted all avenues of conversation, why don't we take a stroll outside," he suggested, rising from his seat and coming around to assist Melissa. Still raging inwardly, she sprang from her chair before he could reach her and sailed out of the dining room. She glanced back only when she had reached the door, expecting him to be right behind her. Instead she saw him shaking hands with the man at the neighboring table and then bending to kiss the out-stretched hand of the woman who had so openly flirted with him.

She fled the dining room and hurried through the lobby and out into the warm night, heading directly for the stables. Sauntering past the stalls housing Calvin's four thoroughbreds, she stopped before her favorite, Little John, and affectionately began stroking him, planting a warm kiss on the white diamond marking his sleek forehead. Little John would be entered at Elmont, New York in the Belmont Stakes. The three-year-old stallion would be competing against a field of strong rivals including Ben Ali who had won the Kentucky Derby on May 14, and The Bard who had recently clinched the Preakness. Recalling the running of the race at Pimlico, Melissa wondered if Kathleen's horse, Pebbles, had been entered after all. Sighing to herself she left the stables.

As she meandered about, criss-crossing the lawns of the hotel, she heard a woman's high-pitched laugh and

313

she saw Calvin sauntering toward her, the woman from the next table clinging to his arm as she navigated her way across the grass, one hand delicately lifting her trailing skirts. With her head held high, the expression on her face set, Melissa was icily composed when she came face to face with the couple.

"There you are, love," Calvin greeted her. "I'd begun to worry about you."

"Had you indeed?" she replied tartly.

Choosing to overlook her arrogant posturing, he turned to the voluptuous, raven-haired woman beside him. "Daphne, this is my, ah, charge, Melissa Howell. Melissa, this is Daphne Somers," he said formally.

"How fortunate for you, Miss Howell," the woman simpered, her smile revealing straight white teeth, "to have a man like Mr. Gabriel looking after you."

"Not quite as fortunate as you, it would seem, Miss Somers," she returned, her tone mocking. At the woman's sharp intake of breath, Melissa gracefully gathered up her skirts and walked haughtily past them, wondering what Calvin found so attractive about such an obvious, vulgar woman.

Once she had returned to her room, she decided to undress. She was restless and edgy and the room was warm, so she tugged the curtains aside and threw open the windows. Looking out into the night, she watched the moonlight gloss the trees and the grassy slopes with its silvery fires. Her flushed skin fanned by the gentle tossings of the breeze, she rested her chin on her folded arms, leaning on the window ledge, breathing deeply of the flower-scented summer air.

She failed to hear the doorknob turning as the door opened and a shadowy figure came into the room and moved stealthily toward her. He reached out and grasped her shoulders, spinning her around to face him. Melissa cried out in terror.

"Why were you so rude to Miss Somers tonight?" he demanded and Melissa's heart began to slow its frantic beating as she recovered from her fright. "You really are becoming a nuisance, Melissa, and I'm beginning to regret not having handed you over to the authorities when I had the chance."

"If you consider me such a hindrance, why not turn me in now?" she flung back at him.

"I've a good mind to turn you over my knee instead," he roared, his fingers digging into the soft flesh of her shoulders. His eyes traveled over her, as if only then becoming aware of her nakedness. He felt the blood pounding in his temples as he stared at the gilded body of the girl befor him. Aware of her effect on him, Melissa's lips curved into a slow, sensuous smile and she twisted within the circle of his arms, turning her back to him and offering her face to the tender moonlight once more. Slowly she raised her arms to unpin her hair and send it spilling in shimmering copper ripples down her back to her slender waist.

"Melissa." His voice was hoarse as his arms tightened around her and his hands caught her full breasts, squeezing their golden softness, massaging their roundness until the rosy nipples tensed and puckered. Melissa leaned back against him, reveling in the nearness of him. Then she turned to face him again, her eyes glowing like twin amber pools as she studied his face. But even as she looked at him, she felt that something had changed between them and that it was Calvin, not she, who was begging for love. She hated him even while her body craved him and even though she would consent to sharing her flesh with him that night, he would never again possess her heart.

Calvin sensed a change in the woman he swept into his arms and carried over to the bed. Although she returned his embraces with an abandon she had never shown before, he felt that she was holding herself back, that he was sharing only a part of her. And for the first time since he was a child, as he held her in his arms, he was lonely. In her ardor, there was also aloofness, and as she drew him to her, he felt she herself was drawing back. He was alone in his burning desire for her. And so he punished her by driving himself relentlessly inside her, plundering her delicate sweetness until he had exhausted himself and his fury and while crying out in his release, he cried out against his defeat at the hands of the woman who lay silent and still beneath him.

When Melissa awoke the following morning, she found herself alone in the rumpled bed. She wondered if she had only imagined him there until she became aware of the burning soreness between her legs. She moved gingerly, wincing as she remembered his thundering assault and her own detached compliance. She dressed and ate breakfast alone and then set out to find Calvin. To her chagrin, she found him standing near one of the paddocks engrossed in conversation with a wide-eyed, attentive Daphne Somers. Melissa straightened her back and assuming an air of indifference, she drifted over to the couple and tapped Calvin on the shoulder.

"Excuse me, Miss Somers." Her smile was charming; her eyes glinting with contempt as she viewed the low decolletage of the woman's pale blue muslin gown, which the capricious summer wind had plastered against her full-blown figure. Calvin notice Melissa's pointed stare and smothering a grin, he turned to the pouting woman, excused himself, and followed after Melissa.

"I apologize for interrupting you, Calvin," she said, her voice heavy with sarcasm, "but I wished to discuss the possibility of your finding a horse for me to ride. Also, I would like to borrow a pair of your trousers until I can locate a dressmaker who can provide me with a proper riding habit." She smiled up at him beguilingly, her angelic expression defying him to refuse her.

"If I didn't know better, Melissa, I'd swear we'd

never met before," he growled, his eyes twinkling as he considered her, "I've never know you to be so sickeningly sweet." But he nodded his head in consent and she threw her arms about his neck and planted a chaste kiss on his cheek.

"Oh, thank you, Calvin dear, what a wonderfully generous guardian you are." She broke away from him, running gleefully back toward the hotel while he returned to the scowling Miss Somers.

That evening, just as they were finishing their dinner, Calvin leaned aross the table and grinned conspiratorially at Melissa. "You'll be pleased to know that I've found you a horse," he announced and her spoon clattered onto the table as she gaped at him.

"So quickly?" she questioned, her eyes alight with anticipation.

"As a matter of fact, yes," he replied smoothly. "It seems one of the guests has been gambling quite a bit and losing heavily at the races. I spoke with him this afternoon and he was only too pleased to part with one of his own riding horses in return for cash."

"Would you show me the horse now?" she bubbled excitedly, springing from her chair, her face wreathed in a luminous smile. Calvin allowed her to tug him from his seat and he laughingly escorted her out of the dining room and down to the stables.

The horse's name was Regent, a magnificent chestnut stallion that reminded Melissa of her beloved mare, Brandywine, left far behind her in Kent. Nostalgia rose as a lump in her throat and she swallowed hard against its pain and turned glimmering eyes to Calvin.

"Thank you for such a splendid animal," she murmured, lovingly stroking the horse's long, graceful neck and flowing, tawny mane. She whispered his name and Regent responded, nuzzling his fine head against her arm and sniffing contentedly at her.

The following morning, Melissa sprinted from the

hotel, mindless of the astonished stares of those she passed. Her auburn hair flowed freely down her back. She sported an old shirt belonging to Calvin tied in a knot around her small waist and a pair of brown trousers tucked into a pair of high, black riding boots several sizes too large. Yet in spite of the incongruity of her appearance, her face shone with a singular radiance. The startled onlookers, gazing at her glowing features, simply clucked their tongues and smiled as they looked away.

Regent was already saddled and excitedly pawing the ground when she reached him. As she swung up onto the horse's back, she accustomed herself to the saddle, bent over and caressed the neck of her impatient horse, and whispered his name. His answering whinny and proud toss of his head sent a surge of anticipation through her and unable to contain her eagerness any longer, she led him from the paddock and out across the vast expanse of green fields awaiting them.

She released her spirit to the wind. Lightheaded with freedom, giddy with the delights of pounding over the open land, Melissa was free at last. The breeze captured her hair, sending it dancing behind her as she flashed across the emerald countryside. Her heart soared, keeping pace with the flying hooves of her charging mount. They plummeted down grassy slopes and bounded to the tops of rocky knolls, racing along with the wind.

Weak from the heady combination of exhilaration and the furious pace of her ride, she finally reined in her horse atop a gentle hill and rested there. Before her spread a variegated panorama of color—the shadings of green pastures, the golden browns of ploughed fields, the purple haze of far off mountains, and the turquoise flashing of a mountain lake. The gentle, undulating terrain stretched in lazy glory at her feet and Melissa drank in the clear, sparkling air, feeling it tingle its life through her body.

She led Regent back through twisting paths burrowing through dense woods, its floor dappled with sunlight, its amber glints splashing onto Melissa's upturned face, warming her, coloring her. Thick, downy moss spread a silent carpet beneath Regent's clopping hooves, and horse and rider moved noiselessly through the jigsaw world of trees, toadstools, and tiny scurrying animals. A squirrel chattered away from a high branch in a towering maple and then busied itself with a small nut held captive between its two front paws. Gurgling water sounded nearby and they meandered alongside the shimmering brook, tracing its wanderings until Regent halted, lowering his majestic head and lapping thirstily at the icy water while Melissa loosened the reins and watched him.

Out in the open again, with the sun sailing high in the cloudless sky, Melissa was bathed in a dampening glow. She wiped her forehead with her sleeve and finally headed Regent back toward the hotel. Her face was hot and flushed, stained by the persistence of the sun's honeyed rays. Her throat was growing parched and raw as she urged her horse into a gallop. Clattering over to the stables, Melissa was suddenly seized by a feeling of panic. She felt certain that someone was observing her movements. The flesh on the back of her neck prickled as she glanced about her. She could see no one about paying her the slightest attention so she shrugged off the feeling of apprehension and reined in her horse at the stables. Dismounting, she stroked the head of her panting, tired animal and left him in the care of one of the grooms.

As she dressed for dinner that evening, she viewed her face in the mirror above the bureau in her room, noting the vitality restored to her eyes and the high color that returned to her cheeks in the afternoon sun. Her rippling laughter filled the room as she thought of her beloved Lettie and the old woman's insistence on scrubbing lemon juice onto Melissa's face in her desperate bid to lighten her tawniness to the accepted alabaster of the well-bred Englishwoman. She gave her gleaming hair a final pat and swept down the stairs to the dining room, eager to join Calvin and tell him of her ride. As she entered the noisy, crowded room, alive with the hum of conversation and the clatter of dishes and glasses, Melissa stopped short. Seated at their usual table was Calvin, deeply engrossed in the words of Daphne Somers, who leaned over the table toward him, her ample bosom spilling from the frothy lace circling her sweeping decolletage.

Melissa stood there, clenching her fists in anger and betrayal, at a loss as to what to do. She had not eaten since breakfast, and the day's riding had given her an enormous appetite. But as she looked despairingly around her, she felt that appetite slowly diminishing. Then she felt a hand gently grasp her elbow and she turned to face a tall, well-dressed man, whose deep-set brown eyes regarded her warmly.

"Forgive me, but I couldn't help noticing your predicament." He glanced meaningfully toward Calvin and Daphne Somers. "Would you care to join me for dinner?"

He appeared so courtly, so politely concerned, that Melissa could do little more than smile her grateful acceptance and allow him to assist her to a chair. As he seated himself opposite her at the small table, a broad smile lit his suntanned face and crinkled the corners of his eyes as he studied her appreciatively.

"I'm Anthony Holmes," he said, "and when I'm not amusing myself at the races in the summer here I'm a fairly respectable banker in New York City." She gaily returned his smile as she introduced herself, her gaze wandering over the straight brown hair heavily sprinkled with silver and the neatly trimmed moustache beneath his high-bridged aristocratic nose. Her heart began to hammer in her chest as she found herself reacting to his physical presence, the veneer of respectability barely concealing the vital magnetism of the man.

"Shall we order, Miss Howell?" His voice was smooth and deep as he addressed her. She started guiltily and halted her perusal.

"Why not order for both of us?" she breathed, reaching for the tall crystal water goblet, quenching the stinging in her throat. Holmes gave their orders to the hovering waiter and then watched the man pour a glass of cold white wine for Melissa before raising his own glass in a toast. "To new acquaintances, my dear Miss Howell." She smiled over the rim of her wineglass, Calvin and Daphne forgotten in the sudden attention being shown her.

She basked in the flattering attentiveness of the older and obviously worldly man, listening with rapt fascination to his tales of life in the turbulent city which nurtured him, generating his unabashed enthusiasm for life. As he spoke, New York was transformed into a glittering wonderland, a maddening whirl of theater openings, elegant dinner parties, and intimate gatherings at the homes of people whose names and faces graced the social columns of every major newspaper in the country. Holmes described the thrill of shopping in vast department stores and living in the vertical splendor of apartment buildings and four-story townhouses lining Park Avenue.

Throughout dinner, Melissa's head spun, twirling in a kaleidoscope of images and colors conjured up for her by the dapper Anthony Holmes. But her dizzying world careened to an abrupt halt when she looked up into the scowling face of Calvin Gabriel who was looming over her as he prepared to pass their table.

"I wondered what had happened to you," he remarked coldly, eyeing the older man, who sat silently observing him.

"I doubt you even missed me, Calvin dear," she

replied, the wine rendering her void of any feeling other than cool detachment. "You were too taken with the very obvious charms of Miss Somers to have noticed much else."

"Don't be vulgar, Melissa," he snapped. "It's not particularly attractive."

"Before we begin to fight, Calvin," she hastily interjected, "may I present Anthony Holmes." She smiled at the older man who rose to his feet and extended his hand. "This foul-tempered gentleman is my guardian, Calvin Gabriel," she said, a slow smile molding the corners of her mouth as the frowning Calvin grudgingly accepted Holmes's proferred hand.

"I'm pleased to meet you, Mr. Gabriel." Holmes acknowledged him with a slight nod of his head. "Miss Howell was just beginning to tell me about you."

"I'm sure she was," he snarled, inclining his head briefly and walking away.

"Your friend is rather possessive, isn't he?" Holmes observed, his forehead creasing in a pensive frown. But Melissa merely smiled enigmatically, secretly pleased by his casual remark.

The remainder of their dinner together passed without further interruption, and as they rose to leave the dining room, Melissa felt unusually fatigued and dizzy, and attempted unsuccessfully to stifle a wide yawn.

"Forgive my rudeness," she apologized, blushing at her halfhearted effort to mask her exhaustion, "but I think the riding and all of the delicious wine have made me terribly sleepy."

"I understand, my dear," he said gently. "I'll see you back to your room then." Taking her arm, he guided her though the lobby and upstairs to her door. They stopped and he released her. "I hope you'll have dinner with me again." He smiled as she smothered another yawn with the back of her hand.

"I would like that very much," she murmured. He pressed a kiss into the palm of her hand and strode back down the corridor. She watched him, his elegant frame, his long legs taking powerful steps as he walked along, and when he had turned and dissappeared from sight, she let herself into her room.

Lying in bed, massaging her pounding temples to ease the ache of her head, she heard voices coming down the hall and stopping at the room next to hers. Calvin's room. The door opened and closed and through the thin walls, Melissa heard a woman's laughter ring out. She flinched as she recognized the distinctive shrillness of Daphne Somers. She tossed about, her thoughts alive with images of Calvin's dark, lithe body entwined with the pale fullness of Daphne's soft and yielding one, her large breasts crushed against his strong, hard chest, his hands stroking Daphne where they had also stroked her. Melissa cried, outraged by Calvin's duplicity, burying her head in the pillows to smother her anguish and blot the tears scalding her. The sounds of their lovemaking filtered through to her. As she listened to Daphne cry out in the throes of her ecstasy, Melissa ground her own body against the mattress, writhing with the agony of Calvin's betrayal. She clapped her hands over her ears, blocking out the loving treachery on the other side of the wall.

chapter 27

Shortly before dawn, Melissa awoke, her body bathed in perspiration. She flung herself from the bed, racing for the open window and the cooling breeze which billowed the filmy curtains. She shuddered in the wake of recollection, remembering her passage through the nightmare which had returned once more to torture her sleep. His inscrutable eyes, behind the protection of his mask, had pierced her, impaling her with a silvering shaft of light sparking from his gaze, and she had felt herself irrevocably scarred. She shivered in the cold his eyes had created around her, frosting her greening world with his icy presence.

But she forced herself to look beyond her terror and she watched as the peaceful beauty of the summer morning unfolded before her. Pastel tints of pink and mulberry hovered on the horizon, muting the uncompromising blackness of night. Nighttime's horrors vanished as the rising sun washed the distant hills with the blush of crimson. Ruby slashes, spiked trumpeters of the golden dawn, streaked the sky with their brilliance. The birds stirred and warbled their greetings to the morning. Somewhere in the distance a horse whinnied, and Melissa lost herself in the promise of the newborn day.

After breakfast, from which both Calvin and Daphne were conspicuously absent, Melissa galloped off on

Regent over the dew-bright hills. As she rode, her precarious peace was restored and she reveled in the freedom that was hers once more. They daringly jumped a moss-covered tree stump and thundered over the cushion of grass, seeking new territory to explore, dodging low-hanging boughs and scrambling among the fallen rocks and stones.

Climbing to the crest of a wooded hill, she slowed her horse and concentrated on the flurry of activity on a branch just above her head. A large blackbird was busily feeding her young, briefly pecking a worm into the waiting beaks yawning in front of her. Melissa smiled and nudged Regent down a steep incline and out across a flower-strewn meadow. They gamboled happily through the sea of white daisies, watching the flight of jewel-toned butterflies as they skimmed above the nodding heads of the flowers. Swinging down from the saddle, Melissa tucked the trailing reins into the belt around her waist and gathered herself an armful of white and yellow daisies to brighten her room.

Astride her horse once again, she sheltered the flowers in the crook of her arm as she guided Regent back to the hotel. Nearing the stables, she heard someone call her name and she turned as Anthony Holmes headed toward her, reining in a dappled gray.

"Good afternoon, Miss Howell," he greeted her amiably, his silver-tipped hair glinting in the sunlight. "I looked for you at lunch today, but now I can see why you weren't there."

"Have you been for a ride or are you just setting out?" she asked, admiring the cut of his ivory breeches and pale taupe jacket, the ivory stock tie at his neck setting off his tan.

"I was just starting off if you'd care to join me," he replied, his eyes resting easily on her upturned face.

She thought immediately of accepting his offer but just then, out of the corner of her eye, she noticed Calvin approaching from the paddock and waving at her to join him there.

"I must refuse your tempting offer for now, Mr. Holmes," she answered, wondering at Calvin's signal. "Perhaps some other time," she hurriedly suggested, regretting the disappointment flickering momentarily across his features. He nodded briefly to her then and headed off, his back straight, his body moving gracefully with the increasing rhythm of his horse.

As she dismounted, daisies scattered about her, falling onto the ground. As Calvin neared her, he bent down to help her retrieve them. Melissa unwittingly brushed his hand with hers as they reached for the same flower. She hastily drew back and he glanced questioningly at her, but her lashes were lowered, her eyes unreadable, as she collected the last of the daisies and straightened again.

"It seems I interrupted something between you and Holmes," he commented as he studied her flushed face. "Sorry."

"Are you really," she retorted.

"The reason for my interruption should please you, Melissa," he barked, his temper flaring at her snappishness. "There's supposed to be an excellent dressmaker in town, and since you need some clothes for the races and the clubhouse dances, I thought we'd head over there. You can do with a riding outfit of your own, young lady," he added, his eyes roaming over the swell of her breasts jutting upward in the shirt he had lent her.

"Give me a few minutes to change," she answered curtly, burning under his scrutiny and quickly turning away.

"I'll wait for you in the lobby," he called after her as she walked briskly back to the hotel.

She sponged herself lightly and then slipped into a delicate, flower-sprigged muslin gown, its gossamer sheerness whisper soft against her warm skin. Brushing her hair, she gathered it into a chignon and anchored it firmly at the nape of her neck before freeing several saucy curls to frame her face. Pleased with the effect, she carefully adjusted the low, square neckline of the gown, assuring herself that her decolletage was enticing and yet demure. Catching up her small purse, she hurried downstairs to meet Calvin.

Relieved to find him alone, but nonetheless curious as to the whereabouts of the ubiquitous Miss Somers, Melissa cheerfully accepted his arm and settled herself across from him in the open carriage. He was freshly attired in a pale blue linen jacket, open-neck shirt, and fawn trousers. Aware of her appraising interest, Calvin simply smiled and looked past her at the hotel receding in the distance. Melissa's brow puckered in a frown at his marked nonchalance and she began to brood, thinking again of the previous night and the sounds of his lovemaking. She felt a slow heat tingle upwards through her body and she hastily veiled her eyes.

Madame Elise, as the French dressmaker called herself, was located in a small, whitewashed shop with startling violet shutters and windowboxes overflowing with pink petunias. A small brass bell tinkled as Melissa and Calvin entered the bustling shop, and a tall, statuesque woman with a flaming red pompadour hurried to them, greeting them effusively. Calvin stretched his long body into a small, satin-covered chair and watched Melissa with an amused smile playing about his lips as she attempted to sift through the bolts of fine cloths the exuberant modiste unfurled for her. She threw plaintive glances his way, but he ignored her beseeching stares and allowed her to make her own choices. Fingering the luxurious materials, selecting from the endless boxes of beads, ribbons, and laces, Melissa finally decided on a riding habit, two day dresses with matching hats and parasols for the races, and two formal dinner gowns with similar shoes and evening bags on long slender chains.

"Mademoiselle shows excellent taste, monsieur,"

the woman smiled, clasping her ring-bedecked hands together excitedly. "But of course she has the exquisite young figure so well suited to these styles." Melissa glowed, enjoying the dressmaker's extravagant compliments, covertly watching Calvin for his reaction. But he merely nodded distractedly and eased himself from the tiny chair. He began to shift impatiently from one foot to the other. He then instructed the woman to have everything ready in a week's time. She hesitated, regarding him doubtfully. He hastily added a bill to the growing stack of money he had already laid into her outstretched hand and the woman brightened considerably and promised that Melissa's entire wardrobe would be ready on time. Calvin immediately grabbed Melissa's arm and hurried her from the shop.

"My God," he groaned, clapping a hand to his forehead, "I don't understand how you women can tolerate it." Melissa gazed sympathetically at him and smiled contentedly to herself. To her surprise, it had grown dark, the entire afternoon having slipped by without her realizing it, and her stomach suddenly began to growl hungrily. Calvin scowled as he tugged out a large gold pocketwatch and glanced down at the time.

"I suggest we find ourselves some place to eat," he said. "Dinner will be over by the time we get back to the hotel, and I could do with a good meal and a bottle of wine right now."

Without waiting for her answer, he started off. Melissa ran to catch up with him, hurrying her steps to keep pace with his long-legged strides. They walked briskly along the town's main street, each of them alertly searching for an adequate restaurant. It was Calvin who spotted one first. Steering Melissa by the elbow, he hurried her across the dusty road and into a small, candlelit dining room, with a welcome aroma of freshly baked bread greeting them as they entered.

Settling themselves at a table near the window, they

ordered their dinner and sipped slowly at their wine, Melissa regarding Calvin's handsome face through the cover of her lashes as he stared wordlessly into his wineglass. Was he wishing she were Daphne Somers, she mused, bewildered by his reticence whenever he was alone with her. With a defiant toss of her head, she drained her glass and held it out silently for Calvin to refill. He glanced at her, the frown clearing from his brow, and poured another glass of the dusky burgundy, refreshing his own glass at the same time.

"Do you know whether Kathleen ran her horse, Pebbles, in the Preakness?" she asked him, growing tired of the unnatural silence dividing them.

"I have no idea, Melissa," he returned rather sharply, the frown appearing again.

"Are Edward and Kathleen living in New York now?" she persisted gamely.

"I suppose so." He shrugged disinterestedly. "They were planning to move into his flat when the doctor said it was safe for Kathleen to travel." He gulped the rest of his wine and poured another glassful for himself. She sighed and toyed absently with the napkin in her lap, grateful when the meal finally arrived and the need for conversation ceased.

As they were nearing the end of their dinner, Melissa glanced up in consternation at the ominous sound of raindrops splattering against the window beside her. The street outside faded to an indistinct blur as a strong wind whipped the rain into a swirling curtain, sending it thundering against the pavement. People scurried to the shelter of nearby doorways and a number of horse carriages clattered noisily past, heading for the livery stables to wait out the deluge. A powerful gust plastered a flying sheet of newspaper to the window next to Melissa and she gasped, nearly upsetting her wineglass as she started in surprise. A flash of lightning split the black skies overhead and a roll of thunder quickly followed, reverberating through the night.

"Damn, now we'll be stuck here," Calvin muttered, pulling out his watch again. "It's nearly nine o'clock, and I'm sure that our carriage was among those tearing down the street before."

"Are you late for something, Calvin dear?" she asked frostily.

"What the devil gave you that idea?" he demanded.

"You keep looking at your watch and frowning," she purred contemptuously. "I assumed you must be about to miss an important engagement. With Miss Somers perhaps?" she insinuated, lifting her wineglass and sipping the last traces of wine.

"You've assumed wrong, my jealous one," he retorted, "and what's more, I think you're a little drunk."

"Perhaps just a little," she murmured, setting down her glass and watching it wobble unsteadily.

"That's all I need right now," he groaned. "Melissa, sit up, for God's sake," he ordered as she sagged dangerously close to the candle set into a holder atop the tablecloth. She straightened immediately, rewarding him with a leering grin. She proceeded to prop her chin up on her hand and stare moodily into the wavering flame. Calvin grimaced as the rain pelted the windows, the lightning flashed, and the thunder roared.

By midnight, she was yawning and not even attempting to conceal her fatigue as the waiter paced up and down waiting for them to leave. Calvin looked outside and although the storm had diminished to a steadily falling rain, there were no carriages about, the streets were deserted, and the houses lining the street were already dark. He signaled to the waiter and carried on a whispered conversation with him as he paid the bill and returned to help Melissa to her feet.

"Come on, princess. Put one foot in front of the other and when I say run, I want you to run."

She stumbled against him as he took off his jacket and threw it across her shoulders and headed her toward the door. As she opened it, a gust of rain and cool air caught her by surprise. She faintly heard him shout, "Run." Then he was dragging her along after him as they sloshed through the wet streets and into a doorway at last. Flinging open the door, Melissa stepped into the lobby of a small hotel. But before she could protest, Calvin was leading her down a dim corridor and into a large room. He fumbled with the lamp and finally urged her farther into the room, whereupon he slammed the door closed behind her and locked it.

"I'm afraid I had little choice, Melissa," he explained, pulling the wet jacket from her shoulders and spreading it across the back of a chair. "This was the only hotel around and the last room they had available," he mumbled as he tore off his dripping shirt and signaled her to begin undressing. "I'll take that big chair over by the window and you can have the bed to yourself," he said.

She huddled in a corner of the room and slithered out of her clinging gown, stripping off her undergarments and soaked shoes. Near the washstand she found a large towel and she dabbed at her glistening skin. Then she unpinned her hair and shook it free, ineffectually toweling its length until she gave up in exasperation and contented herself with running her fingers through the remaining tangles. She tumbled onto the bed, drawing the warm covers over her nakedness, and lying back observing Calvin, who had picked up her discarded towel and was vigorously drying himself with it, unaware of her silent scrutiny.

Wrapping the towel around his waist, he padded over to the bed. He tugged off the light spread and relieved Melissa of one of the pillows. He readied his makeshift bed, blew out the oil lamp, and settled himself into the massive chair. His mumbled goodnight left her vaguely discontented and she squirmed about under the covers, listening to his even breathing as he fell asleep. She fought to drive the thought of his nearness from her mind, concentrating instead on the steady drumming of the rain on the window panes until she willed herself to relax and drifted off.

Uncertain of the passage of time, she felt as if she had been asleep for only a few minutes when the sound of someone screaming awakened her. It was only when she became aware of Calvin's arms around her that she knew the screams had been hers.

"What happened?" he demanded, shaking her into full awareness. "Were you having a nightmare?" He had lit one of the oil lamps again, and as she recovered her senses, she hastily pulled the covers over her trembling body, hiding herself from his probing gaze.

"Do you want to tell me about it?" he persisted, but she shook her head. She chanced a furtive look at him then, examining the eyes which were so disturbingly similar to those in her dream, and again she experienced that familiar stirring within her memory.

She was suddenly cold, and she shivered in the dampness of the musty room until Calvin wrapped his arms about her, warming her with his own body. The convulsive tremors eased and Melissa curled herself against him, her face pressed contentedly into his warm, furry chest. She seemed to doze and he was reluctant to move, even though his legs were beginning to cramp and his back had started to ache. Gently he slid his arms from around her body and got up from the bed, stretching to relieve the tightness in his muscles. Then her eyes flew open and she called out to him, so he slipped back onto the bed beside her, hugging her close once more.

They lay together for several moments, she calmly content and pacified, he growing restless and uneasy, a steady fire throbbing in his loins. When he could no longer tolerate the pressure building within him, he thrust her from him, agitatedly running his fingers through his hair.

"This won't work," he muttered gruffly. "I can't lie here beside you this way, Melissa, without going crazy." In answer, she reached up and caressed the broad expanse of his dark chest, twining the thick, curling black hair around her fingers until he seized her hand. "Stop it," he growled. "I'm only human." But she pulled her hand free and laughingly trailed her fingertips across his stomach, feeling him tense under her grazing touch. "You've asked for this, love," he whispered huskily, his lips lowering themselves to hers. Hungrily, gratefully she accepted them.

Biting her full lower lip with his strong teeth, nibbling on her rich sweetness, he then ran the tip of his tongue around her open mouth, sending dizzying flames sparking through her. Meeting his tongue she traced teasing circles around it with her own while she tenderly explored his face with her wandering hands, roaming its surface, learning its molded angles and planes. He kissed the hollow of her throat and lowered his head to the proud swell of her breasts as she moaned and arched against him, pressing him into the valley between the ripe golden flesh.

He shifted his weight, pulling her on top of him, and she straddled his body, resting her weight on her knees, leaning forward so that her long hair rained a copper shower across his face and streamed onto his heaving chest. He captured the waving tendrils of her curling hair in his large hands, tugging her head down to meet his lips once more. And as he kissed her, he sought the tender bud inside the moist patch pressed against his belly. She trembled and rocked back onto her heels as his finger slipped back and forth across the stinging button, releasing a spiraling heat to permeate her entire being.

She reached behind her and closed her fingers around the pulsing shaft springing from the cluster of soft, warm hair to meet her eager touch. Gently she moved her hand up and down its length, feeling him harden as she stroked him in a steadily increasing rhythm. He writhed beneath her, bucking against the workings of

333

her fingers, finally whispering for her to stop. She slowed her strokings and he gripped her firm buttocks with his hands, raising her slightly to position her above him. Easing himself inside her, he waded through her beckoning warmth and probed further. She lowered herself onto him until she had taken all of him and then he guided her to match his rising and falling and their bodies slapped together as they met and separated and met again.

They plunged together, falling deeper and deeper, slowing momentarily to catch their breath and prolong the ecstatic beauty of their pairing. Then together they rode the surging waves of a pain so intense that they felt their souls touch and shatter, exploding inside one another again and again until they cried out in their mutual release, borne to oblivion and back.

She lay still above him, her limbs throbbing in the aftermath of their shared glory. The heat cooled and the fires coursed more slowly through her veins until they centered only on that part of her where she lay joined to him. Weakly, she flung herself from him. He stirred and sought her lips once more, sealing their exquisite journey with a tender kiss. With one arm draped around her, he soon drifted off to sleep. She lay there, listening to his regular breathing, wishing that he had spoken to her, acknowledging her special place in his life, separating her from the others she was forced to share him with. But he had not spoken to her and she knew that it made little difference to him who warmed his bed. She gulped back her tears and her yearning and stared bleakly into the darkness.

The following morning, Melissa awoke first and propping herself up on one elbow, she studied the man sleeping beside her. His finely chiseled profile was relaxed, the thick black hair curled softly about his face and neck, his arms hugged a pillow, and his muscled legs sprawled across much of the bed. Smiling, she ran

games and as she watched them she grew more restless and ill at ease. When she could bear it no longer, she realized that only a brisk ride through the country would calm her jangling nerves. She sprinted for the stairs, racing back to her room to change into her makeshift riding outfit and then running back outside again toward the stables.

As she mounted Regent, Melissa could feel her spirits beginning to lift and the tension ease from her tautly strung body. She headed away from the confining atmosphere of the hotel and its people only to have an approaching horseman hail her and head toward her. Reluctantly she watched as Anthony Holmes reined in beside her.

"Hello there," he said, his warm smile deepening the creases about his eyes. "I see we both had the same idea." She nodded absently, hoping that he could also see that she preferred to be alone. But he seemed far too pleased with having cornered her at last to let her go that easily. Before she quite realized it, she had consented to ride with him. They set off at a gallop, keeping pace with one another until Holmes pulled ahead of her, forcing Melissa to catch up with him, which she easily did, streaking past him until he finally reached her side once more. She laughed as he approached, continuing their friendly competition. Then she tossed him a teasing wave as she urged Honey faster, racing ahead of Holmes's thundering gray until he again caught up with her, and to her delight, sailed proudly past.

Reaching the stream she had followed once before, she signaled for Holmes to dismount. Together they struggled with their boots, tossed them onto the grass and rolled up their trousers. Then, leading their horses lightly by the reins as they steered them along the bank, Melissa and Holmes waded through the icy water, stepping over moss covered stones and splashing about as they navigated the brook. Finally they climbed back onto the grass and, tethering their horses to a tree, they sprawled out on the bank, skipping stones across the sparkling stream, allowing the sun to warm their faces and dry their legs.

Melissa smiled contentedly, looking up at the handsome man beside her, but she grew strangely uneasy as he suddenly leaned toward her and cupped her face in his strong, brown hands.

"You're a delight to be with, Melissa," he said softly, startling her by the use of her name. As his head moved closer, her heart began to hammer in her chest and her eyelids fluttered closed.

"Such an exquisite young woman," he breathed, caressing her cheek with his fingertips as his lips nuzzled hers, teasingly at first and then increasing their gentle pressure until she felt her head spinning and the breath leaving her. In panic, she drew back, sliding away from him on the grass, raking her fingers distractedly through her hair, embarrassed to meet his troubled gaze.

"Forgive me, my dear." His voice was still tender as he reached for her hand. "I shouldn't have taken such liberties." He released her own weak grip and began rolling down his wet trouser cuffs. She shyly knelt and helped him with his boots. He assisted her with hers and silently they mounted their horses and headed back, the playfulness gone, a tense and awkward silence descending like a curtain between them.

As he walked back with her to the hotel, he again apologized to her and Melissa stopped, tentatively reaching for his hand and covering it with hers.

"There is really no need to apologize." She smiled affectionately up at him, and the tightness eased in his face. "Your attention is extremely flattering, Mr. Holmes, and the fact that you are a gentleman is all the more meaningful to me."

"Then will you have dinner with me this evening?" he asked quickly and she nodded her acceptance.

In the week that followed, she dined with Anthony Holmes each evening and rode with him every day. With Calvin preoccupied with the bountiful Daphne Somers and the daily training of his racehorses, Melissa ignored him and basked in the attentiveness and easy companionship the older man provided. A widower with three grown children, Holmes appeared much younger than his fifty two years. He was a charming dinner conversationalist and an expert dancer, and on the nights that a small orchestra played in the ballroom of the hotel, Melissa scarcely left the floor, sweeping through each dance in his embrace. Despite their burgeoning relationship, he never again attempted to kiss her and she wondered at the conflicting emotions she experienced when she found herself locked in his arms as they danced or strolling with him, hand in hand, around the grounds of the hotel.

At the end of the week, Melissa's new clothing arrived as Madame Elise had promised, and she spent the entire afternoon wading through a sea of tissue paper and boxes, delightedly slipping into each gown and pirouetting before her mirror. Whirling about the room, she watched as the gossamer lengths of delicate fabric fanned out from her spinning body in billowing waves until she resembled some giant exotic flower. Tiring at last, she hung away each gown and replaced the hats and the fragile evening purses in their tissue-lined boxes, storing them carefully in her closet.

The following morning, Calvin announced that he was taking his horses to neighboring Belmont Park for a day of trial runs. Melissa saw him off and then returned to the lobby to find Anthony Holmes nervously pacing about. His eyes lighted as he caught sight of her and he rushed to her and tugged her up against him.

"I've been looking everywhere for you," he admitted and she was puzzled by the urgency in his voice. "I'm afraid that my trip is being cut short, Melissa. There has evidently been a crisis at the bank and it requires my immediate attention, so I'm now on my way back to New York City."

Her stricken eyes met his and she felt a sinking deep in the pit of her stomach. First Calvin and then Anthony, both of them leaving her. Struggling against the unsettling whisperings of despair which hovered about her she stared up at him wordlessly, unable to force anything but a sigh from her lips. He hugged her to him and then set her from him, a wry smile tugging at his own lips below the full moustache.

"If you ever find yourself in New York, will you promise to contact me?" he asked her. She nodded, afraid to trust her voice. "You still have my card?" he persisted, and again she nodded. Then he kissed her tenderly on the mouth and she clung to him and returned his kiss before breaking from his arms and running away from the pain of loneliness welling up inside of her.

chapter 28

Following Anthony's unexpected departure, Melissa found herself at loose ends, deprived even of Calvin's company. For he had decided to transfer his four thoroughbreds to the stables provided for them by the racetrack at Elmont, staying with them for the remainder of the week preceding the running of the Belmont Stakes. Little John was his only horse being entered in the third race of the famous Triple Crown. The other three were being studiously groomed for some of the smaller stakes both at Elmont and later in the season at Saratoga. Melissa's only consolation was the realization that she was not the only one to feel Calvin's absence, for Daphne Somers had also been abandoned.

But it did not take the other woman long to cast about and find a willing substitute, and one night she swept grandly past the table where Melissa sat alone, grinning smugly down at her while clinging to the arm of the tall, saturnine man at her side. Melissa ignored the flamboyant Miss Somers, wondering how Calvin would eventually react to his erstwhile companion's fickleness. She found that she still enjoyed her daily rides alone but it was at night, as she wandered aimlessly about the grounds of the hotel that she keenly felt the absence of Anthony Holmes.

The morning of the Belmont Stakes, Melissa awoke with a tremulous fluttering in her stomach. As she moved from the bed, a wave of nausea rose in her throat and as she fought it, her face seemed to heat with a spreading flush and her body prickled with clammy perspiration. Taking deep breaths, she managed to steady herself and ease her stomach's queasiness. As she rose to dress she attributed her spell of sickness to excitement and forced it from her mind.

After carefully arranging her hair, she stepped into the first of her new gowns, a frothy confection of mint-green muslin. Its low, square neckline and puffed cap sleeves were well suited to combat the stifling heat of the day. She had decided against a bustle, choosing instead only lightly draped panniers of green muslin, embroidered with yellow daisies. The large sweeping hat she settled onto her curls was of the same daisy-strewn fabric with thick clusters of yellow silk daisies nestled against the crown. Gathering up her purse and dainty parasol, she decided to leave the stifling closeness of her room and wait for Calvin's arrival downstairs on the terrace where it was bound to be cooler. As she floated through the lobby, her filmy skirts rippled over her body like a tantalizing wave, causing heads to turn and murmured exclamations of appreciation to follow her movements. Her natural tawny coloring had been further darkened by the sun and it lent her a golden radiance lacking in the milky-toned women who clucked disdainfully at her as she drifted past.

She began to despair of ever meeting up with Calvin, but just as she was returning to the lobby for a second time, abandoning the refreshing breeze on the terrace, she glimpsed his familiar figure bounding toward her. He was tugging self-consciously at his pearl-gray top hat, angled rakishly on his head. He grinned sheepishly at her scowl of disapproval.

"I can't stand these damned things," he muttered grumpily as she reached up to set his hat properly for him. "But you look delicious, Melissa love," he beamed, teasingly licking his lips with a loud smacking sound. "That little dressmaker was certainly right when she said you had the perfect figure for those clothes." His eyes appreciatively scanned her body, lingering on the tops of her breasts which peeked saucily above the low neckline of her gown. She colored at his unexpected flattery and took his arm, dazzled by his attentiveness, giddy with delight to be with him again.

As they drove to Belmont Park, Melissa's heart began thumping with excitement and she toyed anxiously with her parasol until Calvin laid a reassuring hand over hers.

"Relax, princess, there are only two alternatives. Either we win or we lose, it's as simple as that."

"I realize that. But to think that after all of these months of training and preparing, everything is decided in a matter of minutes, somehow it seems rather unfair," she sighed. "One race and then, poof." She snapped her fingers. "It is over and done with."

He laughed, squeezing her hand. "But that's what makes it challenging," he insisted. "Pitting your skill against the best in the country whether you win or not. More than half of the thrill has been in training Little John and watching him perform as well as he has so far."

Despite his words, Melissa believed that much of it was pure bravado, for she was certain Calvin dearly wanted to win. She lapsed into pensive silence as he continued to hold her hand, his own thoughts obviously elsewhere. The carriage finally pulled into the vast grounds of the park and joined the hundreds of coaches and thousands of elegantly dressed men and women swarming through the gates toward the grandstands. After battling through the lines of vehicles, they halted at last and Calvin helped Melissa down. She opened her flower-sprigged parasol, took Calvin's arm, and swished gracefully at his side as they walked toward the large clubhouse.

They were jostled and shoved every foot of the way to their reserved box. When Calvin had seen her comfortably seated, he left her and made his way to the wickets to place his bets on the first race. When he returned and resumed his seat, Melissa impulsively tucked her arm through his and smiled warmly at him. She began to chatter away out of nervous anticipation and paid scant attention to the running of the first races, saving all of her concentration and energy for the one which meant the most to her.

Calvin placed bets on each race, returning to claim his seat shortly before post time. He pressed the paper stubs into Melissa's hand, for luck, he insisted. To her chagrin, they won money on only one of his many wagers when a horse he had bet on came in second and Calvin had been astute enough to have purchased a ticket to place. As he left her side again, sprinting up the stairs toward the wicket to collect his winnings, Melissa contented herself with studying the crowded arena before her.

Thousands of men and women jammed the boxes and the grandstands and spilled over into the enclosures of the field itself. Women in bright summer gowns sporting huge, flouncy hats clutched their parasols as they shielded their faces from the brilliant sunlight. Men in tailored suits, in striped jackets and light trousers all seemed to be wearing straw boaters or formal top hats, and they chomped on cigars and traded knowing comments with their neighbors. Melissa glanced at the man beside her as he swore angrily and tossed his stubs onto the floor, grinding his heel into them. Several rows ahead of her, a happy couple embraced as the man, his boater tipping precariously to one side, bolted up the stairs two at a time, gleefully brandishing his winning ticket.

Before she quite realized it, the moment she had been both dreading and anticipating finally arrived. When Calvin slipped into his seat next to her for the running of the Belmont Stakes, she tugged at his hand, whispering excitedly.

"Oh Calvin, this is the final moment and I doubt if I can even bear to watch it now."

"But this is the one you've been saving all of your energy for," he teased, hugging her to him and draping his arm casually about her shoulders. "Don't you dare back out on me now," he admonished her as she settled snugly against him.

And then the race was beginning and Melissa forgot her nervousness and found herself immersed in the breathtaking spectacle unfolding below her. Onto the track came the horses to begin their dignified parade past the grandstands, and a collective cheer went up from the thousands of appreciative viewers. The flashing rainbow of color spreading across the field was created by the bright silks of the country's greatest stables worn by the diminutive jockeys as they fanned out, leading their prancing mounts around the track in a solemn procession. Calvin's grip tightened on Melissa's shoulder as Timothy Lane, sporting the silver and blue of Stony Briar, passed by, easily handling the majestic Little John, as the horses swung slowly around the giant oval track, heading for the starting gate.

The animals were then readied by the starter who dipped and ran among them, calming them, cajoling them, backing them into their predetermined slots and evening them as best he could for the start of the race. After what seemed to be an interminable delay, the horses were finally lined up for the starting gun. At the signal, they broke from the gate and were off and running.

Most of them were racing neck and neck as they rounded the clubhouse turn and Melissa, straining to follow the figure of Lane, sought out the large number six emblazoned on the cloth beneath his saddle as the horses streaked quickly by. Glints of red and orange, blue and green, yellow and white, silver and maroon glimmered and blurred together as the jockeys crouched over their horses and sprinted by the screaming stands. Heading into the lower turn, there were discernible gaps opening in the ranks as the horses began to spread out, one taking the lead, heading for the inside rail and skimming past the nose of the horse pursuing him. Number three dropped back quickly from first place as number one headed in from the outside rail to overtake a challenging number five. Melissa craned her neck as the horses hammered toward the opposite end of the field, their numbers obscured by the distance and the fences between them and the spectators.

She watched them thundering past the stands once more and found Timothy Lane nosing ahead of one horse to open a slight lead. But it was short-lived as another horse, riding the rail, suddenly pulled ahead of him and Little John dropped back. The horse, whose number designated him as Inspector B, shook off the threat of a horse passing the tiring Little John, and romped alone out of the backstretch and into the stretch turn.

Little John clung tenaciously to his third place position but he suddenly seemed to fade in the stretch and Melissa felt Calvin's fingers digging painfully into her flesh and she winced and pulled away. She prayed that Lane was restraining Little John in order to open up in the final seconds, but he stayed in fourth place as Inspector B careened around the far turn and into the home stretch in a final drive to clinch the race and the Belmont Stakes purse. He streaked across the finish line and as the jockey slowed his mount's furious pace, he led his horse around the track once more and then headed into the winner's circle in front of the judge's stand. The official floral celebration wreath was hung about Inspector B's neck and as the crowd roared its approval, both horse and rider bathed in the glory of their victory.

Calvin's arm dropped from Melissa's shoulder and she looked up at him, tears bright in her eyes, as she reached for his hand. At first he stiffened and tugged away but then he gazed into her face and saw the hurt written there and he accepted her consolation, tenderly brushing her lips with his.

"I am so sorry, Calvin," she whispered brokenly.

"So am I, love, so am I," he returned. But then he shrugged. "What was it that I said about the fun being in the anticipation?" He chuckled and pulled her to her feet. "How would you like a cold drink, princess?" he asked and before she could answer him, she found herself propelled up the steps as Calvin battled his way through the crowd, mindless of the people making their way to the wickets. Calvin tore his tickets into tiny pieces then and tossed them into the air as he walked, ignoring them as they rained down again, sprinkling onto passersby and littering the ground.

Seated at a table near the clubhouse bar, they were sipping at their long, cool drinks in silence when a white-haired man approached their table and clapped a ruddy hand on Calvin's shoulder. He glanced up startled and then he broke into a wide grin.

"I had a lot of money riding on you today and you disappointed me, my boy," the older man said gruffly as he bit off the end of a cheroot and calmly lit it while Calvin sprang to his feet.

"David, you old sawbones, haven't you gotten horses out of your blood yet?" he laughed, throwing his arms about the man, nearly knocking the cigar from his lips.

"Nope, they'll have to bury me before I lose the taste for them, son," he replied, blowing a thick cloud of smoke into Calvin's face. Then his keen gaze fell on Melissa and he smiled broadly. "Are you planning to keep this beautiful young lady all to yourself or do you intend to introduce me?" he prodded Calvin good-naturedly.

"Melissa Howell, Dr. David Endicott," Calvin announced in a perfunctory manner. "David's the best damned horse doctor around," he added as the tall man stooped and raised Melissa's hand to his lips. The thick white moustache tickled her as he pressed a lingering kiss onto her skin. She giggled and drew her hand away. His glinting black eyes stared openly at her from beneath luxuriant white eyebrows and Melissa felt unnerved by his unabashed scrutiny of her.

"Well, young man," he said as he straightened up, his eyes still fixed on Melissa, "you might not know a damned thing about good horseflesh but you always were a great judge of women."

"Speaking of women, how's that little granddaughter of yours? It's been about five years since I saw her. Has she changed much?" Calvin asked and Melissa felt a knot tighten in her stomach.

"My little granddaughter turned eighteen on her last birthday, my boy, and nothing's changed, if you know what I mean," Endicott replied, carefully watching Calvin's face for a reaction to his last words. He was rewarded by Calvin's undisguised discomfort as he reddened and shot the good doctor a warning look from his troubled gray eyes. But Melissa caught the exchange of looks between the two men and the knot tightened inside of her. Calvin cleared his throat and attempted to lighten the situation.

"Belinda was a skinny little devil of a girl," he attempted to explain to Melissa, "always falling into something. You've never seen a girl try harder to act like a boy." His short burst of laughter seemed to falter as Melissa glared uncomprehendingly at him.

"Well, she stopped acting like a boy when she discovered the advantages of being a woman," Endicott interjected, puffing on his cigar, heartily amused by the attempt Calvin was making to placate the young woman beside him. "I've got to be getting back now, Cal, but we're staying at the Mountview Inn up the road a ways so I'm leaving it up to you to come by and call on us. Belinda would never forgive me if she knew I'd let you slip away without her seeing you." He bowed to Melissa and shook hands with Calvin, prepared to set off, when Calvin stopped him.

"We'll be attending the ball tonight at the clubhouse," he said, casting a furtive glance in Melissa's direction.

"Good, we'll be there as well. See you both then," Endicott smiled and with a friendly wave, he threaded his way among the tables and Calvin sat down again across from Melissa and took a deep swallow of his drink.

"You and Dr. Endicott seem to share some fabulous secret, dear Calvin," she commented, her voice tightly controlled, its tone mocking as she confronted him.

"We're not sharing any damn secrets," he snapped impatiently as he scowled over at her.

"How does it involve you and this Belinda then?" she persisted, undaunted by his irritability.

"David and I go back a long time," he answered, a cutting edge to his voice, "and when I knew her, Belinda Endicott was a very lonely little girl. An orphan, if you want to be more precise."

"Another lonely little girl," she returned harshly, ignoring the warning in his gaze as she plunged recklessly on. "And as with Kathleen Ransome, you were supposed to be the one to provide her with some form of loving stability. How many more unloved waifs should I expect to appear from somewhere in your past with some prior claim to you?" she finished bitterly.

"Those remarks were uncalled for, dammit," he barked, reaching for her and catching hold of her wrist, proceeding to twist it sharply as his anger mounted. "I've never been accountable to anyone for my actions and I have no intention of starting now. Do you understand me, Melissa?" he growled, increasing the pressure on her wrist until she cried out in pain.

"I understand perfectly, Calvin," she said in a

scathing voice as she gingerly massaged her bruised flesh. "And since I understand, why not indulge me by telling me something about little Belinda?" Her mouth settled into an inscrutable smile as she attempted to camouflage her turbulent emotions.

Calvin studied her curiously for several moments, trying to divine her intentions, but she sat there quietly, her hands folded placidly in her lap, appearing almost docile. With a sigh of exasperation, he raked his fingers through his hair and gave in.

"David looked after our horses when my father was just starting the stud farm," he began gruffly. "If it weren't for his expertise, we would have lost many of our horses out of sheer ignorance during those first few years. Well, David had a son, Hiliard, who had fought in the Civil War and come home more dead than alive. But he married his childhood sweetheart and they eventually had a daughter, Belinda. Hiliard had lost a leg in the war and had never fully recovered from his wounds, and as a result, he was bedridden much of the time. They all lived near us, in a small house on Stony Briar land, and David and his wife looked after them." His eyes clouded then and his face contorted with pain, but he forced himself to continue.

"One night, while the rest of the family was at a church dinner and Hiliard was alone at home, he must have fallen asleep in front of the fireplace. Some flying sparks evidently set fire to his clothing and by the time he awakened, his clothes were ablaze." Calvin's voice cracked and he reached for his drink, downing it quickly. "He managed to drag himself to the front door and that's where they found him." His eyes were glassy as he stared above Melissa's head. She sat there horrified, silently willing him to stop his tale, but unable to even whisper the words.

"His wife, Ginny, nearly lost her mind, blaming herself for having left him by himself when it was so difficult for him to move around. Less than a year later, she was found in the river. She had drowned herself, leaving behind a four-year-old girl for David and his wife to rear."

"How awful," Melissa murmured, instinctively groping for his hand, but he shrugged her off.

"David's wife died five years ago and he took Belinda to live on a small farm he'd purchased not far from here. We've managed to keep track of one another in spite of the distance, but this is the first time we've seen each other in those five years." His eyes hardened then as he said bluntly, "I intend to see both David and Belinda while I'm here. Have I made myself clear, Melissa?" he challenged her, and once more she was forced to relent, nodding her head in mute assent.

"Good, then seeing as that's settled, I think I'd like to get out of here." He pushed himself back from the table while Melissa struggled with her own chair and scrambled after him.

chapter 29

That evening she dressed for the clubhouse ball with particular care, determined to look especially alluring for Calvin, assuage his ruffled feelings, and make amends for the distressing afternoon they had spent together. But as she brushed out her hair, she admitted that her attempts were for another reason as well, for she feared that she was once again losing the tenuous hold she had on his affections. The gown she had selected was of fine white muslin, its filmy skirt richly embroidered with gold leaves, the delicate threads embossing the edging of the sleeveless bodice and deep, plunging neckline as well. For the sake of coolness, Melissa had instructed Madame Elise to create the gown without draped panniers or a bustle and as a result, the tissue-thin fabric clung seductively to her supple curves as she moved.

She carefully arranged her auburn hair in a mass of sinuous tendrils through which she entwined gold leaves and tiny white feathers. Deftly fastening the last of the little plumes, she wrapped a gold-net shawl around her shoulders and picked up her gold-beaded evening purse just as a knock sounded at her door. She hastened to open it and confronted Calvin, formally attired in a white suit which heightened his dark skin and accentuated his tall, lithe frame. Aware of the pulse fluttering inside her and the slight weakness pervading her, she nonetheless forced a smile to her lips and accepted his proferred arm.

As they were ushered into the brilliantly lighted reception room at the clubhouse, Melissa removed her shawl, slinging it casually over her arm. Chancing a stealthy look at Calvin, she was taken aback by the glowering expression on his face.

"Do you realize that your gown is practically transparent?" he demanded, catching her roughly by the shoulders and steering her away from the other arriving guests.

"Let go of me, please, you are hurting me," she hissed, squirming in his grasp.

"Do you have to parade yourself in front of everyone as if you were a whore?" he snarled, "or are you tiring of my company and deciding to advertise for another patron?"

"I could scarcely consider you company," she countered, mortified by his words, stunned by the reception her painstaking efforts had received.

"Then, if you don't like my presence here, by God find yourself someone more suitable," he replied, spinning on his heel and striding off through the crowd.

She called after him but he belligerently pushed his way through the milling guests and was soon lost from view. Standing there, burning with humiliation, she absently nibbled at her lower lip as she looked anxiously around the vast room, hoping to recognize some of the guests at their hotel. The beautifully gowned women and formally dressed men were all strangers to her. She wandered to a deserted corner of the room and unhappily sank onto a small gilded chair.

Couples danced past her as a small orchestra began to play. Melissa was taken by surprise when a young man, not much older than herself, bowed stiffly before her and asked her to dance. She gratefully accepted. As he spun her about the floor, she laughed and flirted with him, pleased with the effect she seemed to have on him.

She felt peculiarly light-hearted and as she was passed to another eager partner, she made up her mind to enjoy herself despite the irascible Calvin Gabriel. She would manage perfectly well without him.

So she whirled about the room with one attentive partner after another, her face animated and faintly flushed, her skin glowing, offset by the ivory whiteness of her gossamer wisp of a gown. Finally pleading fatigue, she allowed herself to be steered from the dance floor and seated on one of the plush, velvet sofas beneath an open window. She fanned ineffectually at her face with a gloved hand and as she searched the room for a tall figure clad in a white suit, she spotted him at last.

He spun past her with a young woman in his arms, a girl who could have been none other than Belinda Endicott. In spite of her determination to ignore the situation, Melissa was stricken with a pang of unremitting jealousy. As her eyes trailed after the dancing couple, she studied the girl with the golden brown hair arranged in saucy curls entwined with yellow ribbons atop her head. Her piquant, heart-shaped face was tipped to one side as she stared up at Calvin, regarding him with huge, dark eyes. A simple yellow and white striped muslin gown with huge puffed sleeves hugged her petite form and her young breasts peeked shyly from a froth of lace edging her modest decolletage. Melissa smothered a laugh as she watched the unlikely twosome disappear among the other dancing couples and she felt somewhat heartened. Surely Calvin was trying to punish her for her own daring appearance by choosing to lavish his attentions on such an innocent-looking child.

But her smile changed slowly to a frown when she realized that Belinda Endicott was not a child but a woman only two years younger than herself. And no sooner had Melissa been freed of the threat of Daphne Somers, who had returned to New York City with the man she had enticed during Calvin's absences at

Belmont Park, than this woman-child had appeared to further upset the tremulous calm. With a sullen pout, Melissa turned back to the man at her side, feigning interest in what he was saying, while her troubled thoughts remained elsewhere. Just then she noticed Dr. Endicott making his way toward her and she excused herself from the boring young man next to her and returned to the dance floor with the elegant doctor.

"You look radiant this evening, Miss Howell," he said as he expertly guided her about the room. His arms tightened around her as they moved until her breasts were crushed up against the nubby linen of his jacket. She stiffened, squirming in his embrace. Aware of her discomfort, he did nothing to alleviate her distress, but chuckled softly to himself as he bent to whisper in her ear.

"Calvin's a damned lucky man, you know. But then he always did know how to choose his women."

"I am not his woman," she replied, bridling at his assumption, seething with indignation at his effrontery. Again she tried to loosen his grip on her, but he was surprisingly strong for a man of his years and he held onto her with a grip of iron. Then, before she quite comprehended what was happening, Endicott lowered his head and planted a moist kiss on her shoulder. She flinched, staring up at him in disgust while he compounded the insult by throwing back his head and roaring with laughter.

"Don't look so surprised, my dear," he blurted out when he finally stopped laughing. "Anyone as provocatively gowned as you is begging for such advances."

"Your remarks remind me very much of a dear friend of yours, Dr. Endicott, and I resent your insinuations as much as his," she charged angrily. "Now would you be so kind as to release me."

He considered her for a moment and then as a slight flush reddened his face, he mumbled awkwardly, "Allow me to apologize, Miss Howell. I was obviously mistaken in my assumption."

"Your apology is accepted, Dr. Endicott. Now let me go," she commanded and as his grip relaxed, she spun free and hurtled across the dance floor.

"Melissa, wait a minute."

She froze as Calvin's voice interrupted her flight from the humiliating scene with his friend, and she faced him with cold fury glazing her topaz eyes.

"What the hell did you do to poor David?" he laughed, his lips curved in a taunting grin.

"How dare you ridicule me," she spat. "Both you and dear Dr. Endicott are unprincipled scoundrels who need instructions in the proper treatment of ladies."

"I warned you about that dress, didn't I?" he retaliated, "and I've noticed that the other men you danced with had just as hard a time keeping their hands off you as poor David had."

"How would you know when you were busy amusing yourself with a child?"

"That child happens to be a lady—something you seem to know little about," he bellowed.

"Why do you treat me as little better than a whore when you make certain to keep me hidden away and reserved exclusively for your own use?" she lashed out at him, as angry tears welled up in her eyes and threatened to spill onto her flaming cheeks.

"Why should I want to share you with other men, Melissa?" he replied smoothly. "I want you all for myself."

"While I must watch you bed any woman you want," she blazed in defiance.

"That's a man's prerogative, my love," he said bluntly.

"Then exercise that prerogative, Mr. Gabriel, for I will never be your willing partner again," she flung back. Then, to her dismay, he insolently grazed the tops of her breasts with his fingers. At her sharp intake of breath, he murmured, "Are you so certain of that,

Melissa love?" He swept her into his arms and she felt his hardness piercing her through the sheerness of her gown. She clung to him, losing herself to the kiss he pressed onto her upturned, yielding mouth. Their bodies molded together, they glided slowly to the strains of a waltz, oblivious to everything but their mutual desire.

"Calvin," called a girl's thin voice and the intimacy crumbled, the moment lost as Calvin looked up and turned to regard Belinda Endicott, her bow-shaped mouth pouting prettily. "I'm tired of dancing with granddad and you know how strict he is about my dancing with gentlemen I don't know." She smiled coyly at him, her high cheekbones lending her small face a feline grace as her brown eyes narrowed, their thick fringe of lashes veiling them slightly.

Clearing his throat uncomfortably, Calvin managed to introduce the two young women who glared at one another, each studiously taking the other's measure. Melissa boldly returned the girl's unabashed scrutiny, holding herself proudly as Belinda's eyes disdainfully scanned her willowy body so temptingly outlined by the diaphanous muslin.

"Calvin has told me about you, Belinda." She forced herself to smile at the younger woman in an effort to ease the mounting tension.

"Did he also tell you that he'd promised to marry me?" the girl asked coolly, her hand stroking Calvin's arm affectionately. Melissa's smile cracked and slowly disintegrated.

"Child's games, pet, you were six years old at the time," he chuckled, avoiding Melissa's distressed gaze. So that was what had not changed, she mused, feeling a sudden constriction in her throat.

"But why would you have remained unmarried all these years if you weren't waiting for me to come of age?" she persisted gamely. Calvin looked exceedingly uncomfortable and he began tugging at his shirt collar as if it were suddenly too tight.

"Perhaps you should realize that Calvin is not the marrying kind," Melissa spoke up tartly, unable to endure the interplay any longer as she numbly recalled the similar words Amanda Ransome had used to warn her long ago.

"Is that what he's told you?" Belinda taunted, "or are you hoping he'll change his mind and marry you instead?"

"Belinda, that wasn't necessary," Calvin cut in sharply. "Whatever happened to that shy little girl I used to know?"

"She grew up," came Belinda's curt reply and she brushed past him, her brown curls bouncing as she walked away.

"She appears to be a rather determined young lady," remarked Melissa as Calvin took her in his arms once again.

"Belinda's still a child in many ways," he mused, shaking his head in bewilderment.

"And I had thought you were convinced otherwise," she commented, her tone heavy with sarcasm.

"Please, love, let's not fight about this anymore," he pleaded wearily. She nodded her head solemnly and nestled against him as they moved about the floor.

They continued dancing, maintaining a fragile peace, until a man approached Calvin and placed a hand on his shoulder and Melissa found herself in a stranger's embrace once more. As the man whirled her off, she peered over his shoulder and saw a triumphant, smiling Belinda boldly make her way to Calvin's side. Enraged by the girl's manipulation, Melissa endured her new partner for the remainder of that dance and then hastily extricated herself from his grasp.

Scanning the room, her gaze finally lighted on an attractive young man standing alone. Hurrying over to him, she whispered urgently into his ear and pointed out the dancing couple to him. Fortunately for her, he proved to be a willing accomplice, eager to join in her little ruse and he went off smiling broadly to claim Belinda for a dance. When he had succeeded in wresting the protesting girl away from Calvin, Melissa walked confidently across the floor and slipped back into his waiting arms.

"My clever girl," he muttered, his eyes twinkling despite his gruffness as he observed her victorious smile. Then, without another word, he led her from the room, down the clubhouse steps, and back to their carriage.

She hung away her gown and slipped into a sheer nightdress, then set about dismantling her elaborate coiffure. Standing within the faint circle of light cast by the bedside lamp, she languidly brushed out her hair, walking slowly toward the silvering glow of moonlight peering into the room. When she heard his soft rapping at the door, she remained calmly at the window, and as Calvin entered, he observed her, bathed in moonglow, her body temptingly displayed before him. Watching her there, he felt a constriction in his chest, a tightening in his loins. He moved toward her, taking the brush from her hand and running it through her hair with long, steady strokes until it crackled and shone and tumbled smoothly around her.

Tossing the brush aside, he captured her silken hair in his hands, wrapping the gleaming curls around his fingers, pressing his face against its fragrant softness. She turned to look at him and drew him down to her, her lips lightly skimming the surface of his, teasing him, tantalizing him as her tongue traced the outline of his parted mouth. He moaned and drew his fingers from her hair and massaged her tingling flesh, caressing her shoulders and lowering the thin straps of her nightgown, allowing it to slide to the floor at her feet.

His hands moved down her back and cupped her firm buttocks. She felt her knees begin to weaken as a pulsing ache throbbed upward from her legs. Calvin scooped her up into his arms and carried her to the bed, gently laying her on the satin coverlet before loosening the sash on the dressing gown he wore. Slipping out of the garment, he flung it across the chair beside him. Then he stretched out on the bed and resumed his exploration of her inviting body. She trembled in the wake of his traveling fingers, and her thighs parted, urging him inward.

She arched against him and her head thrashed from side to side as a mounting tension built within her. Locking her arms about his neck, she beckoned him deeper and deeper. As he plunged back and forth inside of her, he aroused a quivering passion she had never known before. She began spinning upward from their joining in tiny waves, until she felt them spread into a swirling eddy, carrying her along with it. Caught in its spiraling momentum, she spun beyond her thrusting body toward a pinnacle of delicious agony. He pulled her back from the giddy heights and she cried out to him. But he laughed and hurtled her up again until she flared in a burst of fiery sparks. Shuddering in her release, she sobbed his name and fell from him only to be caught again in gasping ecstasy as she absorbed the fury of his own shattering climax.

Their bodies lay entangled together, their limbs intertwined, her hair a silken cushion for their heads. Easing himself from her arms, Calvin slid onto the covers beside her and turned onto his back, staring up at the ceiling. A cold hand closed over Melissa's heart as she felt him withdrawing from her, and in her fear and her loneliness, she reached out for him. He cradled her against his chest, holding her until she fell asleep.

chapter 30

Calvin returned to Belmont Park several times that week in order to watch the running of his other three thoroughbreds. Melissa, in the meantime, contented herself with daily rides over the familiar countryside atop the magnificent Regent. Returning one afternoon from one of her long excursions, Melissa slowed her horse and headed for the stables when she again experienced the eerie feeling that someone was watching her. As she dismounted and looked around her, she could find nothing suspicious about any of the people nearby, yet she could not shake off the unsettling sensation.

As she crossed the wide front porch of the hotel, she happened to notice a middle-aged man, a pair of binoculars hanging from a cord around his neck, sitting in one of the chairs. Melissa recalled having seen him in the hotel dining room from time to time and wondered if he were the cause of her uneasiness. He seemed oblivious to her presence as she studied him and, with a careless toss of her shoulders, she hurried past him and continued into the hotel.

The following morning, as Melissa swung into the saddle, she was startled to see the same man, the binoculars slung around his neck again, hail her and hurry toward her. Relaxing her grip on the reins, she patted Regent's neck, stroking him gently and calming him as the man puffed to a halt beside them.

"Miss Howell, I believe," he said, and she inclined her head slightly. "I've been watching you for some time now." And he indicated the binoculars. "I must admit to being mighty impressed by your horsemanship."

"Thank you very much," she managed to blurt out, her eyes widening in disbelief at the surprising confirmation of her suspicions.

"Miss Howell, I'll come straight to the point," the man stated. "My name is Nathan Salsbury and although I'm sure you've never heard of me, I imagine that the name of my partner will mean something to you. William F. Cody, better known as Buffalo Bill." At this, she nodded, feeling a vague stirring within her as the man continued. "I act as talent scout and press agent for the show and I'm always on the lookout for fresh talent. And Miss Howell, I believe that you have the kind of talent we can use."

"Do you mean that you want me to join the Wild West Show?" she asked incredulously.

"Can you handle a firearm?" he persisted gamely. "Say a rifle or a pistol?"

"Both," she replied.

"Good shot?"

"Excellent."

"When could you be ready to start with us?"

"Start?" she repeated. "But that would be impossible. I mean, I have no intention of joining such a show," she stumbled over her words as she stared at him.

"We can always use a good horsewoman, Miss Howell. There are many acts in the show. Some drop out and others are added. Changes are constantly being made. One of the most popular acts is our little Annie Oakley. Just think of it," he smiled, encompassing his grandiose scheme with a wide sweep of his arms, "a continuous competition between two women sure shots." He paused, squinting up at her. "That's what they call Annie, you know, Little Sure Shot."

Melissa laughed, shifting her weight about in the saddle as Regent snickered impatiently. "What you are offering is very flattering, Mr. Salsbury, but I could hardly imagine myself involved in something like that. Please forgive me if I sound ungrateful, but I must admit that I find the idea quite astounding."

"If you'd ever seen our show, astounding would be just the word you'd use to describe it, Miss Howell," Salsbury said quietly, "because we bring the west to life, complete with its legends, and the folklore of our native people. Most Americans only read about that kind of life in books, but it's a spectacle which should be seen at least once in a lifetime."

He reached into his breast pocket and pulled out a small white card, handing it up to her. "The show will be playing in Hartford, Connecticut next month and from there, we'll be moving on to New York City in the fall. This is my business card, and if you should ever change your mind and reconsider my offer, you'll know where to find me." And with a polite bow, he walked back toward the hotel.

Melissa slipped the card into the pocket of her breeches and nudged Regent forward, absently giving him his head. Her thoughts, meanwhile, were elsewhere, her imagination stimulated by Salsbury's words. She strained to recall what she had once read about the Wild West Show and the magic it dispersed as it moved from town to town. Her mind quickly filled with images of mounted cowboys, fierce Indians streaked with body paints, and arenas crowded with cheering spectators. As she galloped over the hotel's grounds, she imagined herself, clad in fringed buckskin and brandishing a rifle, galloping instead around a giant indoor ring to the roar of approving thousands. Laughing aloud at her vivid imaginings, she forced the preposterous idea from her mind, the applause of her fantasy dissolving, the only sound remaining being the pounding of Regent's hooves.

Calvin returned from Belmont Park in time for dinner that evening, pleased that his horses were racing well. As he described the purses they had won, Melissa's thoughts again strayed, her ears ringing with the sound of clapping hands and thundering hooves. She speculated as to the wisdom of discussing her encounter with Nathan Salsbury and his remarkable offer with the preoccupied Calvin, and chose to keep silent, ending their meal without her disclosure. As they strolled leisurely about the grounds, Melissa pondered Calvin's reaction to Salsbury's proposal, should she decide to tell him about it. He would probably find the idea amusing but, on the other hand, he might conceivably encourage her to consider it and finally rid himself of her.

"Belinda has apparently convinced old David to allow her to stay on while he goes back to his farm." Calvin's words penetrated the haze Melissa was floundering in and she stopped abruptly and stared up at him. "He's consented providing she stays here at the hotel where I'm expected to keep an eye on her."

"How convenient," she mumbled irritably.

"I hope to God that you two won't be at each other's throats," he growled. "The last thing I want is to chaperone two scrapping females." His voice softened then as he gazed at the stubborn face glaring hostilely at him. "She's a child, Melissa, and a very lonely one at that, so please try to be kind to her."

"She is no child, Calvin, she is only two years younger than I am," she retorted. "How can you expect me to watch you play nursemaid to her while she dreams up clever little schemes to get you to marry her? I refuse to endure that kind of situation."

From the look on his face, she regretted the words as soon as she had uttered them. Panic seized her as his eyes hardened and his voice cracked like a whip as he lashed out at her.

"No one is forcing you to put up with anything, Melissa. And if the situation is so distasteful, I suggest that you find one more to your liking." And he left her, standing miserably alone in the garden, while he walked back to the hotel.

The following day, Calvin announced he was heading back to the racetrack and would return that night with Belinda Endicott in tow, whether Melissa approved or not. She sat in the dining room, staring unhappily at her untouched breakfast, her stomach heaving at the mere sight of the food before her. She felt uncommonly fatigued and after Calvin's frosty attitude toward her, she found she had little desire to do more than mope about her room. Having slept scarcely at all the previous night, Melissa spent the entire day stretched out on her bed, napping off and on, but feeling no better when she awoke to find it was dinner time.

She asked that a tray of food be prepared and sent to her room, but when it arrived she stared vacantly at it, not even tempted to lift a single forkful to her lips. She ignored the questioning glance of the young maid who stopped by to collect the tray and she listlessly slumped in a chair by the window, staring out at the trees below. Closing her eyes, she conjured up the fanciful world of Bill Cody and stepped into its welcoming magic, basking in the love of the faceless crowds surrounding her. Gaudy paints and feathers, fringes and shotguns, teepees and clouds of smoke, wagon wheels and whooping Indians blended together in a kaleidoscopic whirl, and in the midst of it all stood Calvin Gabriel, forcing her out of his life and into a world of make-believe.

The sound of girlish laughter shook her free, dispelling her tangled thoughts, and she knew that he had come back and that Belinda was with him. She listened for the footsteps passing her door and continuing down the corridor and she heard the faint closing of a door at the end of the hallway. Belinda's room. So close. The pain drove Melissa from the hotel. She walked for hours until she could push her weary body no further and then she trudged back to her room and collapsed on the bed, falling into an exhausted slumber.

Melissa forced her swollen eyelids open, blinking in the glare of the sun's bright intrusion, and grimaced as she raised her aching head. Pushing herself from the bed, she struggled to her feet, but a wave of dizziness sent her reeling back and she sat down heavily again. Then, as a spasm of nausea coursed through her, she lay back on the bed and gulped deep breaths of air to calm her heaving insides. Her enforced slow breathing seemed to quell the rising in her throat, but she rested until the feeling passed completely before attempting to get up.

As she entered the dining room, she was relieved to find no sign of either Calvin or Belinda and she managed several cups of strong tea and a hot biscuit without feeling sick again. Passing by the front desk, she asked for Mr. Salsbury's room and learned that he had checked out of the hotel earlier that morning. She scribbled down his forwarding address in Hartford and when she returned to her room, she tucked the address together with Salsbury's business card into her old, battered reticule and slid it back into her cupboard.

Once more she spent the day resting in her room, battling the continuing queasiness in her stomach. Eventually, when she mustered all of her strength and had begun to dress for dinner, Calvin stormed into the room and confronted her as she calmly brushed out her hair.

"I've come to find out if you've reached some kind of decision, Melissa," he stated bluntly.

"What decision, may I ask?" she inquired innocently, the brush gliding methodically through her hair.

"You know damned well what I mean!" he argued. "Do you intend to remain here or have you decided to leave us?"

"I have not made up my mind as yet," she replied sullenly. There was a long pause before he spoke again.

"Will you be joining us for dinner then?"

"Am I to take that as an invitation?" she asked.

"Take it however you like," he snapped. "Dammit, woman, you try my patience."

"In that case, I accept." She smiled sweetly at him as he released a loud sigh of exasperation and slammed the door behind him.

When she reached the dining room, Calvin and Belinda were already seated, but Calvin immediately rose and assisted Melissa with her chair. Forcing a smile to her lips, she looked at Belinda who gazed guilelessly back at her.

"I'm so pleased that granddad is allowing me to remain here awhile longer," she bubbled to Melissa although her radiant smile was directed at Calvin. "And you're such a dear for putting up with me," she simpered, leaning across the table and resting her hand on his.

"What else are guardians for?" Melissa supplied caustically, receiving a scathing glance from Calvin, who then ignored her and centered his attention on the lively young girl with the animated brown eyes.

As Belinda kept up an incessant stream of gay chatter, Melissa stared blindly at the menu in front of her, freeing her troubled thoughts to wander elsewhere. Calvin's sharp command plummeted her back to earth as he asked again for her order. Her stomach quaked ominously as she hastily scanned the large card she held in one shaking hand. She blurted out the first item she chanced to see. She smiled tremulously at him, handing him the menu, and she wondered at the perplexed frown on his face.

"Is something wrong?" she asked.

"You just ordered breakfast, Melissa," he said, giving the menu back to her. "Now would you care to look at the dinner items?"

She flushed in embarrassment, her discomfort increasing as Belinda tittered and then burst into gales of laughter. "I really have no appetite," she mumbled, as she attempted to distinguish the words which had begun to blur in front of her. Shakily, she got to her feet, knocking the chair over as she rose. Calvin sprang to his feet and retrieved the fallen chair as Melissa whispered, "Would you both excuse me, I'm not feeling very well."

"Melissa?" Belinda's voice was concerned, but she was already stumbling away from the table, afraid that she would be sick in front of everyone. When she reached the door of the dining room, she broke into a run.

Calvin found her lying in a crumpled heap beside the washstand in her bedroom. He picked her up in his arms and stretched her out across the bed, soaking a cloth with water and sponging her face and neck.

"You look terrible," he said, settling the cloth on her forehead, and she limply raised a hand to hold it there.

"I feel terrible," she admitted weakly.

"Something you ate at lunch?" he asked, his voice strangely subdued.

"Yes, probably," she whispered, not admitting to him that she had not eaten lunch that day.

"Do you want me to locate a doctor?"

"No, I should be better by morning," she answered, knowing that that, too, was a lie.

"If you need me, I'll be in the dining room, but I'll check with you again after we've eaten." He eased himself from the bed and left the room.

No sooner had the door closed behind him than Melissa removed the dripping cloth from her head and flung it viciously onto the floor. With a sob, she turned over onto her stomach and buried her face in her pillow.

And as she lay there, the truth she had refused to acknowledge over the past weeks could no longer be denied. She was pregnant.

Placing a trembling hand on her belly, she wondered how long it would be before the telltale signs were visible. In despair she knew that her condition would make little difference to Calvin and that she dared not use it to force him into a marriage he did not want. She bitterly recalled the tragedy of Amanda and Bryan Ransome and Cornelia Simmonds, three people whose lives had been marred by bitterness and hatred because of just such a mistake. And she vowed that no man would ever be coerced into marrying her, that he would do so of his own accord and because he truly loved her.

She managed to endure the following days by keeping to her room or sitting in one of the chairs on the terrace, sipping iced lemonade which soothed her stomach. Calvin and Belinda rode together each day and when they asked solicitously after her health, Melissa explained her distress as acute food poisoning. Calmly meeting Calvin's eyes, her gaze unwavering, she gave him no indication that what she was saying was a lie. He seemed to accept her excuse and devoted himself to satisfying the whims and caprices of the untiring and demanding Belinda. In the privacy of her room, Melissa, meanwhile, carefully counted out her remaining funds and began to plan for herself and her unborn child.

chapter 31

One morning, Melissa felt considerably better and had Regent saddled. She spent the day happily riding the countryside she had been forced to glimpse from her window or from the terrace for too long, and when she returned to the hotel with a high flush in her cheeks and a sparkling glow in her eyes, she felt revitalized and renewed. The change in her appearance was evident and Calvin was particularly effusive as he welcomed her back to their table that evening.

"I'm relieved that you're feeling better, Melissa," put in Belinda, but her eyes quickly returned to Calvin's face as if restating her prior claim to his attentions. Melissa seemed oblivious to the other girl and, discovering that she was truly famished, she finished a hearty meal and ordered a second dessert, much to everyone's amusement. But she felt a flutter of fear inside her when she caught Calvin's perturbed gaze, for he was studying her with the same puzzled look he had worn when she had mistakenly ordered the wrong meal a week before.

"Calvin and I have been involved in a running argument for several days now, Melissa." Belinda interrupted Melissa's worried thoughts. "He thinks that marriage is fine for women, but not for men. Have you ever heard of anything as absurd?" she demanded, throwing Calvin a contemptuous glare.

"I think he means that not all men want to marry and that they should have that choice," Melissa replied, carefully choosing her words. "Some men are much better off never marrying for they would probably make miserable husbands." Her pointed glance was not missed and Calvin laughed heartily.

"Well said, Melissa," he said, applauding her. "You've expressed my sentiments exactly."

"But what about children?" Belinda insisted.

"What about them?" Calvin barked, his tone becoming surly as he faced the girl.

"I thought most men wanted children, especially boys, you know, to carry on the family name," she explained. Calvin listened to her words and then flung his napkin onto the table and rose to his feet.

"Not all couples should have children," he snarled. "They only seem to complicate everyone else's lives. Look at my own dear mother or Amanda and Bryan Ransome." His mouth was set in a hard line, his voice edged with venom. "What happiness did they derive from their children or their children from them?" With that, he stormed from the room. Belinda's lower lip trembled and tears welled up in her huge dark eyes as she looked helplessly at Melissa. But Melissa had little time to console the girl for her stomach had begun to quaver and, pushing herself back from the table she bolted from the dining room. Tugging at her skirts, she raced up the stairs to her bedroom, barely reaching it in time.

By the following morning, all traces of the bitter argument of the previous evening had vanished and Calvin invited the two women to join him at Belmont Park to watch two of his horses run, then go to a dinner dance at one of the local clubs. As Melissa dressed for the outing, she carefully scrutinized her body, gingerly touching her breasts and finding them tender and sensitive and somewhat fuller than usual. But her stomach was still taut and firm and she had no difficulty slipping into her yellow and green striped muslin gown, despite the new snugness in the bodice.

The grounds of the racetrack were alive with people and it appeared to be as crowded as it had been on the day of the running of the Belmont Stakes. Eyes followed the tall, striding figure of Calvin Gabriel who had protectively clasped the arms of the two women walking at his side as he escorted them to their seats in his reserved box. Melissa glanced curiously around her at the milling throngs while Belinda devoted her full attention to Calvin.

As the races progressed, Melissa found that she was barely concentrating on them. Her head was beginning to ache and she fumbled with the ribbons on her sweeping sun hat, loosening them to relieve the pressure of the heavy bonnet. Digging into her small purse, she extracted a lace-edged handkerchief which she used as a makeshift fan to cool her face. But as the sun beat down on her, its stinging rays mercilessly assaulting her, she began to grow faint and lowered her head to her lap.

"What's the matter, Melissa?" Calvin whispered, catching hold of her arm.

"I feel somewhat faint," she whispered back. "The sun is so hot." Her lips felt dry, her throat parched as she forced the words out.

"Let's find you some place to lie down," he said, the urgency in his voice unsettling her. She stiffened and straightened again as the wave of dizziness passed and she forced a wan smile in Calvin's direction.

"Perhaps if you could fetch me some water," she murmured, her voice trailing off weakly.

"If you're certain that's all you need," he snapped, and as he rose and left his seat, she was terrified that she had given herself away. Belinda reached over and squeezed her hand reassuringly, smiling at her in her childlike way.

"The heat's really unbearable, isn't it," she soothed. "I'd rather be back at the hotel, having a cool drink on the terrace right now," she added, her eyes alight with mischief. "Shall we sneak off?" she giggled.

Melissa smiled at the girl's brave attempts to humor her, and shook her head. "Calvin would never forgive us," she replied seriously, watching the glint fade in Belinda's eyes. She hastily added, "But I want to thank you for understanding and trying to help." The light returned to the large brown eyes.

Calvin scrambled back to his seat, spilling some of the water from the tumbler he carried, just as the race in which his horse, Moon Dust, was running was about to begin. Handing the brimming glass to Melissa, he hunched forward and trained his gaze on the track below. Melissa sipped on the cool water, swallowing it in small gulps and when she felt better, she forced her attention back to the race.

"Keep your fingers crossed," Calvin muttered as he stared straight ahead of him. "Moon Dust is a good sprinter, but I don't know if she can top Blue Jay, who's favored four to one."

The horses broke from the gate and Melissa spotted the familiar silver and blue of Stony Briar worn by Lemont Wilkie who was riding Moon Dust, aptly named for her speckled gray coat. At the clubhouse turn, Moon Dust was running slightly behind Blue Jay and Melissa concentrated on the see-saw battle developing between the two horses as they headed around the lower turn.

Pounding into the backstretch, Blue Jay fell back and Moon Dust sprinted ahead, and then it was Blue Jay back on top again. Melissa strained to locate the gray as a man stood up in front of her, and she moved forward in her seat to see Wilkie using his quirt, lashing the flank of Moon Dust, closing the gap between them and the leading Blue Jay once more. Into the homestretch they thundered, Moon Dust gradually gaining on Blue

373

Jay until the two animals were running neck and neck. Wilkie crouched lower in the saddle and the gray pulled ahead, opening up a slender lead. The two horses battled for first place and Moon Dust, in a final burst, crossed the finish line, winning the money by a nose.

Melissa dropped the glass with a loud shattering crash as Calvin crushed her to him in an exultant embrace. He pressed a hasty kiss onto her lips and then turned to hug Belinda to him. "Well, ladies," he beamed, "I've just made myself a tidy sum." He leaped from his seat and bolted for the stairs. "Come on," he shouted back over his shoulder, "we're off to celebrate."

"But don't you want to wait until Sinbad runs in the next race?" Belinda called out to him. But he shook his head and beckoned them to follow him.

At the fashionable country club, situated a mile from the racing grounds, Calvin broke open a bottle of champagne and lavishly filled glasses for Melissa and Belinda and for anyone else who happened to be standing near them. He toasted his afternoon's win and gulped down the contents of his glass, hastily filling it to the brim again and downing it once more. With a self-satisfied grin on his face, he tucked the bottle under his arm and marched off to celebrate further by himself. Melissa and Belinda exchanged bemused glances and raised their own glasses, sipping at them slowly and patiently awaiting Calvin's return.

During the long evening, Melissa held herself back from the elaborate buffet while the other guests descended upon it, plates waving, knives and forks brandished, as they attacked the food-laden tables. Silver platters boasted pheasant, partridge, and spiced beef as well as tongue, ham, and a variety of mushrooms unfamiliar to her. For dessert there were rich ice creams, meringues and baskets of succulent fresh fruit. Her stomach heaving ominously, Melissa turned away only to be swept into Calvin's arms and led out onto the dance floor. Despite her weak protestations, she followed him, moving rigidly in his embrace, mindful of the room spinning around her as she followed his intricate movements.

"Is something wrong, Melissa?" he finally asked, uncomfortable with her silence, unaware of her plight.

"No," she answered curtly.

"You've changed, you know," he persisted. "Are you pining for Mr. Holmes, princess?" He waited for her reaction, disappointed when she merely shook her head and continued to gaze off over his shoulder. "What happened to that marvelous temper of yours?" he baited her.

"Are you content only to fight with me?" she snapped, bridling at his persistence.

"At last, a spark," he laughed, kissing her lightly on the tip of her nose. "You know I'm happy to do more than just fight with you, love."

She resented his words and lapsed once more into gloomy silence, refusing to match his wit, tired of posing, wishing he would leave her alone. At the end of that dance, she found herself steered back to the buffet tables and abandoned while Calvin tugged Belinda toward the dance floor and took her into his arms instead.

When Calvin stopped by the chair in which Melissa had spent the remainder of the evening, he announced that he was ready to leave. Wearily, she heaved herself from the comfortable plush seat and followed him out to the carriage. As they jogged along the dirt road, the carriage sank into a deep rut and bounced out again and continued to pitch along at an unsteady pace. Melissa squirmed about on the leather seat as a peculiar feeling whirled through the lower part of her body. A sudden cramp caused her to gasp involuntarily, her hand flying up to her mouth as she winced in pain. Calvin and Belinda glanced at her, but the pain quickly passed and she was able to smile at them.

"It must be all these bumps," she explained unconvincingly, turning away from Calvin's scowling face to stare out of the carriage window at the darkened fields and ghostly silhouettes of trees.

As they neared the hotel, Melissa sat bolt upright, her eyes widening in fear as she noticed an unusual glow illuminating the darkness ahead of them. Calvin, who was seated across from her, observed her expression and turned around in his seat to follow her stare.

"Fire," he cried out. "Hurry, driver!" he shouted, kneeling across the seat, clinging to its high back for support as the coach jolted forward at a dangerous clip, the driver's whip snapping over the backs of his straining horses.

"My God, it's one of the stables," Belinda gasped, as they slammed to a halt. Calvin flung himself from the carriage and Melissa and Belinda scrambled after him. Ahead of them was chaos. Men in ragged lines were passing large wooden buckets along their ranks, dipping them into the water from one of the hotel's huge wells, and passing them back up the lines where they were dumped ineffectually on the spreading flames.

Melissa stood still for only a moment remembering that Regent was housed in the stable beside the one which was a raging inferno. The flames had already begun to eat away at the roof of the second stable and in the glare of the orange flames, she could see men leading blindfolded horses out of the burning buildings, tugging and yelling at the panicky beasts. The shouts of the men mingled with the high-pitched whinnies of the rearing horses as the men pitted their strength against the stubborn animals at the other end of their short tethers.

Snapping and popping, the tongues of fire sprang skyward. Billowing gray smoke spiraled into the air, its noxious vapors enveloping everyone struggling against the hungry flames. Hoisting her skirts, Melissa ran past the lines of black-faced, perspiring men, heading for the open door of the horse barn stabling her beloved Regent.

"Hey miss, you can't go in there," shouted a man, roughly pushing her aside as he led a struggling animal from his stall.

"But my horse is in here," she cried as she plunged further into the smoky interior, coughing as the poisonous fumes hit her full in the face. She blinked her smarting eyes as she tried to find Regent's stall. Running blindly, she called his name, her voice drowned out by the sounds of hooves kicking frantically against the walls of the stable and the terrified neighs of the frightened horses.

Groping for the catch on a stall door, Melissa flung open the gate and grappled with the horse inside, reaching up for its bridle, praying that her memory had served her well and that the animal she was tugging at was indeed hers. Choking down a wave of nausea, gasping for breath, she firmly grasped the bridle and pulled. But the horse balked, refusing to budge. Urging him forward, coaxing him with shaky words, she finally succeeded in leading him out of the stall.

As she hauled the animal after her, she glanced back over her shoulder, glimpsing the color of his mane in the light of the encroaching flames. In relief, she shouted his name and above the roaring, he responded, snapping his head upward and sending the tether flying from Melissa's grip. Desperately, she grabbed for him, catching the end of the tether with her fingertips as he reared up on his hindlegs, backing away from her.

A man leading another horse shoved Melissa out of the way and she stumbled aside, lunging once more for Regent and finally catching his bridle. Sobbing, gagging on the smoke, Melissa summoned all of her strength and tugged on the tether. A burst of sparks showered down on her and a falling timber crashed to the floor as she reached the door of the stable. As she fell through the doorway, she watched her horse break into the open, safe at last. A soot-covered man lumbered toward her and dragged her away from the building just as the roof caved in behind her and as she looked back, the two horse barns were nothing but blazing skeletons.

Away from the heat and the noise, Melissa crumpled to the ground, gazing at her torn and blackened gown, at her grimy hands and her arms which were covered with fine black powder. With a rueful smile, she absently smoothed the singed and tattered skirt. Then she heard someone calling her name and looked up to see Belinda running toward her. She managed a limp wave and attempted to stand up. It was then that the first pain knifed through her and she gasped and sank back onto the ground. A searing explosion seemed to shatter inside of her, leaving a dull throbbing in its wake. Terrified, she groped beneath her skirts and felt the sticky warmth oozing between her legs.

"What's wrong, Melissa, are you hurt?" Belinda cried, frightened by the look of pain on Melissa's perspiring, pallid face. But Melissa lacked the strength to answer and she closed her eyes against the fear and the knowledge that the life inside her was dying. She choked on her sobs and when she could bear it no longer, she cried out to Belinda and the younger girl cradled her in her arms. She reached for Melissa's icy hands to warm them but drew back in horror, seeing the blood which coated them. Melissa's eyes opened again, and she led Belinda's terrified gaze downward, down to the dark stain spreading across the ruined gown, before she sighed and settled back into the welcoming blackness and its release from pain.

"You're going to be fine, Melissa," the voice was saying. "The doctor was here and he took care of you and he promised that it won't be long before you're riding again."

Melissa opened her eyes and found that the voice was Belinda's. The girl was leaning over her, bathing her forehead with a wet cloth. She tried to return the smile she saw peering down at her, but it was too great an effort. She merely sighed and closed her eyes again.

She felt the bedcovers move and then she was aware of someone standing over her. She looked up. His face mirrored her own agony, his gray eyes cried out to hers and she turned away from the pain reflected there and buried her grief in the softness of her pillow. But he would not release her. He refused to let her go. He sat down on the edge of the bed and pulled her into the warm cradle of his arms, waiting for the tears to cease.

"Is Regent safe?" she whispered, fighting for time against the accusation written on his face.

"Melissa," he began, but she cut him off.

"Is he safe?" she repeated and he nodded. She breathed a long sigh of relief. "And the fire?"

"The two stables were completely destroyed, but the hotel wasn't touched."

"And the rest of the horses?" she persisted.

"Dammit, Melissa, I want to talk to you," he growled.

"Are the horses all safe too?" she interrupted.

"Yes." His voice quivered with exasperation. "But before you ask me anything else, there's something . . ." But she stopped him, pressing her hand over his mouth, staying the words she knew he must speak. He wrenched her hand away and his anger masked the hurt in his eyes.

"Just answer one question for me, Melissa." He spoke in a hushed voice as he searched her face for the answer her lips might never reveal. "Why?" he breathed. "Why didn't you tell me?"

"Would it have made any difference if I had?" she whispered.

He sat there stunned, groping for the words she should hear. But he could find no words. His shoulders sagged and he slumped there in the awful silence separating them. His tear-filled gaze held hers for a moment before he walked slowly out of the room.

A week later, Calvin took Belinda back to her grandfather's farm. Melissa kissed the girl goodbye and watched them settle themselves in the carriage. She returned to her room and packed a small valise, leaving no note for Calvin, for her departure would be explanation enough. A carriage delivered her to the railroad station where she boarded the train for Hartford, Connecticut. She had wired ahead and when the train pulled into the station, Melissa stepped onto the platform and into the welcoming arms of a beaming Nate Salsbury.

chapter 32

By the middle of September, the city of New York wore a coat of orange and scarlet; the lush tangle of trees and shrubs in Central Park was aflame with autumn's burnished colors. Along the park's winding paths clattered scores of elegant carriages bearing the city's elite on their Sunday outings, while its twisting maze of bridle paths bristled with the young and fit on horseback. Omnibuses overflowing with noisy passengers lurched up and down the busy streets of the metropolis, fighting for road space with one-passenger coaches, broughams, and phaetons, all drawn by prancing, high-stepping horses, their heads proudly tossing.

Nestled along broad, tree-lined boulevards were the imposing brownstone mansions of the wealthy, while climbing apartment towers, housing thousands, framed the city with a jagged, vertical skyline. New York, epitomized by the island of Manhattan, was a growing, restless giant, awakening and sprawling, absorbing many of the influences of the European continent and adding to them a style of its own.

A city of dramatic contrasts, it was peopled by the millionaire dynasties of Vanderbilts, Astors, Whitneys, and Rockefellers, as well as by wide-eyed arrivals from the ports of the world who knew that for them the streets would be paved with gold. New York's life was recorded in newspapers everywhere, the names and faces of its citizenry splashed in ink before the readers of the nation. A man named Boss Tweed had ruled Tammany Hall and the city's politics with an iron fist. There was a tiny theater-choked area known as Broadway, its stages illuminated by Europe's finest artistic exports—Britain's Lily Langtry and France's Sarah Bernhardt among them. Poets and artists were settling Little Bohemia, creating for themselves a replica of the Left Bank of Paris. Beautiful and brawling, ignoble and illustrious, New York was a burgeoning force with which the rest of the young country would have to reckon.

It was into this magical city that William F. Cody led his Wild West Show, to partake of its wonders while providing its people with a spectacle they might never again witness in their lifetime. With Cody came Melissa Howell, who had been eagerly awaiting their New York opening since joining up with the show more than two months before. She could feel the life of the city pulsing through her veins even as she sat astride her regal white stallion waiting for the procession to begin. Tradition, as set down by the irrepressible Cody, demanded a full-dress parade through the streets of each town the show played. New York was no exception.

To the curious onlooker, Melissa, clad entirely in crimson, could have been either a man or a woman. Sunlight glinted and bounced off the spangles encrusting the jacket, vest, and trousers of the tailored riding habit she wore. A glimpse of auburn hair at the neck beneath the crimson stetson provided no clue to the rider's gender; nor did her features, partially concealed by the spangled crimson mask which hid the upper portion of her sun-darkened face. Spangled crimson gloves covered her hands. Black boots with silver spurs peeped out from beneath her trousers, and the identity of the latest attraction in Cody's Wild West Show, billed simply and tantalizingly as Brandywine, remained a well-guarded secret.

Melissa had been physically weak and emotionally battered when she had thrown herself into the exuberance and hurly-burly of the show which centered itself around the charismatic William Cody. At forty, Buffalo Bill, former Indian fighter, army scout and cavalryman turned author, showman, and promoter of the West as he romantically envisioned it, had welcomed Melissa into his huge family the way a father would welcome a long-lost child. Six feet tall, with long, brown hair curling about his shoulders, Cody sported a drooping moustache and a somewhat straggly goatee. His piercing brown eyes could dance with merriment or flash like liquid fire when angered. But, on meeting Melissa, he had removed his Stetson, swept her a low, courtly bow, and his eyes had worn their warmest look. She had gazed back at this extraordinary man, his muscled frame encased in fringed deerskin, and had smiled a tremulous smile, losing her heart to him from the start.

It had not taken him long to fit her into the show. At her insistence, she wore the clothes of a man and further concealed her identity with the small glittering mask. Cody had cleverly traded on her riding talent and her unique disguise, creating an aura of mystery about the latest addition to his troupe. As Melissa had ridden in the procession through Hartford and performed nightly to sold-out theaters, a legend had been born. Nate Salsbury, with his uncanny eye for detail and his ingenious promotional schemes, saw in Melissa a wonderful opportunity, and he lost little time in using her on the show's handbills and posters. It was not long before the local newspapers and the local townspeople were caught up in the magic woven for them by the shadowed figure on the majestic white horse. WHO IS BRANDYWINE? shouted the bold print on the handbills bearing her image. The people who witnessed her dazzling performances left the show with the same question on their lips.

Through it all, Melissa had managed to maintain her privacy despite her life in a world which traded on its very antithesis, staying away from the other members of the show and keeping quietly to herself. To her surprise, Cody approved of her behavior, insisting that the fewer the people who knew her true identity, the less chance of the show's popular mystery figure being exposed.

Melissa's riding act was gradually expanded to include a varied obstacle course of graduated hurdles. The final hurdle proved to be a sensational show stopper. The wooden bar was wrapped in kerosene dipped rags which were ignited as she thundered around the ring. To the wide-eyed amazement of the crowd, the glittering crimson figure astride the gleaming white horse would leap into the air, soar gracefully over the bar of leaping flames, and ride off amid wild, tumultuous applause.

For New York, Cody had added a shooting competition between Melissa and Annie Oakley, the diminutive Laura Moses who, at twenty and the same age as Melissa, had already been with the show for two years and had long been the audience's darling. Petite with dark wavy hair and a piquant face, Annie strode about clad always in a shirt and cowboy skirt, wearing calf-high tooled leather boots and a broad sombrero perched atop her small head. Her aim was deadly in its accuracy and Melissa practiced her own shooting faithfully each day in an effort to keep up with the other girl.

Melissa's horse whinnied impatiently, one graceful foreleg stamping the ground, and she steadied him, stroking his mane and whispering his name. At last, she saw Cody sweep off his Stetson and raise his arm high into the air. He brought it down swiftly again and the procession was ready to begin. She nudged Target forward as the colorful throng of men and women and animals comprising the Wild West Show began moving down the wide avenue, waving to the crowds gathered on the sidewalks, smiling at the thousands of friendly, eager faces smiling back at them.

Lines of creaking covered wagons and rickety stage-coaches manned by fully costumed cowboys were quickly followed by groups of Indians, their dark faces and chests slashed with streaks of bright paint. Some wore single feathers in their beaded headbands while others were crowned with full feather headdresses, all signifying their importance in their tribes. Cowboys, their fringed chaps flapping, lunged and twisted atop large bucking broncos, one hand, clutching a ten-gallon hat, outstretched for balance, the other tightly gripping the short rein as they fought to keep their seat on the kicking animals.

Squaws, their faces lined with care, creased with age-old suffering, carried papooses across their back as they plodded by on pintos and piebalds. Among them all, moved clusters of shaggy buffalo, high-spirited mus-tangs, and dozens of yapping dogs.

Melissa smiled and waved, acknowledging the cheers and the shouts of "Brandywine, Brandywine" trailing her. She watched groups of youngsters, their hands tightly held by protective parents, straining to view every part of the passing parade. Several boys broke loose from their places and ran along beside the horses, keeping pace with them, reaching up to pat a flank or touch a boot of one of the riders. Slowly the procession wound its way through the streets, heading for Madison Square Garden, where the show was scheduled to appear twice daily until the spring.

As she moved closer to the vast arena which would be their home for several months, Melissa sighed, the smile fading from her face as she shifted to ease the cramping spasm in her back. The fleeting pain re-minded her that despite her existence in the fantasy world Cody had provided for her, she still only partially belonged to it. She eagerly awaited her turn during each performance and was thrilled at the applause greeting her entrance. Each lift from the ground exhilarated her. Each successful spin around the arena throbbed new life through her body, and the daily practices, the continual striving for perfection so exhausted her that she gratefully fell into easy slumber each night. But in spite of it all, she was still painfully alone. Early in the morning when she drifted upward, perched on the threshold of full awakening, she would see his face, remember his touch, and wake with a yearning deep inside her. Her pillows were often wet with her tears.

They had been performing at the Garden for three weeks and Melissa had again established a comfortable routine for herself. She was living in a small hotel, along with a number of the other members of the show, and she enjoyed the brisk nightly walks back to her small room when the cover of darkness provided her with a blanket of anonymity. She was free to bask in the sights and sounds of the city around her which never seemed to sleep. One night, as she prepared to set out for her hotel, there was a knock at her dressing-room door. Glancing around to assure herself that no signs of her costume were visible, she cautiously opened the door. A gasp of astonishment escaped her lips as she confronted a smiling Anthony Holmes.

"Aren't you going to invite me in?" he asked, his dark eyes crinkling in amusement at the look of amazement on her face. She immediately backed into the room, beckoning him inside, and she found herself swept into a warm embrace. He kissed her tenderly on the mouth and then held her away from him at arm's length, studying her. "You're more beautiful than ever, Melissa," he murmured. She smiled and found her voice at last.

"But how did you find me? How did you know I was here?" she blurted out, still trying to recover from the unexpected surprise.

"It was pure chance, I assure you," he chuckled. "I

was having dinner with an old friend last week." He paused. "Nate Salsbury." Melissa's eyes widened. "He's always after me for loans of one sort or another and as an added inducement this time, he insisted I join him for one of the performances. Naturally, he pointed out the latest attraction, and since I'd been reading all of that publicity he churns out, I was extremely curious about the enigmatic Brandywine. Nate obligingly provided me with the name of his masked rider, for a price of course. A sizeable loan and my sworn secrecy."

She shook her head thoughtfully and regarded him with gentle eyes. "It seems hard to believe," she said, her voice hushed, "but it certainly is wonderful to see you again."

"Why didn't you ever contact me, Melissa?" he asked her then.

"I would have, Anthony, in time," she answered hesitantly, "but I needed time alone for a while." Her sweeping lashes lowered, veiling her eyes and cloaking the pain mirrored there.

"That young man of yours?"

"I left him," she said simply. He nodded his head and seemed to dismiss the matter. Then he impulsively seized her hand and tucked it into the crook of his arm.

"How would you feel about me showing you some of the delights of this remarkable town?" he inquired, smiling warmly down at her.

"I would like that very much," she replied and he slid her cape around her shoulders and held open the door for her.

They strolled the long blocks between Madison Square and Forty Second Street, the area known as the Rialto, which was dominated by quaint hotels, gaudily lighted bars, and many of the city's fine theaters. Beneath the flickering of the gas lamps roamed hundreds of people, some spilling out of the emptying theater houses, others making their way to the bars for a late night drink before returning home. One by one the bold marquees, with their revolutionary incandescent lights, began to dim and the theaters seemed to be swallowed up by the night.

Melissa and Anthony followed a group of boisterous theatergoers into a small restaurant, the walls of which were lined with cartoon likenesses and ink sketches of many of the personalities lighting Broadway's stages. Melissa eagerly studied each one, seeking a familiar face, until Anthony laughingly dragged her away, steering her toward the impatient maitre d' who was waiting to seat them.

"Don't be too surprised to find your own face up there one of these days," Anthony remarked, handing her a gold-tasseled menu. "You're creating quite a sensation with that act of yours, you know."

"But then who but a few would even know it was me?" she murmured somewhat wistfully and began to peruse the menu in front of her.

"Tell me, Melissa, whose idea was it for the disguise and why the name Brandywine?" he asked, leaning toward her conspiratorially.

"Bill wanted something unique for me," she replied in hushed tones, "and my situation provided a solution acceptable to both of us. I wanted to remain anonymous for personal reasons, which you might guess at," she added wryly, "and that led to the costume I designed for myself. As for Brandywine—" and her eyes clouded as she spoke the name— "that was the name of the horse my father gave me for my sixteenth birthday. She was a magnificent chestnut with a coat which seemed to glow like molten copper." Her voice trailed off and Anthony cleared his throat awkwardly, bringing her back to him.

"How did you come to meet Nate?" he asked and when he heard her answer, he threw back his head and roared with laughter. "Of course, of course," he conceded, wiping at his eyes. "I bumped into him there a number of times myself. But if I had known something like this was going to be the outcome, I would have introduced you to him long ago." His features suddenly bore a solemn look. "Anything to have enticed you to the city sooner." She felt a quickening in her pulse as she hastily averted her gaze.

During the meal, she told him of her life with the show and of her decision to finally leave Calvin Gabriel. Cautiously avoiding any mention of her short-lived pregnancy, she spoke in a rush, her words spilling out, tumbling freely from her lips as she was finally able to open her heart to someone who would listen to her and understand.

"I had to leave him, Anthony," she finished. "It was either that or continue to watch him flaunting his Daphnes or his Belindas in front of me. I despise him for that," she declared vehemently.

"Of course you do, my dear," he nodded, his eyes skeptical in spite of his outward agreement with her. But Melissa was unaware of the ironic twist to the set of his smile as her attention had been arrested by a superbly gowned and bejeweled woman making a deliberate entrance into the restaurant. Melissa was not alone in her wonderment for the chatter at many of the nearby tables had abruptly ceased as heads turned in the direction of the door. As if an imaginery signal had been given, the woman straightened haughtily and swished into a hushed room with two handsome young men following obediently behind her. Casually flinging the trailing end of a long fur stole over one slender shoulder, she floated serenely to a specially set table in the corner and watched with detached amusement as her two escorts battled over the privilege of seating her.

"That, my dear Melissa, is Lillian Russell," Anthony explained, "the golden girl with the silvery voice as she has been called. She has long been the bewitching star of light opera and she commands as much attention off stage as on." He grimaced, turning toward Melissa again as she met his gaze.

"I wonder how it must feel to have men fawning over you that way," she mused.

"Perhaps this will sound dull in comparison," Anthony put in, "but will one man do for the present?"

"One man will do very nicely, Anthony," she smiled, reaching for his hand across the table and pressing it tightly.

In the weeks that followed, Melissa found herself even busier then before. Cody, capitalizing on the drawing power of his new star, built two additional numbers around her. Although her schedule had become more demanding, she reveled in the outpouring of affection which greeted each of her dramatic entrances and followed her movements as she galloped through the vast arena where fifteen thousand voices shouted as one in their love for her.

One evening, as she was hurrying toward her dressing room to change her clothes before meeting Anthony, she heard footsteps echoing behind her. Glancing over her shoulder, she spotted a sandy-haired young man, a notepad clutched in one hand, trying to catch up with her. Angrily, she wondered what had become of Jared Rawlins, the bodyguard for some of the female performers, who had been assigned to keep reporters and curious spectators away from Melissa at all times. But as she neared her dressing room without any sign of Rawlins, she sped into the room and swiftly bolted the door.

Almost immediately a pair of angry fists began beating on the flimsy wooden door while Melissa stood perfectly still, holding her breath, not daring to call out and give herself away. Then the hammering ceased and the doorknob was tried, worked back and forth and impatiently rattled.

"I just want a few minutes of your time," shouted the voice, "I'm from the *Times* and I could get you excellent coverage. Draw even more people to the shows. Hello.

Answer me, dammit, I know you're in there." He continued his pounding and calling until Melissa heard the booming voice of Jared Rawlins on the other side of the door. In a matter of seconds, the young man's voice was raised in protest and he was unceremoniously removed from his position. A few more minutes elapsed before there was a soft rap and Jared's voice said quietly, "All's clear, Miss Melissa."

Gratefully, she began to undress, tucking away her glittering costume and changing into a soft wool gown. She met Anthony outside the theater and together they walked briskly through the chill night air to Delmonico's restaurant for a late dinner. As they were eating, Anthony busily pointed out various celebrities to her, including several politicians, an actor, and two of the members of the Vanderbilt family. Melissa worriedly confided to him her narrow escape from the inquisitive young newspaper reporter. Then she put the incident out of her mind and concentrated on the man across from her.

One afternoon, as Melissa was slipping into her costume, there was a knock at the door and she stiffened expectantly.

"It's Nate," murmured the subdued voice. With a sigh of relief, she opened the door.

"Good news, Brandywine." He winked as he watched her binding her hair around her head and pinning it into place. "You and I are going to put in a surprise appearance at some of the fancy balls being thrown in town." At her look of astonishment, he continued. "Society folks get tired of the same entertainment, you know, champagne and caviar and some screeching soprano sounding off at the piano." At that, Melissa stifled a giggle and slid her Stetson carefully onto her head, while she continued to stare disbelievingly at Salsbury.

"So I've come up with a solution for their boredom,

namely you," he announced proudly. "Now before you object, just hear me out. The appearances will be brief, a few minutes and no more. I'll be there to answer any questions someone might ask you. We'll simply circulate through the place, giving out handbills and some complimentary tickets to the show, and then disappear. Now what do you say?"

"I think the whole thing is preposterous," she replied. "Why should we risk the possibility of disclosure when everything has been running smoothly up until now?"

"As I said, we'll be in each place for just a few minutes. The lights will be dimmed before you make your entrance and we'll move quickly enough that we can be in and out of there before anyone can get too long a look at you," he explained, unable to disguise his enthusiasm for the idea. "Trust me, please, Melissa. I wouldn't do anything to jeopardize the act. Believe me." His tone was almost pleading and she reluctantly nodded her halfhearted approval.

"Wonderful!" he boomed, hugging her against him. "Just think of the stir this will cause. The newspapers thrive on these stories in their social columns and those reporters will be falling all over themselves wondering where Brandywine will turn up next." He left the room with an exaggerated swagger in his walk, whistling happily to himself.

Melissa found herself preoccupied as she performed that afternoon, her thoughts revolving around the appearances she had agreed to make. The social pages of the newspapers were already filled with items about her, no doubt "leaked" by Salsbury, speculating as to her origin. Each paper surpassed its competitor in concocting the most outrageous history for her. Brandywine was reputed to be an emigré noble from Europe, a descendant of Napoleon, a grandchild of Queen Victoria, a wanted criminal, a one-time beauty hideously disfigured. The stories grew more and more outlandish and the fifteen thousand seats of Madison Square Garden were filled twice daily.

As she was leaving her dressing room that evening to meet Anthony for their usual dinner, she opened the door and walked straight into the young reporter. She caught her breath and his face broke into a triumphant grin.

"At last I've caught up with Brandywine," he smirked, but she recovered her composure immediately and curdled his smile with an icy stare.

"I regret having to disillusion you, but our dressing rooms were recently changed around, due to the meddling of some newspapermen. This is now my dressing room and your friend, Brandywine, has been settled elsewhere. Now if you would excuse me." She pushed haughtily past him as he gaped at her. With her head erect and shoulders straight, she walked calmly down the corridor despite the frenzied hammering of her heart.

"Wait a minute," he called out, hurrying down the hallway after her, "that isn't possible. I've been checking around here for days and . . ." his voice trailed off and as Melissa rounded a corner, she looked back in time to see Jared collar the man and haul him away.

She greeted Anthony with a warm kiss and happily took his arm, aware of the familiar comfort she derived from being with him. Their relationship possessed none of the intense passion she had shared with Calvin but Anthony provided her with a gentle companionship and a steadfastness making her feel cherished and protected, something Calvin had never been able to do. It had even begun to hurt less each time she allowed herself to think about him and she believed that she was breaking free of his hold on her at last.

It was a cold October day when Anthony first brought Melissa to his townhouse on Fifth Avenue. An impressive three-story brownstone, it reminded her of

the Ransome house on Clarendon Street in Baltimore
with its heavy velvet draperies, fringed sofas and chairs,
the cluster of small walnut tables, and the clutter of bric-
a-brac everywhere. Fancifully painted oil lamps lighted
the rooms, while gas-lit chandeliers twinkled overhead,
casting eerie shadows across the dark wood paneling
and the large oil paintings covering the walls. But the
somber interior of the large house was somewhat offset
by the cheerful fires crackling in the grates and the
plush oriental rugs carpeting the highly polished floors.

As she sipped at a warming glass of sherry, Melissa's
body was suffused with a tremulous glow. She wriggled
out of her pumps and sat cross-legged on the thick rug
before the fire in Anthony's study. Anthony settled
himself behind her on the carpet and placed a tender
kiss on the nape of her neck. She shivered and leaned
back against him as his arms slowly enfolded her. She
tensed as his fingers brushed across her breasts. A
feeling of panic intruded upon her sense of arousal and
she struggled to sit up again.

The pressure of his arms increased and he held her
back. She could feel her heart beginning to pound, a
slow flush creeping up into her face as his fingers
massaged her breasts through the soft wool of her gown.
A pulsating warmth spread out in widening circles from
his touch and as she turned to face him, he slipped his
arms around her and pulled her up against him. As his
lips claimed hers, she found herself responding eagerly,
hungrily, suddenly aware of the burning desire within
her which she had kept hidden for so long. Their
mouths clung, their tongues tentatively exploring, as
Melissa felt the blood surging through her veins and a
painful throbbing begin between her legs. She felt his
hardness pressing against her, and as she entwined her
arms around his neck, he gently pushed her back into
the softness of the rug beneath her.

He undressed her slowly, reverently, and then he tore
off his own clothing and stretched out beside her. She

marveled at the tautness of his body for a man of his age, the thick gray hair curling across his chest, his torso trim, his legs well-muscled, and she sighed as his hands cupped her breasts. His breathing grew ragged as he ardently caressed her and when her legs parted for him, he gently urged himself inside of her.

"I've waited so long for this moment, my beautiful Melissa," he crooned as he brushed her lips with his, the full moustache grazed her soft skin. Something stirred deep within her, a feeling of shame, of revulsion and remorse despite the longing to release the mounting tension inside. She moved upward against him as she fought the wish to have him stop and Anthony, as if sensing her doubt, locked her more tightly in his arms, trapping her there beneath him.

She closed her eyes and saw instead the darkly handsome face of Calvin Gabriel. She strained against his unbidden intrusion and gave herself up to the rising whirl of feeling spinning around her. Her body moved with Anthony's as she ached to be satisfied, striving for that cresting ecstasy she had known only with Calvin. She willed her stubborn body into release, but as Anthony drove into her with a final thrust, he shuddered and collapsed on top of her, and she ceased her hopeless battle.

Her pulsing ebbed, pulling back inside itself as emptiness spilled through her, washing her with its cooling ache. Yearning and incomplete, she shifted restlessly as Anthony flung himself down beside her and pulled her close. She tried to mask the frustration written on her upturned face, reluctant to hurt him by her lack of response.

"Beautiful Melissa," he whispered, running his fingers over her features. At her continued silence, a look of alarm sprang into his face. "I didn't hurt you, did I?" She shook her head. The worried frown relaxed and he lay back, closing his eyes. Soon he was asleep. Melissa turned over onto her stomach and stared into the fireplace, loneliness gnawing at her as the sharpness of her frustration gradually subsided. But in the dancing flames, she could see Calvin's face again, and with piercing agony, she knew that she was still not free.

chapter 33

Melissa and Nate Salsbury were scheduled for the first
of their appearances together and after the evening
performance, they slipped into his carriage and rode to
the home of the William Tremonts. Melissa handed her
floor-length cloak to the astonished maid then waited
while Salsbury alerted the Tremonts before following
him to the closed door of the noisy ballroom. Suddenly
the lamps were dimmed, the small orchestra played a
brief fanfare and hush descended upon the assembled
gathering. To the astonishment of the formally attired
men and women, a tall figure in glittering crimson
appeared, smiling and waving and passing out handbills
and complimentary tickets to the Wild West Show,
while moving swiftly through the whispering crowd.

She closely followed the striding figure of Nate as he
cleared a path for her, carefully skirting areas of the vast
room where people were too tightly grouped together.
Sporadic clapping broke out as she whirled through the
room. To her amusement, she heard the murmured
comments as she slipped past.

"Is it a man or a woman?"

"I understand it's a deposed regent from Belgium."

"Belgium, that's odd, I had heard it was Spain."

"My dear, surely you must have heard that it's one of
our esteemed congressmen who's thoroughly bored
with his present position."

Titters of laughter followed some of the absurd remarks and as people shouted out questions to Melissa, they were either ignored or briefly answered by Salsbury, whose replies were as outrageous as the queries.

Then, as quickly as it had appeared, the mysterious figure seemed to vanish, leaving scores of handbills, free tickets and a fresh topic of conversation for the bored and the sated to discuss. Melissa and Nate howled with laughter as they read the social columns in the newspapers each day following one of their surprise appearances. It was not long before reporters began to materialize at private parties all over town in the hope of catching a glimpse of Brandywine and scooping their rivals. To Melissa's increasing chagrin, reporters would arrive at a party ahead of her forcing her to a different destination. Soon even the elusive Brandywine was uncertain as to which party she would be attending on any given night. She and Nate would simply choose from among the many names on the list he had compiled, and hope that there were not enough reporters available to cover every house. To the delight of every host and hostess and their invited guests, even the chance of an appearance by Brandywine sent reporters scurrying to their prestigious gatherings, giving private parties space in the social pages they might otherwise never have merited.

Because of her crowded timetable, Melissa saw very little of Anthony Holmes and she was grateful for the respite. She had still not reconciled herself to their singular evening of lovemaking. Recalling it filled her with guilt and shame. To add to her conflict, Anthony began sending large bouquets of flowers to her hotel, the enclosed cards bearing scrawled verses taken from love poems. She was certain that he was in love with her and although she was very fond of him, she could not return his love. She was afraid of hurting him should she continue to see him.

When she knew she could no longer honestly delay

spending an evening with him again, she sent a message to the bank, asking him to meet her after the evening performance. She sat at her small dressing table, idly brushing out her hair, apprehensive about seeing him again, wondering at the peculiar fluttering in the pit of her stomach. Tossing aside her brush, she picked up her spangled jacket, frowning at the small tear along one of the sleeves which needed proper mending. Realizing that she still had time before meeting Anthony outside, she hurried out of the room to the large wardrobe chamber, hoping to find the little seamstress before the elderly woman left for the night. To her relief, the woman was still there. Melissa handed her the jacket and scampered back to collect her cape and small purse.

Entering the room, she caught her breath, as, seated at her dressing table was a man wearing her hat and spangled mask, and grinning insolently up at her.

"How did you get in here?" she demanded, striding angrily over to him. "Take those things off immediately." She reached for him but he eluded her grasp and sprang nimbly to his feet, artfully dodging her pursuit. Backing into the corner, he swept off the hat and executed a courtly bow before her.

"Charmed to make your acquaintance, Brandywine. I knew I was right about you all along."

"Right about what?" Melissa snarled.

"Let's not play games, Miss Howell, now that I know who you really are," he snapped, tugging off the crimson mask and running his fingers through his sandy hair. His eyes twinkled as he gazed appreciatively at her. "You sure are one hell of a good-looking woman."

"You are making a fool out of yourself, sir, and I insist that you leave this room immediately," she ordered crisply, attempting to fend him off once again.

"How am I making a fool of myself, may I ask?" He glanced quizzically at her, refusing to move from the corner.

"By assuming once more that you know who Brandywine is after I explained it all to you the last time you accosted me," she replied firmly. "I was simply put in charge of having this costume mended and you may speak to our seamstress if you choose not to believe me."

"I don't question that part of it, Miss Howell, but I'm afraid your little charade is over. You see, I've been watching this room every chance I've had, and you've been the only one to enter or leave this room. You come in as a woman and go out as the mysterious Brandywine," he concluded smugly, "and the only clothes in that cupboard over there have been this costume and a woman's gown."

"And how have you been able to accomplish this sleuthing of yours?" she demanded brusquely.

"You're in the habit of leaving your door unlocked and your friendly protector isn't always around to chase me away," he answered, one eyebrow arched cockily.

She flushed indignantly, despairing that he had uncovered the truth about her and that by the following day, the entire city might also learn it. In anger and frustration, she lashed out at him.

"You seem terribly pleased with yourself right now, but I doubt if your readers will appreciate having their favorite diversion ruined because of one overly zealous reporter."

"I don't consider myself an overly zealous reporter," he countered. "I'm a damned good one and my paper has invested a lot of time and money in getting this story. Where others have failed, I've succeeded."

"But if you reveal Brandywine's identity, you destroy a carefully conceived myth, a bit of make-believe which has even helped to sell your newspaper," she cried defiantly. "As show people we have been providing the public with what they want, namely a good show. My own background pales in comparison with the ones people have been making up themselves for

400

Brandywine, and Brandywine becomes whatever a person imagines him to be. Think of what you spoil if your newspaper prints your story."

"Are you sure you're not an actress as well, Miss Howell?" he questioned, "That was quite a passionate performance." Melissa fought the overwheming urge to rake her nails across his grinning face and scrape the sprinkling of freckles from his snub nose.

"How do you know my name?" she demanded then, taking a menacing step toward him.

"I simply asked your protector when he dragged me away from here one night. You were dressed the way you are now, so I guess he saw no harm in telling me. How was he to know I'd keep after you until I got what I wanted?"

"And have you gotten what you wanted?" Her voice burned with rage.

"Not quite," he replied, his gaze casually roaming her body.

"I find you rude and offensive, Mr. . . ."

"Bennett. Evan Bennett," he supplied.

"Well, Mr. Bennett, since you have your story and obviously intend to publish it, would you kindly leave me alone now?"

To her astonishment, he stayed exactly where he was, the satisfied smile slowly fading from his face to be replaced by a pensive frown. Finally, he moved from the corner and walked to her, his voice lowered as he stared solemnly at her.

"You've been more persuasive than you realize, Miss Howell," he said softly. "In fact, your cooperation might even buy my temporary silence."

"My cooperation?" she repeated suspiciously. "How?"

"Having dinner with me this evening would be a satisfactory beginning." His grin returned as he watched her reaction.

"I am not free to have dinner with you this evening or

any other evening, Mr. Bennett," she retorted.

"That's a shame," he said. "Since you'd prefer to see the story in print than spend some time with me, I suppose we have nothing more to discuss. Good night, Miss Howell." He started for the door, but Melissa sprang after him.

"Just a moment, Mr. Bennett," she called, stopping him as he reached for the doorknob. "One dinner and you promise to hold back on running the story?"

He considered her question and then answered her. "Let's just say one dinner would be an auspicious start."

"You are utterly impossible," she exploded in exasperation.

"I'm really not that bad once you get to know me," he insisted as her resolve began to waver again.

"All right, Mr. Bennett, you shall have your dinner. Tomorrow night."

"Tomorrow it is then," he agreed and strutted from the room.

Throughout dinner with Anthony that night, Melissa remained grimly silent, sighing deeply from time to time and scarcely touching the food on her plate. Anthony was disturbed by her moodiness but attempted to distract her with amusing stories about the celebrated people he recognized around them and the outrageous rumors circulating about Brandywine. She made a halfhearted effort at listening but to no avail. Her thoughts were pervaded by the insolent smile on Evan Bennett's boyish face and the threat he posed to her career.

When Anthony saw her back to the hotel, he pulled her into his arms. She stiffened and drew back, forcing her voice to remain steady as she said, "I had hoped to have dinner with you again tomorrow evening, but Nate and I have another one of our appearances to make." She grimaced effectively to cover her small lie. "The poor man is inundated with invitations and I wonder if he regrets having started it all." She smiled as she recalled Salsbury's looks of dismay as messengers arrived throughout the day delivering their invitations. "I think the game is getting out of hand now, though, for I understand that some people have begun offering rewards to their guests if they can manage to learn Brandywine's identity. I wonder how far they might go in order to find out," she puzzled, her distress real as she looked worriedly up at Anthony.

"Are you afraid of physical violence?" he asked, his voice concerned.

"I suppose anything could happen," she sighed.

"Then I suggest you tell Salsbury you've decided against any further appearances. In fact, I'll have a word with him myself," he threatened, but she placed a restraining hand on his arm.

"I promise you that I will speak to him about it, Anthony."

"I'll hold you to that promise, Melissa," he warned, wrapping her in his arms where she stayed as he held her. "You're very important to me and I don't want anything to happen to you," he whispered hoarsely as he pressed his lips against hers. She then broke from his embrace and hurried into the hotel, running a trembling hand across her mouth.

The following night, after her performance, Melissa changed into a simple ivory cashmere gown with a matching fur-trimmed cape. Her eyes were sparkling, her face flushed from the exhilaration of her ride. As she dabbed a spicy cologne onto her wrists and temples, a knock sounded at the door. She waited until he called out his name and then she opened the door and peered into Evan's grinning face.

"Do you ever stop smiling?" she remarked sourly as he stepped into the room.

"Nope. Especially when I'm in the company of such a beautiful woman," he replied easily, drawing his hand from behind his back and presenting her with a small nosegay of flowers.

She accepted them warily, sniffing their gentle fragrance and then smiled her thanks. As they headed down the corridor, they passed an astounded Jared Rawlins, whose eyes widened in disbelief when he saw the unlikely twosome. Melissa grimaced and shrugged her shoulders as Evan tugged her after him and Jared scratched his head disconcertedly as he watched them disappear from view.

"Where are we going?" Melissa asked as Evan hailed a passing hansom cab.

"To someplace I'm sure you've never been," he answered as he helped her into the carriage. "Don't look so skeptical, I'm not kidnapping you."

She settled back against the cushions, clutching her flowers, prepared to endure a boring evening with the young man beside her. He was tugging at the stiff, high collar of his shirt and he looked supremely uncomfortable in the bristly suit he had obviously just borrowed or bought in some thrift shop. She stifled a laugh and he threw her a withering look, ignoring her for the remainder of the ride.

They finally alighted in front of a small restaurant in a dilapidated section of the city Melissa had never been in before. Reassuringly taking hold of her arm, Evan steered her inside where the delicious aroma of garlic and spices permeated the dimly lit room. A portly man with a curling black moustache and a white apron tied around his massive girth hugged Evan warmly and led them to a table in the corner.

"You must come here often," she commented wryly, as the man immediately opened a bottle of wine and poured it into their glasses before shuffling off.

"I practically live here," he admitted. "I have a flat across the street and since I'm too lazy to cook for myself, Luigi obliges me."

Melissa sipped the fruity wine and gazed casually

around the smoke-filled room at the strange assortment of people there. Most of them were shabbily dressed, young, the men sporting scruffy beards and the women with snarled, matted hair falling about their shoulders in neglected tangles. All of them seemed pale and gaunt, almost undernourished in appearance. But as she studied them more closely, she was struck by the animation in their faces, the fervor sparking their eyes, the expressive gesticulations of their limber hands. Sketch pads lay open in front of many of them, ink sketches torn from these books were tacked up on the walls, haphazardly scattered about, spattering its peeling surface with a jigsaw montage. Melissa's roving gaze was momentarily arrested, fixing itself on a young man directly across the room from her who was staring openly at her and rapidly sketching in his pad. Her initial attitude of hostile indifference shifted inevitably to awed interest. When she looked up at Evan, the expression in her eyes had also changed.

"They all come here," he explained in a muted voice, "the artists whose one dream is to be recognized in this city. Some will make it, most won't. Some will die of malnutrition or tuberculosis, damning the world for never acknowledging them. But they'd never abandon their dream. The paint is in their blood, their world is defined by their canvases and when they sign their name to their work, they sign away part of their souls. I can't paint. I wish I could, but what they put down on canvas, I put into words. And I hope that someday more than a newspaper will get the best of my talent. I want to be a good writer just as much as they want to be great artists, and I'll make it or, like many of them, I'll die trying." He tossed back the rest of his wine and filled his glass again.

Melissa sat there speechless, moved by the passion in his voice and she felt a lump forming in her throat. Perhaps she would at last be able to make him understand her own plight, and convince him that his exposure of her would be cutting off a part of her own creativity. Creativity was the one thing he could understand and appreciate, and want no part in destroying. She reached out impulsively and covered his hand with hers. A smile tilted the corners of her mouth as she looked at him.

When they had eaten their fill of Luigi's excellent pasta, they pushed themselves back from the table with a groan and tottered unsteadily outside. They sauntered through the vast parkland of Washington Square which seemed to have been set apart from the rest of the bustling city and tucked away from its clangor and restless activity. It was reserved for a special breed of gentler folk, for the artists and writers, while the rest of the city spun chaotically around their protected little world. Melissa and Evan wound their way slowly through the square, along its twisting pathways, past groups of swaying trees, their dark boughs stripped bare of leaves, while the few still on the ground crunched noisily underfoot.

Although Melissa prompted him to speak about himself, Evan remained somewhat reticent, preferring instead to discuss the book he was writing and the acquaintances he had made in the four years since leaving his native Boston. He admitted to his age of twenty-two, with two unpublished novels gathering dust in his tiny flat and the collection of stray cats and one very old blind dog who lived with him. Melissa found herself happily at ease with the young reporter. She regretted the late hour and the hurried carriage ride back to her hotel.

They stood huddled together in the shelter of the doorway and Melissa once more confronted him, attempting to dissuade him from publishing the story about her. She watched the play of emotions across his face until with a sigh of resignation, he agreed to withhold the story. Bursting with gratitude, Melissa threw her arms around his neck and kissed him soundly on the lips.

"Thank you, Evan," she breathed, allowing him to nestle her against his chest before he set her from him.

"You're quite a woman, Melissa Howell," he muttered, pressing a light kiss onto her forehead. Then he spun on his heel and hurried off. Melissa watched until she could no longer see him before she turned and entered the hotel, still clutching her wilting flowers.

The following night, as she waited for Nate, Melissa nervously paced her dressing room, trying to put together the words to tell him of her decision to discontinue her appearances at private homes. She rehearsed a short speech, discarded it, formulated another one and succeeded in working herself into a state of extreme agitation by the time Nate arrived. As they rode to the house of the Granville Pattersons, Melissa decided to wait until after their appearance to discuss her intentions with him, but she approached the evening's activities with unaccustomed uneasiness nonetheless.

As she waited in the upstairs hallway to make her dramatic entrance, Melissa gazed around her at the house's magnificent furnishings, the priceless paintings on the silk-covered walls and the statuary displayed atop slender marble columns in specially constructed niches. It was as if she were viewing such lavishness for the first time and she was suddenly sickened by what she saw. She smiled ruefully, thinking of Evan Bennett and his friends, tucked away in the squalor bordering Washington Square, living on the remote fringes of such sumptuous wealth. How those artists must dream of attracting some obliging patron from among the people she would soon glimpse on the other side of the ballroom door. She felt a wave of bitterness rising within her and with it the urge to flee before she would be paraded like some pet trophy before the pampered and jaded people she was loath to face.

407

But before she could move, Nate hissed to her, waving her toward him. She took a deep breath, following him into the darkened ballroom, buoyed by the knowledge that it would be for the last time. A blaring fanfare announced her arrival, a sudden glare of light hurtled crimson flashes about the hushed room and as she smiled and waved, distributing the familiar handbills, she felt as if she were moving in a dream.

The faces staring back at her seemed to be ludicrous caricatures of women, with jewels blazing in their hair, at their ears, and around their pudgy throats. High spots of rouge dotted their pasty, powdered cheeks and brilliant scarlet slashes passed for petulant lips. The men were fat, complacent, with hair slicked down over balding pates, cigars stuffed into the corners of their drooping mouths. Melissa's smile became a strained grimace and her hand jerked stiffly and mechanically.

As she swung through the room, preparing to cut short her promenade and make a hasty exit, she felt the blood drain from her face and she knew that her feeble attempt at a smile was failing. For staring boldly at her not ten feet from where she stood, was Calvin Gabriel.

chapter 34

Caught off guard, Melissa tipped over the train of a woman's gown and hurriedly thrust the final pair of complimentary tickets into the hands of the person nearest her. She blundered through the remaining knot of people, not daring to look back or hesitate, fearful of giving herself away. As she hurled herself from the room, she slammed into Salsbury who was just ahead of her.

"What the hell's wrong with you?" he growled, pushing her away.

"I noticed someone in there who might have recognized me," she rasped, breaking for the stairs.

"Wait right there!" His voice echoed through the deserted hallway as he charged after her. "You're supposed to draw the winning ticket in their raffle for the new hospital wing, remember?" he barked. "That was part of the bargain tonight, no advance publicity, no chance of the press showing up. You agreed, Melissa," he thundered, his voice shaking with rage as she shook her head.

"I could never go back in there," she said. "Please, Nate, it would be too risky."

"And what excuse am I supposed to give Patterson?" he demanded.

"You can think of something," she snapped, clattering down the stairs and reaching the bottom step just as

Salsbury reached for her and grabbed her roughly by the arm.

"Is everything all right down there?" a voice boomed from the head of the staircase."

"Everything's just fine, Mr. Patterson," Nate answerered, waving at the large, florid man who leaned over the bannister and peered down at them.

"Well, hurry along then, people are beginning to get restless," he called back.

"We'll be right up," Nate assured him and the man returned to the ballroom. "You owe this to me, Melissa," Nate threatened, his forehead beaded with perspiration as he fought to control himself.

"All right, Nate," she conceded. Forgetting about her carefully planned speeches, she simply blurted out, "But this is the last appearance I make at any home. And that is final."

She marched determinedly across the floor of the still darkened ballroom toward the small raised podium where the orchestra was seated. A spontaneous burst of applause greeted her as she approached the large glass bowl filled with hundreds of pieces of paper. Then there was silence as everyone waited for her hand to close around the winning slip. A drum roll began, adding to the tension of the moment. Melissa plunged one gloved hand into the bowl and withdrew a single piece of paper. She handed it quickly to Patterson who scanned it and promptly bellowed the name of the winner.

There was a short squeal of delight as, amid laughter and supportive applause, a small woman floated toward the dais in a wave of billowing mauve tulle and glittering amethysts. Patterson handed Melissa the large, gold-framed oil painting done by the celebrated Winslow Homer, which she then presented to the smiling, teary-eyed woman. Another wave of applause rippled over the room as the woman disappeared into the crowd and Melissa smiled briefly at Patterson and headed for the door.

"Leaving so soon?" came the deep voice as Melissa reached for the doorknob. His hand instantly closed over hers and without turning around, she knew who was standing behind her. "Of course, the elusive Brandywine never speaks," he chuckled and Melissa shrugged his hand from hers and turned the knob sharply, pulling open the door with a fierce tug. A shattering sound and a muttered oath made her realize that she had knocked the wineglass from his hand, and in that brief moment, she made good her escape.

Racing down the staircase toward the front door, she heaved it open and without stopping to close it again, she headed down the steps. She looked frantically about for Nate or his carriage but she could find no sign of either of them and as Calvin's footsteps pounded down the stairs behind her, Melissa began running down the street. Rounding a corner, she plunged on, the spurs on her boots jangling in the silence, giving her little chance of eluding her pursuer. Her heart hammering painfully in her chest, she ran on, clutching her hat to her head, her breath coming in labored gasps as she darted into an unfamiliar drive and lost herself in its deep shadows.

She crouched behind a low stone wall as she saw him run past. He soon stopped and looked around him, trying to discern the direction she had taken. She waited there, panting for breath, perspiration streaming down her masked face, her overheated body beginning to shudder in the cold night air. Finally, he seemed to abandon the chase and headed back in the opposite direction but Melissa remained hidden until she was certain that he was safely out of sight before she dared edge cautiously forward again. She carefully retraced her steps and managed to locate Nate's carriage, with the driver dozing on the seat, the whip held loosely in his grip. She shook him roughly and his eyes flew open as he struggled to sit up.

"Wake up," she hissed, shaking him again, "I want

you to take me back to the theater immediately."

"But what about Mr. Salsbury?" he mumbled, rubbing his eyes with the heel of his hand.

"You can return for him later," she snapped. "Now start up before I do it myself." She threw herself onto the seat beside him, threatening to grab hold of the reins, and he picked them up himself and clucked to the horse and they started off.

Nate was incensed with Melissa's extraordinary behavior and he refused to speak to her for several days. She bore his angry silence stoically, grateful to have been relieved of the burden of private appearances, despite the obvious disappointment of the city's prominent families. She began once more to dine with Anthony after her evening performances, and she was dismayed by the subtle change in his attitude toward her. He began displaying a possessiveness which stifled and frightened her. She was still recovering from the effects of her chance encounter with Calvin and was glad to fill every moment of her time with activities in order not to dwell on the shock of having seen him again. But at the same time, she studiously avoided being alone too often with Anthony, encouraging him to take her to the theater or for long rides through Central Park, anything to avoid a repetition of their disastrous lovemaking.

As she was preparing for a performance one evening, there was a loud knock at her dressing room door. A familiar voice called out his name to her and she immediately opened the door to Evan Bennett. He kissed her perfunctorily on the cheek and then settled himself on a chair as she finished pinning up her hair and slid the spangled mask into place over her face.

"I've been out of town, in case you were curious," he stated bluntly, toying with her crimson Stetson. She plucked the hat from his hands and settled it onto her head at a rakish angle.

"The *Times* sent me to cover some dull political meetings in New Jersey and Connecticut. I've missed you, Melissa," he blurted out. She said nothing while he shifted about in the chair. "Could we have dinner tonight after the show?"

"Not tonight, Evan," she replied, breaking her silence. "But I might be able to manage tomorrow. Can I get a message to you?"

"I'll come around tomorrow night in any event," he smiled, getting to his feet. "If you can't make it, at least I'll have had the chance to see you." With that, he pecked her on the cheek again and bounded out the door.

But the following night, Evan failed to appear and Melissa angrily returned to her hotel to spend the rest of the evening alone, flipping unhappily through the pages of a book, seeing Calvin's face where there should have been words, and hearing his voice again when all around her there was silence. She began to fret about Evan, suspicious of his behavior, and as the hours passed, she became agitated, realizing that something might have happened to him. Despite her uneasiness, she managed finally to fall asleep, but in the early hours of the morning, she was awakened by a loud rapping. Springing from the bed, she wrapped herself in a long dressing gown and padded over to the door.

"Who is it?" she called, straining to hear the muffled reply. She hesitated and then the rapping began again. "Who is out there?" she shouted and she made out the whispered response, throwing open the door as a rumpled and bleeding Evan Bennett lurched into the room.

"My God, Evan, what happened to you?" she gasped, helping him to the bed and then fumbling with the lamp on the night table.

He stretched out on the bed, his dirty shoes leaving patches of mud on the light coverlet. He ran a grimy hand across his forehead, adding dirt to the blood seeping steadily from a deep gash above his left eye. The eye itself was closed and swollen. His lower lip was cut and a small piece of skin was torn. The blood had already caked in the corner of his mouth. He passed his tongue over his cracked lips and whispered hoarsely, "All in a night's work, Melissa." He winced as he attempted a weak grin, causing the cut on his lip to open again. She hurried over to the washbasin, poured fresh water from the pitcher into it, snatched up a towel and returned to the bed. She wrung out the towel and sponged his battered face, rinsing it with the cool water and then dabbing at the cuts over and over again. She tore a jagged piece from a fresh towel, dampened it, and then pressed it against the oozing wound above his eye.

"Hold that as tightly as you can," she ordered, helping him to raise his hand. Then she struggled to remove his shoes, allowing them to drop noisily onto the floor before she loosened his tattered shirt and pulled off his worn jacket. "Are you hurt anywhere else?" she asked. He shook his head. She patted the cut in the corner of his mouth again and then held the cloth tightly against it to staunch the flow of blood. "You certainly look less fearsome without that layer of mud," she said as she set about washing the dirt from his hands.

He lay there silently, obediently pressing the dripping cloth to his head until he seemed to regain some of his strength. Then he spoke again, his voice stronger than before.

"I'm sorry I didn't show up at your dressing room earlier, but as you can see, I was preoccupied."

"Can you tell me what happened?" she asked, wringing out the towel and renewing her work on his hands.

"The paper sent me out to cover one of the labor strikes. Things got a bit out of hand and before I knew what was happening, everyone was throwing punches. By the time the police arrived, there were more people on the ground then there were standing up. Before I could show them my credentials, I was hauled off to jail with the rest of the mob where I had a devil of a time getting some attention from the damned guards. It took hours before someone came to look at my identification and find someone else to authorize my release."

"And they allowed you to remain there all that time in your condition?" she asked incredulously.

"You should have seen some of the other fellows," he grimaced. "I look good compared to them."

"I think you should try and get some sleep now, Evan," she said firmly as he seemed to be ready to continue with his story. She carefully removed the towel from his forehead, pleased to discover that the bleeding had finally stopped. "This cut is quite deep and I suggest you see a doctor about it in the morning."

He nodded absently as his eyelids fluttered closed. Before long he was sound asleep. Melissa folded the rest of the coverlet around him and then curled up in the room's one large chair and spent the rest of the dark hours alternately dozing off and waking to watch over Evan.

When he awoke, he complained of a violent headache. Despite her urgings that he see a doctor right away, he stubbornly refused. He drifted off to sleep again and she hastily dressed, leaving him still asleep while she left the hotel to buy some gauze and tape for his head. When she returned, he was awake and in better spirits, claiming that his headache had vanished. Eyeing him skeptically, she nonetheless applied a foul-smelling ointment to his cuts, slathering it generously across the gash on his forehead, covering it with a heavy gauze bandage and wide ribbons of white tape. Then she brought him a small hand mirror so that he could admire her handiwork.

"I look like a war casualty," he complained. "How can I go out like this? It was only a scratch, Melissa."

"It was far more than a scratch, Evan Bennett," she

retorted, snatching away the mirror, "and I refuse to be held responsible if an infection sets in. I still insist that you see a doctor and stop being so stubborn."

"Yes, nurse," he teased, flashing her one of his insolent grins.

"And one more word of caution," she put in. "If you want that cut on your mouth to heal, stop that ridiculous smiling." To her dismay, he burst out laughing at her reprimand and she found herself helplessly joining him. She turned her back to him until she had composed herself again. Then she faced him once more. He was still snickering, but she ignored him and helped him up from the bed.

"Do you feel strong enough to go out for some breakfast?" she asked as he hobbled slowly about the room.

"I think I can manage," he replied. "At least I have you to lean on." With another impish grin, he began to slip into his grimy clothes. He then held the door open for her. She sailed through and when he finally caught up with her, they walked slowly down the stairs and out into the morning sunshine.

Together they made their way to a small restaurant nearby, where they drank steaming coffee and devoured freshly baked cinnamon buns and attracted a good deal of attention, with Evan arousing curious sympathy from the patrons and waiters alike. He was thoroughly enjoying himself.

"The mayoral candidates will be speaking in Greenwich Village next Sunday," he said, as they walked back to Melissa's hotel, "and the paper expects me to cover the speeches. Why don't you come with me?" he asked hopefully as they stopped in front of the hotel entrance.

"I will, if Cody has no objections to my missing the afternoon show," she answered.

"Ask him then, and I'll stop by for you at one o'clock on Sunday afternoon," he instructed her. "And now I'd better get home and change my clothes before showing up at the paper. Since I'm already late, I should make quite an entrance thanks to your bandage here." He kissed her gently, tugging her to him for a brief moment. "Thank you for taking such good care of me, Melissa," he murmured against her hair. Then he released her and set off down the street. Melissa smiled to herself and hurried back to her room for a few more hours of sleep.

To her delight, Cody allowed her to miss both Sunday afternoon and Saturday evening performances, freeing her to join Anthony at the Metropolitan Opera House for her first taste of opera in America. She trembled with excitement as she stepped into the apricot velvet gown she had purchased especially for the event. The sleeveless bodice and full, draped panniers were intricately embroidered with tiny pearls. She swept her hair into a severe chignon and then encased the elegant twist in a mesh coronet of similar pearls. The color of the gown warmed Melissa's luminous skin so that it seemed suffused with a honeyed radiance. The topaz drops she fastened to her delicate ears set off the amber fire in her eyes. Dabbing perfume behind her ears, at her throat and in the deep cleavage afforded by the gown's decolletage, she then touched a gold lip pomade to her generous mouth, gathered up her floor-length evening cape and beaded velvet purse and set out to meet Anthony in the lobby.

When he caught sight of her sweeping toward him, he smiled approvingly, his eyes lighting expectantly. He squeezed her arm affectionately and led her outside to his waiting carriage. Formally attired in a dark evening suit, embroidered silk vest, high collared white shirt, and striped cravat, he presented an elegant and urbane contrast to her fresh, youthful beauty. As they made their way into the spectacular opera house, heads turned to admire them. Melissa stared wonderingly at her magnificent surroundings, oblivious to the attention she herself was receiving, as she and Anthony climbed to their reserved loge. Although the Metropolitan Opera House boasted a breathtaking interior, it was an astoundingly ugly building on the outside, constructed entirely of yellow brick in the Italian Renaissance style. A seven-story structure, its stage was larger than the stages of many of Europe's finest opera houses and it was capable of seating over three thousand people. It had been a loving project of the city's "new" millionaire families, among them the Goulds, Vanderbilts, and Morgans, considered uncouth upstarts by the older aristocracy of New York. But the lavish design allowed for more private loges than any theater of its kind, and the new money sat prominently displayed, gloating over their glorious achievement, before the common citizenry spreading below them.

Melissa's wide-eyed gaze swept the cavernous hall with its crystal chandeliers and ornate, fluted columns stretching to the ceiling, the elaborate frescoes adorning the walls, and the deep carpets silencing their tread as they entered their box. Taking her seat, Melissa glanced around her at the fabulously gowned and bejeweled women, the dark suited men with their silk top hats, all moving together as part of a marvelous parade, observing the demanded obedience to opulence. As she settled back in her small velvet upholstered chair, she accepted a delicate pair of mother-of-pearl opera glasses from Anthony and after adjusting them, she joined with the others all around her in peering more closely at the occupants of the other prominent loges.

Anthony was drawn into conversation by the other couple sharing their box and Melissa took advantage of his preoccupation to scan the audience as people hurried to find their seats. Then she trained the glasses on a box near theirs, finding something disturbingly familiar about the pale, blonde woman sitting there alone, her eyes downcast, an ice-blue satin gown hugging her slender frame while a brilliant choker of diamonds shimmered around her throat. Under Melissa's scrutiny, the woman raised her eyes and seemed to stare directly back at her. Melissa drew in her breath as she recognized Kathleen Ransome. She hastily lowered the opera glasses. Her heart began to flutter wildly and the hands which held the glasses were shaking uncontrollably as she forced her concentration away from the other loge and directed it toward the ornate curtain fringing the massive stage.

Finally, out of the corner of her eye, she managed to locate Kathleen's box again and the blue-clad figure still sitting there alone. Biting her lip, Melissa wondered if the other woman had noticed her as well, for even without the aid of the glasses, Kathleen was easily discernible. As she continued to covertly study her, the velvet curtain behind Kathleen parted and several figures stepped into the loge. She looked up, a smile warming her solemn face and Melissa, holding her breath, followed Kathleen's upward gaze until she was staring at Edward Gabriel. He was removing his tall silk top hat and bending over his wife. As he seated himself beside Kathleen, they both turned around to speak to the couple arranging their chairs behind them. Melissa fought down the lump rising in her throat as she saw Calvin there, helping a striking red-headed woman into her seat before sitting down himself. He tugged off his top hat and combed his fingers through his black hair. Melissa looked away, blinking back the tears which were threatening as a bleak feeling of despair settled over her.

Anthony suddenly gripped her hand and apologized for his lengthy conversation. She tensed and turned her luminous eyes to his concerned face.

"You're trembling, my dear," he said softly, increasing the pressure of his hand on hers. "Is something wrong?"

"No, Anthony, nothing," she lied. "I find myself

completely overwhelmed by all of this," she breathed, lowering her eyes demurely. He leaned across her then, gently kissing the sensitive nape of her neck and a shudder of revulsion seized her, shaking her entire body. Anthony glanced at her tensing face with a quizzical look. Frowning in consternation, he straightened up again in his chair and gazed thoughtfully at his program.

Unable to restrain herself any longer, Melissa picked up the opera glasses and trained them again on the box near theirs. She located Calvin's seat and then slowly, tantalizingly, she raised the glasses, tracing the length of his body until they were focused solely on his dark, handsome profile. The world seemed suddenly to shrink, narrowing until it included only the two of them and she lovingly examined each strongly carved feature as he turned his face, caressing him with her yearning eyes until the lights dimmed and he was lost to her.

The performance dragged on interminably, limping toward the first of two intermissions. Melissa found she was unable to concentrate on the pageantry spread before her. Her thoughts were centered only on the man separated from her by a flimsy curtain of darkness. She shifted uncomfortably in her seat, squirming about in an effort to ease her restlessness. More than once, she felt Anthony's steadying hand on her arm and heard his whispered pleas for her silence. Still she fidgeted, plucking at the folds of her gown, running her agitated fingers over the tiny beads sewn onto the heavy velvet, and toying with the long chain on her beaded evening purse. Finally there was a rising swell of applause and the lights returned as the giant curtain swung closed ending the first act.

"May we walk around, Anthony?" she asked quickly, barely managing to keep from bolting from her chair.

"You seemed exceedingly restless, Melissa," he commented sharply as he got to his feet. "I thought you enjoyed the opera."

"But I do," she insisted. "I found the act a trifle long though." With an imperious toss of her head, she walked briskly ahead of him and out of the stifling confines of the velvet-enclosed box.

He caught up with her. She grudgingly slipped her arm through his and he forced her walk to slow, matching his strolling gait. Moving through the crowded foyer, Anthony stopped from time to time, greeting friends, nodding briefly to acquaintances, always ensuring that Melissa was firmly at his side. Melissa acknowledged Anthony's polite introductions with a distracted smile and a hastily murmured word while she cast about straining for a glimpse of the man she longed to see. She noticed Edward first, pushing Kathleen in a wheeled invalid's chair. Then, at last, her eyes found Calvin, striding behind his brother, his arm gripping the elbow of the statuesque woman beside him, her ivory satin gown rustling as she hurried to keep up with his long legged steps.

"Melissa!"

She pressed a dazzling smile to her lips and returned Kathleen's greeting, breaking away from Anthony's grasp and hurrying to her, keeping her eyes trained only on Kathleen's upturned face. Clasping the two cool hands raised toward her, Melissa clung warmly to the other woman who gazed at her with eyes brimming with tears.

"We were so worried about you, how could you have left without a word?" Kathleen whispered. "It was only through Calvin that we learned what had happened to you. Are you living in New York now?" Melissa could only nod her head. Then she was enveloped in Edward's embrace and she found herself laughing and crying and chattering to him as if only moments and not months had been separating them.

"You're more beautiful than I remember, Melissa," he beamed, his warmth encompassing her, comforting her, bathing her in a glow she had long lived without. When the inevitable could no longer be stayed, it was Edward who helped her face it. "You remember my brother, Calvin, don't you?" he said, gently, freeing her from his arms and pressing her forward to acknowledge the man whose gray eyes locked with hers as a slow smile began to spread across his solemn face.

"Of course I do," she replied smoothly, as she offered him her hand. "How good to see you again, Calvin."

"Is it, princess?" he murmured, brushing a gentle kiss onto her skin. She quivered and withdrew her hand, its coolness strangely warm, burning from his touch.

"Isn't anyone going to introduce us?" bleated the woman at Calvin's side. Melissa glanced up at her and before anyone could reply, Anthony broke into the circle, reaching possessively for Melissa's arm. Awkwardly, names were bandied about and although Anthony shook hands with Edward, he disdainfully dismissed Calvin's proferred hand, stating bluntly, "We've already had the pleasure." Calvin smirked and lowered his arm. "Are you coming, my dear?" Anthony inquired, his tone icy as he faced Melissa.

"In a moment," she returned in an equally frosty voice which was rewarded instantly by an ill-concealed snort of laughter from Calvin and a look of bitter reproach from Anthony.

"Very well, then, I'll see you back at our seats, Melissa," he said, his voice tight with anger. Nodding politely to the others, he walked stiffly away.

Melissa turned back to Kathleen, leaning over the girl and murmuring softly, "I never had the chance to properly congratulate you and Edward, but you have both been in my thoughts."

"Edward's proposal came as a shock to everyone, I'm afraid, especially me," Kathleen admitted, a tender smile lifting the corners of her mouth as she glanced toward her husband. "But in spite of everything," she said, indicating her legs, "he's made me very happy, Melissa, just as you promised me." Melissa felt the sting of tears in her own eyes as she recalled her desperate words of hope, uttered to a girl who had lain in bed, crippled and praying for death. She sat before her now, aglow with love and living.

Calvin suddenly coughed, trying to catch Melissa's attention, and when she finally looked at him, he nodded for her to follow him. But she hesitated, not trusting herself to be alone with him. He sensed her ambivalence and swiftly made the decision for her. He took hold of her arm and propelled her away from the others, steering her toward a quiet corner of the vast hall where he stopped, spinning her around to face him.

"Why the hell did you run off without a word?" he demanded, his voice strained with the force of his controlled anger.

"It would scarcely have mattered when I left, dear Calvin," she replied scathingly. "You were otherwise engaged if you recall, and two women were obviously more than you could comfortably handle."

"I'd say you've done fairly well on that score yourself, Melissa," he countered.

"And just what is that supposed to mean?" she flared hotly, bridling at his remark.

"You played a similar game using Holmes and me back on Long Island," he blazed, "and from the looks of it, you knew exactly where you were going when you left in such a blasted hurry."

"I resent your implication," she retorted, turning to leave before she could suffer any further abuse. But his hand lashed out and grabbed her by the wrist. She stopped short, whirling to face him again.

"Not so fast," he barked and she glared at him with eyes charged with fire. "I'm still waiting for some explanation."

"Then wait," she spat. "I have nothing further to say to you."

"What is Holmes to you, Melissa?" he asked bluntly. She started, taken aback by his question. Her eyes narrowed as she tossed her head back spitefully. "He loves me, Calvin."

"And what about you," he persisted. "Do you love him?"

"My feelings for Anthony are none of your concern," she replied coldly. "For you see, Calvin, you are no longer my 'guardian,' and my life need no longer interest you at all." Drawing herself up haughtily, she turned her back on him and walked away. He made no further attempts to stop her.

She returned to the loge and slipped into her chair beside Anthony just as the lights began to dim, heralding the start of the second act.

"You must have been rather surprised to find Gabriel here this evening," Anthony commented casually.

"Yes, I was," she replied curtly.

"He's still standing between us, isn't he, Melissa?" he said, his voice strangely hoarse.

"No, Anthony," she forced out, feeling the words strangle somewhere in her throat. She reached for his hand, pressing it tightly, dismally aware of his pain and helpless to alleviate it. He held her hand throughout the entire second act, and Melissa tried to sit calmly at his side, but her fingers grew numb so tightly clenched between his. Still she forced her body not to shift about. She quelled the urge to scream out and run from the suffocating darkness closing in around her, and she endured the tediousness of the performance by the sheer force of her will until with a burst of anguished relief, it was over and the lights came on once more.

She chose to remain in the loge during the second intermission but encouraged Anthony to walk about in the foyer with the couple who were seated behind them. He grudgingly agreed. Masking his obvious disappointment, he strode through the velvet curtains, leaving Melissa mercifully alone. No sooner had

Anthony gone than she snatched up her opera glasses and trained them on Calvin's loge, locating him and focusing only on his face. She nearly dropped the glasses in dismay when she discovered his own gaze trained back on her. Her pulse quickened as she sat there, pinned weakly beneath his relentless stare. He looked away then, but only long enough to whisper to the woman next to him. Then he was leaving his seat and swinging through the curtains at the rear of the box.

Melissa set aside the glasses and leaned back limply in her chair, her heart thudding, a warm flush spreading through her as she waited. Then he was standing behind her, shifting Anthony's chair so that he faced her. He sat down quickly and took her hand in his.

"I came to apologize for what I said to you," he began, and his voice grew husky. "I'm sorry, princess, if I hurt you. I'll never understand why you and I spend so much of our time together fighting." His puzzled gaze sought hers and she reached up and affectionately brushed back the shaggy hair spilling across his forehead. She felt her love for him coursing turbulently through her body, screaming for release until she thought she would shatter from its force.

He took her face in both of his hands and she looked up at him with liquid eyes, brimming with her ache for him. As a single tear slithered down her cheek, he pressed a finger against it, then kissed the stinging wetness on her silken skin.

"Don't cry, my beautiful Melissa," he murmured. "I've caused you too many tears already."

She stirred against him, wondering at the tenderness of his words, but she felt him suddenly stiffen, moving away from her as he got to his feet. Standing there was Anthony, his features contorted with rage.

"I would advise you to leave immediately, Mr. Gabriel," he ordered brusquely, "and keep a considerable distance between yourself and Miss Howell from now on."

"Are you threatening me, Holmes?" Calvin drawled, casually scrutinizing the older man.

"I would prefer to call it a warning, Mr. Gabriel," he replied smoothly. "Now get out of here."

Calvin hesitated momentarily, but then he bowed formally to a speechless Melissa and, with a final contemptuous glance at Anthony Holmes, he sauntered from the box.

"Was that arranged, my dear, or should I assume he forced his way in here without your prior consent?" Anthony's voice was edged with cruel sarcasm as he turned on her.

"How dare you use that tone of voice with me," she declared, bristling with indignation, loathing the very sight of the man, determined to escape him as quickly as possible. "If you have no objections, Anthony, I would like to return to my hotel. Now," she stated emphatically, rising and gathering up her cloak, handing him the opera glasses.

"Since you obviously had something besides the opera on your mind all night, I'll be glad to see you home now," he agreed, sweeping up his hat and overcoat and following her from the loge. Melissa walked briskly ahead of him, her head held proudly, but as she passed the Gabriel loge, she chanced a furtive glance at the heavy velvet curtains, and she was certain that she saw them move.

chapter 35

In the morning, Melissa lay dejectedly in bed, her body unwilling to face the day. She clung to her pillow, hugging it close, imagining Calvin lying there beside her. Calvin's kiss on her cheek still seemed to burn with a life of its own, the scent of him lingered on her face and hands, a disquieting reminder of his presence. In his absence, he was everywhere. Unable to rouse herself, she drifted in and out of a gentle sleep until she awoke with a start, realizing that Evan would be stopping by the hotel at one o'clock.

But even as she prodded her stubborn body out from beneath the protective comfort of the warm bedcovers and began to dress, she could not shake Calvin's hovering image from her thoughts. She glanced out of the window at the cold, bleak day, the sky overcast and leaden, and she shivered as she padded about in her bare feet. Slipping into a soft cashmere gown, she fumbled with the long row of buttons with icy hands, then wrapped a heavy wool cloak around her, feeling her chilled body begin to warm itself at last.

She was waiting in the lobby when Evan rushed in and she noticed that he wore only a thin strip of tape over the gash in his forehead and that his eye was no longer puffy or discolored. When he smiled at her in greeting, taking her arm and hurrying her out the door, it was obvious that the cut on his lip had also healed.

"You seem in especially high spirits today," she commented as he propelled her along the sidewalk, whistling roguishly, all the time glancing about for an available hansom cab.

"Why not? With someone like you at my side, I'm always at my best," he boasted, pulling her toward a slowing carriage and helping her up. "This afternoon should prove most enlightening, Melissa, and it will give you a chance to see American politics up close." He drew out his note pad and flipped hastily through the pages. "You know, I give those men a lot of credit, running for mayor of this town when there's so much labor unrest and all of these strikes occurring lately. But apparently the one to watch, although he hasn't got a chance in hell of ever winning, is the candidate the Republican Party has put up. A fellow named Theodore Roosevelt." He paused, thumbing through his pad and squinting down at the illegible scrawl covering one of the pages. "He's only twenty-eight years old, but he's a Harvard graduate and has already served three years in the state legislature." He snapped the pad shut. ' Yes indeed, it should be quite an interesting afternoon."

Melissa was paying scant attention to Evan. Instead she busily scrutinized the crowds on either side of the carriage, watching all of the people making their way to Washington Square, streaming by the hundreds onto the grass and pushing toward the makeshift speaking platform. She was surprised and heartened by the turnout for the mayoral candidates but she could not help but pity the man who would eventually win the election, for he would be expected to provide solutions for the many problems facing the troubled city.

Despite the growing prosperity of the established aristocracy of New York, there was an ever-widening gap forming between them and the rapidly expanding working class. The year 1886 was being marked by spreading depression, strikes by employees, retaliatory lockouts by irate employers, and an alarming growth in the ranks of the unemployed. For the first time, labor unions were taking part in the political process, taking sides. The Central Labor Union represented about fifty thousand workers and had already thrown its support behind forty-seven-year-old Henry George, renowned economist and reformer. Abram S. Hewitt, at sixty-four, a former United States Congressman and a seasoned politician, was the choice of the Democratic Party. Young Roosevelt would be fighting an uphill battle all the way.

As Melissa and Evan left the carriage, they quickly joined the swelling numbers of men and women vying for good viewing positions. She clung tenaciously to his arm as they were jostled and pushed about, with Evan shoving back and plodding steadily forward toward the raised wooden platform trimmed in multicolored bunting. Makeshift posters and placards waved above the heads of the gathering people. Shouts of support for the various candidates split the air. Melissa struggled to keep up with Evan as he determinedly plowed on and when he realized that he could progress no further, he stopped and pulled out his pad and pencil. Studying the crowd, squinting critically at the men congregating on the high platform, he began taking down notes.

Standing on tiptoes, Melissa managed to peer over the head of the man in front of her. Scanning the still growing crowd, she looked behind her at the people spilling into the park, noticing at the same time a number of elegant carriages drawing up to the curb. Some of the city's elite had obviously chosen to view the proceedings safely and comfortably at a discreet distance from the rest of the citizenry. Men and women, many clutching the hands of small children, others carrying infants in their arms, stood all around her, straining to glimpse their favored candidates. Melissa felt small and unprotected and she moved closer to Evan. A shiver of apprehension seized her as she spotted a group of surly looking men, obviously laborers, who were standing together in a group, their numbers gradually increasing. Each man joining them carried a placard. She knew that the streetcar employees were striking for shorter hours and she wondered if these men were a part of that protest.

As the first of the speakers was introduced, a hush descended upon the gathering, only to be followed by a burst of applause interspersed with loud jeers as the man began to talk. A short, red-haired man, his prominent jaw edged with a sandy beard, he was agile and lithe, and his small frame exuded a nervous energy as he moved about, slicing the air with his hand for emphasis, his words crackling with confident vitality. Melissa barely heard Evan's whisper identifying the speaker as Henry George before he was rudely shushed by a man who was leaning forward in an effort to see and hear the diminutive candidate. Melissa found her attention wandering as George continued to speak. She shifted from one foot to the other, growing more aware of the number of people pressing closely about her. Evan was busily scratching away in his notebook and she tried to read his script in an attempt to distract her thoughts from the crush of men and women on all sides of them.

Her neck was beginning to ache from the strain of looking up at the platform and the gaunt figure of Abram Hewitt, his face lined, his beard white, who was droning on about his plans to save the city from all the evils corrupting it. She stifled a yawn and nestled closer to Evan only to be pushed away from him by a burly man behind her, who complained that she was blocking his view. Annoyed, she stood rigidly for a while, her arms folded across her chest, until she grew restless again and resumed her awkward shifting.

She glanced back over her shoulder again, studying the line of carriages still at the curb, longing to be inside one of them where it was warm and secluded and out of the cold and the closeness of the crowd. As her discomfort increased, she was scarcely aware of the young man with the bristling moustache thundering in a deep voice from the podium. As he spoke, pounding the lectern for effect, Melissa saw one of the rough-looking men with the placards jostle his neighbor and begin to shout questions at the candidate.

"What about our wages?" the man bellowed. "Is the city goin' to do somethin' fer us or not?"

"That's right!" shouted the man beside him. "We been workin' fer slave wages fer years. What d'ya plan to do about it?"

Suddenly the entire group of men was shouting and waving their placards in the air. Despite the attempts of young Roosevelt to continue with his speech, the men's voices grew louder and more forceful. Melissa tugged apprehensively at Evan's coat sleeve, drawing his attention to the rebelliousness around them.

"This is beginning to worry me," she shouted at him above the increasing din. "What if it turns into a fight and we find ourselves trapped in the middle of it?"

"It will make great copy," he beamed, writing feverishly in his book again, his concentration shifting to the agitators, away from the hapless Roosevelt.

"Evan, I would prefer not to be part of your great copy," she retorted. "Have you forgotten what just happened to you last week?"

"There are plenty of police around to quash any disturbances," Evan insisted. "Now be a good girl, Melissa, and let me write." He shook off her restraining hand and scribbled furiously again.

It was not long before the hecklers were in turn finding themselves shouted down by those around them as people's attention was diverted from the platform and centered on the developing shouting match. To Melissa's horror, one of the men suddenly lunged forward, grabbing a well-dressed man by the collar of his coat. The man instantly took a swing at the fellow, hitting him in the nose and drawing blood as, with a menacing

431

growl, the injured man locked his hands around his opponent's neck and the two men fell heavily to the ground, taking several bystanders with them.

Placards began waving about feverishly as shouts and insults were traded back and forth, and then the signs were being employed as weapons as people were hit over the head and prodded with the wooden poles. Fists began to fly and men grappled with one another, rocking back and forth, locked viciously together. Women started screaming, trying to pull back their men from the fracas. All around her, people were beginning to panic, some jumping in to do battle while others pushed and shoved in an effort to get as far away from the trouble as possible. Melissa began to tremble with fear.

She grabbed at Evan's arm, sending his notebook spinning from his grasp to the ground. With an angry curse, he stooped to pick it up and was instantly knocked off balance. He hit the ground with a loud thud, but began groping about for his pad, dodging between moving legs in an effort to retrieve it. A stocky man with a sneer carved across his broad face snatched up the fallen book and tauntingly held it high over his head, daring Evan to take it. He was on his feet immediately and reaching for the book as the man laughed at him, holding it beyond Evan's straining grasp. His patience sorely tried, Evan slammed his fist into the man's belly and as he doubled over, he grabbed the book and turned to face Melissa with a triumphant smile. Her look of terror warned him and he spun around to find the man lurching toward him, head lowered like a charging bull. He caught Evan in the stomach, sending him sprawling to the ground at Melissa's feet.

She was hauled back by a pair of muscled arms as she tried to help Evan up and people all around her began suddenly to shove and push. She stumbled backward and fell, her hands scraping painfully against the dry bristly grass. Terrified, she fought to regain her footing, her cloak catching beneath a man's boots as she scrambled to her feet, her hair falling into her eyes as she tugged her cloak free. It was as if a human wall had sprung up in front of her because she could not see Evan anymore, and she found herself being forced back again by the surging crowd, carried along by the wave of people running to get out of the park.

Unable to help herself, Melissa was pulled along with the human tide as it rolled and surged, gathering strength as it moved. As she ran, she saw policemen on horseback fighting their way among the hundreds of panicking people in a vain attempt to restore order. Melissa tripped on the hem of her cape and she would have fallen again if a man had not grabbed her arm, steadying her at the last minute. Before she could thank him, he seemed to be swept away before her eyes, and she staggered on alone, frantic with worry over Evan, helpless to do anything other than continue to run.

She finally reached the outskirts of the square where the mob had begun to thin at last, and she raced to the curb where the carriages were still parked, their occupants enthralled by the drama unfolding in front of them. As she hurried along the sidewalk, drawing her flapping cloak more tightly around her, a group of men rushed past her, dropping their placards as they ran in a bid to escape a number of mounted policemen bearing down on them. A horse swerved sharply to avoid colliding with one of the carriages, rearing into the air and almost throwing its rider from the saddle. Melissa backed away quickly, but the irate policeman had spotted her, and assuming that she was one of the troublemakers, headed directly for her.

Fear propelled her and she turned and ran in the opposite direction, racing behind a coach, placing it between her and her pursuer. The driver of the vehicle, sensing imminent danger, picked up the reins and slapped at the horses. They broke away from the curb, leaving Melissa in the open once more. Desperately, she sprinted down the road toward the last of the carriages. She grabbed hold of the handle on the coach door and tugged it open, flinging herself inside.

"Please," she gasped to the startled couple sitting there, "please may I stay here for a moment?"

"Whatever have you done?" sniffed the white-haired woman, staring curiously at the panting girl through a lorgnette.

"Nothing," Melissa rasped. "I was caught in the middle of the fighting and a policeman is chasing me."

"I see," snapped the woman. "Jeffrey, instruct Rodney to get us away from here immediately." But before the elderly man could comply, the door was thrown open. The policeman reached in and grabbed Melissa's arm.

"Get out of there, sister, if you know what's good for you," he commanded, hauling her from the carriage.

"Now see here, officer," the woman began to protest, but he cut her off with a rude remark, slamming the door behind him as Melissa landed heavily beside him. Twisting in his grasp, she struggled and kicked, hitting him in the groin. With a yelp of pain, he released her and she streaked off down the pavement once again. People were still frenziedly pouring out of the park and she headed back toward the surging masses, hoping to lose herself among them.

Tears welling up in her eyes, her hair streaming in tangled disarray, she brushed the fallen strands from her face and continued to run, battling against the crowds pushing her back. She felt a hand close over her shoulder and she spun around, doubling her fists, prepared to fight off the policeman once more, but the man caught her wrists and shouted her name. She looked up through her tears and the hair falling into her eyes and blinked in disbelief.

She was barely conscious of his arms lifting her, of his strength pressed against her as he strode toward one of the carriages on the street. She lay cushioned against his chest, her arms twined about his neck, her head bobbing gently on his shoulder, afraid to open her eyes and find that she was imagining him holding her.

"You were just one carriage away from mine, princess," Calvin murmured, his voice sending dizzying waves coursing through her. Flinging open the carriage door, he set her down on the seat and moved in beside her. She sighed, nestling close to him as the coach started off.

"I watched you take care of the policeman," he said with a wry chuckle. "You're one hell of a fighter, you know." He brushed back the straying curls of auburn hair from her face and pressed his lips against the tears glistening on her cheeks. "No more tears, Melissa love," he whispered before his mouth found hers. She felt the world fly away.

The carriage came to a stop and Calvin helped Melissa down, leading her toward the gray stone façade of an elegant hotel. She made no attempt to resist as he guided her through the carpeted lobby and up a curving marble staircase to a large, lavishly appointed suite. He locked the door and tossed his overcoat onto a velvet settee, then turned to take her cloak from around her shoulders.

"You can wash up in there." He indicated a marbled bathroom, then he disappeared into the bedroom.

When she had scrubbed the dirt from her face and hands and brushed out her hair, Melissa walked timidly into the bedroom. Calvin beckoned her over to the window beside him.

"How long have you been in New York?" he asked softly, drawing her into the circle of his arms.

She hesitated, uncertain of how to answer him. "For several months now," she finally replied. He sensed her reticence and tried to make light of it.

"Aren't you even curious about my being here?" he

wanted to know and she nodded vaguely. "I was in Saratoga when I learned that my father had died," he began, "so naturally I had to return to Stony Briar to take charge of things. I'm up here now settling some of the estate's dealings because it's too difficult for Edward to leave Kathleen alone. So I save him the trouble of the trip down to Maryland and I get a chance to visit New York."

She stirred in his embrace, reaching up to touch his cheek with the palm of her hand. "Your father was sick for so long, Calvin, that it must have been almost a blessing," she soothed him. He let out a deep sigh and nodded his head in agreement.

"You're right, but the house seems pretty empty now with him gone," he said, his voice husky. He held her more securely in his arms.

"How are Amanda and Bryan?" she asked him then, curiosity nibbling at her.

"I haven't had much time to socialize lately," he admitted, "but I can safely assume that things are still the same."

"Not quite," she murmured faintly, despising herself as soon as the words had left her lips, for she felt him stiffen and pull away from her.

"If you meant Amanda and me, that was finished a long time ago." His voice was suddenly harsh.

"I know, forgive me, I should never have said what I did," she apologized, fearing the angry fire lighting behind his gray eyes.

"You shouldn't try to besmirch something you could never understand, Melissa," he warned and she backed away from his rising fury. "Amanda was more of a woman than anyone I had ever met; she was good and kind and loving, and she needed me just as much as I needed her. But once it was over, it was over, and I never looked back." His steely gaze held hers. "I don't regret what we had, Melissa, and I'd do it all again if I had to choose a woman to teach me about love."

She had no words to utter in her own defense. She was helpless in the face of such a declaration and her body echoed her despair. He caught her look of anguish and took a step toward her, his arms outstretched beseechingly.

"Melissa, princess, let's stop this senseless fighting. Please, love, come here," he begged her. But she backed further away from him, bewildered by his changing mood, wary of his intent.

"No," she whispered as he clasped her to him, holding her against his chest. "No, Calvin, please." Her words were lost as his mouth silenced her, his lips insistent, demanding reciprocation. Against his ardor, she was powerless. Against his will, she was weak. She sagged limply against the hardening of his body, her arms finding their way around his neck.

He lifted her easily and carried her to the bed. Then he lay down beside her and gathered her close to him, his lips teasing light kisses across her face until he captured her mouth again. Their tongues touched and melded together. Passion's sweet fire ignited as they held each other, their bodies locking, their limbs intertwined.

"I've missed you, Melissa," he whispered fiercely. "God, how I've missed you." She held fast to the words he uttered to her, daring once more to hope.

His hands groped for the tiny buttons fastening her gown and when she was free at last of its weight, she stretched out languidly before him, her filmy undergarments accentuating her lushness. Calvin's fingertips wonderingly traced the curves of her inviting body. Melissa, her hair spreading like a golden mantle across the pillows, watched him and his open admiration of her with a slight smile tilting the corners of her mouth, her eyes alight with copper fires as she studied him in return. Growing impatient, she began to undress him and her straining fingers tore at the clothes still separating them. He was silhouetted against the fading afternoon light, etched in the dimming of the day, a perfectly molded form which she yearned to devour. She caressed him, feeling the tensing of his muscles as she followed the smooth hardness of his body and cupping the stiffening of his manhood. He groaned as her fingers closed around him.

"Don't hurry us, love," he implored. "We have the whole night still ahead of us." He nuzzled one golden breast with his mouth, sucking the tender, pulsing flesh, delighting in the stiffening nipple so responsive to his touch. Melissa tossed beneath his roving lips, but his words suddenly reminded her of Evan, and guilt gnawed insidiously inside of her as she thought of him abandoned.

"What's wrong?" he demanded as she pushed him away from her and struggled to sit up again.

"I have no right to be here with you," she declared vehemently. "I was with someone in the square this afternoon and we were separated by the crowd. I–I never found out what happened to him."

"Who was it? Anthony Holmes?" he scowled, but she shook her head. "Don't tell me you're playing him false too?" His short laugh was cold and jeering.

"I am playing no one false," she denied. "I was there with a friend of mine, a newspaper reporter."

"And who would you have been with tonight?" he sneered. With a gasp of alarm, Melissa suddenly remembered the show and she jumped from the bed and scrambled to find her discarded clothing. He watched her for a moment and then, with an outraged howl, he sprang after her and threw her back onto the bed.

"We're not through yet, Melissa," he snarled. "You've lighted a fire in me that needs quenching." He held her down, his muscled frame flung sideways across her twisting body.

Sobbing, scratching wildly at him, she fought him, but he easily subdued her and straddled her. With one hand, he pinned her arms above her head, while with

438

the other, he forced apart her stubborn, resisting thighs. She bucked against his groping fingers, hating him for abusing her, despising the animal lust that drove him on despite her pleas. Then, with one brutal thrust, he entered her. She stiffened at the unexpected pain as he drove inside of her. But even as he slowed to a rhythmic pulsing, she felt the treacherous stirrings of desire lick upward through her body.

The flame grew and spread, carrying its surging heat through her singing veins, filling her entire being, and Melissa rose to match the steady pounding of his flesh against hers. Calvin sensed her response and released her hands, gathering her to him, forcing her legs up and around his back as he thrust deeper, drenched by love dew, bathing him as he rode her. Her arms tightening about his neck, Melissa arched and fell as he took her higher, allowing her to share the mounting crest with him and glimpse the glory awaiting them on the other side.

Her body tensed as he seemed to grow inside of her in that final swelling before completion. She absorbed the stinging agony of his arrival at the summit. She spiraled upward to meet him there and her explosion drained her of her strength and of her will. She was tossed back to waking's shore, limp and fulfilled. In the whimpering calm, she floated, suspended above time's pacing, her body one with his, at peace at last.

He untangled himself from their passion and lay beside her, his labored breathing gradually slowing, his gray eyes cooling as he looked at her. She turned her head and gazed back at him, regret etched in her face and she rose from the bed and began to dress. Silence, built of their stubborn pride, lowered as a veil between them and she shuddered in the cold aftermath of their love heat as loneliness settled itself within her once again. She looked back at him just before she closed the bedroom door, but he refused to meet her eyes. With a shattering sigh, she left him there. Her ears strained for the sound of his voice calling her name, calling her back, but the silence was deafening in its mute reply. The door clicked shut behind her and still she waited there, waited until her pride finally drove her away.

chapter 36

That evening, Melissa performed mechanically, her usual exuberance missing, the approving roar of the crowd unable to reach her and dispel the dismal gloom enveloping her. Numbly she moved through her act, aware of the brilliant glare of the lights on her glittering crimson form as she spun around and around the giant arena. But her aim was not as true as usual and several large targets remained untouched. Annie Oakley threw her a questioning look as the two women criss-crossed on horseback around the sawdust-covered floor. But Melissa ignored her. Her riding was uneven and her jumps poorly executed and Target kicked down the top bars of several low hurdles as he attempted to clear them. When Melissa reined in her horse and acknowledged the applause of the audience following her final jump, she caught Cody watching her, his eyes searching her masked face, his brow furrowed in a puzzled frown.

As she headed for her dressing room, Cody lumbered after her.

"Is there somethin' wrong, little lady?" he asked, his deep voice edged with concern as he reached her side and grasped her by the elbow, tugging her toward him.

"Nothing more than fatigue, Bill," she lied. "Perhaps missing two shows was a bad idea after all." She forced a light laugh from her lips. "I seem to have forgotten how to perform properly."

But he did not join in her affected gaiety. Instead he drew her even closer to him, his brown eyes piercing hers. "I'm thinkin' you need some time away from all this, 'lissa," he said gently. "You've been goin' at a hellish pace ever since you joined up with us and I believe a little holiday might be in order right about now."

"But people are expecting me at each performance," she protested, "and with all of the publicity I receive, they might feel cheated if I disappear for any length of time."

"Now don't you go worryin' that pretty head of yours," he soothed. "We'll manage just fine and so will the audience. You just think on what I've said and let me know your decision. Deal?" He smiled down at her.

"Deal," she agreed. He sauntered off down the corridor and Melissa slipped into the dimly lit dressing room, eager to change her clothes and return to the hotel. As she opened the door, she was not even surprised to find Evan sitting on a chair, impatiently drumming his fingers on the top of her cluttered vanity table.

"And just what the hell happened to you this afternoon?" he charged as she flung off her hat and mask and began to unpin her hair.

"As you must have noticed, we were separated by that mob," she snapped irritably, slipping off her spangled jacket and unfastening her vest.

"Well, you certainly ran off quickly enough," he accused, his lower lip thrust petulantly forward as she whirled to face him.

"I was frightened, Evan," she exclaimed, "and I was pushed back until I was shoved right out of the square. Then a policeman started to chase me and—" She stopped, uncertain of what to say. "I barely managed to get away," she finished abruptly, avoiding his eyes.

"I went back to your hotel, Melissa, and I waited and

waited but you never showed up."

"I resent being questioned this way, Evan," she flared angrily. "You have no right to probe into my activities. Now I would appreciate it if you would leave so that I can change out of these clothes." She turned her back to him and started working at the buttons on her shirt.

"I'm sorry, Melissa." His tone was softer, almost pleading. "But I was worried about you, and when you never returned to the hotel, I became frantic."

"I understand, Evan, I truly do," she answered wearily, "but I would still prefer if you left me alone now because I must get back to my room and get some sleep."

"Could I at least walk back to the hotel with you?" he asked. She gave in grudgingly and he finally wandered from the room as she sank down onto the chair and tugged at her boots.

They walked quickly through the cold, crisp air, their breath steaming in cloudy puffs as they strode along, swinging through the deserted streets. Evan was the first to break the silence.

"My editor liked my story about the brawl in Washington Square this afternoon," he said, "and even though he was more interested in the details of the fight than the political speeches, the paper is running the whole story under my byline and giving it front page coverage."

"You must feel rather proud," she commented, her voice more waspish than she had intended. She was immediately regretful as his smile faded to a scowl.

She was grateful when they finally walked the last long block to her hotel. She suffered through the clumsy hug and hurried kiss he pressed onto her frozen lips. Then she scampered into the warmth of the dingy lobby and back to her room. As she struck a match and held it to the oil lamp next to her bed, she was startled to find a bowl of flowers perched atop her bureau. She realized that the concierge must have placed them there and that, as usual, she had neglected to lock her door. But she forgot her carelessness in the excitement of tearing open the small white envelope and pulling out the enclosed card.

Her thumping heart slowed its reckless pace when she recognized Anthony's bold script. She swiftly read the brief apology for his behavior the previous night. With a sigh, she slipped the note into her small, worn reticule in which she still saved the tiny bits and scraps of her life. Dreamily she sifted through the contents of the little purse, rubbing her fingers over the two British coins she had kept as reminders of her home, the small white cards which had been enclosed in the gifts she had received from the Ransomes at Christmas, and Anthony's notes to her, filled with their tender verses. Absently, she caressed the tattered little purse and she found herself getting lost in remembering. How very long ago it seemed that she had set sail from England. She had come so very far, and yet she was no closer to the truth she still sought, no nearer to the reason for her tempestuous flight.

Over the weeks following her encounter with Calvin Gabriel, Melissa drove herself mercilessly, burying the memory of him beneath the rush of activities she pursued and the grueling demands of her work. She made time for hurried lunches with Evan, meeting him at Billy Mould's Bar near Washington Square, a favorite restaurant of artists, writers, and aspiring actors peopling the neighborhood, where they filled themselves with Billy's famous bean soup. In the evenings, after the show, Melissa would dress in her loveliest gowns and dine in elegant surroundings with Anthony, who had, of late, begun giving her small gifts which she was reluctant to accept, but which he refused to take back. When she was with him, she was able to achieve a measure of contentment, drawing strength and comfort from his obvious adoration of her. But once she was alone in the privacy of her room, her moods were bleak and despairing.

A week before Christmas, Melissa confronted Cody with her plan to take several days' holiday away from the rigors of the show.

"Will you promise to be back here in time for Christmas Eve?" he inquired after approving her idea. "You're scheduled to appear at two of the children's wards in St. Agatha's Hospital. Nate's idea, of course. It's to bring a bit of the show to those little ones who can't get to see it themselves."

"I promise," she said, nodding, then scurrying back to her dressing room. His booming voice trailed after her as she hurried down the hallway.

"You have yourself a good rest, you hear?" She waved back at him and slipped into her room.

Over dinner that evening at Delmonico's, Melissa told Anthony of her plan to leave the following morning for Baltimore.

"I wrote to Amanda Ransome several weeks ago, telling her of my intended visit," Melissa explained, "and she just wrote back to let me know that they would be at home to receive me. I know it must seem odd, my wanting to go back there," she said in a hushed voice, "but there are answers I have yet to find and I feel certain they lie somewhere in Maryland."

"What on earth are you talking about?" Anthony put in, staring blankly at her.

"You know very little about my past, dear Anthony," she replied, a vague smile on her lips, "but I left England to find the answer to a puzzle, and I still have not uncovered it. Some day I hope to explain it all to you." She retreated behind a protective wall of silence, revealing nothing more, and he continued to study her, a worried frown fixed on his brow.

"And when do you intend to return?" he asked then.

"I have to be back here in time for Christmas Eve. I

promised Cody I would appear at one of the local hospitals and visit some of the children's wards."

"On Christmas Eve?" he echoed indignantly. "Blast Cody and his infernal show. I'm getting sick and tired of sharing you with that damned cowboy, seeing you only when it's convenient for the show," he raged. "I've put up with it for a long time, Melissa, but I warn you, I don't intend to put up with it forever."

"But I love the show," she protested, "and I owe Bill and Nate a great deal, Anthony. Just what do you suggest I do instead?" she blazed.

"I suggest that you stop parading around like a child who doesn't want to grow up," he stormed back at her. And then he lowered his voice. "What I'm also suggesting, my darling Melissa, is what I've wanted all along. Marry me. Forget this silly masquerade, and live a normal life again, with me."

He leaned across the table, capturing her hands with his, his eyes brimming with the love he offered her. She, in turn, studied the man across from her, strong and handsome, determined to have her, to comfort her and take care of her. But her lips could form no answer, not when Calvin's mocking laughter echoed in her ears, his kisses branded her forever his, and his arms held her as surely as he held her heart.

As if discerning her thoughts, Anthony gripped her hands more tightly and his gaze burned into hers. "I'll make you forget him, Melissa. I promise that I will. Just give me the chance to make you happy."

"Thank you, Anthony," she whispered, "but I have no answer for you now. You should have a wife who can give herself totally to you, not one whose affections are still so torn. Would you give me a little time," she asked softly. "If you love me, please grant me that."

His sigh was deep, defeated, but he slowly nodded his head. "You can certainly have more time, my dear, but don't keep me waiting too long." He smiled ruefully. "I'm getting older, not younger, you know."

* * *

Anthony accompanied her to the train the following morning and after seeing her settled in the compartment, he handed her a small box festooned with a large white bow. She hesitated, but he pressed it insistently into her hands and hurried down the steps just as the train was about to start. As they chugged out of the station, Melissa waved to Anthony's receding figure waving back at her. When she could no longer see him, she leaned back in her seat and stared wonderingly at the box she held. She slipped the mysterious package into her purse, deciding to savor the anticipation of opening it until later in the trip.

Idly gazing out at the passing countryside, at the bare trees and stiff grasses, dilapidated farmhouses, and jagged patches of snow, Melissa gradually found herself relaxing, soothed by the clickety-clack of the wheels and the steady rhythm of the puffing train. The tension knitting her body so rigidly began to ease, and the fatigue, born of the pace she had set for herself, seeped out through her pores. She slept off and on during the journey, mindless of her fellow passengers, the hum of conversation around her, and the occasional jolting of the train as it labored toward Baltimore. Foregoing lunch, she contented herself with biscuits and a cup of steaming coffee in the early afternoon. It was only as the train pulled into the station that she remembered Anthony's gift.

Hastily retrieving it, she tore off the bow and snapped open the lid on the velvet box, her eyes sparkling with delight as she withdrew an exquisite topaz pendant suspended from a thin gold chain. Bubbling with pleasure, relieved that the gift had not been a ring, she fastened the chain and marveled at the large square-cut stone, glinting with deep amber flames, as it nestled against the soft wool of her gown, hanging just above the swell of her breasts.

She waited with her small valise on the station

platform, wondering if Bryan Ransome had thought to meet her at the train. The chill soon drove her inside the small station. She quickly abandoned the idea of ever locating him among the people milling about, and hailed a hansom cab, directing him to the one hotel whose name she remembered. There were no messages from the Ransomes for her when she checked with the clerk at the desk, so she hurried upstairs to her room and unpacked the clothing she had brought with her.

She spent the rest of the afternoon browsing through the many shops she had once frequented, pleased to find that some of the shopkeepers still remembered her. As the shadows began to lengthen and the daylight fade, she directed her steps to the red brick house on Clarendon Street. Suddenly apprehensive about seeing the Ransomes again, Melissa spent several minutes standing on the stoop composing herself until, with a determined set to her mouth, she lifted the brass knocker. A moment later, the door swung open and Melissa faced a young uniformed maid she had never seen before. She was promptly informed that the family was not at home.

"But when do you expect them?" she asked, her heart sinking.

"They didn't exactly say, miss, but I'm sure it won't be until quite late," she replied. Melissa smiled wanly at the girl and walked back down the steps again.

She dined alone at a restaurant which had been a favorite of Kathleen's, then purchased a ticket for the evening's performance at the Ford Theatre. Although it was a frothy comedy which provoked uproarious laughter from the audience, Melissa sat stony-faced in her seat, fretting about the Ransomes, wondering if they had changed their minds and had decided to avoid her. Drifting through the lobby during intermission, she scanned the faces passing by, looking for ones familiar to her. She recognized none of them and returned to her seat. After the performance, she made her way back to the hotel, stopping by the desk to find that no message had been delivered to her. She climbed dispiritedly upstairs to her room.

After a hearty breakfast in the hotel dining room, Melissa buttoned her cloak and walked vigorously back to Clarendon Street, expecting to be greeted again by the young maid. But to her immense relief, Bryan Ransome himself answered the door and clasped her to him in a fond embrace. He ushered her into the parlor where Amanda rose from the sofa to greet her, her lovely face wreathed in a welcoming smile.

"It's wonderful to see you again, Melissa," she declared, hugging her and gazing warmly into her eyes. "We were surprised and delighted to receive your letter, and I dare say we have so much to catch up on." She led Melissa to the sofa, waving Ransome to a nearby chair. Over tea and toast fingers, the interceding months seemed to disappear. As they talked, Melissa gathered that nothing had really changed between Amanda and Bryan, just as Calvin had assumed, but what took her completely by surprise was learning that Cornelia had chosen to spend the winter abroad, moving away from the suffocating family circle for the first time in years, in spite of the intentions she once had.

Over lunch, between the elegantly served courses and the light conversation, Melissa freed her thoughts, searching her surroundings for some clue, some memory which might succeed in jolting her sluggish mind. But there seemed to be no answers in the once familiar scenes around her and she began to fear that her trip had been in vain.

"Melissa dear," Amanda called and Melissa reined in her wandering thoughts, smiling apologetically. "I was just saying that we've invited a number of friends in tonight to meet someone you too should be curious about." Her eyes glittered mischievously as she continued. "We received another bit of surprising news, which is why we weren't at home last evening. As you may recall, Jeremy left behind a young wife and child in London. Well, my dear, Arabella has recently remarried and is in America on her honeymoon."

"And on business too," piped in Bryan. "Jeremy's affairs were in a shambles when he died and I had to straighten them out myself from here. Arabella's arrival makes everything so much simpler now and I can finally wind up his estate."

"So I hope you'll be our guest tonight," Amanda insisted. "Being from England, you should have a great deal in common with Arabella."

"I doubt that," muttered Melissa, recalling the arrogant young woman beckoning to Jeremy on the docks of London so long ago. "But of course I plan to be here tonight, Amanda, and thank you," she replied, easing the anxious frown on the woman's face.

"I'm on my way to the harbor, Melissa. I can see you back to your hotel if you wish," Bryan offered as they rose from the table and left the dining room. Melissa accepted the opportunity to avoid the expense of a carriage herself and she kissed Amanda on the cheek, promising to return again that evening. She followed Bryan to his coach.

"I understand you saw Kathleen and Edward in New York," he said as they started off toward her hotel. "How did you find her, Melissa. Is she happy?"

"She seems extremely content," she admitted truthfully. "Edward is very much in love with her and is doing everything possible to make her happy."

"I'm so grateful to hear that," he sighed, "for God knows I tried to discourage the match, knowing how Kathleen felt about Calvin. But Edward can be a damned persistent fellow when he wants to be, and for once I'm glad I let him have his way."

"Is Calvin here in Baltimore?" she asked, her voice trembling as she spoke his name.

"No, not right now. He's involved with expanding Stony Briar and traveling back and forth to New York settling Tyler's estate." From his tone, Melissa realized that he was still unaware of his wife's long affair and she was loath to press him further.

When Melissa alighted in front of her hotel, she went immediately to her room, pulling out the apricot velvet gown she had worn to the opera with Anthony and spreading it across the bed to smooth any of the creases it might have sustained while packed away during the train journey. Leisurely bathing and arranging her hair, she finally slipped into the gown shortly before eight o'clock, allowing her enough time to arrive at the Ransomes. She fastened the topaz earrings she had brought and then hung the magnificent topaz pendant around her neck, watching it flash and sparkle between her golden breasts.

She felt a nervous fluttering in her stomach as she rode to the house, and when she handed her cloak to the same maid whom she had seen the previous day, the girl remembered her and smiled.

"Melissa, you look so beautiful," Amanda bubbled, hurrying over to her as she stood shyly in the front hall. "Come along with me. There's someone here I want you to meet." She threw her a pointed look and Melissa hastily prepared herself to confront at last the woman who had been Jeremy's wife.

As Amanda steered her into the parlor, Melissa hung back, not quite ready to come face to face with the widow of the man who had raped and used her. But it was too late and she found herself led to the former Arabella Ransome, whose honeyed purr raised the hackles on the back of Melissa's neck.

"Melissa," she crooned, "I feel as if you and I have already met. Your name has been the subject of much conversation of late."

"Has it indeed?" Melissa replied, coolly regarding the woman whose green eyes gleamed with a brilliance

451

to match the large emeralds blazing at her ears and around her slender alabaster throat. Her dark blonde hair was gathered in a severe chignon, wispy tendrils escaping to frame her ivory face. Her blonde brows arched warily, her slim nose flaring slightly above a full, sensuous mouth. Gowned in white satin, the underskirt fashioned of heavy white lace, she appeared for all the world to be a bride, yet missing was the tender blush of innocence and the eyes were hard and cold.

Melissa turned away then, acknowledging the warm greeting of a couple she had met at the previous Christmas party, grateful for the reprieve from the disdainful woman whose scathing glance still followed her.

"Oh there you are, darling," she heard Arabella saying. "Melissa, there is someone here who is most anxious to meet you. May I introduce you to my husband, my dear?"

Grudgingly, Melissa forced herself to turn around again and a strangled gasp caught in her throat. Standing before her, his arm around the waist of his smugly triumphant wife, was Philip Wentworth.

chapter 37

"Melissa, my pet," drawled Philip, his thin lips spreading into a slow smile, "I never thought to see your beautiful face again." He raised her shaking hand, brushing a kiss lightly across the back of it while his blue eyes bored coldly into hers.

"Philip," she managed weakly as he released her hand.

"Quite a shocker, eh, my dear?" he laughed harshly. "When the Ransomes spoke of a delightful creature named Melissa who had stayed with them, who would have guessed it was you? I certainly never expected to set eyes on you here. But then, if one waits long enough, one usually gets what one wants." He turned his glittering gaze toward his wife. "Like Arabella and myself. Her poor husband did us both a favor by drowning, did he not, my darling?"

"Shall we toast dear Jeremy, my love?" She laughed maliciously, raising the wineglass she was holding. Philip obligingly joined her. A knot of revulsion tightened inside of Melissa as she glowered at their callousness. They were suitably matched, she thought disgustedly, each equally deserving of the other.

"How is my home, Philip?" Her voice seemed loud and harsh to her own ears as she succeeded in capturing his attention once again.

"Howard House still stands, Melissa, fear not," he

smirked. "Though it is a fair sight more prosperous than when you left it."

"And Lettie?"

"Alas, old Letitia chose not to remain at Howard House. With an excellent letter of recommendation from me, she found employment elsewhere." He brushed off the subject with a disdainful wave of his hand.

Seizing the moment, Melissa suddenly realized that her chance encounter with Philip might be to her advantage after all. He was growing restless. Sensing his growing uneasiness, she placed a restraining hand on his arm as he seemed about to edge away from her.

"Philip," she began, a quavering tone to her voice, "do you remember the night of my masquerade ball?"

"Yes, Philip," Arabella cut in rudely, "refresh my memory as well, dear. Was that not the evening sweet Melissa insisted on announcing your betrothal?"

"I did nothing of the kind," Melissa retorted heatedly, yearning to scratch the complacent grin from Arabella's face.

"But dear Melissa," she persisted, "it was apparently quite common knowledge that your father owed Philip a great deal of money. You were to be the enticement to pay him back."

"That is a lie!" Melissa cried, outraged by the woman's insinuations.

"Enough, Arabella." Philip abruptly silenced his wife. "Stop carrying on in front of complete strangers when it is none of their concern." His voice was strained and tight as he addressed the gloating woman.

"Sorry, darling," she sniffed petulantly, "but from what you told me about that affair, Melissa had quite set her cap for you."

Philip's laugh was derisive as he met Melissa's astounded gaze. "Hardly, my dear. She was obviously smitten by some brute of an American."

"American?" Melissa repeated, reaching again for

that elusive memory. "What American?"

"Ah, how fickle you women are," Philip sighed. "How quickly you forget."

"But I have forgotten," she insisted, "and you must help me to remember. Please, Philip." He glanced quizzically at her, his mouth curling into a perplexed scowl as Arabella stepped between them, brushing aside Melissa's plea.

"Your theatrics are becoming tiresome, Melissa," she remarked cuttingly. "Come along, Philip darling, Amanda would prefer us to mingle with the rest of the guests." Before Melissa could protest, they strode off together, leaving her gaping after them.

Deeply distraught, infuriated by the lies Philip had obviously been constructing for his wife, Melissa stood alone, trembling and on the verge of tears. Sensing her distress, Amanda hurried to her and drew her off to a corner of the room, waiting until she regained her composure.

"Amanda, you must answer me truthfully," she pleaded, a stricken look in her topaz eyes. "What has Philip told you about me?"

"Very little, Melissa dear," she replied gently, "except to say that you were neighbors in Kent and that you were to be betrothed. I now know that your name is Howard and not Howell and that your father died leaving you deeply in debt, with everything going to Philip."

"Is that all he said?" she persisted. Amanda nodded. "Have you spoken to anyone else about this; about me?" she stammered.

"No, no one, I promise you that, Melissa. We met Philip for the first time only two days ago and both Bryan and I have agreed to keep this to ourselves. You have my word on this," Amanda assured her. "Is there something else? Are you in some kind of trouble?" she questioned but Melissa shook her head distractedly.

She knew that she had to devise a way of separating

Philip from the tenacious Arabella, and she spent the remainder of the evening seeking him out, but to no avail. Arabella clung deliberately to his arm, never straying from his side, moving him from guest to guest with calculated ease. As the couple prepared to leave, Melissa dared once more to attract Philip's attention and she accosted him openly as he stood at the front door.

"Please, Philip, I must speak with you," she begged, grabbing hold of his arm.

"Melissa," Arabella snapped, hurrying over to her, "Philip spared you before, but if you persist in hounding us, I promise that you shall regret it."

"Arabella, there is something that I must discuss with him," Melissa insisted, her tone adamant. "It will take only a moment, I assure you."

"Melissa, what the devil is it that you want of me?" Philip spoke up in exasperation.

"I want to know about the night of the masquerade," she began once again.

"Philip," commanded Arabella, "I am ready to leave." He glanced at his wife's angry face and hastily opened the front door.

"She has a great deal of money," he quipped, "even more than I have, Melissa, and I must hasten to do her bidding." He guided his wife out the door ahead of him, tossing back over his shoulder in a muted whisper, "Two o'clock. Gramercy Hotel."

Melissa nervously counted the hours, too anxious to eat any breakfast, too excited about her meeting with Philip to dare swallow a mouthful of lunch. At last she had found someone who could provide her with the answers she sought. The prospect of finally being able to fit together the missing fragments of her memory was almost more than she could bear. She scarcely recalled the long walk as she finally neared her distination. At precisely two o'clock, she found herself standing across

456

the street from the Gramercy Hotel, eagerly scanning the building for some sign of Philip. She had been reluctant to wait in front of the hotel itself in case the Wentworths were indeed guests there. She dared not risk a chance encounter with the possessive Arabella.

The street was crowded with clattering carriages and the sidewalks brimmed with people moving about from store to store. Melissa was jostled and shoved by scurrying women clutching small children and by men striding purposefully along, newspapers tucked neatly under their arms. She was growing worried as the minutes ticked by and she began to despair of his ever appearing. Then she spotted a familiar figure walking briskly along the street toward the main entrance of the hotel. He peered into the lobby through the large glass doors and when he turned around, Melissa called out to him, waving frantically.

He signaled her to remain where she was and then he was lost from view as a number of carriages sped past in front of her. A loud rumbling sound attracted her attention and she glanced up in time to see a hansom cab careening around the corner. The driver had navigated the sharp turn too quickly, losing control of his horse. In terror, she realized that he was bearing down on Philip and she screamed out a warning. Caught in the middle of the road, Philip attempted to dodge out of the way of the oncoming carriage, but he was too late.

Melissa watched as he crumpled to the pavement. The coach thundered past and she began running toward him. Reaching his side, she threw herself to her knees and flung her cape over his still form to keep him warm. She heard someone shouting for help but her eyes remained transfixed, staring disbelievingly at the steady trickle of blood oozing from his head. His eyes stayed closed, his face ashen.

She barely remembered arriving at the hospital amid moving blurs of white. People in starched white uniforms darted past her, crisply issuing orders, bustling efficiently about, leading her to a hard wooden bench and leaving her there. Numbly she recalled the Ransomes's address. They were summoned and she stared vacantly at Amanda's troubled face before it was somehow transformed into the contorted features of an accusing Arabella.

"This is all your fault!" she raged. "Because of you, my husband is lying unconscious in a hospital bed. Damn you for doing this to us, Melissa!" she cried, tears streaming down her cheeks. "You and your blasted questions could cost Philip his life." She suddenly lunged forward, her clawing hands reaching for Melissa's paling face. Bryan Ransome interceded, managing to subdue the hysterical woman, and lead her away.

Amanda sank down beside Melissa on the bench, attempting to soothe the distraught girl, but Melissa was inconsolable. "What Arabella said is true," she moaned, covering her face with her hands. "It really is my fault."

"Nonsense!" Amanda retorted. "It was an accident, Melissa. You can't blame yourself for something you couldn't possibly control."

"But it never would have happened if I had left him alone and not pleaded with him to speak to me. Dear God, what would I do if he died? How could I live with myself?" She wept uncontrollably in Amanda's arms.

For three days Philip lay in a coma hovering precariously between life and death. Melissa spent each day at the hospital, prowling the long sterile corridors and fidgeting uncomfortably on the bench outside Philip's door. Arabella swept haughtily by her, refusing to even acknowledge her existence. She spent her time sitting dutifully at Philip's side, barring everyone but the doctors and nurses from her husband's room. Haggard from lack of sleep, dizzy with fatigue, Melissa remained tortured by guilt. The days seemed to extend into a waking nightmare for her.

Then it was December twenty-fourth and she knew that she would have to return to New York. She paid a final early-morning visit to the hospital and learned that Philip's condition had improved slightly, but that it was still too early for a proper prognosis. With heavy heart, she embraced Amanda and extracted from her the promise to keep her advised as to Philip's progress. Bryan saw her off at the train station. When she boarded the train, she collapsed into her seat and slept through the entire journey back to New York.

She was still exhausted when she arrived at Madison Square Garden that night. She staggered clumsily about her dressing room, struggling to get into her costume. She was grateful for the protection of the spangled mask, for it hid the pale gauntness of her face and covered the purple bruises of fatigue beneath her haunted eyes. Leaving her room, she wove unsteadily down the hallway, colliding with Cody. He wrapped his arms around her and hugged her up against his lanky frame.

"Well, little lady, did you have yourself a good rest?" he asked as he escorted her over to one of the waiting carriages already filled with some costumed members of the show.

She merely nodded her head. He clapped her heartily on the back and opened the door for her. Tripping up the step, she lurched uncertainly and fell heavily into the leather seat beside a grim-faced Indian. She smiled weakly at him and huddled next to him as the coach started. She was soon dozing as they bounced along the road through the night. The trip was short and it ended abruptly at the hospital where scores of eager children were waiting for them. The Indian nudged Melissa. She wakened with a start and left the coach.

With the others, she walked slowly up and down the rows of metal beds, smiling and waving, handing out small fancifully wrapped packages to the wide-eyed youngsters who had been allowed to stay up late in order to celebrate such a special Christmas Eve. The wonder in their pinched faces, the gratitude mirrored in their pain-filled eyes deeply affected her, relieving some of the horror of her days in Baltimore. The raucous peals of laughter and squeals of sheer delight greeting the troupe acted as a healing balm for Melissa's aching heart. For a while, she was able to forget.

When she stumbled into the lobby of her hotel, Anthony sprang from his chair and bounded toward her. And with a cry, she threw herself gratefully into his arms.

They spent Christmas Day together in his home, barricaded from the world outside, warmed by the fire snapping in the grate, and sipping hot rum in his study. When she had collapsed in his arms the previous night, it had taken little persuasion on his part to scoop her up and take her to the welcoming sanctuary of his house where he had immediately tucked her into bed in one of the guest rooms. When she awakened at noon, he had presented her with a delicious breakfast of eggs, smoked ham, hot buttery scones, and a spicy, aromatic tea, all served to her on a silver tray while she sat comfortably in bed.

As she lay before the cheering fire, clad in one of Anthony's dressing gowns, now fortified by the hearty meal and the steaming drink in her hand, Melissa knew peace for the first time in many troubled days. She told him little of her disastrous trip to Baltimore, and he discreetly refrained from questioning her about it. He simply contented himself with her nearness, pleased that she needed him. Surrounded by his protective love, and nurtured by his patient tenderness, Melissa marveled at how swiftly the terrible ache within her was assuaged.

* * *

She left the security of the cocoon Anthony had provided for her and returned to the show, but she immediately asked Cody to free her from performing in the afternoons. After some deliberation, he finally agreed, and she quickly adjusted to her new schedule. She delighted in spending her days discovering the wondrous city in which she lived. Anthony began taking time from his lunch. Occasionally walking with her through Central Park, they would watch the skaters flashing past them on the frozen lake. Fur-wrapped women, warmly cloaked men, and laughing, tumbling children spun and whirled together while chatting couples, their arms linked around one another, their skate blades glinting against the blue-white surface of the ice, glided gracefully by. Melissa and Anthony would walk briskly through the biting cold, their breath hanging in frosty clouds in the stinging air, and then head for a heated restaurant to sip hot chocolate and thaw their numbed fingers before setting off once more.

Melissa had still received no word from Amanda as to Philip Wentworth's condition so, shortly after New Year's Day, she sent a cable to Baltimore urging some response. Amanda wired back to say that Philip had finally regained consciousness and that the doctors had assured him a complete recovery. Tears of relief overwhelmed her as she read the stark black words printed on the yellow paper clutched in her trembling hand. The heavy weight of her guilt was eased at last. She wrote a long letter to Philip, and despite some initial hesitation, asked him once more about his recollections of that fateful ball. She posted the letter and anxiously awaited his reply.

She had not anticipated Arabella's persistent intrusion, and it was only when the letter was returned to her unopened that she understood what a formidable obstacle Philip's new wife was. Melissa wrote once again, this time enclosing the letter in one addressed to

461

Amanda. Again she was frustrated. Amanda sent the letter back, writing that Philip and Arabella had already left Maryland, journeying south, without leaving a forwarding address.

Railing angrily against the meddlesome Arabella, Melissa viciously tore up the letter, ripping it into smaller and smaller pieces and throwing them into the fireplace. With resentful tears welling up in her eyes, she watched the tiny bits of paper ignite and flare, the greedy flames licking hungrily around the tattered edges, until in a roar of heat and a blur of gray smoke, the paper was consumed. Dismally she saw the last piece curl and flutter in fiery death. With her letter died the only hope she had of learning the truth about her past.

chapter 38

Evan Bennett bounded in and out of Melissa's life with youthful exuberance, bringing with him an infectious enthusiasm for which she was grateful. His reputation was building steadily at the *Times*, and he began spending more of his time out of the city, covering political events, chronicling the continuing labor unrest and writing colorful vignettes about the common working man. Melissa, meanwhile, eagerly read the daily papers, seeking his byline, clipping his articles, and pasting them into a book for him. One afternoon, when a light sprinkling of snow dusted the city, Evan pushed her into the steamy warmth of Billy Mould's and excitedly broke his news to her.

"Melissa, I'm going to England," he burst out, a grin spreading across his face. She found herself smiling back at him despite the sudden rushing of the blood to her head.

"England," she breathed, the shock of his words setting her temples pounding.

"Yes, my beauty, England. I'm off to spend the next three months covering Queen Victoria's Golden Jubilee."

Melissa gazed at him in disbelief, feeling a sudden constriction in her throat. "How marvelous, Evan," she whispered, wondering at the fluttering in her chest.

"Why don't you come with me?" he blurted out

then.

"Come with you. How?" She was incredulous.

"As my wife," he stated bluntly, hurrying on as he caught her look of stricken shock. "Look, Melissa, my passage and accommodations are being paid for by the *Times*. I've saved up enough money to buy your ticket for you, and you must have something put away from your work with the show and together . . ." He paused for breath and Melissa broke in immediately.

"Evan, wait, please, before you continue with this," she pleaded, the distress obvious in her quivering voice. "This is all so sudden, I had no idea that you would ever consider something like marriage. We never once talked about it. We were friends." She knew that she was babbling incoherently but she seemed powerless to stem the words spilling from her lips. "My life is here now, with the show. I have commitments, and Evan, dear Evan, thank you for your mad proposal, but how could I possibly accept it?"

He sat across from her, his face an inscrutable mask, the look in his eyes unreadable. Then he smiled at her and the light returned to his eyes. He reached across the table and clasped her hands in his.

"You're right, Melissa, it is mad," he said softly, "but I don't leave for another few weeks and you can always change your mind."

When they left the restaurant, the bitter January wind plucked at their clothes and sent them scampering to the sides of the taller buildings to shield them from the fierceness of the howling gusts. The force of the wind pressed Melissa back as she bent against it. Snowflakes lashed at her unprotected face, and as she bucked against the strength of winter, she thought again of Evan's words. England. Would she ever again view her home, ride the rolling hills of Kent, breathe the sweet purity of its country air. Or was she condemned to live the ·itinerant life of the performer, moving continually from smoke-filled city to shabby town, sleeping in strange surroundings, never knowing the security of one home, doomed forever to be a wandering soul without an anchor to the world around her?

"Is my idea becoming more appealing, my red-nosed beauty?" Evan called out as Melissa burrowed deeper inside the high collar of her cloak. "Just think of it, Melissa—royalty from every part of the world, politicians, stage personalities, all streaming into England for a year-long celebration. The whole country will be having a birthday party."

Once more, she found herself living his words, imagining the splendor of the British court, the titled men and women being presented to the remarkable old woman who had reigned for fifty years and whose unmistakable stamp was borne not only by her own country, but by the entire world.

Dining with Anthony one night, Melissa casually mentioned Evan's imminent departure, omitting the young reporter's proposal to her. She watched closely for his reaction. He contemplated her words for but a moment.

"Would you like to go to England, Melissa?" he asked. "Has the young man, by any chance, suggested that you accompany him?" She colored at his astute assumption. He chuckled softly, puffing contemplatively on his long cheroot. She nervously ran her fingertip along the rim of her tea cup as she avoided Anthony's bemused scrutiny.

"If it's England you're interested in and not your reporter friend, why don't you and I visit it together," he suggested quietly, "on our honeymoon."

Melissa's hand knocked over the tea cup, spraying the amber liquid across the tablecloth and onto her fingers. Clumsily, she righted the cup, dried her hands, and met his puzzled gaze.

"Why does my mentioning marriage upset you so

much?" he demanded.

"Because I feel so uncertain about everything," she blurted out unhappily. "I have no right to keep you waiting, Anthony, but I still cannot give you the answer you want."

"I'm not asking for that much, am I?" he argued. "I only want to make you happy, share my life with you. I want to enjoy your youth and your beauty and your sparkle, and just love you. You might never feel for me the way I do for you, but I have enough love to carry us through a lifetime together."

"Anthony," she murmured, her heart twisting wretchedly, "I have no words to match yours, I only know that you have been my strength now for such a long time. I am deeply grateful and extremely moved by your feelings for me. But please," she whispered, "give me a little more time."

"A month, Melissa, and no more," he replied, his voice firm.

Melissa began to brood. Straining under the pressure both Anthony and Evan were unwittingly exerting on her, she grew irritable and snappish, longing to reach some decision but frightened of making a wrong choice. To further increase her anxiety, she felt herself living in a strangling web of fear, for she was certain that someone had started to follow her, dogging her steps, tracing all of her movements.

One evening, as she walked toward the theater, she experienced the same uncomfortable feeling she had suffered on Long Island when Nate Salsbury had been watching her through his binoculars. Darting quickly around the corner, she waited for a moment and then peered cautiously out around the building she had hidden behind, expecting to surprise someone there. The sidewalk was deserted. Swallowing hard, waiting for her heartbeat to slow, Melissa stood in the shadow of the building a moment longer, then set off at a run, arriving at the theater breathless and perspiring.

"Somethin' wrong, Miss Melissa?" Jared Rawlins loomed up in front of her as he opened the back door and let her in.

"I think someone has been following me," she gasped as she hurried inside. He looked past her, then sauntered out into the alley running alongside the theater. She waited in the safety of the lighted corridor until he eventually returned, shaking his head.

"If there was someone out there before, there ain't no sign of him now," he assured her. "But I'll keep a lookout for anythin' suspicious." She thanked him and raced down the hall to her dressing room to change.

Mounted on her horse, waiting in the wings, she watched the end of the elaborate Pony Express act. She nodded affably to several of the cowboys riding past her on their way out of the arena. Then Cody's voice boomed into the silence they had left behind and Brandywine thundered into the blinding glare of the specially constructed lights and warmed to the boisterous ovation waiting to greet her entrance. Fifteen thousand voices reached out to her. As she performed, their cheering acceptance filled her, dispelling for a while the loneliness which haunted her.

Exhausted as she made her way to her dressing room, she failed to notice the shadowy figure against the wall as she approached. Slipping into the room, she tugged off her hat and slumped into a chair, unpinning her hair and shaking her head, allowing the tangled mass of curls to spring free of their confinement and cascade down her back. She changed and walked out into the cold January night. Her head was bowed, her eyes downcast. She did not see the hiding figure scribbling into a small book, then following a discreet distance behind her.

For the remainder of that week, she felt the presence of a trailing shadow and then, to her alarm, Rawlins began to appear at her dressing room door each evening, holding out a beribboned, oblong box to her. The enclosed card always bore the same words, AN ADMIRER, written in black ink, obviously penned by the same hand. In the box, nestled there amid a crush of heavy satin, lay one perfectly crafted white silk rose.

In exasperation, she finally confronted the baffled Rawlins. "But, Jared, surely you must notice who delivers these boxes," she protested when he repeatedly denied it.

"Nope, Miss Melissa, I swear it." He shook his head. "Like I was sayin' before, the box is always settin' outside the back door when I get here for the afternoon show."

She impatiently dismissed him, and stared grimly at the growing collection of silk flowers which she then crammed viciously into one of the small drawers in her bureau. Nibbling anxiously at her lower lip, she pondered the identity of her secret admirer, frightened by the fact that whoever it was knew that Brandywine was a woman. Outside of the show, that left only Anthony and Evan.

Over dinner at Delmonico's, she finally confided in Anthony, carefully watching his expression in an effort to discern his own guilt or innocence.

"Perhaps it's your young reporter friend," he suggested, "and it's merely his way of trying to convince you to go to England with him."

"I doubt that." She shook her head. "Evan would scarcely go to all that trouble or expense. Are you certain that a prominent city banker is not my secret admirer?" she teased playfully, still scrutinizing his face.

"Admirer, most definitely," he laughed, "but I've made no secret of it, my dear, as you well know." He settled back comfortably in his chair and sipped slowly at his brandy when he noticed the startled look in Melissa's eyes and the sudden paling of her face. He turned in his chair and his own eyes locked with those of Calvin Gabriel.

"Now there's an admirer not to be overlooked," he remarked caustically, straightening in his chair again and gulping the rest of his brandy. "He has an uncanny way of showing up all the time, doesn't he?" Anthony mused.

"It must be nothing more than coincidence," Melissa assured him in a halting voice. "After all, despite the size of the city, Delmonico's is one of the better restaurants and most people have heard of it."

"Yes, yes, it's all very possible," he cut in irritably, "but I still don't trust that fellow."

Melissa sipped at her brandy while restraining the impulse to look at Calvin again. Her pulse was racing wildly and she felt a flush burning through her body, the effects of which were only partly attributable to the liquor she was drinking. Unable to resist any longer, she dared a hasty glance in his direction. He was watching her, a half smile on his mouth as he raised his wineglass to her in silent salute before he touched it to his lips.

"Shall we go, my dear?" Anthony said. Melissa tore herself from the spell of Calvin's hypnotic gaze and rose from the table. She walked slightly ahead of Anthony, studiously avoiding having to pass Calvin's table, but the frantic hammering of her heart eased only when she reached her hotel room.

The days seemed to be whirling by, spinning from Melissa's grasp at an alarming pace. Not only was time running out before she would have to answer Anthony's ultimatum, but Evan had renewed his efforts to convince her to sail with him to England. Calvin's sudden reappearance had further unsettled her and she felt as if she were being torn apart. Her only avenue of escape lay in her nightly masquerade, when her inner turmoil was blanketed by the roar of the crowd, the challenge of her performance.

The evening before Evan's scheduled sailing, Bill Cody summoned Melissa to his dressing room and waved her to a chair. Tugging off his hat and soundly scratching his long tangle of hair, he settled himself on the edge of his dressing table and studied her pensively for a moment.

"I have some news which might come as a damned nice surprise for you, little lady," he said, stroking his drooping moustache with his long, bony fingers. "How would you feel about taking an ocean voyage?"

"To where?" she asked, taken aback by his unexpected question.

"How does England sound to you?" She was struck speechless and stared openmouthed at the man in front of her. "Yep, I've always had me a hankerin' to bring the show over to them colonial dogs and let them see how things really were around here once. It was Nate's idea, naturally, tying it up with old Victoria's Jubilee, and I'll be damned if he didn't go ahead and arrange the whole blamed thing. We leave at the end of March."

"I—I don't know quite what to say," she stammered wonderingly.

"Well, you don't have to say a thing until you're sure about what you want to do," he said. "There's still plenty of time to decide. But I'll be lettin' the word out tonight so that everybody can have time to make up their minds. I can promise you one helluva good time if you come with us, Melissa girl, so think on it and let me know."

She staggered from his room, reeling from the shock of Cody's words, unable to fathom her confounded reaction of excitement, relief, and uncertainty. She felt weak from the weight of the possibilities open to her. Her troubled thoughts crippled her performance and she narrowly missed disaster. Clearing the flaming hurdle, she almost lost her balance on Target's back. Her chest tightened with fear at the gasped response of the audience as her horse landed awkwardly, one

470

stirrup flapping ominously after Melissa's boot slipped out of it.

Racing to her dressing room, she noticed another oblong box propped up against the door. She kicked it savagely down the corridor. Flinging herself into the room, she tore off her hat and threw it down. She was just beginning to strip off her mask when a sound outside her door made her stiffen. Hurrying to lock it, she reached it in time, because the knob was suddenly turned, first one way and then the other. Slipping one of the pistols from her holster, she aimed it at the door, waiting. The knob stopped its rusty squeaking and she heard the sound of muffled footsteps disappearing down the hallway. Soon all she could hear was the loud thumping of her heart.

Tiptoeing to the door, she unlocked it and opened it cautiously, scanning the deserted corridor, wondering where Jared was whenever she needed him most. Holstering her gun, she closed the door again, bolted it once more and hurriedly changed her clothes. She left the room and was making her way to the back door when she nearly collided with Rawlins.

"Jared!" she exclaimed. "There was someone lurking about in the hallway before. Did you see anyone leave just a few minutes ago?"

"Come to think of it, I did see someone go by me, but I figgered he was one of the boys from the show," he explained. "He sorta waved at me, friendly like, so I waved back and didn't pay him no mind."

"What did he look like?" she prodded him.

"I didn't get a good look at him, 'cause his collar was turned up high. But he was tall with a dark coat and he was wearin' one of them Stetsons."

"Was he young or old?"

"Miss Melissa, I can't rightly say for sure," the man grumbled. She knew that it would useless to pursue the matter any further. She said good night and left the theater.

471

Tossing and turning in her sleep that night, Melissa found herself racing along endless corridors and twisting down winding passages to escape a man whose black cloak billowed out behind him as he thundered after her. She hurtled through a narrowing maze with the sound of his footsteps relentlessly echoing behind her own and she ran until she thought her lungs would burst and her legs refuse to carry her any further. With a strangled cry, she slumped to the ground and waited until his footsteps slowed and his cape swirled out around her huddled form to envelop her in its voluminous folds. Her entire world was draped in its blackness. She looked up then to know at last the identity of her tormentor, but when she gazed into his face, she saw only a pair of silvery eyes gleaming from behind a small black mask.

The graying light of a winter morning bleached the veil of darkness and gentled the threat of night's horror as Melissa awoke. Drenched in the aftermath of her terror, she drew strength from the welcoming shafts of day which pierced the drawn curtains. She slid gingerly from the safety of her bed, touching the cold floor, grateful for its solid touch. She dressed quickly, picked up the heavy book she had prepared for Evan with all of his clippings tucked inside. Then she hailed a hansom cab for the long ride to the harbor.

A blustery wind tore through the streets near the waterfront, spinning boxes about, tossing papers and bits of garbage into the air, slamming the flying debris against hapless pedestrians and the walls of crumbling buildings. Sailors in heavy blue jackets, their wool caps pulled over their faces, were busily hauling crates and stacking them on the pier, stamping their feet and rubbing their gloved hands together in an effort to keep warm. Carriages clattered by, dogs sniffed among the toppled pails littering the cobbled alleys, and the steamship office was crammed with people waiting to board their vessel.

Amid the chaos and the confusion, Melissa stood with Evan, their voices raised in order to be audible above the noise and bustle of his fellow passengers.

"Here's the name and address of my hotel in London," Evan shouted, slipping a piece of paper into Melissa's hand. She tucked it into her purse. As she offered him the book she had kept, she felt suddenly and unaccountably shy. His eyes seemed to mist over as he accepted it, leafing quickly through the pages, scanning the articles bearing his byline, all of them carefully trimmed and pasted down, the dates of their publication written at the top of each page in Melissa's fine flowing script. He cradled the book in his arm and kissed her tenderly, drawing amused cheers and claps from some of the people standing near them. Melissa flushed uncomfortably and drew back thinking that it was time to mention to him the possibility of her own trip to England. But before she could speak, Evan whispered huskily, "I still wish you were coming with me, you know. Although we've never talked about our feelings, I'm sure you realize how much you mean to me, Melissa."

She found herself growing uneasy, anxious to tell him of her tentative plans, loath to hear a declaration of his affection for her when she could not return it.

"I know I can't offer you very much right now," he plunged on, disregarding the warning in her eyes, "not as much as someone like Holmes can, but I love you and I want you to be with me."

Her discomfort mounting, the strain and the pressure of the past months sweeping over her as she fought for control, she tried once more to tell him.

"Evan, your friendship has been very special and although I like you and . . ."

"I had thought of us as more than friends, Melissa." He cut her off brusquely.

"But I never led you to expect . . ."

"Yet you made a good showing of being more than a

friend when you kept seeing me, or was it just so I wouldn't change my mind and print that story about you?" His voice was surprisingly harsh and bitter. She scarcely believed it was Evan talking to her that way.

"You are succeeding in distorting everything," she lashed out at him defensively.

"Melissa, I'm sorry," he pleaded, reaching out for her, but she squirmed from his grasp, yearning only to be free of him and his demands. Like a caged animal breaking desperately toward freedom, Melissa bolted from the crowded, stifling room and stumbled out into the battering wind.

She started to run from Evan's longing, his adoring gaze, the touch of his hands on her. She ran through the pitted streets, heedless of the shouts of the dock workers as they tottered past her with their heavy crates, mindless of the carriages lumbering by, the drivers calling out to her as they dodged around her streaking form. She ran until her legs buckled and she collapsed, heaving and gasping for breath, onto a barrel leaning up against the wall of a crumbling warehouse.

Miserably she stared out at the harbor, its choppy waters stained slate by the sunless day, whipped into molten peaks by the biting wind. Ships riding at anchor bobbed about with the erratic rhythm of the waves and the port seemed so like the one which had seen the start of her fruitless voyage nearly two years before. With the tall masts of the vessels splitting the mottled skies, the call of the gulls, the shouts of the seamen, everything seemed to be the same. As she sat there, shivering in the cold, she wished herself safely back in her native England, back before her father's life had spilled from him and her own world had ground to a painful halt.

She began to shake uncontrollably and forcing herself from her awkward perch, she hobbled across the street toward the beckoning shelter of a shabby restaurant. Stepping into the dismal place, she located an empty table and ordered a pot of tea from the scowling waiter. She thankfully gulped down the steaming brew and the chill gradually eased inside her. She ordered a second pot and sipped more slowly at it while she gazed curiously around her.

Roughly dressed sailors clustered together in friendly groups, some lounging against the long wooden bar in front of a sleepy-eyed bartender, while others sprawled about at the small round tables. Several primly dressed, matronly women sat quietly sipping tea at a table near the window, while a garishly dressed prostitute meandered up to the bar and balefully eyed one of the men. When Melissa finished her tea, she searched through her small purse for some money to pay for it. Then she gathered her cloak around her and headed for the door, taking one last warm breath before going back into the cold again.

chapter 39

With strong determination, Melissa banished all thoughts of parting with Evan from her mind. She felt relieved that she had never revealed Cody's plans to take the show to England, and was thankful to have been freed at last from the suffocating demands of one suitor. Her month of indecision was rapidly nearing its end. When Jared entered her dressing room one evening with the too familiar oblong box tucked under his arm, Melissa knew what her decision should be. Perhaps Anthony was right after all. Perhaps the time had come for her to discard her double life and return to some form of normalcy once again. With a defeated sigh, she pulled the lid from the box and separated the creamy satin folds. Her eyes suddenly widened in disbelief when she drew out the crimson rose of delicate silk lying there.

With shaking fingers she opened the small envelope and extracted the enclosed card. Like the rose, its message had also changed. TIME IS RUNNING OUT, the stark black letters screamed from the whiteness of the card. With a cry of alarm, Melissa threw down the offending flower as if she had been stung. Did he mean to kill her, using the note as a warning of his eventual intention? She spun from her chair, knocking it to the floor. A split second later, Jared Rawlins crashed into the room, his gun drawn.

"What the hell's goin' on in here?" he thundered, staring at the wild-eyed woman before him.

"I think he means to kill me!" she cried.

"Who does?" his voice was incredulous.

"This man, this secret admirer, whoever he is," she gulped, distractedly running her fingers through her hair.

"You think maybe it's the same fellow you said was followin' you?" he demanded. "You think he's the one's been sendin' you them flowers?"

"Why not? It would seem logical," she mumbled, pacing nervously back and forth as she tried to think.

"You suppose we oughta tell Bill about this?" he asked as he slid the gun back inside his jacket.

Melissa shook her head. "Not yet," she said, "I would feel like a fool if it turned out to be a perfectly innocent prank and not what I imagined it to be." She bent down, retrieved the rumpled note and read the words again. Now she wondered it it had been Anthony's doing all along, despite his denials, and whether this final message was merely a reminder of their deadline.

"You think you'll be all right now?" Jared wanted to know.

"I think so," she said smiling faintly, and she locked the door behind him as he left.

Her performance was poor again that evening. She anxiously scanned the arena as she rode past the cheering stands, watching for anything unusual, any suspicious movement which might pose a threat to her safety. Distracted, she performed erratically, narrowly avoiding a collision with Annie during a fast-paced sequence, missing many of the targets Cody himself threw into the air above her head. He scowled darkly at her as she rode from the arena at the end of her hurdle-jumping exhibition, and when she had changed out of her costume, she ran from the theater to avoid an unpleasant confrontation with the man.

She met Anthony at Delmonico's and soothed the chilling fear within her by hurriedly drinking two glasses of a delicate white wine. The wine spiraled through her, heating her, emboldening her, and with Anthony smiling adoringly at her from across the table, she felt protected and safe. Sipping more slowly from her third glass of wine, she gazed affectionately at him, seeing him as her salvation, her champion, forgetting that she still suspected him of sending her the anonymous cards and the exquisite silk flowers. She leaned toward him, finally ready to accept his offer of marriage.

"Anthony," she murmured, his face distorting into a wavering image of itself as she squinted at him. "I want to talk to you about something, dear."

"Yes, Melissa?" he replied, an expectant smile on his handsome face.

She tried to move closer to him through the haze that seemed to be enveloping him. "I think," she began, "that is, I feel—" But she burst into a giddy peal of laughter and fell back in her chair, staring helplessly at him. "I feel terribly tipsy," she hiccuped, hastily covering her mouth with her hand.

Anthony regarded her questioningly, and then looked away as a black-clad waiter approached the table and bent over to whisper in his ear. He nodded and got to his feet. "If you'll excuse me for a moment, Melissa," he apologized, his brow furrowing thoughtfully. "It seems that there's someone waiting at the door with a message for me and he refuses to come inside. Strange," he muttered, as he hastened from the table.

No sooner he had left than the same waiter walked briskly over to Melissa and handed her a small envelope. How like Anthony, she thought smiling, to invent a reason for leaving the table, and to then have the waiter slip this note to her. She tore open the envelope and the smile froze on her lips as she read the same message which had accompanied the crimson rose, the same four words printed in black ink by that same unseen hand.

She barely had time to recover from her shock when Anthony hurried back to the table, his face flushed with anger. "There was no one out there," he snarled, throwing himself into his chair and glowering at her. "What kind of a fool trick was that?" he asked, swallowed the rest of his wine, and slammed the glass down.

"Anthony," she whispered hoarsely, blinking to clear her blurry vision, "I think this charade should be stopped now."

"What the devil are you talking about?" he snapped.

"The notes and the flowers," she said. "You have made more than made your point."

"Make sense, Melissa," he growled irritably. "My patience has already been sorely tried."

"The silk flowers and the anonymous notes which have been sent for weeks to my dressing room," she insisted, growing exasperated with him. "The ones you suggested had been sent by Evan. Evan is gone, but the flowers are still arriving."

"Melissa, on my honor, I swear to you that they have not come from me," he protested. "I'm afraid you'll have to look elsewhere for the answer, because I've had nothing whatsoever to do with it."

"Oh Anthony," she wailed, flinging the card over to him, "whoever it is knows who I am, that Brandywine and I are one and the same. You were called away so that waiter could bring me this note."

Anthony read the few words and glanced around for the waiter. Locating him, he caught his attention and beckoned him over to the table.

"Who gave you this envelope?" Anthony demanded brusquely, waving it in front of the startled man.

"A gentleman, Monsieur," the waiter replied, swallowing nervously.

"What gentleman?"

"Why, just a gentleman," he repeated. "He gave me some money and said to give the envelope to this woman." His pointing finger indicated Melissa.

"But first you were to lure me away from the table?" Anthony persisted, and the man nodded his head. "Was this gentleman in the restaurant at the time we came in?"

"He left shortly after you and the lady were seated. He told me to wait until you had finished your meal before approaching you." The man shifted from one foot to the other, gazing uncomfortably around him. "I am sorry if I have been the cause of some misunderstanding, Monsieur," he murmured as he started backing away.

"Not so fast, my man," Anthony barked, and the waiter hastily returned to the table. "Could you give me a description of this gentleman?" He pulled out his billfold, withdrew a twenty-dollar note, and held it up to the man.

"I am afraid you would get little satisfaction for that, Monsieur," said the waiter, as he shook his head, refusing the proferred bill. "I admit I was more interested in the money he offered me than in his face." With that, he walked away.

Anthony crammed the money back into his wallet, sighing resignedly. "I'm sorry, my dear, but it seems we won't learn anything more from that fellow. However, I suggest that tomorrow morning you and I have a little chat with a police captain I know and see if we can't get to the bottom of this once and for all."

"At first I felt certain that it was simply a prank. Then I actually believed that you were the one behind it all," Melissa fretted. "But now I have no idea who it could possibly be."

"We'll have the answer soon enough, I assure you," he said, "but for now, I think I'd better get you back to your hotel."

They walked together down the corridor toward her

room, and when she opened the door, he glowered at her and began to admonish her severely.

"After all this business about anonymous notes and flowers, you still leave your room unlocked?" he blustered as she flinched at his attack. Sheepishly, she nodded her head. With an exasperated groan, he followed her weaving figure into the room and stood silently as she lighted one of the lamps.

"Since you seem so distraught, why don't you pack a few things and come home with me tonight?" he asked her as he parted the curtains and gazed out of the window at the street below.

She pondered his suggestion for a moment, then shook her head. "Thank you, Anthony, but I think I can manage by myself." She walked over to the table beside her bed and pulled a pistol from the drawer. "As you can see, I have some protection."

He cornered her there and took her in his arms, pressing a yearning kiss onto her mouth. "It's been so long, my sweet, won't you reconsider?" But she slipped from his embrace and emphatically shook her head.

"Then at least promise that you'll bolt the door when I leave and answer it for no one," he said strictly. "I'll be by for you first thing in the morning. Sleep well, my dear." As he closed the door behind him, she slid the bolt into place.

Shedding her clothes, she stepped into her nightgown and then sat down on the bed. She lowered the glare of the lamp on the night table, leaned back, propping herself up against her cushions, and stared bleakly about her. She toyed idly with the gun in her lap, running her fingers along the cold metal of the barrel, consoling herself with the knowledge that she was well armed and an expert shot. She would not hesitate to use the gun should the occasion warrant it.

A slight scuffling sound outside her room caused her to sit bolt upright on the bed. She watched as the doorknob was worked from side to side, and when that failed to open the door, a loud knock followed.

"Who is it?" she called out, raising the gun and cocking it.

"A message for Miss Howell," came the muffled reply.

"From whom?" she demanded.

"I don't know, Miss," came the hoarse answer.

"Slide it under the door then," she ordered brusquely.

"I was told to deliver it personally," the rasping voice persisted.

"It seems rather late to be delivering messages," she barked angrily. "Come back tomorrow."

She thought she heard the sound of a cough until she realized that the person outside her door was laughing. It was Anthony, she thought irritably, attempting to frighten her enough so that she would consent to return home with him. Padding noiselessly to the door, she pressed her ear to it and waited. The knock sounded again.

"What is it you want!" she snarled, backing away little by little.

"Melissa, for God's sake, open up this door," came the muted voice between bursts of muffled laughter.

"Who is this?" she cried indignantly, all fear gone, leaving a burning curiosity in its place.

"Why don't you open the door and find out?" cajoled the disguised voice. When she made no move to comply, the tone became threatening. "I'll break the door down if I have to."

"I warn you, I have a gun," she countered, stepping back just in time to avoid being hit as the door flew open, knocking the pistol from her hand. She lunged for the fallen weapon and whirled to face the intruder.

"I surrender! Don't shoot!" he shouted before he doubled up with laughter. Melissa sprang to her feet.

"Calvin Gabriel, I ought to shoot you where you stand."

chapter 40

"Melissa love," he laughed, gasping for breath, "put that damned gun down before you hurt somebody." He swiftly closed the damaged door.

"Just what are you doing here?" She glared at him, still warily clutching the pistol.

"Delivering a message," he replied, with a studied look of innocence on his dark face.

She turned her back on him and flounced to the bed, flinging herself down and staring resentfully at him.

"And what is this message you are supposed to be delivering to me?" she asked haughtily.

"Just this," he declared, tugging a crimson silk rose from inside his overcoat.

Her eyes widened incredulously. "You?" she gasped.

"Consider this a peace offering, princess," he said, sitting down on the bed beside her and pressing the silken flower into her hand.

"But why?" she murmured. "How did you even know about me or where to find me?"

"Simply enough. I had a detective following you."

"A detective?" she cried. "So it was you all along?" She stared down at the rose in her hand and she suddenly felt the overwhelming desire to laugh, but a hoarse scream was wrenched from her as she hurled the flower onto the floor. "What made you do it?" she shouted at him. "Why Calvin, why?"

"Curiosity at first. I simply wanted to find out who the mysterious Brandywine was," he replied, "and after I learned that it was a woman, I thought I'd play at being her secret admirer for a while." His gaze clouded then. "To think that I had you cornered at the Pattersons' that night and never realized it. But why did you run away when you obviously recognized me?"

"Did you ever stop to consider that perhaps I had no interest whatsoever in speaking to you?" she said coldly.

"I see." He lowered his gaze, shifting uneasily beside her. Then his eyes brightened again as he strove to placate her. "Can you imagine my reaction when my man told me he had tracked Brandywine to Delmonico's one night and he pointed you out to me?" His laugh was mirthless as he glanced covertly at her expressionless face.

"Why did your message suddenly change?" she demanded of him then.

"I figured once your friend, Evan Bennett, was on his way to England, Holmes would press you for a wedding date. Has he?"

"That is none of your business."

He shrugged. "Fair enough. But time *has* run out. I've just finished up my business dealings here, and I plan to head back to Stony Briar tomorrow."

"And why should that concern me?"

"Because I'm asking you to go back there with me."

The frankness of his words caught her off guard. "Does that mean you're asking me to marry you?" she whispered.

His snort of laughter made her cringe in humiliation. "I was only hoping to continue the arrangement we had before, princess."

She could scarcely control her rage. "After what has happened to all of us, you dare to come here and ask me that!"

"Do you mean you honestly prefer Anthony Holmes to me?"

"He is something you would know nothing about," she cried. "He is a gentleman, considerate and kind. You—you—" she sputtered helplessly. "You disgust me, Calvin."

The gun was back in her hand again. As she faced him, her voice was suddenly deadly calm.

"I want you to leave this room immediately, Calvin. You have delivered your last message now, and I want you out of here." She motioned for him to stand up. "If you refuse to leave, I might be forced to shoot you as an intruder. One glance at the door to my room should make it quite clear that you did force your way in here."

Calvin seemed to consider her words for a moment before nodding his head. He eased himself from the bed. "All right, Melissa, I'll leave." He eyed the gun warily as he headed for the door. "I'm sorry you don't approve of my proposition, but then, I guess the better man's won out. I'm also disappointed to find you didn't enjoy your mysterious suitor as much as I'd hoped you would."

She followed him to the door, keeping the gun pointed at his back with every step. With his hand on the knob, he turned.

"A goodbye kiss, princess?"

Before she realized what was happening, the gun was spinning from her hand and she was being thrown onto the bed. How stupid of her to assume he would have given in so easily, she chastised herself as he pinned her down with the full weight of his body, and crushed his lips to hers.

"Stop it," she protested, pushing at him with all of her strength. "Stop it. I loathe the very sight of you. Stop it!"

"Stop fighting me, Melissa," he growled, burying his mouth in the hair which swept across her throat. She moaned and his lips claimed hers once more, his

485

tongue thrusting inside of her mouth, searing, probing, exciting her despite her resolve not to give in. He cushioned her scantily clad body against the hardness of his own, then began to move slowly back and forth on top of her. The roughness of his clothing chaffed the softness of her skin, as her filmy nightgown rode higher and higher on her body. Trapped by his mounting passion, she pressed against him, rocking with him, her nerves alight with the building sensations hurtling through her.

"Help me get these clothes off," he urged, drawing away from her, but she lay still beneath him, refusing to move and assist him. With a curse, he struggled to his feet, stripping off his clothes and tossing them carelessly onto the floor. Melissa lay sprawled across the coverlet, her nightdress tangled about her waist. He leaned over her and ripped it from her unresisting body.

In the dim aura of the lamplight, his gray eyes singed hers with their growing intensity, holding her captive until she seemed to be responding to him of her own free will. She followed his lead, clutching him to her as his lips branded her flesh. His hands traveled lightly over her skin, awakening the tingling fires which had lain dormant for so long within her. Tenderly cupping her breasts, his strumming fingertips coaxed the nipples into stiffened points. His lips closed around them, playfully nipping the quivering mounds of golden flesh. Melissa shuddered and arched her back, forcing more of her lushness into his eager mouth.

Her fingers dug into his arms as she tensed and strained beneath him. Kissing the tautness of her belly, sending sparks of heat quivering through her, he gently parted her trembling thighs and kissed the secret moistness there. A gasp escaped her as her agony grew, spiraling upward as she curved to meet his probing tongue.

"Please stop," she gasped. "No more." She tugged helplessly at his thick black hair in an effort to halt him.

"What's wrong?" His voice was husky, deep with yearning as he raised his head.

"We must stop now," she whispered, fighting down the burning ache inside her. "Please try to understand."

"Understand what?" he demanded. "That you want me just as much as I want you, but that Holmes is standing in the way. Well, he's not here now. It's only you and me, Melissa."

"But I would be betraying him," she pleaded, afraid to meet his stormy gaze. "He wants me to marry him and I could never hurt him this way."

"Marry him," he snorted, grabbing her wrists. "You keep telling me that he wants to marry you, but what about your feelings, Melissa, do you want him or don't you? Answer me!" She remained silent, unable to form the words. "Just as I thought." He released her wrists and his voice became soft and taunting. "Does he make love to you like this, princess?" he crooned, his tongue tracing teasing circles around her parted mouth, his fingers gently kneading her breasts. He smiled in triumph at the tight, bobbing nipples.

Stunned, she lay limply under his moving tongue, willing her body not to respond, but as his fingers claimed that aching spot his lips had warmed a moment before, she quivered helplessly and her thighs parted of their own accord. She was lost. Caught in the tantalizing web he was spinning for her, she allowed his desire to encompass them both, lifting her beyond herself and the claim earth had on her.

Calvin drove deeper and deeper within her, carrying her along with him as they whirled upward toward the ecstasy awaiting them. Their bodies, slick with perspiration, slapping hard against each other, twisted and tossed together, holding tightly to the reins as they rode, prolonging their exquisite pain. Melissa felt the control slipping from her grasp as she gave herself up to the delicious spasms rocketing through her. She shuddered again and again as she spun in dizzying circles through the eddies of their passion. Calvin, feeling the clutch of her release, straddled his soaring steed for but one moment longer until he reached, at last, that stinging pinnacle of his own.

They lay together, their arms entwined about each other until he stirred and drew the covers around them. Stretching out beside her, he stoked her flushed and gentled face. His hands whispered through her hair, feather light, as he caressed her. Sated, her entire body bathed in the tender shower of their loving, Melissa curled up against him and fell asleep in the circle of his arms.

When they awoke early the following morning, they made love again, this time more slowly, savoring the delicacy of each moment, their driving hunger of the night before replaced by tenderness and the luxury of time. As they rested once again, Melissa turned onto her stomach and looked into Calvin's face. Her hair tumbled across his broad, dark chest. She combed her fingers through his hair and her lips nibbled at his ears, his nose, and the sensuous fullness of his mouth.

"My hungry love," he growled, catching a handful of her lustrous hair and pulling her down. His lips caught hers in a long, tingling caress.

They did not hear the door push open and they were not aware of the presence until Anthony Holmes's sharp intake of breath thrust them instantly apart.

"Anthony," Melissa gasped, drawing the sheet over her nakedness, her face burning with guilt and shame as she looked at him with stricken eyes.

"I seem to have come by at a most inappropriate time." His voice was tight and hard, controlled in its icy condemnation of the woman facing him.

"Anthony, I must explain," she began.

"The situation needs little explanation, Melissa my dear," he said scathingly, his gaze fixed on Calvin. "I should have known we hadn't seen the last of you, Mr.

Gabriel."

"What are you doing here, Anthony?" Melissa's quaking voice called. He looked back at her.

"If you recall, we were going to pay a visit to the police this morning," he replied sharply.

Sudden recollection blanched her face and she huddled further under the covers, beginning to shiver uncontrollably. "There is no longer any need to go to the police," she explained haltingly. "You see, it was Calvin who was behind it all."

"And for what purpose, may I ask?" Anthony demanded of the still-silent man sitting calmly in bed observing the interplay.

"I can't see that what I do is any of your concern, Holmes," he answered coolly.

Anthony's gaze returned to Melissa once more. "I'll step outside to give you a chance to dress. Then I want a word with you—alone." As he turned to leave, Calvin's voice stopped him.

"That won't be necessary, Holmes," he said, springing from the bed, ignoring the older man's incredulous stare. "I have a long trip ahead of me and you can have your bride all to yourself now." He began pulling on his clothes.

"Calvin." Melissa's voice was a strangled plea as she called out to him. He continued to dress as if he had not heard her cry. Shocked into defiance, smarting from his cavalier treatment of her once again, she lashed out at him. "Leave! Just act as if this has nothing to do with you at all. You despicable man, you spoil everything you touch, playing with people and then discarding them without a further thought to their feelings." Tears were streaming down her face as she shouted hoarsely, "How can you just walk out of here now?"

"She's right, you know, Gabriel," Anthony cut in, taking a threatening step toward Calvin. "Don't you consider it rather cowardly to run off and leave Melissa here to face me alone? What should she do if I decided to withdraw my proposal of marriage?" At Calvin's blank look, Anthony continued, "I'll tell you what she should do. Since you got her into this compromising situation, I would think it only fair that you get her out of it. You should be marrying her yourself, Mr. Gabriel."

"Marriage for me?" Calvin burst out incredulously. "I'm afraid you've approached the wrong person, Holmes."

"You know, Gabriel." Anthony's voice was menacingly low. "It's a shame that dueling is frowned upon these days, otherwise I'd demand satisfaction and settle this on a field of honor."

"Stop it, both of you!" Melissa shouted. "How dare you both stand there and haggle over me like two fishwives. If I have anything to say about this, I say both of you be damned. I want you out of my sight right now." Both men turned to stare in disbelief at her. "Get out of here now and leave me alone."

His face ashen, Anthony spun on his heel and strode from the room. Calvin looked balefully at the tousled beauty glaring so hatefully at him from the bed. As he was about to approach her, her low-voiced threat froze his steps.

"If I ever see you again, Calvin Gabriel, I promise to use my gun as I should have last night."

Anthony reentered Melissa's life one night as she was leaving the theater after the show. He seemed older, the lines in his face more firmly etched, dark circles of fatigue ringing his eyes.

"Hello, Melissa," he greeted her, his voice muted and dull. "I've missed you very much."

"I know, because my life has been changed too," she said sorrowfully.

"I had hoped you might have dinner with me," he explained, indicating a waiting carriage. She nodded wordlessly and he guided her to the curb and assisted her into the warmth of the coach.

He chose a small, unfamiliar restaurant, where they would be able to speak privately without the threat of interruption. Melissa found that she had very little appetite and she barely touched her food. Anthony stared morosely at his.

"I think I can appreciate how you feel about Calvin Gabriel, Melissa," Anthony began, "because despite what you have always maintained, you're in love with him and have been ever since we first met. But I think he made it clear that he would never marry you, no matter how greatly he might desire you." He paused then, taking a deep swallow of his wine before continuing. "I love you very much, Melissa, in spite of what happened and I'm still asking you to marry me."

Melissa twirled the fragile stem of her wineglass between her fingers, aware that the time had come at last. Sadly she raised her eyes to his.

"I cannot marry you, Anthony. At the end of this month, the show will be sailing for England and I shall be going with them." At his sharp intake of breath, she nodded her head. "It took me a long time to finally reach this decision, but I am now committed to it and relieved that the uncertainty is over. Cody plans to be performing in England for six months. By then I should know whether to remain there or return to America." She hastily gulped down the last of her wine and when she dared to look at him again, her eyes were veiled with tears.

"Forgive me, dear Anthony," she whispered, "for all the pain I know I must have caused you. But leaving this place is the only choice left to me now." She turned away from the agony in his eyes.

They rode back to her hotel in gloomy silence, Anthony staring vacantly out the window, Melissa lost in the turmoil of her own thoughts. At the canopied entrance, he held her tightly in his arms and kissed her one last time. He studied her upturned face and with a quivering sigh, he set her from him and climbed back into the carriage. Waving his hand to her in a final, tender salute, he closed the door and the coach moved off. Melissa watched it disappear into the night before she gathered her skirts around her and hurried into the hotel.

chapter 41

She moved mechanically through the remaining shows, avoiding contact with everyone, including Cody, oblivious to the mounting excitement all around her. Trunks were being packed, extra costumes made, acts refurbished and new performers added to the cast of the show. For any one of the people choosing not to make the ocean voyage, a replacement was quickly found. Among the replacements was Chief Red Shirt who would take over for Indian Chief Sitting Bull. Nate Salsbury confirmed the booking of the steamship *State of Nebraska* to carry the company and all of the show's properties over to England.

Melissa was sitting in her dressing room just before the start of the evening performance when an urgent knock sounded at the door. Wearily, she moved to answer it, but before she could even start across the room, the door was flung open and Calvin Gabriel rushed in. His gaze roved appreciatively over her glittering costume as she glared at him with undisguised hatred in her eyes. Her hand moved instinctively down toward her holster.

"You won't need your gun, Brandywine," he cautioned, "I only came here to talk to you."

"We have nothing to say to one another," she snapped.

"On the contrary," he argued, "we have a great deal

to talk about."

"Stay right where you are," she threatened, the gun instantly in her hand, as she moved past him to the door. "Jared," she called out, "get in here right away!"

"Melissa, please hear me out," Calvin urged, stepping toward her. The ominous click of the hammer as Melissa cocked the pistol stopped him. He stood silently, his hands hanging limply at his sides as Jared Rawlins charged into the room.

"What's wrong, Miss Melissa?" he panted, glancing over at the tall, dark-haired stranger glowering back at him.

"Get this man out of here," she ordered tersely, "and see to it that he stays out." Jared immediately drew his own gun and gestured for Calvin to follow him.

"Melissa, call off this fellow," Calvin pleaded. "I'm warning you, you'll regret it."

"The only thing I regret is having met you, Mr. Gabriel," she hissed as Jared hauled him from the room. She slumped weakly into her chair, cursing him for the disruption of her life once more, with only one more week remaining before she sailed. Resting her head on her hands, she gave way to her misery, sobbing wretchedly, and despair settled like a lead weight inside of her. Jared called to her from the doorway and she hastily dabbed at her face.

"He's gone, Miss Melissa," he announced quietly, "I don't think he'll be troubling you again."

"Did you hurt him?" she asked, suddenly alarmed.

"Nah, I just pushed him out the door, kinda forceful-like, but I didn't hurt him none," he said, grinning at her, and sauntered off down the corridor.

Despondently, she made her way to the wings to await her cue. Because Cody had been changing the order of some of the existing acts for the British tour, Melissa's hurdle-jumping had been shifted from the middle of the program to the end, with her dramatic fiery leap closing the show. Trotting easily around the arena, awaiting her signal from Bill, she slowed her horse and watched the final hurdles being set into place. Anxiously scanning the crowds, she headed toward one of the exits and halted Target, patting him gently as she gazed around her. And then she saw him. Standing across from her, his eyes fixed on hers, his arms folded across his chest, he leaned casually up against a wall.

She looked away, tears welling up in her eyes once again. When she heard her name shouted by Cody and repeated by the tumultuous crowds, she rode into the glare of the brilliant lights blurring before her. Her eyes stinging, her entire body trembling, she led Target into the first jump. Numbly she felt herself soaring into the air and landing heavily, applause swiftly following as around the course she rode. Dimly aware of her movements, unable to concentrate on the approaching hurdles as she neared them, she pulled down the bars on one of the jumps and smarted as the crowd gasped.

Tears were streaming freely down her covered face, blinding her as she rounded the last turn for the final jump. Sobbing, she kicked the horse into a faster gallop and the flaming bar loomed closer and closer as she thundered toward it. She knew that she had misjudged the distance as soon as she felt Target lifting off the ground. The smell of the oil-soaked rags assaulted her, filling her nostrils. The heat of the licking flames scorched her as her feet slipped from the stirrups and she was catapulted through the air. Screams and shouts echoed around her as the ground came rushing toward her at a dizzying speed, and she slammed to the earth and sank into the darkness waiting to enfold her.

Somewhere music was playing, and people were laughing and dancing amid garlands of flowers and trellises of climbing leaves. Wineglasses were filled with sparkling champagne and black-clad servants moved silently about. Melissa swayed alone to the rhythm of the music until she was swept into the arms of a black-haired figure sporting a small black mask.

His silver gray eyes bored into hers, the cleft in his chin deepened as he smiled, and his voice rippled melodically, bearing an accent foreign to her ears. He held her tightly in muscled arms and when his lips bruised hers, she felt the glow of passion being born in her. Suddenly he slipped away, his laughter ringing in her ears, leaving a vague pulsing deep within her, and a welling emptiness in his place. Searching for him, she pushed through the crowd around her and made her way through an open door to find her father, his brow bathed in blood, lying on the floor.

She looked up, seeking the man in the black mask whose silvery eyes had claimed her for his own, but he had disappeared. And then she was running through darkened streets with two men chasing her. She ran until she stumbled and fell screaming to the ground.

Her eyes flew open, meeting the troubled gaze of gray eyes looking back at her and she cried out in fearful recognition. She tried to raise her head, but the blinding pain forced her back again. Blinking, dispelling the shadowed veil suspended in front of her, she gazed up into the face of the man who had stepped out from behind the curtain drawn across her past. The nightmare haunting her sleep receded forever.

"Melissa," Calvin Gabriel's voice called out to her, the voice she had first heard on the night of her masquerade ball, but she turned her head away. She saw Cody then, his face lined with worry and she smiled weakly up at him.

"Where am I, Bill?" she murmured.

"It's this fellow Gabriel's room," he answered gruffly. "The arena was hoppin' with reporters and too many curious folks, so we bundled you up and brought you here. You gave us all a mighty bad scare, little lady," he grimaced, stroking her forehead with his large, calloused hand, "but the doc says you're gonna be fine."

"Does everyone know about me now?" she whispered through dry lips. Cody nodded his head solemnly.

"It was all that long hair of yours," he laughed. "But don't you fret none. They haven't heard of Brandywine across the pond yet, and we aim to keep it that way."

Melissa sighed deeply, closing her eyes and wearily waving everyone from the room. She needed the time alone to collect her thoughts and think about what she had to do. A sudden tremor rippled through her and she shuddered in the aftershock of discovering that missing fragment of her life, jolted into place by the impact of her fall in the stadium. Calvin Gabriel—her lips trembled forming the words of his name. Calvin, the man she had felt she had known before, and the masked intruder in her dreams were one and the same. Calvin, the black-haired American, the swaggering stranger who had courted her that night in England, was the man she had given her heart to in America, and the man she had sworn to seek out and destroy. A bitter laugh escaped her while the anguish sharpened in her breast, honing for her the strength she would need to carry out her promise.

"Melissa," his voice called to her again when she had thought herself to be alone. "Look at me, Melissa," he commanded. "Dammit, woman, open your eyes and look at me."

And slowly, she forced her eyes open again and looked at the man who was kneeling beside her. His mouth was set in a grim line as she studied her, his gray eyes stormy and uncomprehending. The horror he read in her returning gaze made him wince. He pushed himself to his feet and walked to the window. The first tentative rays of light brushed the sky with a faint pearling glow and Melissa realized that she had been unconscious the entire night. Her body responded stiffly as she again tried to sit up and she noticed that she was wearing a man's dressing gown and that her torn costume lay crumpled on a nearby chair. Her gaze fell on her guns, and she hastily glanced back at Calvin who stood staring bleakly out of the window, his back turned to her, his head resting on his folded arms.

Her feet slid silently to the floor and she glided stealthily toward the chair, heedless of the furious pounding in her head. Her fingers closed around the butt of one of her pistols and slipping a bullet from her gunbelt, she crept noiselessly back to the bed.

"Where do you think you're going?" His shout caught her by surprise, but her hand was shielded by the bulky folds of the dressing gown she was wearing and she was able to slide the gun into a pocket without his noticing.

"I wanted to see if all of my clothes were here," she answered in a hushed voice. "I really should leave now, you know."

"You'll leave only when I say so," he barked, crossing the room and walking toward her.

She edged closer to the bed and as he neared her, she flung herself across the heavy spread, feeling the gun pressing uncomfortably into her side as she attempted to hide its telltale bulging inside the pocket of the robe. Her hand closed tightly over the single bullet. To her dismay, he sank down on the bed beside her.

"Leave me alone," she snarled through gritted teeth.

"Not until we talk," he retorted, and she slithered across the satin coverlet until she had moved as far from him as possible. "Melissa, there's something I want to say to you," he began, running his fingers through the thickness of his dark hair. But he stopped abruptly when he saw the threatening glimmer in her eyes and his troubled gaze turned quizzical.

"What's wrong? Why are you looking at me that way?" Her silence angered and frustrated him and he sprang from the bed and began to restlessly prowl the room.

Melissa waited until his back was turned to her once

more before slipping the bullet into an empty chamber of her gun. Getting to her feet, she raised the pistol slowly, seeing before her the completion of her long journey, the end of her quest.

"Calvin." She spoke his name firmly and he whirled around.

"What the hell are you doing?" he cried, his face paling as he stared at the gun in her hand.

"This is for my father," she said simply as she squeezed the trigger.

His eyes widened in surprise and pain and he seemed to hang suspended momentarily in the air before slumping to the floor, a crimson stain spreading across the whiteness of his shirt.

Melissa averted her horrified gaze from his body sprawled across the carpet and hastily gathered up her clothing, threw her long cloak around her, and drew the hood over her face. She closed the door quietly behind her and walked briskly along the corridor toward the staircase. Clutching the tight bundle of clothing beneath her cape and grasping the bannister with her free hand, she descended the dimly lit stairs and scurried out through a side door which led into a deserted alleyway.

Gasping for breath, her head throbbing, she felt her stomach begin to heave. The rising nausea doubled her over and, sinking to her knees, she gave in to the spiraling waves of sickness coursing through her. And then she raised her tear-stained face and cried out in her agony to the father she had avenged and the man she had loved, inextricably bound forever by the spilling of their blood.

chapter 42

The morning of March 31, 1887, dawned crisp and bright. The people thronging to New York's waterfront witnessed a spectacle the likes of which they would never see again. Groups of cowboys, dark-skinned Indians, horses, cattle, gaudily painted wigwams and wooden wagons, were all clustered together at dockside. A rangy man with streaming hair and a long moustache took charge of the proceedings. With infinite patience, William F. Cody coaxed the frightened and superstitious Indians on board the steamship *State of Nebraska*. He urged the horses and the livestock aboard and waved his hat high in the air to signal Nate Salsbury, who was bustling back and forth among the hundreds of well wishers and curiosity seekers.

Amid the turmoil and excitement, stood a solitary figure. Auburn hair framed a ghostly face in which burned a pair of extraordinary topaz eyes. Melissa Howard gazed at the people gathering on the deck beside her and she burrowed deeper into her long, wool cloak. Her huge eyes held a vacant stare, her full lips were tightly drawn in a face whose beauty was scarred by grief. She scarcely remembered the week slipping by her, for she had remained secluded in her hotel room, forbidden by Cody to perform in order to ensure a complete recovery from the fall she had suffered. She had received no visitors, read no newspapers, and had eaten and slept hardly at all, managing somehow to keep her tortured mind mercifully blank.

She took a tentative step forward and leaned out onto the ship's wooden railing, gazing pensively down at the murky waters of the harbor below. In a matter of weeks, she would be back home in England, back to where it had all begun for her. Sudden tears misted her eyes as she thought of him, of his gray eyes holding hers, the fury of their passion, the futile love which had so tormented her. Raising her head, she glanced at the people clambering aboard and her heart twisted in fear as she watched two uniformed policemen making their way up the gangplank and stepping onto the deck.

One of the men nudged the other and they started toward her, signaling her to remain where she was. Her immediate impulse was to turn and run, but her body had turned to stone. She stood there, with only the rapid thumping of her heart giving proof that she was alive at all.

"Are you Melissa Howell?" one of the policemen asked. She nodded imperceptibly. "Miss Howell, we're here to place you under arrest for the murder of one Calvin Gabriel." Before she could reply, her arms were seized and she was hauled from the ship and down the gangplank to the dock below.

Looking desperately about her, she sought Cody's familiar face, but there were too many people and the crowd was too dense. If some curious onlookers saw the terrified girl and the two policemen, they assumed they were all part of the show. It was a short ride to the somber brick building which housed one of the city's jails and Melissa sat stiffly between the two taciturn policemen, her eyes staring directly ahead, refusing to contemplate her pending fate. She found that she no longer feared death but, despite her attempted composure, a muscle twitched in the side of her face and she shuddered.

They tugged her up the stone steps into the station

and pushed her past a burly officer who sat perched behind a massive desk with a huge ledger open in front of him. She heard her name called out by one of the men accompanying her. She was led into a small, dingy room containing several wooden chairs and a large table. There were iron bars covering the two small windows. As she looked around her, she was grimly reminded of the day she had been interrogated at the police station in Baltimore. Only this time, she thought dully, she was no longer innocent of the crime they had charged her with. She walked to one of the chairs as the two policemen sauntered from the room, the door slamming shut behind them.

Sinking weakly into the chair, Melissa buried her face in her hands, taking one deep breath after another, steadying herself in anticipation of the ordeal ahead of her. Eventually, the door was opened again and quickly closed. Slow footsteps began making their way across the room toward her huddled form.

"Miss Howell," rasped a man's voice and she slowly raised her head, thankful that it would soon be over. In the dimness of the room, she was startled by the whiteness of the sling supporting one of his arms. His face, when she looked up at him, was gray with fatigue and his battle with death.

"You almost succeeded, princess," he said faintly, "and you're supposed to be an expert shot." His mouth twisted into a wry smile and he stood over her, watching the pale face before him turn ashen.

Unable to form a sentence, Melissa stared open-mouthed at the living apparition before her.

"Why, Melissa?" he whispered then. "Why did you try to kill me?"

She ran her tongue along her parched lips, trying to force some words from her numbed mouth. A hoarse scratching finally emerged. "My father." She watched his face but his puzzled frown revealed nothing.

"Your father?" he repeated. "But I never knew a

Howell in England."

"But you knew Sir Edmund Howard," she mouthed weakly, the name an aching twinge inside her.

"Sir Edmund Howard." He ran the name over and over again until he exclaimed finally, "I remember now, I had some business dealings with him a few years back. He had wanted me to buy up his entire estate but I didn't have the kind of money he needed. He was apparently in debt to a neighbor of his and about to lose everything to him." He shook his head thoughtfully. "I felt sorry for him, but there was nothing I could do. I was only interested in some of his prize studs." His voice trailed off then and Melissa cut in sharply.

"And that was all there was between you?"

"Yes, that's all," he answered. "But I still don't understand what Sir Edmund Howard has to do with any of this."

"Sir Edmund Howard was my father," she said softly, and with halting speech, she related to him the events of that night at Howard House. He listened, his face registering his dismay. He pulled out a chair and settled wearily into it.

"But when I last saw him, he was alive," he protested. "He was very upset and obviously wanted to be alone, and since there was nothing more to discuss, I simply left him in the study and returned to my hotel." He shifted uncomfortably in the chair and dabbed at his strained face with a handkerchief. "I'm supposed to be resting in bed," he commented, grimacing sheepishly. "Melissa, I sailed the following day for Baltimore, never knowing that he was dead. I swear I know nothing more about it."

She studied him, noting the pain in his eyes and the anguished set to his mouth. But she was still not convinced that what he had told her was the truth. As she watched him, the look he gave her was suddenly angry.

"You're accusing me of having had something to do

with your father's death." It was a statement, not a question, and Melissa nodded her head.

"I believe you murdered him."

"Murdered him? But why? I didn't even know the man. I only knew about him through the reputation of the Howard stables. Even the Ransomes knew about the stables. That's the reason I was in England in the first place, to buy horses for our estates. I even discussed the purchases with some guy named Wentworth at the house that night. He seemed damned upset at first, because he thought I was there to bail Sir Edmund out of debt. When I realized he was the one Howard owed so much money to, I wished I could have come up with the kind of money he needed, just to spite the bastard." His throat went dry and he suddenly began to cough. One spasm led to another until his face was red with the exertion of it. Melissa became alarmed. The coughing finally subsided and he wiped his forehead with the back of his hand.

"Go on," Melissa urged him.

"There's nothing much else to say." His voice was hoarse now. "Wentworth was relieved when I assured him I had no intention of standing in his way of taking over the Howard estate." He looked down at his feet then, a sheepish grin tugging at the corners of his mouth. "But there was a young woman there I'd treated pretty poorly. When I set out to look for her just so I could apologize, Wentworth got angry again and practically had me thrown out of the place."

Melissa was stunned. Just listening to him speak seemed to be hurtling her back in time, back to that awful night, and knitting together the pieces of her jagged memory for her once and for all. She finally began to understand. She understood now why Philip had been so angry that night and why he had continued to bait her, refusing ever to dissuade her in the belief that an American had actually taken her father's life. How like Phillip to have played so cruel a game. She wondered now if he had ever meant to help her at all when they had met in Baltimore months before.

"Then it's true," she murmured. "My father did kill himself." She closed her eyes, blinking back the tears and the terrible pain which seared her as no knife could ever do. She thought of the time she had wasted trying to disprove the truth. Now she had no other choice but to learn to live with the truth at last. Her father had chosen the coward's way and she could feel only pity for him now.

"Dear God." Her voice broke. "To think I could have killed you and never learned the truth."

Moving slowly and awkwardly, Calvin went to her and gave her his handkerchief. She pressed the lightly scented linen square to the tears which were flowing unchecked down her cheeks and watched as he eased himself into a chair. After what seemed an eternity, he finally asked her the question she knew it was time for her to answer now.

"Why, Melissa? Why did you wait for two years before trying to kill me?"

She blew her nose, wiped her eyes and tried not to feel too much like a fool. "Because I had lost my memory." The words had scarcely left her lips before she found herself unable to stem the flow of all the words tumbling after them. Calvin leaned back in his chair, his eyes never leaving her face, as she revealed to him what she had never revealed to anyone.

"So you were that tempestuous little vixen who'd lost her voice that night," he chuckled, shaking his head in disbelief. "You must forgive me, princess, for not remembering the sweetness of those stolen kisses when I met you again. How differently things might have turned out if one of us had at least been able to remember."

Her temper flared to the surface at his familiar bantering. The tears and the worry were quickly forgotten as she jumped to her feet. "You have succeeded once again in playing another of your ridiculous pranks, having me brought here like some common criminal. You have taken enough of my time and since my ship is about to sail, I intend to leave this place immediately." With that she marched determinedly to the door.

"But you are a criminal, my dear Melissa," his voice called, halting her. "Instead of murder, you'll now be charged with attempted murder, if I press charges, that is."

"And will you press charges?" she asked him.

"That all depends on how eager you are to return to England," he answered. "We never did have our little talk, you know," he reminded her.

"We have nothing left to talk about now," she snapped, casting an apprehensive glance toward the door again.

"Melissa, my love, as I warned you once before, you'd better hear what I have to say." He struggled to his feet and walked to her. Gently tipping her face up to his, he said softly, "In your hotel room that morning, Anthony Holmes taught me something about being a gentlemen. He was right, you know. I'd placed you in a compromising situation and I never should have left you there." He paused, clearing his throat awkwardly, the faint smile on his pale face strangely shy. "When I returned to New York and confronted you in your dressing room that night, I had made up my mind to ask you to marry me. But you never gave me the chance, and so, princess," his tender loving voice murmured, "I'm asking you now."

"Why? Because you feel it to be the proper thing to do?" she cried, backing away from him.

"No, Melissa." He shook his head and reached for her again. "I'm asking you because I love you. I suppose I've always known it and like a fool I waited until it was almost too late for us."

With a sob, she flung her arms around his neck,

mindless of his wince of pain as she buried her face against his chest. She could feel his heart racing, coupled with the joyous beating of her own. She raised her face, radiant through her tears, to his and welcomed his kiss upon her lips.

"And I love you, Calvin Gabriel," she answered him, uttering at last the words she had long saved for him alone.

Somewhere in the distance, a whistle sounded, and a steamship weighed anchor, heading out of New York harbor and across the sea to England.

POSITIONS By Bill Adler

PRICE: $2.75 LB966
CATEGORY: Novel

A SIZZLING NOVEL OF WHAT WOMEN
CAN DO WHEN THEY REACH THE TOP "POSITIONS"

Three women changed the Hollywood scene. They had it all—beauty, brains and talent. Their stepping stones to the top were male egos, and they rose to rule the very men who desired them.

KELLEY LEE plunged into a career writing film scripts, and out-sold the best of her men.

DARLENE NORTH became a top talent agent, who bought and sold beautiful people—and most of her friends.

ANNA MANNERS fell prey to the worst in show business, and bounced back to become the biggest bitch of the silver screen.

AFTER SUCCESS, THEY WANTED LOVE
–BUT CAN A MAN LOVE A WOMAN WHO CAN FIRE HIM?

THE REAPING

An ancient superstition reaches out, catching you in a net of horror and suspense

The Reaping

LEISURE
1035
$2.50

BERNARD TAYLOR

"Taylor works wizardry again here."
—PUBLISHERS WEEKLY

He was hired to paint the portrait of a young woman at Woolvercombe Mansion, but Tom Rigby didn't know she was after more than a painting. He wondered about the identities of the strange inhabitants of the house and the bizarre events that began to happen. And suddenly he was catapulted into a rendezvous with terror and violence, as the power of the supernatural wielded its horrifying spell!

By Bernard Taylor

CATEGORY: Occult
PRICE: $2.50
0-8439-1035-6

THE INSTITUTE

By
James M.
Cain

AUTHOR OF THE POSTMAN ALWAYS RINGS TWICE,
DOUBLE INDEMNITY & MILDRED PIERCE.

"NOBODY ELSE HAS EVER QUITE PULLED IT OFF THE
WAY CAIN DOES, NOT HEMINGWAY, AND NOT
EVEN RAYMOND CHANDLER. CAIN IS A
MASTER OF THE CHANGE OF PACE." —TOM WOLFE

James M. Cain
The
Institute

THE FORBIDDEN LOVE THEY SHARED DREW THEM INTO A
VORTEX OF VIOLENCE AND DEATH!

PRICE: $2.95
0-8439-1034-8
CATEGORY:
Novel

*T*he brilliant career of James M. Cain, the celebrated
author of "The Postman Always Rings Twice,"
"Mildred Pierce" and "Double Indemnity," reaches a
shattering climax in this power-triangle of love,
lust and greed.

When Professor Lloyd Palmer seeks financial backing from
wealthy Richard Garrett, he meets and falls in love with
Garrett's seductive wife.

Marguerite Tanner

Marguerite had struck a bargain with life, trading her beauty, her only asset, for security. Now she had achieved the goals she had set for herself as a penniless young girl — wealth, position, a successful husband, attractive children. Then dynamic Lou Armitage entered her life. Consumed by a passion she could not control, Marguerite willingly risked the destruction of the very world she had so carefully constructed!

By Elizabeth Dubus

PRICE: $2.95
0-8439-1037-2
CATEGORY: Novel

SEND TO: **LEISURE BOOKS**
P.O. Box 511, Murry Hill Station
New York, N.Y. 10156-0511

Please send the titles:

Quantity	Book Number	Price
_____	_____	_____
_____	_____	_____
_____	_____	_____
_____	_____	_____

In the event we are out of stock on any of your
selections, please list alternate titles below.

_____	_____	_____
_____	_____	_____
_____	_____	_____
_____	_____	_____

Postage/Handling_____

I enclose_____

FOR U.S. ORDERS, add 75¢ for the first book and 25¢ for
each additional book to cover cost of postage and handling.
Buy five or more copies and we will pay for shipping. Sorry,
no. C.O.D.'s.

FOR ORDERS SENT OUTSIDE THE U.S.A., add $1.00
for the first book and 50¢ for each additional book. PAY BY
foreign draft or money order drawn on a U.S. bank, payable
in U.S. ($) dollars.

☐ Please send me a free catalog.

NAME _____

(Please print)

ADDRESS _____

CITY _____STATE _____ZIP_____

Allow Four Weeks for Delivery